~ *A Stone Ranch Prequel* ~

I0665819

ANN'S VALLEY

CAYT LAWSON

This is a work of fiction. Names, characters, places and incidents either are products of the author's imagination or are used fictitiously, and any resemblance to actual persons, living or dead, business establishments, events, locales is entirely coincidental.

No part of this book may be reproduced in any form or by any electronic or mechanical means, including information storage and retrieval systems, without permission in writing from the author, except by a reviewer who may quote brief passages in a review.

Written by Cayt Lawson
Cover Art by Fiona Jayde Media
Interior Design by Ryan Flowers

By Cayt Lawson

Stone Ranch Series

Ann's Valley (A Stone Ranch Prequel)
Seduced by the Saint
Kissed by a Devil

COMING SOON

Stone Ranch Series

Wanted by the Ranger
Loved by an Outlaw

Sisters Disreputable Series

Love's Song
Love's Wings

I dedicate this book to my husband, Ryan. He is my rock and my inspiration. I never would have imagined my writings as anything other than a personally gratifying hobby if it weren't for him encouraging me to share my stories. Thanks for always believing in me, pulling me up when I fall, and pushing me to do better.

Prologue

London, England
Duchess of Linley's Ball
April 10, 1832

"Will you meet me, Ann?"

The handsome American, whom she had fallen in love with over the past weeks, leaned against one of the heavy columns leading to the balcony. Ann could see the colorful blur of dancers swirling behind him in the ballroom, but her heart was too aflutter and intent upon what James had finally asked of her, to pay them any heed.

She had been hoping he would promise for her before his necessary return to America.

He was only in London on business, after all. Ann couldn't quite recall what his business was about. Something to do with exporting tobacco. His family owned a plantation in South Carolina, so she supposed that made sense.

She truly should listen more closely to the man she loved, Ann berated herself – and why was she standing there like a ninny, wondering about his Family's business anyway? He had finally proposed to her! James had offered for her!

He hadn't offered in the way she'd hoped, obviously. An elopement? Secreting away north to exchange vows with no family present?

She didn't mind escaping a large wedding, and the social obligations one entailed, but would her mother ever forgive her? It's not as if she had other siblings for her mother's plans to be met through.

And her father? What would he think about them sneaking around in such dishonored fashion? Then again, her father hardly approved of James. He'd made that clear on numerous occasions. So, if one thought about it, her father was truly to blame. He'd left them little choice but to elope.

Ann rolled her fingers about in the palms of her hands as if the silk gloves she wore were capable of absorbing the accumulating moisture from her clammy hands, and shook her head clear of any doubts.

"Yes. Yes, I will meet you." She met his eyes decisively.

James reached for her silk-gloved hand and raised it to his lips, in the ever so charming manner he always possessed, and her heart did another flip within her chest. She remained standing before him, her hand in his, her honey brown eyes locked with his silvery blue, and a brilliant smile on her lips until the spell was broken with her father's approach.

"My father's coming toward us," She spoke.

"Until next we meet."

James flashed her one of his irresistible, devil-may-care smiles and made smooth his exit just as her father reached them.

"Evening Lord Abersty," James gave an arrogant nod of his head and disappeared into the crowd of dancers.

Her father's eyes stared stonily after James for a brief second before turning to Ann, his handsome worn face wearing a sterner expression than she was accustomed to receiving from her father-until recently. She readied herself for a scolding and stepped further into the cool night air offered from the balcony. Her father moved to her side.

"What is the meaning of this? Consorting with *Mr.* Morgan? You are deigning too much of your attention on this man and there's starting to be talk about it. I would not have you marry this fortune hunting American. And I will not have you embroiled in scandal! Since there is no chance of a marriage between the two of you, you will cease acknowledging his very existence."

She was tired of defending James' attributes to her father. She couldn't help that she'd fallen in love with an American. Her father should understand. It was heavily frowned upon for him, a second son of an Earl, to have married a farmer's daughter, yet he did not allow society to dictate his heart. And neither would Ann allow her father to control hers.

She reigned in her irritation with her father and smiled, "I shall do my best to please you, father."

Lowering her eyes, she knew her words were only partly true. She did wish to please him, but she also knew that he would forgive her. In time, he would come to accept James, if for no other reason than to remain a part of his daughter's life.

She felt her father's hand at her elbow, guiding her back to the ballroom where her mother waited nervously.

"Ann, there you are." Her mother whispered with relief.

"Yes, mother, all is well. Although, I fear a headache is setting in. I think I will retire for the evening."

"Oh, but it's too early. Surely it would offend the Duke and Duchess. Besides, you have been absent most of the evening. Gossip is already stirring. No, I really think you should suffer it out."

A very unladylike snort escaped Ann's mouth, "Hardly 'most of the evening'-"

"First, you mistakenly allowed two dances to that *American*," her mother interrupted, "and then you disappeared with him," her mother added more quietly, but every bit as vehemently.

Ann gritted her teeth in frustration, causing her head to actually throb. "We were in plain sight on the balcony, as father can well tell you since that is where he found me. I am sorry mother, but I think it is a megrim and the pain is becoming intolerable."

Her mother studied her face searching for the slightest fabrication to her plight.

"She truly does appear piqued, Edmond. Perhaps we should leave."

Her mother sounded disappointed and Ann felt a brief wave of guilt. Ann supposed she took the season for granted, forgetting that her mother had never received anything of the sort as a young woman. She'd witnessed her mother having a joyous time on the dance floor with her father many times over the course of the last two months and she did not wish to deprive her mother of more such moments.

Her father sensed her mother's reluctance to leave as well, "No reason for us to turn in early Rosemary. Ann may take the carriage home and send Peter to return for us later this evening." Then he turned to Ann, "We shall make your excuses. Go, home and rest."

As Ann turned to go, her father added, "But tomorrow, we shall have a very important discussion about how we expect you to behave for the remaining duration of the season."

Ann's blood heated, but she nodded shortly in feigned acquiesce and made her escape. Her heart pounding, she delivered herself to their carriage. Once back at their town residence she instructed Peter, the driver, to return to the ball for her parents. She then ensured the household servants had not been made aware of her unexpected arrival. Once Peter was out of sight, she wrapped her cloak firmly around her with the hood obscuring her face from any passersby on the street.

Then stole away into the other carriage secretly awaiting her, into the inky darkness of the night.

Chapter 1

Atlantic Ocean
October 12, 1832

Lady Ann Morgan, the daughter of the Earl of Abersty, lay curled up on her cot below deck of The *Clara Stella*, shivering from the damp cold as she clutched her rounded belly and willed to keep her sickness at bay. She didn't feel much a Lady anymore; in part, because her current circumstances had her living like a gutter rat and for another, she had married below her station and therefore could, and in her heart *should,* be addressed *Mrs. Morgan.*

Ironically, she was currently being addressed as such, but only because she had used her husband's name as an alias to gain passage onto the ship in hopes of delaying her father's indubitable search of her.

She'd wanted to be plain Mrs. Morgan, but when she and James had eloped, he'd requested she keep her title, arguing that it would aid in growing his business in London. Her father, a powerful man with many connections could serve James' company well, so it seemed silly to refuse his request.

Ann turned to Fiona, the only other passenger-and female-on the ship sharing a chamber with her, "Did you find out from the Captain, how much longer we have until we reach America?"

Ann's voice was dry and crackled when she spoke, no doubt from all the retching she'd done during the storm.

"Captain Ludwick decrees at least three more weeks, so long as we do not encounter any more storms."

Ann groaned, repulsed at the thought of spending three more weeks aboard the rat-infested rain barrel the Captain called a ship. The *Clara Stella* - a beautifully chosen name for such a hideous entrapment. Such was life, Ann supposed; evil often wore the face of beauty.

An image of James' sun bronzed, smiling face surfaced briefly in her mind. At least she'd been smart enough to marry the man before losing her innocence to him. She wished *he* had been smart enough to find his way back to England as he'd promised, blast him!

He'd written to her upon reaching Charleston. At least he had managed to accomplish that much. Even though it had only been to inform her that he would not be able to return for her until spring.

His *wife!*

He'd written -no, *instructed*- her to keep their marriage a secret until he returned for her in the spring. *'To make life easier for herself whilst remaining under her parents' roof'* he'd written. Ha! To make *his life* easier, surely. Especially, when he had the only copy of their legal marriage documents, with him, on the other side of the ocean!

She'd decided then to take matters into her own hands. Of course, he hadn't known when he left her there to rot, how well he'd sown his seed. Instead of posting a return letter to inform him of their unplanned circumstances, she'd waited as long as possible (that being until even the scullery maids had begun to notice her expanding waist size and -unfortunately- coming to accurate conclusions and gossiping amongst one another), before carrying out plans of her own. Plans that included her boarding a ship and taking herself along with the special cargo she carried, unbeknownst to him, to his home in America.

She imagined his surprised reaction when she showed up at his doorstep, "Hullo, I'd like to make a deposit: Myself. -And your baby."

She gave a wry twist of her lips at her own dark humor.

It's not as if she could very well have remained in her parent's home. She couldn't bear to have her father look upon her in disgust and betrayal. He'd adamantly forbidden her to further see James and she'd went off and married the man and allowed him *all husbandly liberties.*

No. No, she absolutely could not have remained in the same house as her father. She would make things right and when she returned home, she would be able to face her father with pride and dignity once more.

The ship rocked and swayed some more, interrupting Ann from her thoughts as water that had seeped through, splashed onto her bedding. Ann gritted her teeth in annoyance.

"The babe sure doesn't have a liking for the sea." Fiona stated. She'd been good company and a great help to Ann. Most importantly, neither one felt like sharing overmuch about their pasts, which made her a perfect companion for the journey.

Ann grumbled her response. Fiona chuckled, not at all deterred by a moody *breeding* woman.

"Och, the constant dampness is irritating in and of itself. I'm right glad I'm not in the increasing way that you are. I don't think I could have braved this voyage, had I been. And alone at that."

Ann had come to know the fiery little Irish woman well enough in the weeks they'd been confined together to know she wasn't judging Ann or intending to pry for information. She'd been Ann's only helpmate thus far on the journey and she would be ever thankful for the woman's kindness.

There were times though, especially concerning her burgeoning belly and the babe growing within, that she wished for her mother's presence. Indeed, one would think her out of her mind to cross the Atlantic in her condition. No doubt, it revealed how desperate her circumstances truly were.

Most of the time, though, she longed for her father's company. His soothing voice and knowing wisdom. As well as her beloved Uncle, always a constant companion. She smiled, recalling the day of her first ball and the last memory she had of her father looking on her with pride...

Somerset, England

Abersty Country Estate
November 2, 1831

"I still cannot believe that shot! Quite literally two birds with one, well, shot I suppose. But can you believe it?"

Lady Ann Dunneroy trailed behind but could still hear her uncle over the sound of her horse's hooves softly clopping the dirt, boasting about her mark on the morning's hunt. She chuckled softly, still in wonder a little herself. She had been aiming for an impressive head shot on the lead pheasant; It had been an unbelievably lucky circumstance that another bird had flown and matched perfect flight with the one she'd aimed for so that her shot pierced them both through the eye. She didn't deem it necessary to correct her uncle's presumption, either, when after investigating the harvest, he began hooting with unbridled pride and amazement over her kill.

It was never a bad thing for her Uncle to be bested by her in a hunting competition and to have his unwavering arrogance knocked down a peg. Besides, even one bird with a shot like that, was a prize worth boasting about.

Ann began singing quietly as she was prone to do when alone, wrapped in the solitude of nature's beauty. Over her soft hum she heard Uncle Rupert again, "Honestly Eddie," (her father abhorred the nickname his brother granted him in their childhood, and it nettled him that Rupert still called him by it; which consequently was why Uncle Rupie continued to do so.) "I say, the student has surpassed the teacher!" He exclaimed.

Her father only smiled. It was a bittersweet afternoon for them after all. Today she would have to begin to cease her -as her mother would say- "manly pursuits".

Trade in her rifle for a ballgown, as it were.

Ann sighed. She was to debut at her first ball this very evening. Seventeen years seemed unfairly young to Ann, to have to begin seeking matrimonial goals. Her mother and father had agreed though. And so, Ann (with much arguing at first) relented.

It is not as if she truly had a choice, anyway.

Ann glanced back again longingly, to the moors now distant behind her. She may have to don an over frilled and flounced, enveloping gown and enter more ballrooms than she'd care to, but she did not have to marry. She may even decide to not marry until her fourth year, she mused. Her father was rich as Croesus, it's not as if he couldn't afford to turn her out for four seasons. She wrinkled her nose amusingly over such a petty -but just- plan for revenge against her father. In fact, she thought it only fair her father accompany them on all the shopping expeditions her mother planned. The corners of her lips lifted with her evil plans.

Ann snorted, as her thoughts wandered back to marriage. It's not as if it would take much effort to remain unmarried. The renowned label "Dunneroy's Little Spitfire", such as she had been termed with (or earned, as her mother would testily remind her) was sure to follow her all the way to London!

She'd ridden against many of the gentleman she would be expected to partner for dances. And bested them all at hunts and races her father put on at his lodge events. She'd always been allowed to participate, much to her mother's chagrin.

Her father and uncle being second and third sons, respectively, without any expectations of gaining the earldom, both chose the soldier life; and excelled in their positions immensely. Their eldest brother had met his untimely demise before Ann had born, and her father being next in line, had gained the titles and responsibilities that went with it.

Ann had been told through stories that her father and Uncle Rupie had been kept distant from their eldest brother whilst growing up. But her father becoming the earl did not break the bonds of the soldier brothers. Ann knew brother relationships of jealousy existed, but her father and Uncle Rupert shared no such animosities and were as close as two brothers could be.

Both ex-soldiers-and Calvary officers, such as they were-determined it prudent to begin instructing Ann in the arts of survival at the tender age of five. Thanks to their teachings and Ann's devotion to her unorthodox education, Ann knew her way around weaponry. She could assemble makeshift firearms and outshoot, well, all the gentleman of her acquaintance - including her father and Uncle in recent years.

She could ride as if born seated to a saddle; jumping hedges and brooks since she was first able to explore outside of the corral. That's where her true passions lie. It was her dream to own the best horseflesh in all of England and Scotland combined.

She mostly enjoyed a slow canter throughout her favorite winding trails amidst the dense forest, but she had been taught to ride as if the fiery gates of hell were descending upon her if need be.

As early as ten years old, her father and uncle began abandoning her in the wilds of Exmoor to fend for herself. That's what Ann had been led to believe, of course, on her first test. She later learned they had remained near enough to keep guard of her the entire time.

She could still recall the frightening sounds of the night, embellished by her youthful imagination. Her horse's anxious hooves pounding in place beneath her as her shaky hands tightened around the cold leather of the reins. The chilled breeze of night air wisping loosened hair from her braid into her face in stinging whips and the darkness descending upon her as the sun exited the sky. Alone and frightened. But determined.

She had not faltered through her fear; instead she utilized the skills her father and Uncle had taught her and made it through the night unscathed. The next morning as she rode up the path leading to their grand manor, her father and uncle rode to greet her, both of their faces beaming with pride at her success.

Later they designed more challenging tests. Sometimes she was to survive an entire week with whatever meager items they deemed to supply her with. Eventually, they stopped coddling her by keeping watch.

Her father denied it, but her Uncle informed her that her father had chewed his fingers to stumps with worry for her those first few times she set out alone. Her mother had intentionally not been made aware of those special occasions.

Each time, Ann had surpassed their expectations and with that earned their respect in the way that a man, *a son*, might.

The forest and wilderness became like a second home to her. More than that, it felt a part of her. And Ann cherished her time in the woods as well as the special bonds it had forged with her father.

She basked in her role of her father's favorite "son". It was no matter that she was his daughter and only child. She adored her father and from as early as she could remember had strived to make him proud. It was an unorthodox role for a daughter, she surmised, but she reveled in it. Her father was her best friend and closest confidante, with Uncle Rupie a near second.

Which is why it had felt somewhat of an abandonment, when her father had taken her mother's side and backed her mechanisms to force Ann into a lady, proper. But that was the way it was with marriage she supposed; the husband was secretly run by his wife.

Only, she knew that statement to be untrue. She may be a tad bit wild and spoiled, she'd admit, but she wasn't daft. Her parents had a loving relationship, rare amongst the ton, from the glimpses she'd observed and stories she'd been told.

Their neighbor, Baron Rennington was a cruel man and violent towards his wife. Nearly as bad, in Ann's opinion, were men not physically abusive, but of the mentally dominating sort. She'd met a few of those sorts at her father's hunting lodge during sporting events her father hosted.

They were all one and the same; advising her father to put her in a dress and teach her the art of a silent tongue to go with her pretty face. Her father, never baited, always remained silent knowing and having faith in Ann to deliver her own comeuppance. She would often spy her Uncle Rupert taunt them silently with his devilish twinkling eyes as if telling those men, *you're no match for my niece.*

She always felt a certain satisfaction when trouncing those particular gentlemen. Their losing comments were always the same, often remarking upon Ann's inability to acknowledge she was in, fact, female. To which Ann could do no more than roll her eyes.

She was well aware she was a woman. And she did plan to marry one day. But she wouldn't settle for anything less than love. After witnessing her parents' devotion to one another all her life, how could she possibly live otherwise?

She just didn't want to marry *yet*. Was that so much to ask?

She surfaced from her maudlin thoughts as she sensed her father's presence beside her, his tall mount matching the slow stride of her gelding. He knew today weighed heavily on her.

He was a stark contrast to his carefree brother. His humor was quieter, his gruff words softly spoken; never one to raise his voice. When he spoke, it was always with intent and purpose and often words were unnecessary between them. Just as him riding beside her then, offering her strength, knowing her mind's struggle.

"Your mother has given into your wild ways all these years. She thought she had born a daughter that would partner her around the manor and in the taming of us rough men, but instead I fear I stole you away and made you one of us. I don't regret it. But I think even you can be kind enough to give your mother this one boon. She has longed for some time to have you for her own friend in her world; a Lady's world. Surely you can give her this time before you go on to live a life of your own?"

Her relationship with her mother was more complicated. She loved and respected her mother. She even understood her mother's worry for her. She just abhorred the activities her mother chose to do with her time. Unfortunately, those very activities were duties Ann would be expected to perform one day as lady of her own household.

Her father's words struck guilt in her heart, though. She hadn't thought her mother deprived of time spent with her? It wasn't as if her mother *never* stepped foot from the house. She accompanied them on picnics and fishing trips. Honestly her mother always seemed to love time spent out of doors as well. She even had her own special garden that was off limits to everyone else -even the head gardener. Ann couldn't understand why her mother continued to strive to be what society dictated a "true Lady" to be, when it was obvious she felt the restrictions herself.

She supposed her mother felt she had something to prove. After all, she'd been naught but a farmer's daughter when she and father had married. Before he came into his title and was but a traveling soldier himself. Didn't she know that in the country, one needn't give a fig about the opinions of the *haut ton*? Ann certainly didn't!

She shouldn't be assuaged with guilt, however. It's not as if all Ann did was ride wild over the estate and learn how to dig her own latrine. -Something of which she was quite proud of.

Most of the time, she bloody well was kept confined to the manor walls learning the very skills she detested. Her father taught her the useful skill of sewing, while her mother taught her the finer art of embroidering. Which was utterly useless, if one asked Ann.

She knew bawdy soldier songs (mostly learned from her Uncle Rupert) while her mother forced piano lessons unto her. Ann would have happily compromised and endured musical talents foisted upon her, had her mother allowed her to learn her choice: the mandolin. A mandolin could be carried from her saddle, she'd argued.

Obviously, she had not endeared her mother to agree with her logical reasoning.

She knew how to bake and season wild game to make it last, rather than how to select fine wines or direct a kitchen staff for a house party.

Ann cringed. She rather suspected, she would be made to catch up quickly on those studies over the course of her dratted season. Along with other unimportant knowledge she was to pretend she gave a wit about.

"A well-oiled door should never creak, Ann."

"There should never be spots on the silver. And the balustrade and doorknobs should always be shining."

"A lady does not slouch."

"Nor does she sneak pastries from the kitchen."

All her mother's lessons came heralding back into her mind, like a hammer thwacking away at a stone wall. Ann knew her duty though. She had never failed any challenges her father extended to her and she would not fail in this.

Ann didn't want anything to do with the aristocracy that looked down upon her mother and labeled Ann a hoyden because she excelled at talents beyond the drawing room. But she would step into their world with the epitome of the finest lady and have the pleasure of seeing them choke upon their own venomous tongues.

She turned to her father, then, who had been looking on her with unusual sympathy in his eyes. With the new goal to turn the heads of the ton burning in her blood, and renewed spirit glowing from her eyes, she smiled with wolfish determination and spurred her horse ahead at full speed.

"Race you back!" She hooted exuberantly over her shoulder in a flash past her father and Uncle Rupert.

Rupert smiled back to his elder brother knowingly and shared a silent communication. Edmond worried for Ann's debut into society, but Rupert had every faith in their Ann. Her spirit would not be broken so easily; as her recent display of vivacity just projected. With pride filling their chests, both men dug in their heels and chased after Ann, neither one accustomed to losing a race.

Peals of laughter rang out over the flying dust as they all brought their mounts to sliding stops in the circle drive in front of the manor.

"Well, Uncle Rupie, that's twice in one day you were bested by little ol' me," Ann gloated

"I know not why you single me out," Rupert grumbled as he hopped to the ground and busied himself with loosening his horse's cinch, "Your father didn't fare any better."

"Yes, but he's not a poor sport like you and not nearly as easy, or fun, to nettle." She shot back impudently and shared a smile with her father.

Three groomsmen came to assist them with the horses.

And Ann's renewed sense of vigor dissipated with the cloud of dust around them at the sight before them.

Her mother, The Countess of Abersty, stood at the top of the smooth stone steps leading to the main entrance of the manor, tapping her tiny slipper clad feet in furious rhythm.

Rupert sensing the scene that was sure to unfold, cleared his throat nervously, "Actually, I had better see to my own horse. I think he may have thrown a shoe in the last stride of our race."

Ann and her father shared glances, both knowing that statement to be bollocks. Rupert would have inspected his mare instantly upon their arrival, had that been the case.

"Coward." Ann directed to him under her breath. He grinned back unabashedly, before saluting and turning on his heel back towards the stables.

Ann was amused to see her father nervously stroking his short, full beard as if searching for words that wouldn't set off the dynamite that was her mother.

Their two-day hunting trip had been a surprise for Ann; she hadn't known about the plans, thought only to be sharing a ride with her two favorite men before her forced departure from their country homestead. Then they'd arrived at their favorite clearing and her uncle jumped down and pulled supplies that had been hidden behind the brush out into the open.

Apparently, the trip had been a surprise to her mother as well.

Unusual for her father to keep her mother in the dark about these trips. She wondered herself, the explanations he had given for their absences.

One look at her mother however, told her whatever the story had been her mother no longer believed it.

Her father braved to speak, "Rosemary,"-

Her mother turned her cool gaze to her father and then turned primly on her heel and marched into the house.

Her mother was the queen of communicating through facial expressions alone. This one clearly said, *"We will not discuss this on the front steps and create a public display of ourselves."*

Ann was caught off guard when her mother turned her attentions firstly to her upon entering the foyer.

"Ann!" Lady Abersty exclaimed with no small amount of exasperation and accusation. "Tonight is your debut into society and you have arrived home with little time to prepare and in a state of complete mess. Your hair is windblown and snarled with-good grief-leaves and twigs!

"And Edmond! What is the meaning of this?" Ann winced at her mother's unusually shrill voice.

"Now, Rosemary, don't start squawking at us."

Lady Abersty raised a delicate brow in warning to Lord Abersty, loaded with contrary objection to being resembled to anything that could "squawk". Ann nearly snorted an unlady-like laugh but stifled it in time. She was in enough trouble as it was. Lord Abersty winced in recognition of his error and knew he would pay for that comment later.

"She has plenty of time to ready for tonight's event. It's her first ball, but it's not as if she will be entering a ballroom in town; It's nothing more than a country entertainment." Her father reasoned.

"Yes, and for most of the debutantes this season, a small ball in the country will be like tip toeing over a puddle, but for our Ann it will be as if she were thrown into the rushing waters of the Thames!"

"Do give her more credit than that."

"Truly, Edmond? Most of the guests attending have never even seen Ann attired in anything other than breeches!"

Now, *Ann* knew that for an exaggeration. She wore a frock to every church service. -When she attended them...

"Rosie," her father began.

This time Ann winced for her father and waited for her mother to object to the use of her most abhorred pet name, but instead her mother ignored it, all but for a peevish look that momentarily crossed her face.

"Edmond, you promised that once Ann came of age, you would put an end to these wild ways. She is not your son, but your daughter. She was supposed to make her debut last year when she turned sixteen, but I fell for your cajoling and relented, giving her one more year to, well, run wild like a hoyden, I suppose!"

Ann and her father both grinned widely hearing her mother use such a term. Which her mother promptly ignored.

"How will she ever become a Lady and a mother herself one day, if you keep allowing her to keep company with hounds and horses? No gentleman wants to settle down with a woman so wild."

"Any man would be lucky to have our Ann."

"Yes, and what gentleman is going to approach her with a marriage proposal, knowing she can probably out-shoot, out-hunt, and out-ride him? Young men are intimidated by," her mother coughed, "Er-hm, *Ladies*", her mother fixed a pointed stare at Ann, letting her know she was applying the term loosely in Ann's case, "with such a strong-willed disposition as Ann."

"Mother, I am sincerely not at all interested in marriage and becoming a baby factory."

Ann knew what to say to needle her mother. It was true Ann had no desire to become a bride or a mother so soon, but she couldn't help but hope for a love as grand as the one her parents shared, for herself, and she planned to hold out until she found it.

Her mother gasped in outrage! "Ann, such language is unacceptable."

Lady Abersty turned back to Ann's father, "Do you see, Edmond, what spending time with you and the, dare I say - gentlemen- you associate with at your hunting lodge have done to our daughter? She has been corrupted. Congratulations: the son you never had!"

Ann's mother waved her hands towards Ann with dramatic flourish, her pale strawberry blond hair loose in its chignon, swayed in effect.

"Oh, mother, do calm down." Ann kissed her mother on her pale cheek as she brushed by her. "I am on my way to don one of those blasted ball gowns you ordered for me, right now." Ann gave her father a conspiratorial wink.

Her mother tried to interrupt her with another raise of her brow, indicating she was not pleased with Ann's choice of words.

"No worries, mother," Ann drawled, "I will be readied in time and be all that is desired in a Lady: graceful, polite, delicate and, of course, dull and lacking all intelligence."

Ann's amber colored eyes twinkled devilishly at her mother, who swatted her fan at her in feigned aggravation (or rather, not so feigned), causing Ann to laugh as she dashed up the stairs.

Lady Abersty blew an exasperated breath towards the domed ceilings of their home, then pursed her lips accusingly towards Lord Abersty, but her eyes remained smiling with the same devilish twinkling as of her daughter's.

"You forgive me, Rosemary." Lord Abersty pulled his wife into his arms, the same charming way he had done for the past twenty years.

Clara Stella

Fiona's rough brogue woke Ann from her reverie, "If you don't think you'll be needin' anything, I think I'll just catch a few blinks meself, while the waters are calm, if'n you don't mind."

Ann opened her weary eyes and watched Fiona fold her damp, crumpled gown from earlier and place it in her trunk, before scooting it back under the cot and strapping it into place. Then, clad in her stocking feet and a drier change of clothes, Fiona climbed under her own covers. Her corkscrew, curly, orange hair flopping wildly as she did.

"No, thank you Fi. I hope to sleep this night as well, if the waters allow." Fiona nodded and turned over succumbing to a peaceful sleep. Ann wished she could do the same.

She wrapped her arms around her middle, drawing comfort from within and let a stray tear trickle down her cheek. She couldn't seem to keep maudlin thoughts of her family and home at bay lately. Nor could she keep her heart from feeling betrayed by James. More than once since eloping with James had she wondered if she had made a mistake. Perhaps she should have heeded her father's advice.

Surely, she hadn't been naïve as her father claimed, though he didn't know the worst of it. She'd felt suffocated by the ton, until James entered her life. She'd felt fun and alive again only in his arms and when gazed at from his eyes.

She recalled so many memories of witnessing stolen kisses between her parents; her mother the Ruler of Decorum, herself, Ann smiled. She had thought she'd found that same kind of love with James. Her parents made their objections clear, but Ann was certain they would fall in love with him too once they grew to know him better, and so she had continued to accept his suit, ready to battle for him if she must.

It was during this time, that she had ever felt as if she were truly disappointing her father. Her parents had always fondly referred to her as a "spitfire', "hoyden", or "hellion", but her father had never before called her a fool. That word had cut her deeply and set the rift between her and her parents.

Neither quite knowing how to mend it, both sure they were in the right.

Her arms dropped lower to cradle where her and James' baby grew. She laid her head down to her damp pillow and closed her eyes tightly against the tears; silently hoping for the rocking and swaying of the ship to lull her.

Ann kept her eyes closed in attempt to achieve the sleep, in which Fiona found so easily. Instead she dreamed of him...

Patterson's Ball
London, England
February 12, 1832

Well this had hardly been worth her time. Ann twirled a loosened spiral of her chestnut colored hair out of boredom. Mostly an outcast and therefore a wallflower at most of the soirees she'd attended, she was often left moldering in the corners. Her season had begun precisely the way her mother had predicted; therefore, Ann had been initiated to the wall flower set upon arrival. Her reputation as "Dunneroy's Little Spitfire" had indeed *preceded* her to London. Ann had not expected nor aspired to be the belle of the ball, but that is not to say that she wouldn't enjoy a dance or two, so long as she was stuck attending these tedious parties.

Suddenly the dance floor grew silent as the next sets of dancers took their places. The silence was slightly unusual, and it had all manner of heads turning towards the center of the floor followed by the murmuring of hushed voices.

It was no doubt unladylike to fervently hope for a scandal to liven a party. But even being only Ann's fourth ball, she was that desperate for action more diverting-than plucking the leaves from her hosts' potted palms-that she found herself craning her head.

Her eyes traveled the rows of decorative heads turned until she discovered what, or rather *who*, had everyone's attention. She felt her own intake of breath as she stared uncouthly at the stranger occupying the dance floor.

He was a rather beautiful specimen of man. Even from where she stood, she could see his sculpted physique framed beneath his evening attire; his hair and complexion could both be described as golden. He ignored the blatant stares as he led a trembling young lady unto the dance floor. Ann was as entranced by his charming smile as the rest of the captivated crowd.

It was the golden quality that gave him away. That sun bronzed skin that screamed *American*. She allowed her eyes to continue to appraise him, after all she was a good distance away what harm could happen? It could hardly be classified as bold if she was hiding slightly behind the leafy plants while she perused him.

Before her eyes could obey her to divert her attention elsewhere, they spied his rather interesting leather boots. Ann knew them to be called moccasins. It seemed rather a bold and uncharacteristic move to flaunt one's American heritage in the middle of a grandeur London ballroom. Ann's lips quivered into a satisfied smirk. She wasn't the only one defiantly resisting being transformed into a made over dandy of the *ton*.

Oh! His silver gaze met hers square on across the room. He was certainly direct. And in a world where obtuseness was demanded, that was not a good thing. She certainly didn't want to be the next reason heads were turned. She forced her eyes to quickly turn away. There was nothing she could do, however, to calm her racing heart. She hadn't been safe behind the potted plants after all.

It was rather embarrassing being caught out by the very man she had been eying like prime horse flesh at Tattersall's. She needed to recover her nerves lest she draw unwanted attention to herself.

Her breathing was still matching the pace of her heart. Calm breaths, shallow breaths, she told herself. Probably nothing would come of it.

"Hello."

Ah! Ann knew she resembled a gaping fish in that moment. *He approached her? Her?* Oh, no. this was not at all what she needed. She just wanted to make it through this blasted season and return to her beloved home in the country to the fine horse that awaited her.

She failed to hide her annoyance, "Hello."

She managed not to wince at her own tone. Truly, it wasn't his fault she was forced to attend these dull affairs. Nor was it his fault she had been caught gawking at him like a ninny.

She cleared her throat and attempted to say more (and in a polite fashion), but it seemed all of the English language deserted her. What was wrong with her? She wasn't shy. She was bored with the monotonous conversational topics allowed for debutantes and therefore *chose* to remain in the corners, unbothered. Well, that, and because she tended to be too forthright; not a redeeming quality to have here amongst the *ton*.

But she had never been shy, and she always had something to say (another disfavored quality she possessed according to a greater population that, unfortunately, scoped further than the *ton*), even if she sometimes, wisely, withheld her thoughts.

Wasn't she just complaining that she'd at least like to enjoy dancing if she was to remain cooped up at these *entertainments*? Blinking like an owl was not going to endear her to any future offers.

Before she could expound unto why he was addressing her in the first place, she reached for his hand and blurted, "Let's dance."

She cringed inwardly; *ladies* did NOT request dances from gentlemen. Her heart stopped fearfully. If he rejected her now, in front of all the watching eyes she felt upon her like flames licking at her back, she would forever be a laughingstock. She supposed she could retire to the country then as she desired, however she didn't handle failure well and she *did* intend to marry one day, after all.

She forced her gaze to move within her frozen body to meet his. If her father was watching this melodrama, she would ensure she at least appeared to go down in flames bravely.

She squared her chin at him and waited for him to respond. If only she could control the heaving rise and fall of her chest as she awaited her social hanging.

His face reflected surprise, then fascinated delight and she was able to exhale with relief when he led her away from the growing crowd around them. Of course, crowds of people were probably nothing new for this golden Greek god of a man.

Should she thank him? That would imply that she had needed rescuing and Ann Dunneroy was never so helpless that she couldn't save herself. She notched her chin a little higher. No, she didn't think so. She would never have needed rescuing if he hadn't sneaked up on her like a devil fox. Okay, so perhaps her bold eye contact had beckoned him to her, but that had been a mistake, albeit a rude one.

It was too late now; she was paying for her crime. Or was she? If dancing with a perfectly handsome stranger was her punishment, then perhaps she should let her eyes rove more often. This last thought appeared on her face in a secretive smile.

"What are you smiling about?"

Oh, even his voice was handsome. The deep and resonating kind; the kind one could listen to telling stories into the late hours of the night by a warming fire...

Okay. Stay clear of those thoughts Ann, quit behaving so foolishly. And find your tongue for goodness sake! She shook her sable mane lightly and delicately cleared her throat, as if to erase the previous encounters from her mind and begin afresh.

"And why should I share my secrets with you, Mr....?"

"Morgan. James Morgan," he supplied and smiled in kind, "Fair enough. How about we begin with your name? I can uncover your secrets later."

Arrogant man. Ann liked him. She felt a kindred spirit in him; a fighting spirit.

"Lady Ann Dunneroy."

"Dunneroy?   Abersty's   daughter?"   Shocking comprehension dawned on his face.

Apparently, he had already heard about the 'Hoyden of Abersty'. Ann narrowed her eyes defensively.

"Yes, the daughter of the *Earl* of Abersty." She challenged him, haughtily.

"Quite so. The Earl's only, and very *rich* daughter." He grinned unrepentantly, in a way that melted the frosty veneer she had stormed up.

"Indeed. And are you a fortune hunter, Mr. Morgan?"

"Isn't everyone?"

"Spoken like a true American."

His grin flashed again in that strong jaw of his. "My family has been investing in tobacco for some years now. We've managed to be fairly successful." The dimple deepened in his cheek and she knew his family had been more than "fairly successful".

"You don't wear modesty well, do you Mr. Morgan?"

His answer was a deep rumbling chuckle. His enigmatic energy was palpable and alluring. Although, it garnered a lot of unwanted attention, Ann couldn't keep from smiling back in return.

"I forget myself. Money and business are too delicate of topics for English ears and most especially so for a Lady's."

"I happen to find the topic very intriguing." She wanted to know more about him.

"Yes, I suppose *you* would." The last was stated in a way that seemed to cocoon them off from the rest of room; as if he already knew her secrets and she was more special for them in his eyes. Warmth spread all the way down to her toes.

The descent of the song was already being played much to Ann's regret. Soon she would have to step from the strong arms she was growing readily comfortable in. She could sense too, his objection to the end of their dance.

"What do you say we shock the *ton* once more and dance with me again?" What festivity will you be attending tomorrow evening?"

She hadn't planned on attending Lady Clarydon's Ball. She had spent most of tonight thinking of convincing excuses to get out of going, in fact. Besides, she shouldn't allow James Morgan the impression that she was so easily won over.

"Lady Clarydon's Ball." She blurted, surprising even herself. "That is to say, I might deign to be present at Lady Clarydon's ball tomorrow evening."

"Please do." He chuckled again, knowingly, causing a most unwanted girlish blush to heat her face. "I would be most distressed if I am deprived of another opportunity to be insulted by your brazen tongue."

The satisfied smile that curved her lips was quickly replaced with one of immediate shock and pleasure when, as the dance came to its close, he raised her hand to his lips and pressed a bold kiss to the back of it. It had been quick and discreet, but she would never forget the brief warm meeting of his tongue there. The wicked grin he was wearing just for her lit his eyes and all the promises in them arrowed straight through her heart.

"Until we meet again, Lady Ann."

Ann woke suddenly, at the feel of water upon her face. *Not another storm!* Quickly she sat up and wiped the wetness from her face only then realizing it was her own tears she was dashing at. "Wonderful, it appears I'm trading one form of saltwater for another."

She would not be getting that restful sleep tonight. Ann reached for the rubber boots made in loan to her by one of the captain's shipmates. She'd brought night slippers but had quickly realized the futility in that ensemble when crossing an angry ocean. She tugged the overly large boots on and chuckled at the absurd picture she must make. A little English miss in her sleeping gown and giant rubber sailor's boots. – A drowned rat, more like, one of which looked like had swallowed a melon whole.

Her legs wobbled beneath her as the ship groaned and swayed under her feet. She managed to grab her warm cloak that was mostly dry thanks to Fiona, who had been seeing to both their care. She wrapped it tightly about her and lightly stepped up the stairs, weary of attracting any unwanted company. She had only been able to afford second class cabins, if she was to conserve what she had saved of the pin money she'd received from her father over the past months.

That was the bulk of her financial provisions. The rest had been accumulated from sending much of her valuable belongings with a trusted source of her lady's maid, who pawned them for her. She had been saddened to see some of her jewels go that had been gifts from her parents along with some other sentimental objects, but it had been necessary. Ann only hoped these sacrifices would be worth it in the end.

Ann peeked out the door, when she was sure no one was about this side of the ship she walked to the rail. It felt good to inhale air that did not seem mildew and stale as it felt below deck and her lungs breathed hardily. The stars reflecting off the ocean was truly a beautiful sight, and if she didn't hate the ocean so, she might admit she actually found it quite lovely.

She stared out across the endless blue, where the smooth sapphire jewel they sailed mirrored the glittering gems in the black velvet sky and it was indeterminable where one ended and the other began.

Ann sighed at its majestic beauty. She could hardly fathom that she existed amongst such gloriousness, let alone that she was where she was in that moment; on a ship, cast out for lands unknown.

Oh, James.

She didn't know whether his name was a curse on her lips or a lonely, yearning whisper.

Ann, once so certain, was frightened of so many things now...The pregnancy and birthing and not having her mother at her side...Sailing to lands unknown to her, alone... The question of James' intentions...

The more she thought about her circumstances, the more foolish she felt, and insecurities wrapped around her like a London fog. She would be a mother in a matter of weeks, and she must make the right decisions, but what were they?

How she missed her own mother. Ann hoped her parents had received her letter of explanations, or *lies* rather, and feared naught for her. She loved both of her parents dreadfully and her heart ached with grief over where her rash actions had led her.

Water lapped at the side of the ship and sprayed over the edge, thoroughly misting Ann in the process and dousing her memories with the cool shock of reality. She was too heartsick in that moment to feel vehemently towards the indifferent waves.

The ship rocked forcefully then and sent Ann knocking into the sidewall. She found her feet quickly and put her hands to her swollen belly in alarm. She didn't know a whole lot, or anything at all really, about whelping children, but she was certain slamming the protruding anatomy into the wall of a ship was not healthy for it.

She didn't feel differently and there was no pain, so she assessed all must be well. Fiona had told her that the protective barrier around the baby was quite strong, and it must be so, she thought.

Ann pushed herself from the side and began making her way back down to the cabin area below deck, thinking of her and James' child. Would James want their child? He must, she decided, finding her grit. All would turn out and this will have been nothing more than a little hiccup in their lives.

Ann had it all worked out in her mind: she and James (once she found him) would delay their return to England until after the baby was born, inevitable at this point. Her parents, though originally opposed to the match, would no doubt welcome her and their grandchild back with open arms. Ann smiled at the blissfully happy reunion she pictured in her mind and sighed. Yes, all would go as planned. It had to.

Otherwise, what would she do?

She could not dwell on such uncertainties, now. She only wished her heart could be as easily convinced as her mind. Ann rubbed the chill from her arms as she wished she could do to the doubts that haunted her and climbed into her cot where she finally drifted into an exhausted slumber.

Chapter 2

Charleston, South Carolina
November 2, 1832

She could see the bay now; only twelve kilometers or so away from port. Blessedly, her time aboard the Clara Stella was near its end. Though Ann's health had fared better during the past three weeks she was still thankful no additional storms had decided to hurl themselves into the little clipper's path and delay her parting from it.

Surprisingly, a budding romance between her friend and the captain had occurred during the voyage. She was happy for Fiona and nearly as happy that the relationship had aided in producing upgraded accommodations for them aboard the ship. Once Fiona and Captain Ludwick's engagement had been announced to everyone on the ship, Ann and Fiona were moved into a small cabin above deck that proved far more luxurious than their previous housing arrangement- mostly because the room remained ninety percent drier than had their room below. It was also far more spacious, what with Fiona spending most of her time sneaking into the Captain's quarters.

It was interesting to Ann, witnessing -what was obviously- a love match between Fiona and her Captain. It had Ann questioning again her love for James. Did she still love him? Had she truly ever loved him? Or had she found a kindred wild spirit trapped in a London ballroom and become infatuated with his tales of adventure? Of a certain, she'd been charmed, but she was no longer certain they had ever shared anything deeper.

She supposed it was a moot point now; they were married, after all, and she was carrying his child. Breathing deeply, she reaffirmed her plan in her mind. She would find him, and she *would* love him. It was simple really and she refused to settle for less.

"Och, that is a fierce look of determination upon your face." Fiona laughed, "I've not seen you look so battle ready since you first boarded. What a fearsome little mother you shall make." Fiona squeezed Ann's hand communicating her genuine love for her friend.

Fiona would not continue past Charleston and instead would be marrying Captain Ludwick and remaining on his ship with him. That she would miss the companionship of the fiery Fiona was a massive understatement. But Ann couldn't dwell on their parting, lest her strength be depleted. She needed to steel her nerves for the unknown, not be lost to a melancholy. Fiona, as always, understood Ann's thoughts and kept her words light, although both hearts were heavy.

"I want you to know, I spoke wi' me Elliott. I do not know the particulars of your predicament, but I do know, that you are here alone, Ann. And carrying a wee babe. Elliott knows what of a doctor in Charleston. Says he's right kind and will take good care of ye." Fiona continued, a worried expression marring her brow, "We also want you to know, the Clara Stella will be docked for a week. So, if ye decide you'd like to return to England wi' us, you've only to send word while we're here."

Ann nodded, unable to form words. She and Fiona had shared little of their secrets, though it had not impeded their growing fondness for one another. Ann had explained to Fiona, however, that she was coming for her husband. She told Fiona she had not time to send notice ahead of her passage that she was coming early and thus her husband was unaware of her arrival.

It was nearly the truth. She'd omitted the fact that her husband didn't actually invite her presence at all, early or otherwise. Nor did she inform Fiona that her husband had no idea he was to be a father in a matter of weeks.

"Look, Ann there it is! We've arrived!" Fiona pointed excitedly towards the harbor. They both turned, taking in the picture before them equally in silent awe.

Ann and Fiona waited patiently with their luggage out of the way of the crew as they docked; the anticipation and excitement building inside Ann with each second. She fair fidgeted as she sat upon her luggage and took in the sight of Charleston.

This was America, she smiled brightly, all trepidation and prior foreboding, pushed aside in this moment.

The sun shone brightly on this day as if encouraging Ann to move forward and to reach for this new life; *her new life*, with both hands. *All in now*, her father would have said.

All seemed brighter here, and so full of life. Even the fishy smell of port did not seem as malodorous as in England. Below, the land pulsed with life, people thronged around the ship and scurried here and there busily, and the vital atmosphere was infectious. She would be okay, she told herself.

Captain Ludwick made his way to where she and Fiona sat. He was smiling at Fiona and looked for all the world as a star-crossed lover should look. They had eyes only for each other. Ann felt guilty for feeling discomfort, an unwelcome visitor in their presence, instead of only joy for them. As if broken from the spell, Captain looked to Ann.

"Are you ready?" Captain Ludwick asked as he picked up her bags in one hand and offered her his other.

"Ready as ever I will be." Ann smiled nervously.

"Well then, let's disembark. I'm sure steady land will be welcomed under your feet once more, no?"

She blushed, embarrassed as Captain Ludwick teasingly alluded to her wretched sea sickness during the voyage. Ann placed her hand on Captain Ludwick's arm, "Thank you. Thank you for your kindness. I am very pleased Fiona has found such a gentleman."

Fiona smiled and stood near Ann's other side, and together Fiona and the Captain gave Ann strength as they departed the ship.

Ann braved a glance about her as she trudged between Fiona and the Captain. There were many black skinned people grouped together and in ill health from what Ann could see. A couple of white men appeared to be inspecting them. Ann had of course heard that slavery still took place in the Americas, and yet she was unprepared for the sight.

Back home, the abolition of slavery had been being fought for by the public for over forty-five years and was very nearly won. Her father had always supported the cause and was active in the fight to instill laws that would end not only the African slave trade, but slavery in all, for good.

Even though slavery existed throughout the British Empire, never had she witnessed the practice before now. Disgusted, she averted her eyes, training them ahead. The buildings and homes she saw much resembled those in England and her heart squeezed with thoughts of home, but she pushed on into the busy street.

The Captain had generously hired a hack and paid the cab fare for the three of them, for which Ann was grateful. They made their way slowly away from Dock Street and up Market Street where it was just as busy and crowded. People dashed everywhere frantically, and shop owners called out in attempt to sell their wares. In all outward appearances, Charleston was much like the grimier streets of London. Except, it wasn't London. It wasn't England. And it wasn't *home*.

They made their way into the heart of the town, where Captain and Fiona deposited Ann at the posting inn.

"Are ye certain ye doona wish for me to stay with ye?" Fiona asked in earnest.

"I'm certain. You go on and enjoy your shopping. I'll catch up with you."

Ann spread her lips into what she hoped was a convincing smile. The last thing she wanted was for her friend to stay and discover how much of a goose Ann truly was.

It had been the Captain who had suggested Ann head to the posting inn first thing in order to send word to her husband of her arrival. Such a suggestion made a lot of sense. -If one knew the address of whom one sought.

Ann, however, did not.

Her husband's letter to her had been marked with a fictitious return address so that her father's household would not be alerted to her and James' secret messages. She did not know James' address. All she knew was James and his family managed a successful plantation in Charleston. She had banked on the hopeful reasoning, that surely, if it was as profitable as James alluded to, someone would know of him or his family and be able to help her contact him.

Only now was she realizing how asking about town for her husband might make her appear a tad deranged. She imagined most wives did not lose their husbands.

She was here now, though. What else could she do?

Captain Ludwick's voice cut in, "We shall be just visiting those shops up ahead," He gestured, "Come find us once you've finished your business." He smiled to Ann politely, then eagerly whisked Fiona off towards the shops.

Ann filled her lungs with the salty air, finding her courage as she entered the inn. She walked up to the desk.

A pert, doughy man from behind it pushed his glasses up his nose, "May I help you?"

Tentatively, unsure of the most effective words to use, Ann began, "Yes, I... I am recently from London and am to meet my new husband, Mr. James Morgan. Only, I thought to surprise him by booking passage earlier than expected, and well, now I...am unsure how to get into contact with him."

She flinched inwardly over how impossibly silly she sounded.

"I was hoping you, being the postmaster and therefore all-knowing in the elite personage of Charleston, may know of an address of which I may reach him?"

Good, Ann, she congratulated herself, *flattery should loosen his tongue and she'd even managed to slip in that her husband was of some importance.*

But instead the greasy rotund man stared back at her in disbelief. "You don't know your husband's address?"

So much for flattery easing her way around her obvious blunder. She gritted her teeth, "No." She forced herself into a calm and asked again, "I'm sure you have heard of the Morgan's in these parts somewhere. Of the Tobacco Plantation Morgan's?"

"I'm sorry Miss, I don't know of any Morgan's in this area or the surrounding counties neither."

Ann felt her insides drop as if from a cliff side. Her shock and worry must have shown on her face for the blunt postmaster before her spoke more gently, "Perhaps check with the bank across the street. Bein' your husband's family is in the tobacco industry, they might be clients there."

She nodded, dazed, but still remembering her manners thanked the man. Slowly she made her way onto the wooden planked walk outside the building and across the street to where the bank was located.

Unfortunately, the bank was of no help either.

Ann had been so certain it would be fairly easy locating her husband. After all, he'd told her of how lustrous his family name was, how prosperous was their plantation. Could he have lied? She'd expected for the postmaster to perhaps have a list of Morgan names, after all it seemed a fairly common name. She'd thought the trial would be in determining the correct *Morgan*. She'd never imagined having *no* leads to follow. She'd crossed an entire ocean...

She found Captain Ludwick and Fiona easily enough and continued on with them. Mostly Fiona shopped, excitedly. Even if Ann could have afforded to indulge in a few fripperies, she was still too shaken by the realization that she may not ever find James, to enjoy the outing.

As the day had grown long, Captain Ludwick, suggested they dine before continuing on to Dr. Fletcher's. He generously rented a day room at Rosie's Inn and allowed for she and Fiona to clean up and dress more appropriately for their evening meal.

Fiona was able to don one of her new gowns. Ann was certain Fiona was not accustomed to such finery. She stood smiling brightly into the looking glass admiring her transformed appearance.

Ann smiled softly, "You look stunning."

"Thank ye. Now if only I could *sound* a proper lady." Fiona's smile faltered, nervously.

"Your Elliott loves you for you. He didn't purchase you these lavish gowns in order to change you. He simply adores you and wanted to dote upon you."

Ann smoothed a wrinkle here and there from the fine gown as she reassured her friend.

"Besides this isn't England. I'm told Americans don't put much stock into the notions of 'lords and ladies'. You shall dazzle everyone in the room."

Fiona smiled to her friend, but it faded shortly, and turned into a line of concern. "He's not coming for ye, is he Ann?"

Ann didn't pretend to misunderstand the probing question and looked away ashamedly.

"I doona know your circumstances, since you have not chosen to confide in me. That is fine. We both have our secrets. I know that. But it does nae sit well wi' me, leavin' you behind. I mean, look at ye. You're due to birth in a month's time."

"Nearly two-" Ann lamely tried to interject.

"Even so. You should return home, Ann."

"Captain Ludwick said himself, his doctor friend would be more than capable of delivering me safely." Ann argued back defensively. She didn't need anyone else scrutinizing her choices right now, even if it was only out of fondness that Fiona worried. She did enough of that herself.

"I shall be fine. If I need anything, I have contacts back home to which I may seek help from."

"Aye, an entire ocean away," was her friend's scathing retort, before leading out of the room to where Captain Ludwick awaited to escort them to dinner.

Ann remained behind a second longer, lines worrying her brow. More had been said in her friend's short statement than had actually been spoken. Fiona had wanted to point out Ann's foolish belief that anyone from the other side of the world would be of any help to her.

Ann already knew that. Just as she knew she would never contact her family for help no matter how dire her circumstance became. She'd not crawl back with her tail between her legs like a chastened hound. No. She'd not be returning unless her dignity would be returning with her. And until she found James, that simply wasn't a possibility.

Ann could not seem to summon any enthusiasm throughout the evening. Luckily, Captain Ludwick and Fiona seemed more than enough content with only each other for conversation. Despite her and Fiona's little spat, Ann dreaded their future parting. Waiting for that moment, however, was only increasing Ann's anxiety. The meal seemed to drag on, in Ann's mind. She barely tasted her food, only aware of chewing and swallowing in order to pass the time. Her stomach seemed to churn with dread, and Ann wished for the meal to end so they could proceed to Dr. Fletcher's.

The Captain had taken the time before supper, while Ann and Fiona were bathing and dressing, to visit the doctor, who he assured Ann was happy to board her. While she was appreciative of the help, Ann wasn't certain Captain Ludwick was aware that she hadn't much in the way of funds. As far as he knew, her husband would be coming for her soon and there was nothing to truly worry about.

Ann worried all through the meal wishing for it to be over. Then suddenly it was, and Ann felt it was too soon.

Fiona's lilting voice broke into Ann's internal rising panic, "Are ye ready?"

Ann nodded despite the butterflies in her belly fluttering an opposite response. Once she reached Fletcher's, Fiona would be returning to the safety of the ship. The vessel returning home. Ann would be left behind.

Alone.

Ann's emotions were whirring within. She needed to keep herself held together. She couldn't allow herself to unravel like a falling ball of yarn. If she could leave her parents and all that was familiar to her -her entire life- behind, and cross the Atlantic, then surely, she would survive parting from her newfound friend.

Once more, with her thoughts careening from hopeful to anxious-fueled fear, they piled into a hack and arrived before the doctor's residence in no time at all, despite the busied streets. -Though Ann rather suspected the acclaimed time had cost her backside.

There the three of them stood on the cobbled street. A few blocks out of town, the doctor's home and business matched those of the modestly built ones surrounding it. It wasn't necessarily a shabby neighborhood, but it didn't have the splendorous look of the bay side part of town.

Captain Ludwick stepped ahead of the ladies up onto the rushed mat lying on the stone step to rap on the solid, wood paneled door. The heavy door was encased into the wall of the building with gray brick arched above making for a little roofed overhang. Above that was an engraved sign that appeared to be made of wood as heavy as the door itself. The sign simply read: Dr. H. Fletcher.

"So, this is it."

Fiona's voice pulled Ann back from her study of the modest abode. Tears glistened in Fiona's eyes. "Ye can be sure I'll be checking in on ye when next we port. I'll write to Dr. Fletcher's address. So be sure to tell him where to forward to once your husband comes for ye."

Ann returned Fiona's smile knowing her last statement for the apology it was. Fiona was letting her know she had faith in Ann to see her plans through; and that faith bolstered Ann. They embraced one another warmly.

"I will," Ann said. She stepped back and looked at her friend, smiling her courage in thanks for her friend's loyalty and kindness.

Just then, a young lad appeared on the street, calling out to the Captain as he ran toward them.

"Captain! Captain, quick. This is for you." The Captain swept past them hurriedly to reach the boy and take the message from his dirtied fingers.

"Damn. It's urgent." The Captain swore, uncharacteristically. "I'm sorry Mrs. Morgan, but Fiona and I must be back to the ship immediately."

Without any further explanation and no time for Ann and Fiona to say a proper goodbye, Fiona, the Captain, and the boy rushed away down the street.

Ann's heart began to pound as she gaped after their retreating forms. Her two friends had abandoned her on the doorstep of a stranger like a lost kitten.

Before Ann could think what to do, the door opened.

"Yes? Hello, Miss, how may I help you?"

An older, over-portly man with tufts of white hair sprouting wildly above his ears and small spectacles resting upon his cherry colored nose and cheeks, stood in the doorway. He greeted Ann with a welcoming, if tad weary, smile.

Ann peered desperately in the direction her friends had left her. She had truly been abandoned and left in a most uncomfortable position. The man before her, whom she presumed to be the doctor, was friends with Captain Ludwick, who was no longer present to make the introductions.

"Hullo, my name is Ann Morgan," she found herself fiddling nervously with one of her carried parcels, "I am a friend of Captain Elliott's fiancé. He told me he had made arrangements with you or, er, discussed with you -"

"Ah, yes!" The man's smile widened, and his dull eyes sparked a bit, "Mrs. Morgan, hello! And I am Dr. Howard Fletcher. Pleased to meet you. Come in, come in."

He turned around proceeding into his home, gesturing for Ann to follow.

"Indeed, Elliott visited earlier and informed me that you may be in search of a comfortable housing arrangement."

The part of the house she had entered seemed like a small cottage type dwelling, all raw wood and rustic. No fancy tables, or décor of any kind. Indeed, the kitchen area was attached to where people dined, and one could view the family quarters from there as well. T'was very different from her home in England, thought Ann, and an ache of nostalgia crept into her heart.

"I hope Captain Ludwick explained that I am willing to work for my keep."

Her hands traveled of their own accord to her swollen belly. The Doctor's eyes followed briefly before returning to her face, an understanding smile on his lips. Her spine steeled, and she straightened taller. She'd not have him think her trying to use her advanced state of pregnancy to gain favors.

"I still have nearly two months before the baby is due, and I am in perfect health. I assure you I am able and most willing to assist in any way necessary in order to pay for a respectable room and board."

"Yes, yes," The doctor smiled warmly to her, understanding in his eyes. He knew Ann would not accept charity and he respected her for it, "I can see that."

Although he had no intention of working a pregnant woman to death, he would find chores that were fit for someone of her condition in order to soothe her pride; as he could tell that was the only way to appease the stubborn woman before him. He'd have rented the room free, however, just to have company around again. It had been too many years since his wife's passing, and their child decades before that. Life had begun to seem mighty dark for him of late.

"Well, I think we could make an excellent team, as I told Elliott earlier today. And I am more than pleased to have the help."

He smiled gently again. Then as if surprised, "Where is Elliott by the way? I cannot believe the boy would forget his manners and allow a beautiful young lady such as yourself to journey across town unescorted. And not greet me, to boot!"

Ann smiled when the Doctor referred to the strapping Captain Ludwick as a 'boy'. And again, as the Doctor appeared angry on her behalf, as if the few blocks from the main part of town could be termed a "journey".

"He did, actually, escort me that is and intended to greet you as well, but I am afraid an emergency situation arose that caused him and Fiona to harry off unexpectedly."

"Ah, probably to do with whatever cargo he is trading. Well, that is no matter. You are here and safe." He smiled once more. "If you don't mind Mrs. Morgan, I am an old man and have cared for patients all day. I would love to further discuss our plans but fear it must wait until the morning. If that is agreeable with you? Might I show you to your room, where you may get a restful night's sleep?"

Ann was certain the man was reading into her fatigue and kindly suggesting retiring for the night for her sake, but she didn't think it would be respectful to argue. There would be plenty of time tomorrow to hash out the details of her stay, and she *was* quite tired, after all.

"Certainly. Thank you."

She was led across the wood planked floor towards the far end of the entertaining room to a door. The door opened to a poorly lit hallway, but Ann could still discern the numerous doors on either side of the hall and imagined those were patient quarters, rather than for housing guests.

"These first two rooms are the guest room and my own," The doctor informed her, "The rest are examination rooms and the like, for my practice. Your room is to the left, here. My room is directly across the hall."

She stepped into her room. It was not grand lodgings, but after weeks aboard the *Clara Stella*, it looked like heaven. The furnishings in the room were few, but lovely, clearly designed for a lady, and at odds with the masculine features of the rest of the house.

"I'll leave you in peace, to retire for the evening. If you should need anything, I will be in the sitting room for a spell yet, while you get settled."

Before he could retreat, Ann cleared her throat awkwardly, "And where might the bathing chambers be and the 'necessaries pot'?"

The Doctor chuckled over her discomfiture and directed Ann to the proper locations of each before leaving her to her own devices.

Ann nearly sighed with longing for the opportunity to sleep on a large stuffed mattress, with fresh bedding, again. She set her luggage down on the other side of the room, deciding she would sort through and find places for her things once plans were confirmed on the morrow. She quickly changed into a sleeping rail and climbed under the coverlet and large quilt, sinking into the comfort of the mattress. She smiled to herself, feeling secured in where her actions had taken her for the first time since leaving home, and drifted to sleep.

The next morning, Ann dressed and stepped from her room in search of the Doctor. She put her hand to the cool wood paneled wall for support as she gathered her courage to lead her new life with this stranger.

Kind as Dr. Fletcher was to take her in; she couldn't help but feel awkward and uncomfortably shy. The last thing she wanted to be was a burden, though, so Ann did what she had always been taught to do. She squared her shoulders like the soldier her father had trained her to be and carried herself into the next room and to her new, strange life. She made her way to the kitchen where she could hear the short rotund man scurrying about.

"Oh, hello, dear." He said when he spied her. "I was just about to prepare us some tea. We won't have long before clients begin to arrive."

The white tuft of hair on his forehead was in disarray, his face pink and moistened with little beads of sweat as he scurried about his business.

Ann cleared her throat nervously, "If I may, Dr. Fletcher, I would be more than happy to finish making the tea and take on any other responsibilities that would assist you."

"Well, thank you dear girl. I almost have this set though. We may as well sit a moment while it peaks and have a little chat to better acquaint ourselves with one another."

His thick, fatherly hand gestured to one of the rustic chairs before the table, "Have a seat, have a seat."

His smile was encouraging, and Ann felt some of her nerves dissipate as she seated herself. "I want to thank you so much for welcoming me into your home. I plan to work very hard in return for your hospitality and generosity."

"Well, you are very welcome. And I could for surely use the help. I'm getting too old to be running all of this practice by myself."

His knees creaked as he sat the chair opposite of her, as if to prove true his last statement, but he continued to smile kindly on her.

"It has been a while since any ladies have lived under this roof, so forgive me if I have forgotten how to be delicate around such topics. I just want you to know that Elliott explained to me, during his visit, that you are searching for your husband and may not be staying with me long. I want you to know that you are welcome to stay for as long as you wish."

"Thank you."

She glanced down nervously to her hands, uncertain of how much she should unburden herself to this stranger, but deciding he deserved to know something of her situation.

"I fear something dreadful may have happened to my husband...."

She let her sentence trail off and they both understood what was not being said. That she feared even more that he had abandoned her.

She raised her chin a notch, "He didn't know about-about the baby."

"I see." The doctor said pityingly.

Damn James. She'd never been pitied before and she didn't much care for it.

The doctor perhaps sensing this spoke again, "Well, I will do all I can to help you find him, if that is your wish. I suggest we go about this search discreetly, however. You never know what answers we may find..."

Another unspoken message between them. Ann knew he was warning her that she may not like what she learned if she went in search of him.

A thought she was already familiar with and all too aware of, but she was thankful for the doctor's kind warning, nonetheless.

"Yes, I agree. And thank you."

The doctor reached his large warm hand over hers and squeezed it gently.

The tea kettle whistled, and he walked Ann through the kitchen, showing her where the utensils were, cups and all else and then they settled once more and sipped through the pot of tea together.

After, Ann was more than eager to pull her fair share of the weight in order to repay Doctor Fletcher for his generosity and they set off to prepare the patients' rooms. She studied and learned her duties well and Fletcher was glad for the company.

Over the following weeks, Ann and Fletcher fell into comfortable routines and came to know one another well. He treated her like a daughter in that time and it was a welcoming comfort, considering her circumstances, and she knew she would forever be grateful for this man's kindness and for that of Fiona and Captain Ludwick's as well.

She began assisting Fletcher with his patients, though he never allowed her to overtax herself and continued to look after her with fatherly concern.

The people of the town welcomed Ann as well, or at least those of which she met. She rarely left Fletcher's home, in part due to the embarrassment of her situation, but also because it was just too difficult walking into town at her advanced state of pregnancy.

Nancy, a silver haired, robust woman who liked to spend her time at the clinic with one embellished ailment after another was a patient Ann had grown quite fond of. She suspected, too, that Nancy had a secret love interest in the doctor and that was the cause for Nancy's so called, "illnesses".

Predictably, Nancy made her appearance half past the noon hour that day.

"Hello Ann, dear. How are you faring today?" That was another thing to become accustomed to in America. One did not stand on ceremony here and titles were not referred to.

"I'm well, thank you Nancy. And yourself?"

"Well, I thought I might be coming down with a touch of something and perhaps Howard would have a remedy for it. Also, of course, I just wanted to check on you. I know it won't be long before that little one arrives."

In the three weeks, Ann had known Nancy, she was always coming down with '*a touch of something*'. Ann would have been irritated with such behavior if the woman hadn't been as sweet as fig pudding.

"Oh my, you are looking a bit green around the gills today, too. Where is Howard? He will want to check you."

Conversations with this woman would make most anyone dizzy, thought Ann.

"Fletcher is seeing to Miss Calpurnia at the moment and I assure you, I am a most appropriate shade of..." Ann failed to find an apt description.

"Green." Nancy finished for her and gave her a pointed look, before charging down the hall calling for Doctor Fletcher.

Oh dear, Ann, thought. Miss Calpurnia would not take kindly to Nancy barging in on her appointment. Titles may not be well respected, but wealthy snobs were still to be found; and wealthy or not, privacy was still preferred within a physician's office!

"Wait!" Ann called, but when she began to step after her, a cramp seized her immobile and she could do no more but clutch her abdomen as fear sparked within her.

Dear God, the baby is coming.

Nancy came trotting back towards her from the far end of the hall in a flurry of skirts, with a worried Fletcher on her heels and a bewildered Calpurnia. The aches in her back grew too fierce and she remembered little else.

She did not faint, though she dearly wished her body would release her from such pain and Ann believed a temporary state of unconsciousness just might work! Her body wasn't willing to send her into the relief of darkness though and seemed instead to have her trapped in a fog.

Fletcher and Nancy scurried about the room around her after positioning her on a raised bed. Ann even glimpsed Miss Calpurnia offering aid when she could, although she looked as utterly horrified as Ann felt. She could see their lips moving and knew they were communicating with one another and perhaps even with her, but the pain was too immense to register or focus on anything else in the room.

She couldn't believe she was bringing her child into the world, on a narrow bed in the uncivilized Americas away from home and hearth. Her mother and father nowhere near to provide comfort and support as she'd always imagined.

Her mother should be at her bedside holding her hand, soothing her with the tale of her own triumphant birthing experience. Sharing with her, methods that would ease her pain and ensure their safety. *Her husband, with her father awaiting the joyful news and the arrival of his child.*

She cried out as another contraction gripped her like a vise and contorted her body until she felt as if claws were ripping the flesh from her bones. The half scream, half growl that filled the room, did not seem familiar to her ears and she could scarcely believe the sound had emitted from her own lips.

"Ann, dear, you must conserve your energy." It was Dr. Fletcher's face before her eyes, though his image appeared fuzzy.

She squeezed her eyes tight against another contraction that pierced her body. That's when she knew.

She was going to die.

"Mother...Mother...I'm so sorry...so very sorry..."

Her breathing became more labored until she was gasping for air. Her body was torn between the wracking sobs and the contractions that seemed ever relentless. The fog was closing in on her, yet the pain was not lessening. *Would death be this painful, always?*

She felt someone's hand grasp her own. *Her Mother?*

"Mother..."

"I'm here for you, Ann. Please, darling, you must conserve your energy. Your weeping is sapping all your strength."

The gentle hand brushed her sweat dampened hair from her brow. *Not her mother. Nancy.*

"You need to breathe now. Come, breathe with me dear."

Ann tried to focus on Nancy, she tried to form her lips as Nancy did, and inhale deeply, but the pain was too great.

"I cannot! No, no, no..." Ann cried and tossed her head violently, from side to side, becoming angry at the unforgiveable pain.

"Ann, listen to me. Look at me! If you have enough air to release nonsensical words, you have enough breath to do this correctly, now pull yourself together!" Nancy commanded.

"Calpurnia, grab her other leg and push it up towards her body. Are you ready Fletcher?" Ann heard Nancy's assertive voice directing the room.

How could she treat her so? Didn't she know she was dying? Her body convulsed violently on another contraction and she heard Nancy yell, "Push, Ann! Get that baby out! C'mon!"

When Ann's body squeezed, Ann gritted her teeth and pushed her muscles as deep as she could.

"Good, Ann. Again."

A low scream tore through Ann's throat as she pushed again.

"Here it is." She heard Fletcher's voice.

On the next push, she felt the baby purge from her body and the pressure that had been bearing down on her relented at last. Ann breathed, exhausted.

"It's a girl!" She heard Nancy shout, gleefully, "A beautiful baby girl, Ann."

She'd done it. Dear God, she'd done it. She was alive. Nancy stepped to her with the little toweled being, but just as she was about to reach for it, another contraction squeezed her.

"She's not done yet. The placenta needs yet to be expelled," Fletcher instructed Calpurnia to take the infant and Nancy stepped back into position to assist Ann.

It wasn't over? Ann wanted to give in to her grief but did not think Nancy would allow her to concede defeat now.

"Come dear, you can do it. This should not be as difficult as was the baby. It's almost over now," Nancy encouraged her.

Then to Fletcher she declared with surprise, "That doesn't look like a... Why, it's another baby!"

Ann groaned in half childish fit against the unfairness of it and half terror of repeating the ordeal again.

Nancy was at her side once more, urging her on, "Again, Ann. You can do it. Push!"

Ann didn't know where she found the strength, but she did, and she brought forth another child. Another daughter, she heard Nancy happily shout. Ann sank to the mattress, utterly exhausted and depleted. She heard Fletcher speak to her soothingly and announce that she passed the rest of which needed to come.

She was a mother. She had two daughters. And she lived. A smile bowed her lips and her eyes too heavy to remain open, closed as she drifted into black oblivion.

Chapter 3

Philadelphia, Pennsylvania
March 1833

Grayson Stone hadn't set foot in Philadelphia in the past two years since his wife's death.

May she rest in hell.

After learning of his wife's many deceits, he'd taken off and headed west, leaving her and her rich, malicious family behind. The problem was, he'd had to leave his son behind, too.

His wife, Vivian, had trapped him into marriage, and her father's power wielding over the political world of Philadelphia ensured divorce was unobtainable. At least not without sinking Grayson in the process. Grayson would not have let even the aspect of ruination deter him from slipping from Vivian's tight coils, if not for their son. So, Grayson had escaped the only way he could. He'd shared his idea of a new path of revenue -the only possibility of leaving with his father in law's consent- and headed west to pursue trapping. He promised to put a family mark in the trade and strike it rich, which greatly appealed to his greedy wife and her father.

Ironically, that is exactly what Grayson did. Then Grayson was rewarded again when he learned that not only had his father in law passed away from the cholera in his absence, but his wife who had been visiting her father had also contracted the sickness and perished.

When he'd received that particular letter from his wife's spinster aunt, Agatha O'Malley, his heart had nearly stopped in fear: fear to read on and find that his son, Luke, was ill as well.

But Luke had been spared. Apparently, as his wife had visited her father, she'd become sick so quickly that she'd been unable leave his residence and his entire house, servants and all, had been quarantined until there was no longer any sign of the cholera.

Grayson had wept then.

He had wept with relief that his son was still healthy and alive. He wept in grief for his son who had lost his mother. Even if Vivian had been a terrible person and horrid wife, she'd still been Luke's mother. Grayson imagined Luke saw and loved his mother innocently through a child's eyes. He thought his son's heart must be broken and Grayson ached for him.

He grieved too, for the marriage that he never had. He wondered if Vivian had any regrets before she went to her grave...

His anger and loathing for her had built during the years after which he'd learned of her many transgressions. Each betrayal like a block layered upon one another, ascending to the sky.

But with news of her death, all of his fury and resentment tumbled those blocks like a crumbling tower.

The pieces were all still there, but with nowhere to go, they now just sat heavily in his chest.

He needed to put her out of his mind. Today wasn't about resurrecting sore memories; it was about reuniting with his son. *His son...*

The bulk of memories he had of his son had been before Luke's fifth birthday, before Grayson set out west. After that he'd only visited his son once more as that was the only time Grayson could make the arduous trip back East to see him. Even after Vivian's death, when Luke was nearing seven years old, Grayson couldn't spare the time to make a visit. It would have set back his plans nearly a year. Grayson thought it prudent instead to remain and continue building his empire so that when he did return, their union would be permanent. He hoped one day Luke would understand.

The trapping life was unpredictable and isolated in the extreme. That is why he'd rationalized leaving Luke behind when he left. It was barely an existence for a grown man let alone a -then, five-year-old boy. And it's not as if he left him with strangers. The first two years, he'd had his mother, then after her death, his great Aunt Agatha. She'd agreed to see to Luke's wellbeing, comfort, and education while Grayson started their new lives out west.

Grayson was sure Agatha had been more than pleased with the arrangement, as it had allowed her to move into their grand home on High Street in Society Hill. -Far more richly appointed lodgings than she'd been accustomed to, as her brother had not shared his wealth with her. The finances he'd ensured her was another reason Grayson believed Agatha would care well for Luke in his absence. He'd set up a monthly transfer of funds for both Agatha and Luke, with Agatha acting as designated guardian. He should have been in good conscience knowing his son would be privileged to the best education and life of luxury the great Philadelphia had to offer while he was away.

But guilt gnawed away at his insides over the past years anyway. He'd written, of course, in the time he'd been away and sent letters back East as often as he could. That he rarely received letters in response to his own fed the guilt and a feeling of unease began to spread through him.

In the beginning when no letters arrived for him, he thought perhaps his son was angry at him for leaving. -Or worse, angry at him for not having been there and able to bring his mother back from the sick bed. Occasionally, though, he would receive a letter from Agatha assuring him that all was well, and that Luke was just a healthy, active, busy boy. Still, it hadn't set well with Grayson and the worry built up inside him until he decided he'd settled his home well enough in the west and could finally bring Luke to come live with him.

He didn't want to inspect that decision more closely; afraid it was made entirely in selfishness to have his son near him again. He hoped he wasn't making a mistake and taking Luke from a life that was sure to offer him more advantages than would living remotely in the mountains with his father.

Grayson nudged his horse to the side as a wayward buggy drove recklessly into his path. The buggy carried on down the road unapologetically. Some things never changed, Grayson thought with the shake of his head, his overgrown locks of hair tickling his neck as he did so.

Then again, he thought, some things changed so much they became unrecognizable from what they once were. He was no longer a smitten boy or hurt and confused young man. One grew up fast in the wilds of the Rockies, or you didn't grow up at all. He felt himself change with the land when making his way west. As the soft land of the prairie, where long grasses easily given direction from the wind, turned to hard unyielding rocky slopes of the mountains, so, too, did Grayson; in order to survive he'd had to harden with it. He was no longer without direction, but a man with purpose and as immovable as the mountains in which he planned to remain for the rest of his life.

He'd set out west with the intent of escaping his marital chains without knowing at the time how much he would come to love the wild land. In the time spent there, he'd become a part of it. He hoped Luke would come to feel the same way in time.

He was as nervous as he was excited to see his son. Three years was a long time when it came to the life of a child, and Lord knew, it felt like far longer than that since he'd last seen his son.

He hoped his son had kept up his riding skills in that time. He'd purchased him a horse for his fifth birthday, but it had to be stabled across town, not conveniently located for a small boy. He'd instructed Vivian and then Agatha to ensure weekly lessons. It would certainly be helpful for the journey ahead of them if the boy had been attending his lessons.

Would Luke be excited to see him as well? He would certainly be surprised. Grayson hadn't thought it practical to write ahead when he and a letter would arrive in the same amount of time. Honestly the letter would probably have arrived later. Neither Agatha nor Luke knew of his imminent arrival.

Grayson slowed his horse when his old house came into view. It contrasted sharply in comparison to the other grand homes on the street. Grayson wondered why the upkeep on the house had not been maintained. Surely, he'd sent enough funds for the repairs. In one letter Agatha explicitly requested funds to re-whitewash the boards on the outside. Grayson's stomach churned with dread as he neared his drive.

His boots crunched where they met the tiny stones that made up his drive as he led his horse behind him to the door. No servant came to open the door at his arrival or offer assistance with his horse. Peculiar that. Hodges should have come to the door. Grayson had never known the butler to allow a person to cool their heels in the street in the years he'd lived in this house. Grayson rapped at the door.

"Yes, yes! I'm coming!" barked the woman's voice, "Who would dare call at this hour?" The voice growled as the door swung open.

This hour? thought Grayson. It was midafternoon at the latest. A piggish-looking woman, from her stout shape wrapped in pink, to her upturned nose, stood in the doorway. Her dark eyes, round with recognition, in sharp contrast to her stark white pallor. No, her eyes revealed something else as well, thought Grayson: fear.

Agatha recovered her alarm quickly, attempting to replace it with a showy smile.

"Grayson! What a surprise!"

He didn't smile in return. With scrutinizing, perceptive eyes, he took in his surroundings; a house fronted with gray, cracked, weathered boards, steps that bowed with warp in front of the door, weeds in place of where flowers once bloomed on either side of the rotted porch... He was beginning to get a good idea why Agatha was alarmed to see him standing before her.

Grayson hoped for her sake that his son had been cared for properly, unlike the home she'd allowed to dissipate around her. Although that was enough to flare Grayson's temper.

Grayson had to unclench his teeth, "Where is Luke?"

"Why, at the stables of course." Agatha's smile wobbled on her plump face as she tittered nervously.

Grayson didn't say another word, but the look he leveled her with told her in no uncertain terms that he would return and be seeking answers. He mounted his horse and dashed off to find Luke.

When he arrived at the stable yard, a nervous thought shamed him, *would he be able to recognize his own son?* A groom hurried to him sensing he was someone of importance.

Luckily, Grayson had taken the time to bathe and shave and purchase new clothes otherwise the groom would have probably taken one look at Grayson's dirty buckskins and turned his nose up to him. Such was the way of the world in the rich man's Philadelphia. He'd thought to look more human and less part bear though, in greeting Luke after so long.

The groom hurried to him, "May I help you, sir?"

Grayson flipped him some coin. "I'm looking for a boy. My son. Luke Stone. I was told he would be here."

Concern wrinkled the brows of the groom, but he nodded for Grayson to follow him and led his horse to the barn. As they entered the large opening that allowed for a smooth, wide, aisle down the middle separating rows of stalls, Grayson saw what appeared to be a small boy carrying sacks of feed that were far too heavy for a body of such size, and his unease grew. He looked to the groom that still held his horse.

The groom looked on stoically and replied, "This is the only boy of which visits the stables on regular basis. I do not know if he is your son of a certainty. We were never given a last name."

Anger steeled through Grayson, but he tried to keep it in check so as not to frighten the child. He swallowed, "Luke?"

The boy didn't hear or didn't realize he was being spoken too.

"Luke Stone?" Grayson called again, more firmly.

The boy set the grain down, turned, and tossed his shaggy, dirty brown hair out of his eyes to see who had called his name. Grayson's heart stopped. Even through the grime covering his face, and worn, ill-fitting clothing covering his body, Grayson knew it was his son.

His son. Looking like a neglected street urchin. Working for his keep? The Groom must have sensed the feral mood, taking over Grayson, for he spoke tentatively, "We were told he was to work for riding lessons. We assumed he was some rich bloke's by-blow." Grayson held up his hand for the man to cease speaking. Guilt and regret filled him up inside until it was thick enough to choke him. He walked slowly to his son and lowered to his knees before him.

"Luke."

Luke looked on him confusedly at first, a stranger before him. And then recognition dawned, "Father?"

Grayson wanted badly to pull his son to him and hug him and never let go. He tried to read on Luke's face if he wanted the same or if he blamed Grayson? Maybe even hated him? Hell, Grayson blamed himself.

Instead Grayson, voice too weak to speak, affirmed with a nod. Luke's eyes, green like Vivian's, but guileless and innocent, looked to him uncertainly. The image of his son's face he'd kept close in his thoughts the past years, had been soft and boyishly rounded. Freckles had smattered across the bridge of his nose onto his cheeks, and a playful smile always ready on his lips.

That sweet face was replaced now with one that had lost its boyish flesh; transformed into the more carved features of a young man. His eyes told him he had known hardship and fear. He no longer wore a smile. Grayson's heart ached. And rage forged like a fire within. He had to keep the flames at bay though. His son had clearly paid enough for his absence. Grayson would not add to that by unleashing his fury in front of him.

Grayson swallowed, wanting for a way to comfort him -or maybe himself? -placed his large hand on Luke's small shoulder. "Will you come with me?"

Luke's eyes, more perceptive than most children's his age, understood the question for what it was: a father seeking forgiveness and acceptance. Luke answered by throwing himself into Grayson's open arms. They wrapped one another in a tight embrace and in that was a pact to never part again. Grayson ensured Luke knew he would not leave him behind ever again.

Grayson cleared the knot in his throat, patted Luke's back then held Luke before him to see his face as he spoke, "Do you still have that horse I gave you before I left?"

Luke nodded.

"Did you learn how to ride?"

Luke nodded again, more enthusiastically.

Grayson smiled, "Good. Real good, son."

Luke smiled, happy to have earned his father's approval. Grayson didn't yet deserve such loyalty and respect from his son. But he would make it his goal to earn it.

Grayson didn't even look at the groom, still afraid of causing bodily harm to him and anyone else who'd played a role in his son's treatment, as he asked, "Where's my son's horse?"

"He's this way, Pa," Grayson felt his son's hand in his, tugging him further down the aisle towards a stall before the groom could reply. "I've taken real good care of him. Just as you instructed me."

Grayson peered into the stall. Indeed, the horse had been better cared for than had his son.

"Yes, I can see that you have. One can take the measure of a man by how well he treats his horse and you have done a fine job."

Luke looked to him and Grayson thought he saw a spark of happiness in the boy's eyes. Even though his smile only drew into a small curve of a line, Grayson could tell his son was pleased by the compliment.

Grayson hollered to the groom, "I'll need this horse saddled." Then, he thought to add, "And it had better be saddled with the tack I purchased and had stored here with the horse."

"Yes, sir." The groom scurried, fearfully, to do his bidding.

Luke began to open up slowly, as they made their way back to their High Street residence. Grayson had guessed correctly. By the life Luke was describing, Grayson figured Agatha had developed a gambling addiction. According to Luke, she stayed out all hours of the night, which explained her irritation for having to answer the door in the middle of the afternoon. The servants began disappearing. Even the cook left. Agatha had had to hire a replacement cook, Luke explained. Although, he opined, the new cook wasn't nearly as good or as nice as Mrs. Langley.

"I missed Mrs. Langley when she left. She used to sneak me dessert or small meals on the nights Aunt Agatha would send me to bed early and forget to feed me."

Grayson's stomach churned again at the thought of his child feeling hungry and abandoned. His feelings must have shown on his face.

"Please don't be angry with her, Pa. It wasn't stealing if she were giving the food to me, was it?"

"I'm not angry with you or Mrs. Langley. I'm angry at myself for not being here."

Luke's silence made it apparent he'd wished for his father's presence as well.

Grayson couldn't stop the snipe that escaped, "It doesn't appear that your Aunt Agatha ever forgot to eat any meals."

Luke snickered at that. The first sounds of laughter Grayson had heard from him. Grayson vowed, though, that Agatha had had her last meal on his coin.

Agatha was less friendly upon Grayson's return and instead tried to enact a facade of hauteur with him.

"Well, I really don't understand your irritation with me. I did all that was asked of me. I ensured his riding lessons continued, fed him, clothed him, taught him."

"You hired a tutor?"

"Well, of course not, you never sent the funds for that. But I made him read the books you left behind in the library."

"I sent more than enough funds and you well know it."

"Well, perhaps while living on your mountain, you forgot how costly it is to live in high society," She sniffed.

"Or perhaps you didn't think I would leave my mountain and took advantage of your position."

Grayson leveled her with a threatening glare. "You have twenty-four hours to gather your personal articles and remove yourself from this house."

"Well! Well I never!" She exclaimed dramatically. "After all I have done for you. -Raising your child, a little beast no less. Taking care of your home. And all on a limited budget. Why it's criminal how you've treated me!"

Grayson had to, once again, quell the rage inside that wanted to snap this woman in half.

"Treated *you*? You are lucky to still be standing here, because I am about a thread away from committing murder," he growled with forced restraint. She looked taken aback for a second and her yapping ceased for a few blessed moments.

"I'll get a lawyer. I have my own money, you know." She followed him, harping again, all the way to the door. He was glad he had Luke wait outside with the horses.

"Twenty-four hours," were his final words to her before he turned his back on her for good.

He took Luke to a hotel in town. As it turned out Luke needed an entirely new wardrobe, but they wouldn't be in Philadelphia long enough to have one made. Some readymade clothes would have to do. Luke didn't seem to agree that the rags he was wearing needed to be replaced, but he didn't quibble when Grayson told him to dress in the new garb he'd purchased.

Grayson also took Luke along with him to the bath house before putting up at the hotel for the night. Both of them got their overgrown locks sheared off and Grayson had his full, dark beard trimmed up. Luke's dirtied hair washed clean returned to the sandy blond Grayson remembered it to be. Luke was beginning to resemble his old self.

He'd never be the little boy Grayson had left behind all those years ago, though. Too much had happened and too much time had gone by; no amount of new clothes and scrubbing could wash away that.

The next day, Luke accompanied Grayson to the various businesses Grayson had to conduct. He met with the local banker to inform him he was putting his house up for sale and where to send the proceeds from the sale when it occurred. He also sought out a legal counselor and ensured Agatha would no longer receive a cent from him and that any repercussions from her would be taken care of, not that he predicted she would attempt to make a case out of her fabrications, but unlike her he didn't gamble with his life.

Thankfully, Agatha had heeded Grayson's words and had vacated herself before he returned. He noticed some of his family's furnishings had disappeared along with her but didn't much care. He was too pressed for time to continue squabbling over details with the horrid woman.

Luke didn't appear overly sad to be leaving his home behind. But, like Grayson, Luke seemed to prefer to keep his emotions below the surface. He wasn't easy to read, his son. His eyes kept finding Luke as if he couldn't believe they were finally seeing him again and didn't ever want to look away.

At only nine years old, Luke sat stoically in his saddle atop his horse, placing all his trust into the hands of his father, a man he barely knew. His son had nearly grown into a full man without him even being present. It was a hard tack to swallow.

But he was grateful for such a strong boy. He hoped in time, the gap between them would narrow into nonexistence.

"Are you ready?"

"Yes, sir." Luke nodded bravely. Then asked, "How far is it to Cumberland Gap, from here?"

Grayson chuckled. It was going to be a long journey.

Ann soon learned the trials of motherhood, doubly so! But with the help of Doctor Fletcher and Nancy, she felt she was finally catching on. Her absolutely lovely and perfect daughters, Catherine- named for Ann's paternal grandmother- and Lavinia -for Ann's maternal grandmother- had grown at astonishing rates. Nancy often chuckled and exclaimed how like a couple of piglets they were and doted on them as if they were her own grandchildren, much like Fletcher. They were always hovering about them and ready and waiting to receive them into their arms. Ann smiled to herself as she thought of the two of them; without them she would have been completely lost.

Nancy had her way and moved in right away after Catherine and Lavinia were born, to help with chores. Ann had felt it too much charity and though she appreciated Nancy's efforts, had tried to negate her from putting herself out any more than she already had helping Ann.

"Please, Nancy, truly, you have done enough, and besides, I-I haven't the means to pay you for your services. It is not...acceptable."

"Nonsense, you have become like a daughter to Fletcher in the short time you've come into our lives and, well...to me," Tears glistened in Nancy's eyes when they met Ann's, which she quickly wiped away, "The only payment I demand is to hold those two, sweet, little angels, you have given us."

Ann knew Nancy, widowed and whose own children were too busy and too great a distance away to make time for her, was lonely and how she secretly loved Doctor Fletcher. She realized there would be no turning the woman away.

"I don't know what I'd do without you," Ann went to her and gently squeezed her hands. Fletcher, who Ann thought secretly adored Nancy as well, had no objections to Nancy's moving in.

In the evenings when Fletcher was finished with appointments and supper was cleared from the table, they would all sit and take turns snuggling the babies while Ann entertained them with stories. Sometimes she read from books that Fletcher had or from some Nancy had fetched from her own abandoned home. Other times, Ann would make up stories or tell them about her life in England.

The girls began making their very different personalities known right from the beginning. Catherine, or Kit as she was called most by her "adopted" grandparents, was calm and observant; her gray eyes always wandering as if taking everything in and thinking constantly.

Lavinia or "Livvy" (her name too, had been shortened into a pet name) on the other hand, never seemed satisfied and was rarely content. She fussed and when she wanted fed, she wanted fed that instant and would scream until she *was* fed. She was also far more active than Kit; always waving her little fists about in those jerky infantile movements and kicking her tiny little legs when she was happy (or impatient and angry). Ann smiled as she gazed down at her sleeping beauties.

She loved them more than words could say. And although Nancy and Fletcher had helped her considerably and made a home and family for her and her girls, Ann wanted more for them. Somehow, in her rash and foolish behavior she had failed them. And yet, had she not acted as she had, she would not have them at all.

The months flew by; Kit and Livvy growing like weeds all the while. And not once during that time, had she, Fletcher, or Nancy even come close to a lead on James' where-abouts. It was as if the man had vanished off the face of the earth.

Worry for the future of her daughters weighed heavily on her mind. She needed to come to a decision soon, for all their lives depended upon it. Thoughts of giving up her search for James brought her melancholy and she could never entertain them for long. She could not resign herself to a life of failure. Her only choice, truly, was to continue in her search for James.

Sheer determination fueled her most days. Even as winter seemed to stretch on and on.

Ann had been surprised over Charleston's mild winter, very different from England. She was beginning to think winter had waited in Charleston until spring, to arrive, but Nancy informed her that the falling temperatures of late were unusual for March. It seemed the early spring brought with it chilling breezes wrought with sickness to spread around. Ann worried for Kit and Livvy's health being so near to those ill, but Nancy was as strict with their care as any Army general and ensured they were always kept far from the patients and in a cleanly environment. The following day proved to be extremely exhausting, as patients flowed in one after the other seeking remedies for their cold humors.

Fletcher was kept busy seeing to the concerns of stray patients late into the evening hours, never one to turn away those he could help. The unshakable Nancy even appeared to be frazzled and fatigued.

She entered the seating room after checking on the babies, wiping her brow, "Lord in heaven, but it would seem all of Charleston took ill today."

Ann was in the Kitchen area, still wiping down some of the dishes from the patient's rooms. She'd kept tea and coffee brewing all day for those well enough to consume it while they awaited Dr. Fletcher. She had a kettle of water boiling now for her and Nancy.

"Do not forget, we are not all possessed of such a sturdy constitution as you. Especially we foreigners." Ann quipped back teasingly.

Nancy ignored the teasing and quickened to ensure the 'foreigner' whom most concerned her wasn't suffering from any maladies, "Oh never say you are feeling unwell too!"

"Don't be a goose. I may have been born a Lady, but I descend from sturdy working-class stock on my mother's side. Besides, England is blusterier than this come this time of year. I daresay I am accustomed to a lot worse."

"You still are a Lady, Ann." This was spoken weightily, and the message was clear. Ann was grateful for the reminder, but she needn't feel sorry for herself. Nancy must have shared such sentiment because she added, "But you are a rare breed, that's for sure. I have never met someone raised in a station of delicacy turn out so rock stubborn as you dear."

Ann wrinkled her nose and pursed her lips at the friendly jibe.

"I am feeling every bit of my advanced age this evening." Nancy groaned and slowly lowered herself into her chair.

"Ann, could you be a dear and take this basket to Cora's? I'm not certain my legs could carry me that far on a night such as this. With so many people fallen ill, I fear Fletcher may be running low on herbs."

Ann smiled, "Of course."

Nancy handed her the large wicker made basket, used for trips to the market. She was sure to fasten her cloak and slip her hands into the wool mittens Nancy had knitted for her before the winter season arrived. Nancy never allowed details to escape her attention. She was quick to assess that Ann had traveled light and hadn't thought to bring practical and weather appropriate attire. And bless her kind heart for it!

Nancy assured her she'd look in on Kit and Livvy -not that Ann doubted their care under Nancy's watchful eye- and Ann was out the door. It was too brisk for Ann's taste for all she should have been accustomed to such weather, as it resembled that of the cold season in England. Even milder most days. Nevertheless, Ann tightened the thick wool cloak under her chin to keep the cool wind from her neck and made her way down the street.

Her trip, as always, was interrupted many times by chatty neighbors. She was surprised to find so many out on such an unusually chilly day. Some were quite friendly, but Ann noticed most were simply eager to spread gossip, again much like her neighbors home in England. She finally made it to Cora's; a woman Nancy swore grew the best garden this side of Charleston and whom they always made their raw purchases from. She also harvested the best herbs.

She didn't mind conversing with Cora, who was a widowed mother of four young children trying to get by on her own. Conversations with her always helped to lift Ann's spirits and strengthen her. She was a sweet woman and Ann rather thought that even if she didn't grow the best herbs that Nancy would still insist on purchasing from her. Ann smiled thinking of Nancy and her many kindnesses.

"Good evening Cora."

"Oh, good evening, Ann."

"Nancy assured me just weeks ago, that the weather in Charleston never reached these temperatures."

"Oh, then it was her foul tongue that cursed them down on us." Cora grinned merrily and tossed her thick braid over her shoulder.

"I wouldn't be surprised if all of South Carolina was feeling the humors today. I don't think there was a moment without a patient to attend to at Fletcher's, certainly."

"I take it you are here to restock on powders?"

"Indeed, never say you are out too?"

"No, no. I always keep a special reserve for the Doc." Cora smiled. "Echinacea and Golden Seal?"

"Yes please."

"Come in out of the wind while I measure some out."

Ann stepped into the familiar little home. Her four children were seated patiently around the wooden table, similar in style to the one at Fletcher's residence.

"Hello children."

Ann didn't like that she was interrupting their supper. Cora valued this time as she was certain the children did as well. So often Cora was needed in the store front as was necessary to provide meals such as what they were partaking in at the moment.

"Hello, Mrs. Morgan."

"That looks like a fine warm stew you are enjoying. Did you help your mother prepare it, Lara?"

Lara was the eldest, at the ripe old age of nine and a half. Secondly, was a six-year-old boy, Louis; then four-year-old Benjamin, and lastly was two-year-old Suzannah. Lara shook her head yes, modestly.

"I'm sure it's very tasty then. Your mother has told me that you plan on opening your very own bakeshop one day?"

Again, Lara bobbed her blond head affirmatively. The children were all so dear and polite.

"Well keep eating, don't let it get cold." Ann smiled to them. Cora returned then with the bottles of root powders. It didn't take long to make the purchases. Ann thanked Cora and said her goodbyes to her and the children then slowly strolled back towards Fletcher's.

She hadn't yet turned from Market Street when something caught her eye; a golden light flashed by her in masculine human form. Instinctively she reached out as the man rushed by. *James!*

Chapter 4

"James!"

"Excuse me miss, do I know you?"

Ann's heart had leapt into her chest and pounded furiously at its cage within her when she saw James. Now, suddenly, it was as if stopped altogether.

Not James.

Although a striking resemblance in size and coloring; this man's eyes were a bit smaller and his nose a bit sharper than the man she had given her heart to all those months ago.

Her heart tried to resume a normal rhythm. "I'm dreadfully sorry; I thought you were someone I knew."

She turned to resume her pace back to Fletcher's, when she heard him speak.

"Did I hear you call me James? You wouldn't have thought me to be James Morgan, would you?"

She stopped abruptly and lifted her gaze sharply to the man's. With her lips parted in surprise, she tried to form words, "Y-yes. I-I mean th-that is-"

"Yes, well, I am often mistaken for my cousin." He took his hat off and swept it in front of him in a sort of bow. "My name is Jonathon Morgan."

Desperation rose up to choke her. This man was James's cousin! Surely, he knew where James was.

Calm yourself, Ann. This man is but a stranger and for all you know, his cousin could be a different James Morgan. But the resemblance was so canny; it had to be her *James.*

"Nice-Nice to meet you, Mr. Morgan." She wasn't sure how she managed to stutter out the polite social niceties, when her mind was a whirlwind of unanswered questions. She could barely resist the urge to blurt out her questions and demand answers.

"I am Ann. Ann Morgan."

It was his turn to resemble a startled fish. Had she just implied she was James' wife? Jonathon studied the girl. Very pretty he thought, exactly his cousin's type too. Of course, pretty young ladies were really every man's type. He knew his cousin well though and none of James' other conquests had ever claimed marriage to him... What was she about? She must have felt his eyes narrow in on her suspiciously, because the tip of her tongue darted out quickly to moisten her beautifully plush lips in nervous fashion. Interesting he thought.

"James and I met in England, nearly twelve months past. And married." She added hastily.

The chit was lying he knew, but something about her compelled him to go along with this revelation. For now. It was something about those honey colored eyes and the defiant strength shining from them as she stared him down. The only indication that her fierce composure was a front for vulnerability was the nervous flicker of her pink tongue to those kissable pillowy lips of hers again.

Jonathon had to quell the urge of desire stirring through him. He was a gentleman, after all. It's not as if he was going to ravish this woman on the street. Good Gad, did he just use the word, *ravish*? He shook his head; *it's been too long since your last trip to Maggie's*, he thought. Perhaps he should seek out a whorehouse here in Charleston...

She registered something in his eyes, as he studied her. For a moment his sharp silver gaze smoldered, not with skepticism as before... Then she recognized it. He was looking at her as a man would a woman. A man who *desired* a woman. Fear pulsed through her instinctively, but she tampered it down with something stronger, anger.

How dare he look at her as if he wanted to bed her, when she had just announced herself to be his cousin's wife! The covetous look that had filled his eyes a moment ago flickered away as quickly as it had appeared. Unease still tingled through her though as she continued to challenge him with her eyes.

He coughed then as if clearing his throat, "Well, then, *Mrs. Morgan*, welcome to the family. What a surprise this is." His eyes seemed to peer more deeply into hers then. "James never mentioned you upon his return from England."

"Yes, well, our marriage was to remain a secret until-until he was able to return back to England. You see, my parents didn't really approve of the match at the time."

That was unsettling. *James hadn't imparted news of their marriage to his family? He never impressed to her that their marriage was to be kept secret from his relations...*

"Ah. And you are now here, in South Carolina..." His eyes remained polite, but the crook of a smile forming as if he knew of her secrets, made her feel vulnerable.

She could feel the strength dissipating from her body as surely as the wind leaves the sails of a ship. She was exhausted. She had been frightened and exhausted for the past eleven months. She could no longer keep up the pretense of diplomacy. She needed answers now.

"When he did not return, and I did not receive any letters, I became worried for him. I decided to travel here and determine his state for myself, imagining the worst, of course. Do you know... Is he-?" she left the word *alive* unspoken. For what if he had perished and she'd wronged him by harboring feelings of anger and resentment towards him, when she should have been grieving for him instead?

"Oh, James is very much alive."

James was alive. Suddenly the biting wind blowing furiously, seared her flesh as surely as Jonathon Morgan's statement had pierced her heart. Strands of her hair wisped and blew viciously across her face, but her eyes never blinked as she stared inexorably back at this man. This man who had James's blood running through his veins.

The heavy winds must have been holding her upright, because as soon as the angry gusts dissipated, she felt her knees buckle beneath her.

"Oh-ho now, Miss!"

"Mrs. Morgan." She corrected weakly as he gathered her in his arms. She clutched her basket of herbs, lest they crash to the cobbled streets. Suddenly, the busy street was a blur. Hacks and carts continued to roll past, and horses' hooves clopped the ground. People strolled by in every direction, but for Ann the world remained still.

Suddenly, desperately, she clutched the lapels of the man who was holding her. "Where is he? I must speak to him. Please!"

"Yes, yes, of course." Jonathon soothed. He reached his arms beneath her and scooped her up like a child.

"I can walk. Truly. Just take me to him," she protested.

"Are you staying with someone? Have family with you? Where is the residence to which you are staying?"

Jonathon continued before she could protest, "James is not presently in Charleston. Let us continue this conversation somewhere warmer and off the streets, shall we?"

She was feeling a tad foolish now. Here this man she had only just met was, cradling her in his arms and she carrying on like a madwoman.

She cleared her throat and calmly replied, "Yes indeed, tis a fine plan. I assure you, though, I can walk on my own."

He gently settled her back to her feet and waited patiently while she righted herself and felt composed once more. She was loathed to allow this man to walk away along with the opportunity to discuss James.

It was late in the evening, hardly a respectable hour for gentleman callers. And, of course, she wouldn't want him to discover the girls. Then again, she was certain she could enlist Nancy's help. Nancy was fatigued, she knew, from the long practice hours, but surely for something as important as this, it couldn't be wrong to request her assistance.

Distractedly, she responded, "Th-thank you. For catching me. I'm not typically so weak spirited. Tis only, I have traveled so far and..."

"Yes, quite understood."

"Are you in the habit of rescuing damsels in distress?"

He laughed then, and his countenance transformed into something less severe, almost handsome. Though it was difficult to compare other men to James, almost unfair. James was built to perfection. If human form were an art, James was a godly masterpiece.

This man, although he shared some of James's features, was not instantly eye-catching remarkable. He had the same pale shade of gray eyes like James, but his were not framed with the same long coal-black lashes. His face was less symmetrical. His nose almost hawkish from the side, narrow from the front. His chin did not possess the dimple nor was it as squarely masculine as James's, although it wasn't an unattractive face when viewed upon as a whole.

"No. You would be the first actually. And I must point out, that it was my choice words that nearly sent you crumbling to the ground."

Ann cringed a bit at the depiction, detesting the show of weakness. She couldn't afford to be weak, she had more than just herself to safeguard.

"Thank you all the same. You offered to speak further with me. Would you find it acceptable to walk with me back to my home now? When we arrive, I could put a pot of tea on and we could talk."

"Yes, that sounds most agreeable." He extended his arm to her and she placed hers within his.

It felt good. It felt *right* to him, walking alongside this woman, with her arm in his. He smiled and wondered how James could have ever left her on the other side of the ocean. But of course, he *knew* why.

The wind continued to blow heavily, and Ann was grateful for Jonathon's warmth at her side. It was too blustery to illicit any conversation and so cold she had to grit her teeth together to prevent them from chattering. The only words exchanged were when Jonathon insisted he carry the basket the rest of the way. She didn't hesitate to hand it over to him. She was glad for the freed hand that she may keep her hood clutched into place.

"We're here," She announced softly once they reached Fletcher's.

Now, how to politely ask this man to stand outside and await her in the cold while she ensured Nancy could help and that her daughters were well asleep and hidden for the night?

Before she could grasp the knob of the door it opened before them, spilling firelight into the street, a cry from Nancy along with it, "Ann! Whatever has taken you so long? I've been worried sick!" Then shock widened her eyes as she acknowledged the strange man beside Ann.

Well, no need to stall the introduction at this point. Ann spoke swiftly before Jonathon could introduce himself, "This is Mr. *Jonathon Morgan.*"

Ann raised her brows and widened her eyes when she delivered his name, hoping Nancy would understand the silent message.

Nancy, though, was still barring the door, stricken with shock, "Mr. Morgan. *Mr. Morgan!*"

Ann looked to her beseechingly, "Yes. Mr. *Jonathon* Morgan." Ann released a small coughing sound. "I ran into him on the street. He is a cousin to my husband." She coughed again, trying to communicate to Nancy the importance of his presence. "I was hoping it would be okay to invite him in for tea."

Again, Ann implored Nancy with her eyes. *Are my babies safely out of sight?*

Nancy must have come to her senses. "Yes, yes, of course. Do come in, both of you out of the cold."

The sound of Ann's relieved sigh was lost to the wind and shut away behind the door as they entered into the warmth of the room.

"Ann, if you and Mr. Morgan would like to seat yourselves in the kitchen and you see to the tea, dear? I just want to inform Fletcher of our guest before joining you."

She would indeed inform Fletcher of their *guest*, but Ann knew she was also checking on Kit and Livvy and allowing Ann some private conversation with Jonathon. *Bless Nancy!*

Ann turned around and hung her cloak on one of the many hooks lining the door. The entry way of the home served as the patients' waiting room of a sort. Jonathon removed his jacket and hung it as well. He remained silent, but Ann could feel his eyes on her studying her.

"A-herm. Right this way, please." She led Jonathon past the seating area where she and Nancy's rockers and Fletchers stuffed chair sat facing the warming fire and into the attached kitchen. She gestured for him to take a seat at one of the hard chairs at the table and then began boiling the water.

She nervously clanged the kettle against the pipes and tried not to slosh and waste the water as she sat the kettle on the broilers. She hoped Mr. Morgan attributed her clumsiness to cold fingers instead.

Jonathon sat at the table warming his hands. That walk had been damned cold to say the least. He watched Ann fumble around nervously, preparing the tea. She was astoundingly beautiful, even whilst her nose was yet cherry red from the cold. *James, you scoundrel, what sort of trouble have you happened on this time?* He recalled the brief conversation with his cousin on his return from England. Ann must be the woman with the golden eyes he'd referred to.

It was unconscionable to Jonathon that his cousin could behave so reproachfully, especially after the debacle he'd caused at home. But perhaps, his cousin's wicked ways would for once, reward *Jonathon*. Jonathon continued to study her while she had her back turned to him.

Her windblown hair, tousled from its confines, hung loosely down her back. It was not an especially remarkable color, an average shade of brown, but paired with the sunshine strands that streaked it and those spectacular eyes; no one could deny she was a great beauty.

Her form was disguised by her many layers of gown, but Jonathon remembered the feel of her in his arms, which is when he decided that is where she was meant to be and began formulating a plan as how to win her for himself.

He heard her clear her throat. He'd already come to understand that was how she squared herself for battle. He watched her spine straighten as she turned towards him.

"Well, while the water boils, perhaps you and I could get some questions and answers out of the way, shall we?"

His smile was similar to James'. It quirked up more on one side giving the appearance of a mischievous boy who'd just successfully pulled off a prank endeavor. Ann felt her heart tighten painfully at the memory and she tried to squelch the aching pangs stirring.

"Of course." The gentleman that she was coming to know him to be stood while she took her seat and then reseated himself.

"Where is he?" Directness had ever been her path of choice.

"On his way to Texas, I'm afraid." His kind eyes watched her patiently.

"Texas?"

"Yes, it's a part of Mexico. Americans have been settling there more frequently in the past six years. James believes he can grow cotton successfully there."

There was no sense adding that James had effectively destroyed his parent's tobacco plantation in Virginia when he earned the reputation of a blackguard and a cheat. People tended not to want to do business with those types. Ann needn't know those particular details, however. Not yet in any case.

His aunt and uncle would recover once they found a new merchant to sell to. They would have to travel out of state most likely, but Jonathon had recently been over their finances with them in James' absence and determined that traveling expenses would not sink profits entirely; despite the fact that James had cut a swathe far and wide making it difficult for his aunt and uncle to find people willing to continue business with them.

James had a penchant for seducing the daughters of said business associates and he'd finally seduced the wrong one. He'd been nearly forced at gunpoint to make things right and in the moments after had fled to England.

That action had done little to repair the damage to the Morgan's family reputation. When he returned his parents had still been furious with him. They had nearly been ostracized by all of Dorchester in the wake of his cowardly absence. James was then forced to abandon his family plantation altogether and move west. He'd finally trapped himself.

Jonathon received a letter from James nearly a month past that explained a rather unexpected turn of events, however...

"He may still be in St. Louis, Missouri. That is where he was last I received word from him. In his letter, he explained that he might soon be traveling on to Texas."

"So, he may still be in St. Louis, then? Where is that exactly?"

His eyes looked on her pityingly, "Why it's nearly nine hundred miles from here, I'm afraid."

"You've received correspondence from him. Might I have his address, that I may pen him a letter? I'm certain once he knows about-about...That is once he knows I am here, he will want to travel back..."

"Listen Ann, if I may call you so?"

Ann nodded her consent curtly, so that he may proceed quickly. She wasn't *Lady Ann*, here and it seemed preposterous for James' cousin to call her *Mrs. Morgan. Especially when that wasn't even her legal name...*

"I know you are not who you say you are."

Her spine grew rigid and if she possessed hackles, she would have felt them raise. Just who did he think she was?

Jonathon continued on in her silence, "I know you are not *Mrs. Morgan.*" Then, more gently, added, "You couldn't be James' wife, you see, for he married shortly before he ever set sail for London."

Chapter 5

All the air in the room vanished until Ann felt she would suffocate. Her stomach churned, sickly. The blood in her hands that had finally warmed moments before turned cold; and from the concerned look she was seeing from Jonathon, the blood had drained from her face as well.

No, no, no. This couldn't be! He could not have... Her body began to tremble. *All of her plans to reunite them... She'd voyaged across the Atlantic for him! She'd given up everything she held dear: her family and home...*

"Ann?"

Selfish thoughts warred within Jonathon. The blackguard-rogue part of him he hadn't known he possessed until meeting this woman, insisted that he should press his suit now while she was vulnerable. The gentleman reprimanded him for such disgraceful thoughts and told him to tell her more. She deserved to know the whole of it. In time, he hoped she would perhaps turn to him of her own accord.

He reached for her shaking hands; they were so cold. That's when he noticed she was shaking everywhere.

"No, that isn't possible. We married. There was a minister... We signed a legal document... I don't understand..."

"Ann, listen to me. I'll help you. You've nothing to fear from me. I will not impart any of your secrets to the world."

His soothing voice broke through the havoc that was her mind. *He would help her, he said... She didn't want to be alone anymore...* She ached too much. It hurt to breathe.

What had she done? The full weighted consequences of her actions were only now falling down to crush her. Every decision she had made had been to prevent that from happening and to protect her daughters. She wouldn't be able to return home. She'd never see her parents again. Could she even remain with Doctor Fletcher and Nancy, or would she taint their good names too? People would find out; they always found out. Is there any place she could run?

"Ann, look at me."

His voice faded into the frenzy of thoughts whirring in her mind. She fought to cease them. She turned her eyes to his and tried not to think of how similar they were to James'.

"No. How do you know the supposed wedding you speak of was legal. Perhaps my marriage is the lawful one. I spoke vows before God and there were witnesses. We signed papers." She could feel panic rising in her voice. She needed to focus on breathing. It would not do to lose herself to the rising fear.

"Ann, he married a woman - was forced to marry -the daughter of a very important man a few counties over from here. His family - we - were all in attendance. The bride's father ensured that it was legal, I assure you."

"Then, then, how? Why?"

"Unfortunately, James has a certain reputation. I'm not sure what tricks he employed-"

Ann had heard enough. She couldn't, wouldn't believe it. She'd spent every moment she could with James in the months before she eloped with him. How could she have misjudged him so? She held up her hand to stop Jonathon. She need not hear more about James's sordid reputation.

"Why did he not return to -his wife- then, when he returned home?"

"When he returned from England, he discovered that her family was planning to move to Missouri and James felt it could be a new beginning for him as well and moved with them."

Ann felt as she did the time she fell from her horse Knight, and all the wind expelled from her lungs in a whoosh.

Jonathon continued, "He didn't have a lot of choices, she was his wife after all, and her father wielded more power than James."

She began shaking her head no. Perhaps he did love Ann then? If he didn't love his wife? But what did it matter? He should never have made her believe he loved her if he'd been married. He'd lied to her. She'd offered him everything and he'd taken it. Her heart was breaking anew, and she felt freshly betrayed and abandoned all over again. Perhaps for the first time, as before she hadn't known how deep the deception had been and was able to hold onto the tiniest threads of hope.

"Ann, I'm not saying this to hurt you."

She felt him gently stroking her hands.

"I told you I had received a letter from James recently. He sent news that may be of interest to you."

"What could he have written that could possibly be of interest to me now?" Her voice was hoarse and filled with the tears and anguish she was trying to swallow.

He watched her straighten in her chair as she recovered her strength. Only a lone tear escaped and trailed down her soft cheek. Jonathon followed its path with his eyes, wishing he could reach his fingertips to it and make it disappear. Wishing he could spare her the pain his wretched cousin had caused and heal her with his touch.

He dreaded what he was next about to say. If she knew, she could well decide to continue after James and surely James wouldn't be so big a fool as to walk away from her again? Then Jonathon could never have her...

He spoke before losing his nerve, "James' wife grew sick on the journey and died shortly after reaching St. Louis. James is widowed now and no longer married."

He waited and watched her eyes for their reaction. Would she choose James again? After what he'd done to her?

Just then, the robust woman who opened the door to them on their arrival, lively rounded the corner into the kitchen and joined them.

"How's tea coming?"

She wore a smile unaware of the turbulence of the conversation. Jonathon retracted his hand away from Ann's guiltily.

The smile Nancy wore disappeared instantly upon seeing Ann's face. "Ann! Oh, dear." She turned towards Jonathon accusingly, "What has happened?"

"No, no, Nancy, I'm fine." Her sniffle betrayed her attempt at stoicism.

"I've never seen you around these parts of town before, for all you say your name is Morgan." Nancy looked disapprovingly and suspiciously at Jonathon.

"No, I am here on business." He answered the elder protective woman dutifully and respectively but turned to Ann as he continued.

"I am here, actually seeing to James' family's affairs. My Uncle's that is. I was on my way back to the hotel when you stopped me, having just delivered some paperwork to the solicitor's office."

"He revealed his last name to me, Nance, before I requested it from him. He looks remarkably similar to James. I believe he is who he says he is."

Nancy, yet suspicious, chirped, "Cousin you say? And yet so similar a resemblance. That is common with brothers..."

"Yes, we did appear as brothers to most people who didn't know our relations. Our fathers were twin brothers, identical to one another. And as it turned out, James and I both favored our fathers."

Nancy and Ann shared a look. Dr. Fletcher had informed her that twin births were common in some family lines. If James had been around, she may not have been so surprised at the birth of her own twin daughters.

Jonathon defended again, "I have documents with proof back at the hotel. I also have James' last letter to me, there..."

Ann looked up and let her eyes lock upon him then. Her glorious, sparkling, champagne colored eyes.

"I had originally planned to travel back to Dorchester on the morrow, but I will extend my trip so that we may continue this conversation. It's become rather late and Miss Nancy appears as if she could use some rest."

He smiled and looked to the feisty woman standing at Ann's shoulder. Nancy understood that he was sparing Ann's pride and not addressing the awful emotional state she was in and nodded graciously to him.

"Might I call upon you here, after noon time tomorrow?"

Ann hardly wanted to wait that long, so eager was she to hear every detail of James' life before and after he came into hers; and even more eager for details so that she may formulate another plan for her life. She was unbearably fatigued from the physically taxing work from earlier that day assisting Dr. Fletcher and even more so from the emotionally exhausting confrontation with Jonathon Morgan. She looked to Nancy to determine if such a meeting was permissible.

She felt herself nodding acquiescently, "Yes, I find that agreeable."

Jonathon nodded to her once more and stood from the table. She stood as well and escorted him to the entryway where he retrieved his jacket. She was so near he could smell the sweet fragrance of her hair. She smelled of honey and faintly of cloves. He had to stay his hand from reaching for a tendril of that flaxen streaked hair and running his fingers through its silken lengths.

She appeared but a ghost of the woman he'd met on the street. He longed to touch her once more, comfort her in some way, but the tyrant figure of her female protector stood watch. He settled, instead for words that he hoped were reassuring.

"Please rest and do not fret anymore tonight. We can talk more tomorrow, and I will help you in any way possible."

"Thank you."

There were more words she should have spoken, she knew. 'Thank you' seemed all too inadequate for all this man, a perfect stranger no less, had done for her today. She couldn't seem to bring forth any more energy, however, to fulfill the proper social etiquette. What was the proper etiquette for a surprise meeting with your illegitimate children's second cousin?

"Well. I will see you on the morrow then."

He bobbed his head politely to the tyrant in the corner and once more to Ann and took his leave back into the cold of the night.

She could no longer focus. Nancy, worried over her distraught state, walked her to her room. As they entered the hall, Fletcher appeared.

He sighed unaware of all that had transpired, "What a day, what a day. That was the last patient for the evening. Even a doctor must sleep occasionally. Especially an old one like myself."

When he didn't receive the smiles, he had endeavored to rouse, he noticed something was terribly wrong.

"Ann? Nancy, what's wrong with her?" He took in Ann's weakened appearance, her eyes tired and shock stricken.

"I'll explain after I help her to bed Fletcher," she said.

Nancy helped her change into her sleeping gown and pulled the quilt over her as if she were a child.

"Don't worry dear. You're not alone in this. We will figure everything out in the morning."

Ann was too exhausted, and she welcomed the escape into the sleeping world of darkness. She was asleep before Nancy reached the hall and closed the door.

Ann dressed quickly and met the early morning with renewed strength. She peered down into the large crib; the one Fletcher had constructed specially for her daughters after discovering they preferred sleeping together. Her babies, still so small, lay stretched out alongside one another. Kit lay with both of her arms in the shape of a 'Y' above her head and hands curled into chubby little fists. Livvy, the same, except one of her arms extended and covered part of her sister's face. Ann smiled down at her perfect, sleeping, darlings.

Nancy was right: she was hardly alone anymore.

Nancy was startled when she entered the kitchen that morning and found Ann already seeing to the day's preparations. She looked well recovered from last evening's events and Nancy recognized the determination in her movements and wondered what Ann had decided upon.

Ann turned and smiled to Nancy, "Good morning, Nance."

"Good morning." Nancy replied cautiously.

"Is Fletcher risen yet?"

"I don't believe so. He may not be for a while, poor man. He was utterly exhausted from yesterday's patient load. No one is scheduled for the morning and let's hope there are no emergencies, so that he may sleep his fill."

Then carefully, but poignantly, she asked, "How are you this morning?"

Ann stilled from wiping down the table and set the rag out of her hands. She sighed, "I am... ready to do what is necessary."

"What have you decided?"

"I am not going to meet with Mr. Morgan this afternoon."

Nancy looked incredulous, "But, what do you mean? He knows how to reach James."

"Yes, and so do I. He told me last night that James is in St. Louis."

"No, Ann. Please do not say, what I think you are going to say." Nancy's chin wobbled, and her words sounded choked from her, tearing at Ann's heart.

"I'm sorry. I must."

Tears filled the gentle woman's eyes despite her efforts to restrain them.

"But what of," Nancy covered her heart with her hand as if it was physically being ripped from her chest and she sought to keep it, "What of the babies?" She finally managed.

"It will be difficult, but I can hardly leave them behind." Ann answered, grievously.

"When?" The word sounded torn from her.

"The stage leaves by the noon hour, this day. I plan to be on it."

Nancy looked stricken and Ann knew well the pain, for she felt it tearing through her own body. She knew it would cause all of them heart ache, but this was her only viable option. It was the last chance to be able to give her daughters a whole life, one with their mother *and* their father. James' character was questionable, thus far, but she had to maintain the belief that once he knew of his daughters' existence, he would do what was right; perhaps even come to love them.

As if they knew they were being discussed, an aggrieved cry, more of an angry fussing noise, came from Ann's room. Ann began to cross the kitchen to retrieve her daughters and dress them for the day, but Nancy stopped her.

"No," she said simply. Ann needed hear no more, she understood. Nancy needed to be with them to hold them all she could before they were gone from her.

Ann wiped the tears from her own eyes. She couldn't allow herself to give in to the pain and sorrow of once more uprooting from those she loved and traveling to more foreign lands, or she may not be able to follow through with her decision.

She came to America to *find* James and that is exactly what she was going to do. He would marry her *-legally, without a doubt this time-* love their children and she would go back to England one day and back into the embrace of her loving parents.

The choking grief tried to overwhelm her with pain. She slammed her fist fitfully into the counterpane, would that she could do so to the grief that threatened to consume her. She had to find Fletcher and explain to him, her new plan to travel to St. Louis. He was not going to approve any more than had Nancy, but it couldn't be helped.

After conferring with Fletcher, she set out to find Nancy and to begin preparations for her journey. She walked into her room and saw Nancy sitting upon the bed holding Livvy and telling her a story. Kit was busy trying to pull the booty from her foot on the floor. When Nancy spotted Ann, she hugged Livvy to her once more then set her on the floor next to her sister.

"Did you tell Fletcher?" Nancy asked.

"Yes."

"I take it, he was unable to convince you to stay."

"You know why I must go."

"Did Fletcher tell you of all of the trials awaiting you on such a journey? St. Louis has not had time to become as civilized as Charleston, Ann. Once you cross those mountains, you will be entering lands overrun with Indians and men that are, well, not gentlemen. It's not safe for you or these little ones, Ann. I beg you to reconsider."

"Nance, I know how difficult this will be for all of us. Fletcher told me that if my plan is unsuccessful that the girls and I-we may return to you both." Ann's stoic front broke into anguished tears. Nancy rushed to embrace her, giving in to her own tears.

"Of course, of course child. Oh, dear Ann, my sweet girl. Don't even *think* of not returning to us, whether you find this James Morgan, or not."

Nancy continued to hold Ann tightly clasped to her chest with one arm as her other hand smoothed the back of Ann's plaited hair to soothe her.

In Nancy-like fashion, she did not allow herself to be seen in a state of weakness and woe for long.

"Now, if you are certain this is what you want to do, we must begin packing at once."

Ann had reclaimed her monies (that she had meticulously sewn into her various gowns and trunks as way of providing secret storage compartments), once she came to trust Fletcher and discovered she'd be remaining with him for some time. She didn't have time to re-stitch coins back into place. She didn't necessarily want her money separated from her nor all of it stored in one location and easy to become lost or stolen, however either. She presented this problem to Nancy who, reliably, had a solution.

"We shall store it in the girls' pack."

The 'pack' had been the term given to the contraption Nancy constructed soon after the babes were born. She said she had viewed something similar once from a native Indian. The Indian mother had carried her child more securely on her back, rather than in a linen sash carried at the side, she'd explained. Because there were two of them, however, Nancy had constructed it to carry one in front and one on her back, but it could also be rotated as she did not fix the straps into place. That allowed, if Ann desired, the ability to turn them, bring them closer together and carry both babes in front.

She tended to prefer the latter carrying position, with each baby slightly beneath one of her arms and covering each side of her chest. It made hand work more difficult for she had to reach around both babies, but for traveling she felt safer having them on the front side of her where she could better discern their safety.

The pack consisted of a leather frame structure to ensure security. Stitched by Nancy's capable hands with animal sinew that it may be of most endurable quality and strength. Large pockets, in which to place the babies, were sown in, made from double folds of linen to provide flexibility as well as allotting for easier clean up and able to hold up better to moisture. The girls were already feeling constrained at nearly six months of age, despite the fact that Nancy made sure it had ample room for them to grow further.

In the center of both the front and the back was a wide support of leather that covered Ann's middle like a vest and at the bottom was equipped with the loops that the straps from the sack portion where the babies were carried, belted through. It was this design that allowed for the rotation of each baby pack. The center vest area held pockets for storing hankies and the like; utilized much like an apron.

Nancy was a brilliant, clever woman. Ann never doubted how blessed she was for having her in her life. She smiled to Nancy and nodded her accordance with the plan, and they set out to finish packing.

Ann had to relinquish much of the trunk space for her daughters as they would require more necessities to get them through than she would herself. She allowed herself two plain, sturdy dresses, borrowed from her lady's maid back home; but since the birth of her daughters had been taken back in some to accommodate her shrunken size. She had not been thrilled to discover that she no longer measured at the size she did prior to her pregnancy, even though she had waited a good solid five months after Kit and Livvy had been born before taking the dresses in.

She had more important things to worry about than her figure at the moment. Perhaps life would allow time in the future for such frivolities. If her plans finally met fruition!

Aside from the two working gowns, she allowed herself one of quality; it had been selected by her mother and it brought back nostalgia and loving memories of time spent with her. It was not the most fashionable gown and Ann had thought it unlike her mother at the time to order such, when her every motivation was that of impressing her peers.

She had told Ann that it would be much more comfortable to wear and be perfect for their return to the country. She had explained to Ann that once entered into the social realms, she would never be able to escape. There would always be watching eyes waiting for Ann -*especially Ann*- to fall.

Ann's mother was new to a title and to life of splendor. *Well, not that new*, Ann rolled her eyes. Her mother had been rubbing elbows with them for all of Ann's seventeen years and they had never fully accepted her. The ladies and even the lords that occupied the *haut ton* could be so cruel. Not a one of them without flaws of their own and yet eager to reveal all those of everyone else.

What Charleston considered its elite society was much the same. She recalled a certain patient of Fletcher's, Calpurnia Grenrow; apparently her cousin had married very high up indeed, a viscount no less. Calpurnia ensured every one of her acquaintance knew of it too. She put on airs as if it was she who was bestowed the title of Lady. Oh, how Ann had itched to inform her that she herself was the daughter of an Earl and therefore should be addressed as *Lady Ann*.

She'd had to refrain in order to continue with her current pretenses and remain *Mrs. Morgan*. Funny, how at the time, the pretense was little more than name formality. Now that she knew she'd never been married, well, it took on quite a new dimension of deceit.

At least Nancy had been able to find enjoyment in the knowledge. She and Calpurnia were enemies of a sort. Calpurnia was of the age of Nancy and had married a Baker's second son. She'd become widowed after the first five years of that marriage and had produced no children. She'd remained unmarried all these years and held a discreet reputation for being a rather promiscuous widow. It was obvious to all who witnessed Nancy's interaction with the also widowed, Doctor, that the way she cared for him ran deeper than friendship; obvious to all but Fletcher. Nancy had told Ann in confidence one afternoon, that she disliked Calpurnia.

She had said, "That promiscuous bit of baggage can go after the doctor all she wants. Fletcher could never be interested in one with such a viperous tongue."

In truth, Fletcher hadn't been ready to share his heart with another woman at all; he had loved his wife deeply. Ann could hear his love for her in his voice when he spoke of her. Ann was glad his love for his wife had been strong, but she ached for

Nancy when she was present to hear such conversations, as she knew how Nancy longed to be loved by him that way too.

She didn't think Fletcher should spend the rest of his days alone either. His wife was gone, and he had a lot of years left to live; one should be loved all the years they walked the earth. Ann smiled as she thought of her parents and how happy they were. Then she recalled James and felt bereft again.

Well, Nancy at least hadn't had to deal with the haughty Calpurnia much, ever since Calpurnia had been present and enlisted to help deliver Ann's daughters against her every desire. She'd never had children of her own after all and it had been quite traumatic for her to witness the ordeal.

Nancy had later informed Ann, with a mischievously pleased smile, "I don't think she enjoyed that experience over much. I imagine we won't have to endure the *pleasure of her company* quite as often as before."

Pulling from her thoughts, Ann held up her precious gown and looked it over once more. She'd only ever donned it once and had been pleasantly surprised by how it transformed her appearance. It was a simple Empire-waisted gown with slightly puffed sleeves, nothing about its design unusual other than it being a fading fashion when she had ordered it. It was the color of it that had turned the simple gown into something striking; the hue of brandy wine, and it flattered her complexion well.

Her amber eyes had warmed, and her sunshine streaked brown hair had looked as soft as caramel. She hoped she could still fit her post birth altered form into it! It was one of the few gowns that had not been white, cream or pastel colored to mark her as a debutant in society. She was glad her mother had insisted on this particular dress. She'd been excited to wear it for James upon his return for her. He called her 'Lady Golden Eyes' and she knew he would approve of the golden image she made in the gown.

A pity he never returned, destroyed her life, and now she had to chase him down across a foreign country like a desperate wolf. She had to resist crumpling the gown into a mess and punching it into the trunk in her fit of anger. Instead she exhaled and calmly folded it and placed it between her two plain gowns, as that was all the protection she could afford it.

She watched Nancy pack many clouts for Kit and Livvy; Ann couldn't wait until they could manage a chamber pot!

Next, Ann pulled out the small case in which she stored her father's dueling pistols. The ones she took from his safe the morning she stole away into the early morning mist to board the *Clara Stella*.

Now that seemed so long ago.

Guilt shouldn't reside within her for she knew her father would care only for her safety and be glad she thought to take some protection with her, but it was difficult to shake all the same. She felt a stray tear trickle down her cheek, but she didn't bother to swipe it away. She wondered if her parents thought her dead after all these months.

She vowed she would pen a letter and post it to them once she reached town. It wouldn't reach them for months, but when they received it, she hoped it would bring them some peace. She thought of Fiona then, too. What had become of her friend? She'd not heard from her or Captain Ludwick all these months. She prayed her friend was faring well wherever she was.

It didn't take overly long to pack everything they would need (well, that of which could fit) into two serviceable sized trunks. Ann only had two hands and that only when Kit and Livvy were strapped to her like monkeys.

A vivid image Ann recalled of a mother gorilla with her tiny baby clasped onto her like a leech as she ambulated around her enclosure, sprung to her mind from her visit to the Zoological Society of London in Regent Park four years past. She remembered the trip vividly. The zoo had not actually been open to the public at that time, but her father, rich as Croesus that he was, had invested in its studies and therefore she had the privilege of an escorted visit inside the mysterious structure. She sighed, another memory to cherish of her beloved father.

In the next instant she berated and reminded herself that she *would* see her father again. That was the point of this crazy escapade. No. *Adventure*. That was how she should view it, as an adventure. Then when she found that vile adulterer and made him her husband, she could thank him. It wasn't every woman who had the opportunity to journey across an ocean and tour the entirety of a foreign country.

Alone.

No more, she shook her head. Only positive thoughts.

"Well, I think we are done, Nance."

Once she had finished packing, Ann stole away with Fletcher to speak with him about a serious matter – the revelation of which left him with a boyish smile and a spark in his eye that told her more than words that he would be truly happy and loved in her absence.

Nancy escorted her and the babies to the coaching Inn located behind the new SCC & RR Co. rail station on Line Street. Ann wished the rail went further than Hamburg, she dreaded riding the stage, especially with two little ones to care for. Nancy, on the other hand was glad Ann wouldn't be boarding the "Noisy contraption".

"There was another before this one, you know. It was called *The Best Friend of Charleston*. Humph! Some best friend it turned out to be: it exploded! Terrible, just terrible. You'll be much safer taking the stage."

"Mr. Louis!" Nancy's shrill voice encountered no difficulty in getting the young man's attention over the ruckus of the stable and the steaming train boarding passengers at the front. "Now, will there be someone to assist Mrs. Morgan with her trunks and baggage once she reaches her destination?"

"Of course, ma'am." He tipped his hat to the old curmudgeon.

"Well, there had better be for the price she paid for these tickets."

Although it was true, the tickets were costly, and she'd been charged additionally for each child their own ticket, it wasn't this young man's fault assisting them with loading her luggage. Ann smiled to him apologetically.

"Then of all things, they tried to charge you for both trunks! My word, what is the estimable town of Charleston coming to?"

Ann thought to share an amused smile with the luggage boy, but he appeared rather nervous instead.

"It's alright Nancy, you handled it as you always do."

"That's right I handled it. Told that ticket man what for is what I did. Imagine someone trying to wrangle one over on *my Ann*."

Tears filled Ann's eyes and she turned promptly to embrace the dear woman. She felt Nancy's arms squeeze her back, as well as she was able with Livvy and Kit squirming uncomfortably between them.

"Now, now, none of that my dear." Nancy retreated from the embrace and patted her shoulder comfortingly before wiping the welling moisture away from her eyes.

"I'll write to you as soon as I arrive to St. Louis, I promise." Ann said almost frantically and clutched Nancy's sleeve.

How could she do this without Nancy? To leave those she loved all over again? She needed to steel herself against the new wave of grief struggling to pull her under. She'd embarked on this very journey not all that long ago on her own. She needed to finish the mission she came here for.

"That is not the least bit comforting Ann. It will be at least two months before your letter gets back to me, by then who knows where you will have trekked off too!"

"Nonsense. No matter what James decides to do after learning of his family, I will come back to you. I just cannot move on with my life until I know that I tried to unite my daughters with their father. He has a right to know. And they have a right to be loved by their father in return."

Nancy cupped Ann's cheek with her hand, "As do you, have a right to be loved in return."

"Thank you," she whispered and pressed a kiss to the inside of Nancy's palm where it rested on her face.

"Coach ez leavin'!" Their goodbye was interrupted by the driver climbing up to his perch.

The young man who had loaded their luggage came to Ann's side now.

"Are ye ready to go, Miss?" He asked politely.

She nodded her consent and allowed him to assist her into the two-person car. She arranged Kit and Livvy in their packs so that she could twist towards the window.

She saw Nancy, standing so forlornly, that Ann's chest tightened with all the reservations about her decision, wanting to fling herself from the car and run back to her friend. She put her fist to her mouth unwilling to allow crying sobs to interfere with her last words to her friend.

She wanted to shout how much she loved Nancy and how grateful she was for all that she'd done and for loving her as a mother would a daughter. There wasn't time, however.

She was sure Nancy knew Ann's heart.

Instead she leaned over the window casing and shouted, "Go home to Fletcher. He has *something of importance* to ask of you. You two take care of each other until I return."

Ann's smile grew as she took in Nancy's confused state. "You'll understand once you return."

Nancy's confusion turned to that of surprised realization.

"Don't wait for me, though. I want to hear all the details when next we meet!" She heard the driver crack the whip and felt the lurch of the coach in motion, so she quickly blew a kiss to Nancy and they both waved until they disappeared from sight.

Nancy had battled conflicted emotions all the way home from the station. She wanted to cry with despair over the departing of Ann and her darling babies and perhaps she would have given in to the temptation to do so had Ann not declared in front of the whole coaching Inn, the type of news she had secretly coveted privately for the past six years. *What was that Ann up to?*

She'd hurried home and sure enough, there had been Fletcher waiting for her, not on bended knee, of course, they both were far too old for that such nonsense. And so they spent the next hour holding and comforting one another, spilling tears of both happiness and sorrow. They decided they would marry that very afternoon if the preacher was available.

Nancy was just gathering her pelisse and reticule to go in search of Pastor Davis when a knock sounded at the door.

"Blast. Even the ones that cannot read should be familiar with the sign. No more patients today." Fletcher grumbled as he made his way to the door.

"I'm sorry, unless it is of dire emergency; I am not seeing any more patients today."

"I'm here for Ann."

That was when Nancy heard him.

"Mrs. Morgan, I mean. We assigned a tea date this afternoon, is she still available?"

The old doctor at the door looked at Jonathon with weary and almost pitying eyes, released a frustrated sigh and motioned for him to enter. As he stepped into what resembled a foyer, he was made aware of Ann's stoutly protector from the previous evening.

"You may as well not hang your coat, sir. Ann is not here."

That came as a surprise. She'd seemed more than eager to meet with him yester eve, before parting, to discuss more her situation concerning James. He'd thought she would be ready and waiting when he arrived.

"Well, would it be too much of an imposition to await here for her return?"

"No, no, no. I mean yes. I mean, you misunderstand." The woman shook her head with frustration. "Ann will not be returning here. Not for some time anyway. She took the stage before noon today...... She's gone."

Chapter 6

She's gone.

The words hit Jonathon like a bag of bricks.

He brought his thumb and forefinger up and lightly pinched the bridge of his nose and then smoothed the lines forming over his brow.

"She-She's left?" He couldn't believe what he was hearing. "She's set out for Missouri... On her own?"

It was inconceivable! How could this woman, who was obviously Ann's caretaker, have allowed it?

The woman must have sensed the accusations steaming from him, for she rolled her shoulders back defiantly.

"Ann is a very capable woman. She traveled across the entire Atlantic by herself and she was-" Nancy ceased the words flowing from her. This man still did not know about the children and for some reason Ann hadn't wanted him to know of them yet.

"'Was' what?"

"Determined. Very determined. Just as she is now."

Nancy averted her eyes to the floor. She was unsure about this gentleman. She wasn't prone to trusting easily and she had to be very careful regarding her precious Ann and the dear babes. She very much disliked this man's cousin, James Morgan. Detested him, really. It wasn't fair to judge this man by the same cloth, however.

Nancy looked to him carefully and asked, "Why are you so interested in her whereabouts?"

Jonathon seemed to be searching reflectively within himself for the answer to this question as well.

"She has been wronged by my cousin. It's the gentlemanly thing to see that she is afforded the respect due to her. If my cousin will not do right by the gal, then...then..."

"Yes, Mr. Morgan?"

"Well, then I intend to, of course. My cousin has been laying shame to our family name for years. And I have been cleaning up his messes and trying to reestablish the respect once associated with the Morgan name for just as long."

"So, you would marry Ann out of duty?"

He coughed uncomfortably. "A-hem, yes, of course."

Of course, that was why he would marry her. He'd only just met the woman yesterday. It didn't matter that she was the most gorgeous creature he'd ever seen or that all of his thoughts since meeting her have been occupied with whether her lips would taste of the honey that the scent of her hair had indicated.

The woman looked at him through squinted eyes that seemed to be searching him for more, as if she knew he had already developed feelings for Ann.

"If she finds him, he could decide he wants her for himself after all, you know."

The woman's words unsettled him, made his starched suit feel too tight and he absently tugged at his collar to loosen its noose-like hold around his neck.

"That seems very unlikely. Ann is hardly the first young woman he has misused so."

"Oh?" Nancy said, "You did not offer for the other ladies your cousin ruined?"

It was true. Most of the women James dallied with, however, had had an underground reputation already. Only their papas believed them to be still possessed of their innocence. He'd felt bad for the few ladies who thought James had serious intent toward them, yet Jonathon had never stepped up and offered his name for their protection.

He'd been young, he placated. He hadn't thought to settle down with a wife for a few more years at least. He wasn't even thirty yet. Still, there was something about Ann and the strength and determination that emanated from her. Her beauty and those unforgettable eyes. Even James had remarked upon them upon his return.

That was the first James had ever divulged details from any of his conquests. Perhaps he did care for Ann, but his marriage to Lorraina had inhibited him from legally marrying Ann. Would he now that he was free once more? If Ann showed up in St. Louis in front of him, would James fall at her feet as he should?

Somehow Jonathon didn't think James could ever love anyone more than he loved himself. No matter how special a woman walked into his life.

Jonathon would not make that mistake though.

"I must go after her. She shouldn't be alone. Christ! Any matter of vile things could happen to a woman alone. Traveling by stage no less!"

"So, you will go after her?" Nancy asked eagerly. She was more convinced that this man could help Ann. He seemed to feel something stronger for her than he was willing to admit, or maybe wasn't aware of yet. She didn't like her headstrong Ann traveling across those mountains alone either.

"If I am to catch up with her, I need to leave quickly. Did she take State road?"

"Yes, from the Line Street Station. Please hurry. And take care of her. Bring her back home safely."

The young man fled out the door.

Ann would be displeased with her, she knew, but Nancy felt it was for Ann's own good. Society could be cruel to a woman traveling alone, and fate even more so. Nancy felt Fletcher take her hand and squeeze it gently, lending her strength. She knew they were both praying for Ann's safety.

Jonathon spared time he didn't have to pen a note to his aunt and uncle. Ever the dependable and devout gentleman, he growled to himself. He spared details, telling them only that urgent business of a personal nature required his presence in Missouri. They would no doubt associate that urgency with James who they knew also to be currently located in Missouri.

They would probably worry for him, but it couldn't be helped. They'd grown quite fond of him over the years, and he them. His aunt and uncle had taken him in when Jonathon's own parents had met their untimely deaths in a coaching accident.

He'd spent the last ten years on their farm working alongside his cousin, ever since he was fifteen. Well not precisely alongside him. It was soon realized Jonathon had a head for numbers and he took over the business side of things. He was never much built for physical labor. James had been the one gifted with the physique ladies admired. Jonathon preferred his paperwork duties to that of toiling away in the dirt alongside the others anyway.

Despite their differences and James' rebellious tendencies, he and Jonathon had become close friends. It wasn't until recently that James' wild ways had begun to separate them. He knew his aunt and uncle were consummately worried for James as well. They really deserved better from James, he thought. So did Ann.

Jonathon swallowed his fears for Ann's safety. The roads were a mite safer now, but little innovations have been made to the cars over the years and Jonathon remained mistrustful of their safety provisions. Of course, that wasn't the main concern when traveling by coach. Brigands and robbers knew they were easy pickings, none more so than a lady traveling alone.

He cleared out his room at the hotel, paid up with the clerk then hurried to post his letter. After that he sought out the stable yard in search of a good mount to rent. He could travel much more quickly and safely on his own.

Ann noted the clouds darkening overhead. Oh, that was just what she needed! Rain to soak her and the babes through on top of the nauseating terrain they were enduring. Ever since leaving the main towns behind, the roads had been nothing but ruts and sand! She and the girls were constantly being flopped left to right as the coach swayed roughly back and forth and up and down over every bump. Livvy let out a cry as she startled from the boom of thunder in the distance.

She heard the driver shout something back to her. He was blathering something about the approaching storm. The man had been annoyingly silent the entire trip except to make caustic remarks about women without the brains to stay put. She didn't much care for the unpleasant man's company and she was glad for the majority of the time when he was silent. Now he was accusing her of bringing on the storm, apparently.

"I's told ye it warn't smart, a woman travelin' alone. Settin' off in a storm no less."

The man spit and nearly tumbled from his perch as they rounded a bend in the road. Ann steeled herself against the side of the car and squeezed her eyes shut against the bruising she'd already endured.

"You's not right smart are ye?"

"I prefer *uninformed*. Why did not you explain at the station that the weather wasn't well enough to travel in?"

"What with the chill in the air and the blowin' winds this week I figured as you already knew'd," He shouted back over the wind and the creaking of the coach and jangling of the harnesses.

"Well, it seemed a perfectly sunny morning when I set out for your services." She tipped her nose into the air and stifled a *harrumph!* She turned her attention back to soothing Livvy who had been unable to sleep due to the hard ruts the driver seemed incapable of hitting at speeds other than full capacity!

He informed her that they could run into others and have to maneuver around herds of sheep or cattle if he didn't push the team. She wished she had set out earlier as to have avoided this particular driver as well as the traffic. She didn't want to spend all of her coin on the trip there and the least number of establishments she had to spend the night at the better. If she had more coin, she'd be singing a different tune, for she couldn't wait to step from this contraption!

Cramped in these packed quarters on hard seats and jostling into the hard-walled panels. She was ever hitting the window frame and as both of her arms were used to protect the girls, she had only her head sometimes available to catch her. She tried maneuvering her legs so that she could steady herself and resist from flying forward by pushing against the seat that faced her.

It didn't help that her trunks were on the floor as she had wanted convenient access to them and could hardly get to them had they been strapped to the top of the conveyance. They rattled and bounced sometimes all the way up into the seat. All of her muscles ached from the constant use to keep her and her daughters seated, and they hadn't even made it to the first stop.

"What do you mean that's the only horse you have? It looks near to starved!" Jonathon barked in disgust.

"That's wot we've got gent. Take it o' leave it."

"When's the next client due in?"

The unshaved man reeking of whiskey shrugged his shoulders, then spit and presumptuously stretched out his hand to shake a deal with Jonathon. Jonathon cursed. His hand rubbed the back of his stiff neck and he could feel an ache beginning to drum through his head.

"Alright, alright. I'll take the lamed beast," He spat, "But I'll not pay the high rate you spoke of. This mare doesn't look as if she'll make it to the next Inn, let alone all the way to Columbia."

"Eh!" The filthy, be-ragged and bewhiskered man had the nerve to sound insulted, "T'aint lamed!"

"No, just near to starved," Jonathon grumbled.

Jonathon begrudgingly paid the man. He didn't wait for someone else to saddle the ribby horse but did for himself. He pitied the poor animal. He'd not be able to ride it hard. Hopefully they could make it to the next Inn and a healthier mount would be available there.

He tied his belongings, few as they were. He'd travelled light thinking it only to be a short two day's stay in Charleston. He swung up into the rented saddle. The leather seat had been worn into a smooth hard surface that felt as if he were riding on stone. He hoped to change that at the next inn as well. He really should think about investing in a horse and saddle of his own.

He wondered how far ahead Ann was.

Ann's Valley

Grayson and Luke had finally made it to Cumberland Gap where Grayson was to meet his partner, Jacques Dubois. He and Jacques had agreed to lead a team of wagons west with them. It hadn't actually been on the way for Grayson, but people paid good money to be led by men who knew the country, and no one knew it better than Grayson and Jacques Dubois in these parts. Grayson also wanted to ensure safe traveling for Luke, so if that meant taking a detour so be it.

Luke proved to be a trooper and a natural in the saddle. He seemed happy to ride day and night. It wasn't very surprising as Grayson had learned Luke had spent most of the past two years in the stable yard with horses. Grayson couldn't tell if Luke was shy by nature or if it was a product of his neglected treatment in his absence. It still riled Grayson when he thought about what his son must have endured over the past years.

Grayson garnered from the information he'd been able to draw out of Luke, that he'd not been physically harmed during that time, although it sounds as if he may have been half starved if it hadn't been for their old cook. His Aunt Agatha had never shared any of Grayson's letters with Luke, so Luke had been hurt and angry he admitted, during the first year after his mother had passed.

It wasn't until he'd spied Aunt Agatha reading one of them that he learned the truth. She usually burned the letters after reading, but that day she'd been interrupted by a caller. Luke hadn't intended to snoop, but he'd caught sight of his name over her shoulder when she'd been reading. Once she left the room, he'd snatched it quickly and quietly and hidden it in his room. That was the only letter he'd been able to snatch over the years, but it had revealed a lot.

According to Luke, Aunt Agatha had often maligned Grayson and accused him of not sending money for Luke's care. After reading that letter, he'd learned the truth. Luke shyly told Grayson that he'd been happy to learn that he hadn't forgotten about him.

The shame hit Grayson hard. But it was all in the past now. Grayson promised him they'd remain together from here out. Luke had slowly over the long, enduring, trip begun to open up and occasionally, in glimpses, revert back to the child he was. It would just take time, thought Grayson, for trust to build in his world again.

Grayson was never so happy that he'd not squandered any of his time out west. He'd worked hard and diligently over the years making as much profit as he possibly could. It wasn't an easy feat when there were limited companies to trade with and furs were on the decline.

Last year at the rendezvous, Grayson had noted an influx of young bucks arrive with the idea in their minds of striking it rich. Grayson only shook his head knowingly. He wasn't worried about the newest wave of young men being any competition. Most would give up once they realized life in the mountains was always a life or death battle with nature. And nature usually won.

Most mountain men were content just living the solitary, rough lifestyle. And if you weren't happy with that alone, he could have told those young bucks, may as well just head on back east. Most of the trappers and fur traders Grayson met, didn't have a farthing to their name. Any profit they made was quickly recycled into booze and loose women supplied to them at the rendezvous.

The companies were smart, they knew how to cater to a man's vices and keep him where they wanted him.

Grayson hadn't partaken in the excess behavior, however. He'd been too focused on his freedom and later, building a life for himself and Luke. He'd been lucky too, to have established a friendship with William Ashley, early on. He and Dubois purchased shares in Ashley's company, and along with a number of other men managed to build quite the empire. They grew to rival even the great, dominating Hudson Bay Co., which was about as good as it could get.

Grayson and Dubois had both recently sold their shares of the company back to Ashley however, both knowing fur was on a decline. They'd already made their riches. Grayson could get by easily enough.

Grayson had harbored doubts about bringing Luke into the wilderness with him, but after spending so many years feeding his soul with fresh mountain air and living amongst natures most secreted beauty, he'd become too much a part of it to ever leave.

Ann's Valley

It was still wild, but it was no longer new to him. He'd been tested by nature and not only endured but thrived. What was a harsh wilderness for some, was now home for Grayson. He had a healthy respect for nature; it was no longer a battle for him.

He was confident in his decision, now, to bring Luke after learning of the life he'd been living. They would make it just fine: together.

Hours later, Ann breathed a sigh of relief when they finally stopped in Columbia. She'd worried for all of their safety after night had settled upon them. The clouds that had threatened rain earlier followed them and kept it a black moonless night. As of yet the clouds had not relinquished their drowning fury and Ann supposed she must be thankful for that. However, it was dangerous traveling at night, especially so with no light to guide them.

The driver nearly leapt from his perch when they arrived, causing the stablemen working there to make quickly for the reins.

"Take care o' the horses wod ye, I've got to warm me bones somefin' fierce!"

The dastardly man did not even mention his client and her babies still in the coach! Ann growled.

"Excuse me. I'd like to get out of this blasted thing too!"

"Oh, right miss. Right away." Another young man came forth to assist her with the door of the cart while the first one held the hungry horses. The horses knew they were here for a resting stall and a meal and Ann was certain they were eager to get out of harness too. The young man assisting her was polite and kind and she felt wretched for having snapped at him.

"Thank you, sir," she said as she stepped from the car, babies in-tow.

The man's eyes widened when he saw two babies. He waited as if to see a man exit with her. She refrained from saying, "Search all you want, no husband will be coming out of that coach, but if you find one, bring him in with the rest of the luggage, would you?" She chuckled to herself, must be the exhaustion allowing for her to make light of her situation. She'd have to become accustomed to people gawking after her, wondering why a woman with two babies was traveling alone without a husband.

Sure enough the next trial that awaited her was that of obtaining a room for the night.

"Listen, sir, I have traveled a long way." *All the way from England in fact!* She added silently. "I am tired, and I have two irritable babes to tend to. I don't care what state the room is in, so long as it can accommodate the three of us for the night."

"This is a respectable establishment." The man turned his nose up to her.

So, the man thought to put on airs, did he? He who had never rubbed elbows with the haut ton thought he could intimidate her?

Ann smiled serenely back to the offending man.

"I'll have you know, that not only will my husband be displeased with the treatment I am receiving from your 'respectable establishment', but so will my father, the Earl of Abersty once he learns of it!" She was near shouting by the end of her threat, which wasn't very lady-like, and therefore counterproductive to the point she was trying to make. It seemed to have affected the man, however.

His frail frame trembled before her as he endeavored to keep his composure.

"My apologies Miss."-

"*Mrs*. Morgan." She interrupted with a delicate arch of her brow.

How many times had she witnessed her mother berating someone-usually Ann-with the same look? It appeared the look came with motherhood. Ann would have laughed, if she hadn't had to remain serious and threatening.

"Of course, Mrs. Morgan, my apologies. It would appear we do have a room available."

She raised her brow a little higher.

"Errr," the thinly man stammered, "A grand room. I think you will find it very luxurious."

Without her further having to press him he added, "And!- And affordable."

He smiled to her nervously while she remained staring back at him with the most condescending look she could manage. She must have pulled it off successfully for it had been effective. But then she'd been educated by the most elite of the ton; a world this man would never have access to.

She allowed a small hard smile, "Well, that's more like it."

The man behind the counter twitched then hollered to a boy nearby, "Parker, please show Mrs. Morgan to her room, the one closest to the copper."

Oh, could he truly be referring to a tub? This was indeed a respectable establishment she thought. Now she wanted to run the boy down, get to her room as fast as possible and figure out how to order that bath! Who knew when she'd have another opportunity to bathe herself and the children?

She kept a dignified pace, however. The girls were fussing, one at each of her sides. Kit of course was the quieter of the two and suckling on her fist. Livvy was a mess of tears wetting her angry red face as she muttered little cries, that Ann knew would soon to turn into ear piercing wails.

The bath would have to wait, it would seem.

The boy led them into the room. It was larger than the room she lived in at Fletcher's. The curtains were of a gauzy material and the chair and stand in the room stood on matching petite legs. Everything selected to give the appearance of splendor and rich tastes.

She'd grown to feel most comfortable with more utilitarian, rustic surroundings. She missed Nancy and Fletcher and the comforts of home, still the bed looked rather inviting and the coverlet appeared cleanly.

"Will this do for you miss?" She heard the boy squeak; no doubt he witnessed her cold display downstairs and didn't want to encourage her wrath.

She smiled sweetly to him, "Yes, this will do very well thank you."

Before he could skitter all the way out the door, she asked, "Are the kitchens still available this late of night?"

He stopped in the hall and turned to her, his hands nervously folding and unfolding the hat in his hands, "Uh, yes ma'am. I mean miss. I was on m' way just now to tell the cook to prepare three meals."

"Why, you are quite the gentleman," She smiled to him again in a way she hoped would soothe some of his nervous twittering around her. She hated to think she behaved so wretchedly downstairs that she frightened small children.

"I'm grateful for your assistance. Please do request cook to prepare a meal, albeit, just one meal I'm sure will be sufficient." She smiled again and nodded to the boy, so he knew he was dismissed.

He smushed his crumpled hat back onto his head, "Yes, miss. Right away." He returned a quick smile before darting off down the hall.

Before she could turn around another young man filled his place at the door. It was the same young man from outside who'd assisted her from the carriage. It appeared he'd carried her luggage to her room.

"Where would you like these, Miss?"

She directed the gangly boy, somewhere in his teenage years he must have been, to place her trunks on the bed. He then stepped over and lit the fire in the hearth. The room hadn't felt awfully chilled, but nights in early spring still required fires for warmth, so she was pleased with the boy's thoughtfulness. He didn't linger any either and quit the room as quickly, but politely, as possible.

She chuckled to herself. Either she looked a terrifying witch, or these young boys didn't know what to make of the two babies. Some people were intrigued by twins, Ann had discovered in Charleston, and some people were horrified, believing in superstitious nonsense. Doctor Fletcher had told her, himself though, that it was rare to have twins that were both equally healthy. She was grateful for that. They required much more work and patience than she felt she could muster some days, but she loved them both beyond words.

Livvy, growing impatient, let out a shriek that must have surprised even herself for she ceased crying and looked mightily startled.

Ann laughed, "Yes well, that's what you get when you try to break the windowpanes with your howls. Come now." She pulled them both from their confines. Poor Kit was always seen to secondly because she was so well behaved. It truly wasn't fair to the poor dear. She set her on the rug on the floor. Ann found Honey Bear out of one of the folds on her vest carrier. Honey Bear was a tiny bear Nancy had sewn from strong linen cloth, stuffed with horsehair, and with tiny black wool patches cut in the shape of eyes and a nose. Nancy hadn't wanted to use burlap, saying it'd be too rough on their faces and no buttons for eyes as the girls were sure to choke on them, she'd insisted.

Ann hadn't understood the significance of that at the time. She well knew now, however; both girls had taken to chewing constantly on anything they could fit into their mouths, including the collar of Ann's dress. Often her latest fashions were of sporting baby drool. It's no wonder so many in the aristocracy hired nurse maids to tend to their children full time.

She placed Honey Bear in Kit's chubby, slobber-wet hand. Kit replaced her fist with Honey Bear to her mouth and began gumming it right away. Next, she brought Livvy around to feed her. She was in the process of weaning them. It would have been more economical to continue feeding them from her breast, but her milk supply had never seemed able to keep up with their demands well. At about four months of age, Nancy began assisting with feedings by mashing carrots and other edibles into mush she could spoon to them. Luckily, they seemed eager for the foods Nancy fed to them and didn't have trouble keeping it down. Nancy was always telling Ann how blessed they all were that she had two healthy babies that were easy to care for. Ann didn't think raising them was very easy at all, but according to Nancy it could have been much more horrific of an experience.

Ann was glad to have removed the pack from her. Good gracious she must resemble a mule with both girls strapped to her sides!

Both girls were fed and contented, so Ann placed them both sitting up on the rug and then seated herself in the nearby chair. Oh, how glorious its padded cushion felt on her backside compared to the hard seat in the coach her rear had pounded against all the way to Columbia! She stretched out in it reveling in its provided comfort.

She watched her girls on the rug and felt her eyes growing heavy from exhaustion aided by the heat of the fire. She must have begun to nod off because she awoke at the sound of knocking on her door.

"I have your meal miss." It was the awkwardly teenage boy who'd carted up her luggage.

She opened the door and thanked him, "Also, would it be too much to ask to have a bath prepared?"

The boy blushed, and she realized in her directness she'd unintentionally embarrassed him by speaking of bathing in his presence.

Truly, it was no wonder young women had to follow so many sets of rules when society was raising individuals to believe that breasts and other female parts were a hushed secret. As if not speaking of them would alter anyone's knowledge that men and women were anatomically diverse.

The boy stammered, "Y-yes, ma'am, I mean, miss. I mean, no miss it isn't too much to ask. Not a bother at all."

Ann had to keep from rolling her eyes; it's not as if she'd uttered the word breasts or proposed to bathe in his presence or any such ridiculousness. She tried not to feel irritated knowing he was in discomfort over the conversation. She desperately wanted that bath and she didn't care how many foolish boys she had to cause to blush and stammer to get it.

She watched him back out of the hall on jellied legs, "I'll just ah, I'll just inform the cook's Missus. Right away."

"Thank you, please do so." She was happy to shut the door after him.

Blast and double blast! Jonathon had had no luck in catching up with Ann. He made it only as far as Summerville when he'd been forced to stop and trade in his mount. The trading post nearly wouldn't accept the nag! Jonathon had furiously argued with the man, explaining that it was rented from stables in Charleston, and he'd have to take his grievances to them. Summerville's stables were rented out and the nag he'd rode in on was quit, so he had no options except to wait. He was informed no riders were expected in until morning, so he went off in search of housing for the night.

There was only one place that rented out rooms, he discovered, and it was a tavern attached to the stables. The good people of Summerville who occupied this establishment were lucky enough to consume their food whilst smelling the strong odors of soiled straw where the livestock bedded.

Wonderful. Jonathon shook his head astounded with the idea that anyone would build a tavern on the front side of a barn. He'd be glad to leave this place and soon.

He asked around a bit after paying for lodgings and partaking in, what appeared to be, a rather over-stewed stew from the kitchens. No one he asked had seen a woman traveling alone stop through which meant Ann's coach was making good time while Jonathon was stalled in *Stenchville*.

To top it off, the sky looked as if it were about to storm. If it stormed and *if* he would be fortunate enough to rent a horse on the morrow, the road would be slick with mud and Ann would gain greater distance between them. With any luck the rain would fall wherever Ann was and slow her down, as well. He couldn't imagine she'd made it as far as Orangeburg yet, certainly he'd catch her on the morrow.

Ann soaked in the tub early that morning before departing. It could very well be the last time she'd bathe for days or...weeks even. The kitchen staff did not seem overly inclined to indulge her in another bath, after having taken one last evening. The bathing services were intended to be included in the rooming fee, but apparently it wasn't looked kindly upon for guests to request more than one filling and heating of the tub per stay. Well, they would survive, no doubt. Besides one could hardly term last evening's experience a "bath".

Her bathing arrangements the night before had been wretchedly appalling at best. The girls had been irritable from being cooped in the carriage all day and had wanted to crawl over every inch of the dusty floor. Dusty! Some 'respectable establishment' Ann snorted.

Ann nearly drowned Kit trying to bathe her whilst keeping Livvy from scorching herself on the hot bricks in front of the fire angrily spewing ash about. And She'd drenched her undergarments in the process.

Kit had sputtered and cried in outrage for having her head dipped below the water; understandably infuriated with her mother and she let her know it by wailing all the way to the upper floors of the Inn when she resurfaced.

That was no exaggeration, as shortly after, the Cook's wife who had directed the bath, knocked at the door demanding loudly for Ann to quiet her "little beasts". Apparently other guests took to complaining very quickly when disturbed into the late hours by screaming children. Ann had been warned then that her time was being restricted due to the raucous and she only had fifteen minutes to quit the room entirely.

She'd only had enough time to rinse the grime from her person and hair and no time to lather with soap; which had not been provided at any rate. –Another commodity not afforded at the *Respectful Columbia Inn*. Add that to the list along with, no dusting, and poor manners! She rinsed herself quickly and took to scrubbing the dust coated gown she'd traveled in as well as the girls' travel worn garments instead of bathing herself.

Ann had barely wrung the water from the last of the articles of clothing before Mrs. Cook came to hurriedly usher Ann from the room. With as much dignity as possible and refusing to be rushed and treated disrespectfully, Ann carried her two daughters -of which were both crying at that point- as well as her dripping laundry, with her chin high and walked smoothly to her room. She quickly draped her clothes over the petite framed chair in front of the fire and settled both girls in for the night.

But Ann no longer housed regrets about rousing the amenity of the servants last night. Not now that she was soaking in steaming water scented with her own precious soap from home. The soap was made by one of her father's tenants; Molly, a kind woman who always had a smile for Ann. She made the soap especially for Ann before her trips to London, so that Ann would have remnants of home, for all in Somerset knew how Ann dreaded to leave them for the dirty crowded town life. She made the soap with flowers that grew nearby that gave off a spiced honeyed scent Ann cherished. Since crossing the ocean and staying in Charleston, Ann had used it sparingly, but sometimes just taking it out to smell was enough to make her feel closer to her beloved home again.

Ann breathed in the heady aroma and laid her clean rinsed head back against the rim of the tub basin. Kit and Livvy lay rosy white and clean in a bassinet in the corner of the room, sleeping; for that of which Ann was so very thankful. Yes, this was much more ideal than last evenings events, peaceful even. Ann sighed.

Ann stared out the coach window, wishing dearly she was still relaxing in the tub at the Columbia Inn. Goodness, was that really four days past? Yes, she thought as she looked down at her grime covered arms holding her sleeping babes, unfortunately it was so.

So far, her journey had been quite uneventful, with only one misfortune to date. One of the horses came up lame before their stop to Greenville and they'd had to stop in Laurensville to replace the animal. It had cost Ann two extra dollars for additional lodgings that she hadn't wanted to expend, but as it was necessary, she'd had no choice.

No additional mishaps from then on, however and Ann had to admit to being impressed with the drivers and their ambitious driving. They seemed adept at handling the worst of road conditions.

Although there had been some close calls if one asked her.

A couple times her heartbeat sped to match the pounding of the four horses' hooves, pulling as the carriage careened too far to one side. In those moments she felt sure her driver was taking unnecessary risks, but four days later and having survived the Catawba trail, she decided, they must have known what they were doing after all.

She chuckled to herself as she imagined the complaints Nancy would have voiced during certain moments of the journey. Then she immediately regretted conjuring up thoughts of her beloved friend and pushed down her heart ache, determined to see this trip through.

Just then the vehicle began to slow. Angling her head out the window, she called to the driver, "Why are we stopping?"

"This is it ma'am. As far as I can take you. We've reached Cumberland Gap."

As she craned her head out the window, she began to see the little village. Even more impressive were the mountains behind it. She'd already traveled through some mountainous terrain, but nothing compared to the intimidating sight before her.

The sway of the vehicle stilled as the horses came to a stop in front of a large log cabin.

"This be the Olde Mill Inn, Miss. They'll see to your needs of a certainty."

Ann looked about her doubtfully. Obviously, her driver was ready to wash his hands of her. Ann truly couldn't begrudge him for that. The girls had cried relentlessly from Laurensville to Greenville. Even Ann had had fleeting thoughts of diving from the carriage. Not to mention, although polite, the driver had been obviously disgruntled at having to make more stops for Ann to change the girls' nappies. She managed the wet ones from within the carriage, but the ones of a more odiferous nature simply had to be taken care of out of doors.

The driver plopped her bags into the dust at her feet and spun away from her. Wasn't he going to carry them into the Inn for her?

No, apparently not.

No sooner had she pulled her carrying bag and shut the door, the carriage began rolling away. Well, if that didn't beat all! She huffed and blew dirty strands of fly away hairs from her eyes.

Grayson Stone saw the carriage ride in at breakneck speed and stop in a cloud of dust. He worried trouble might come walking out of it, so he remained hidden in the shadows near the window to assess the situation in case he needed to get to Luke quickly.

He was unprepared for the sight that met him when the coach door opened: Aphrodite in the flesh.

Golden eyes glittered in the setting sun as they searched through the settling dust around her. Her mane flowed in rich waves that framed the delicate line of her jaw and draped downward parting unto either side of what Grayson couldn't help but notice, were the exposed creamy tops of her breasts. Grayson's mouth parted in awe, for surely, he was in the presence of a true goddess. Everything about her seemed to glow, from her golden eyes to her rich brown hair that softened into an array of tawny shades like burning embers or like sweet maple syrup.

He swallowed; trouble had indeed stepped from that carriage.

He continued to study her from his secluded position, taking care to remain unseen. She stepped from the conveyance and shook out her crumpled skirts. By the looks of it she had been traveling a long time. Her unique coloring had conjured a fanciful image upon initial sight. On closer inspection, she resembled more of a feral animal than a goddess. Dirt covered her from head to toe. Her glowing locks cascaded in snarled windblown masses. Hardly the fetching picture he thought she had made upon first exiting the carriage. He couldn't deny, that despite her wild hair and disheveled attire, she was still beautiful. The dirt smudges did not disguise her high prominent cheekbones or the delicate straight line of her nose and definitely did not detract from those luminous eyes that peered around cautiously.

She reached back in and grabbed a large contraption that she slipped over her head. It wrapped around her frame and large packs hung from either side. She drew back into the carriage for something else. A baby. Of course, a woman like that would already have a man in her life.

It should not have bothered Grayson. He was through with women. Other than the occasional whore when one could be found, that is. He'd been married for thirteen miserable years and that had been plenty enough for him. He'd planned to be miserable for the duration of his life, but God had seen fit to release him from those oaths.

It seemed a sin to be thankful, morbid even. It wasn't as if he was happy Vivian had died, he was just happy to no longer be married to her. He couldn't regret the entire marriage, though. Guilt always followed the occasional feeling of relief over Vivian's death. She had given him the most precious gift in this world; his son, Luke, and for that he tried to respect the memory of her.

The dust laden Aphrodite captured his attention again, for when he glimpsed back, she had two babies strapped to her sides! He waited a moment more out of curiosity for the man who was responsible for that baggage, but nobody else exited the carriage. The driver appeared then with luggage and plopped them at her feet. Ignoring her questioning gaze, the man pivoted quickly from her and next thing Grayson knew, the carriage was lurching forward on down the road.

There she stood in the middle of the dusty path, with two infants at her side and a pile of luggage at her feet. No maid or companion. And no husband.

He wasn't certain if the anger that swelled up inside him at that moment was due to the young mother's carelessness with her children, her guardian's carelessness for her, or because of the unwanted urge to protect her that came over him.

He had his own plans and they didn't include getting involved with another woman.

He struggled internally to ignore the compulsion to help her and briefly entertained the idea of disappearing to his own rooms and leaving her to fend for herself. Until he witnessed her next movement.

Ann twisted 'the pack' so that Livvy rested against her back and Kit to her front and very inelegantly attempted a squatting stance in hopes of reaching at least one of her trunks. Her eyes surveyed the area around her discreetly, for any other life forms that might be witnessing her undignified pose and sighed her relief when the dirt paths in sight proved empty.

Okay, one more time she told herself and squatted as low as possible. In doing so her knees spread wider and-rrriiip!

The sound of her overskirt tearing apart stopped her swiftly mid squat.

Dash it all, that was just her luck! She looked around once more fearing someone may have heard her dress ripping or worse, viewed the incident. Thankfully, there was still no one about. Well, she was ending that foolishness right there. It was obvious the squatting method would not be successful. Bother, she would have to leave the trunks in the road while she made arrangements with the Inn. At least the town, if one could call it that, didn't look terribly busy with passers-by. In fact, it looked all but barren. Not a soul around. No one to help her, not even a servant from the Inn! Someone inside the Inn had to be aware that a potential customer had arrived.

She stomped her foot; ladylike manners be hanged! Still fuming, she collected herself and stepped towards the Inn with decidedly unladylike thoughts in her mind as well. *Stupid arse of a driver! Couldn't even assist a lady with her bags. Curse all these bags anyway. Curse James! No, curse all men!-*

The woman's unconventional methods, arisen out of the obvious need to secure her luggage, stopped his steps from proceeding to his rooms and instead led Grayson to the door, where he watched her efforts shred -literally- to pieces and her distress became unbearable to ignore.

He growled, agitated with the circumstances he found himself in. Damn women. They were nothing but trouble.

"Miss?" A man's deep resonating voice interrupted her silent tirade. At least, she hoped it had been silent. Her groan just then definitely wasn't. Had she been cursing aloud again? The choked words she'd heard grated indicating the man speaking them was irritated; which undoubtedly might be the case if she'd insulted him while cursing his gender. She winced, hopefully it wasn't the Inn keeper.

She looked up to see an unexpectedly handsome man leaning against the doorway of the Inn, eyeing her. A tall, *very* handsome man. Handsome seemed too docile of a word to describe the man. Attractive would be more apt, she thought, her body tingling with an instantaneous sexual awareness as she took in the sight of him. Muscled arms folded over the expanse of his chest as he watched her from his relaxed pose against the door frame, one muscled, leather clad thigh crossed over the other. She swallowed, her mouth suddenly dry.

Goodness, what was she thinking? The last time her mouth had gone dry at the sight of a man, it had led her to all sorts of trouble. Did she really have to be reminded that she was already chasing a handsome devil clear across, not one, but two countries!

That's when she felt his dark imposing stare upon her. His stormy gray eyes glinted at her in a glowering fashion she certainly wasn't accustomed to. It was rare when a man wasn't bestowing looks of admiration her way, let alone casting looks of disapproval such as this man was doing.

That truth didn't come from conceit or vanity, only awareness.

Unfortunately for her, it derived from the awareness of shallow men's marked attention of her person. In fact, that was one more complaint against men she could add to the list.

Never mind that she had just caught herself admiring the opposite sex.

The voice grunted, followed gruffly by, "Looks like you could use some help with those."

She intended to ignore the fact that the tone of his voice indicated grievance instead of a willingness to help (entirely at odds with his words), until another thought seized her.

She stilled, mortification heating her cheeks; had this incredibly handsome man witnessed her skirts ripping?

Chapter 7

Ann saw the man push himself from the wall. He was at her side in just a few agitated strides.

"Where's your husband? Shouldn't he be accompanying you during travel?" He sneered at her.

The audacity of the man. Her spine stiffened then. "Well, that's really none of your business, is it?" It was rather difficult to look down her nose at a man who had to have been a good ten inches above her, but she gave it her best effort.

"No, of course not," sarcasm edged his words, "I'm only a hapless bystander forced into the undesired role of serving you."

Here Grayson was, aiding this woman whom he'd wanted nothing to do with. He practically seethed his discontent with the thought that he may end up more entangled by this foolish woman for this one charitable act and he didn't find it necessary to conceal his annoyance from her. Perhaps she would see fit to avoid him in the future if she took offense to his surliness.

Her mouth gaped open and her eyes stared back incredulously.

He watched her face screw up in obvious indignation over his last retort. Her lovely winged brows drew together with fury and he readied himself for a verbal lashing.

"Why, you insufferable beast! I don't recall requesting your assistance." She bit off caustically.

He looked up at her ready to childishly engage in a bout of insults with her, but all retorts arrested from his mind when his attentions became ensnared by the sight of her eyes. It was rather hard not to become aware of those eyes, with them flashing at him in a glorious fit of fury.

They glowed like the embers of a fire, enflamed by her anger. Something about them intrigued him and it had nothing to do with their unique coloring and everything to do with the strength blazing forth from within.

He couldn't resist stirring the flames a little more, "Perhaps you'd like for me to leave your bags here in the road?" A muscle ticked in his jaw as he waited for the woman to spitefully comply and release him from his obligation.

Instead she stuck her nose in the air like the spoiled debutantes he'd seen in Philadelphia and spun on her heel towards the lodging, casting haughtily over her shoulder, "Nonsense. Escorting my luggage to the door is the least you can do to amend for exhibiting such rude behavior."

Her unexpected response surprised him. Grayson couldn't help but smile at the straight-backed form marching away from him. Admittedly, he felt a slight admiration for her ability to maneuver him. His eyes admired more than that as they followed the curve of her spine down to where her hips flared out with what he could only imagine being curves of the more luscious variety.

Those kinds of thoughts were exactly the kind he couldn't welcome. The mental reminder froze his smile into a tight line across his face and cooled his ardor as effectively as if he'd been submerged into a springtime mountain stream.

Her trunks thudded to the floor where he dropped them at her feet as she stood in front of the main desk. He tipped his hat to her out of an ingrained politeness he didn't *always* disregard and ignored the faint scent of honey that clung to her hair as he brushed past her in the direction of the guest quarters. He made three strides in the direction of freedom before overhearing:

"I see. Surely this isn't the only hotel establishment in Cumberland Gap?"

Grayson stopped when he heard her dejected voice but kept his back to the confrontation behind him. He was so close to being rid of her; he should just keep walking. His hand sought the frame where the connecting hall joined the entry room as if to propel him forward before he did something he would regret. He looked up to the ceiling and rolled his eyes, knowing, it was too late.

She cleared her throat seeking the strength for yet another battle, "Mm, I see. So, this is the only lodgings around that offer rented rooms and you're... full?"

Grayson could hear from where he stood, the skepticism dripping from her words.

"Yes ma'am, I'm afraid so. All the rooms are occupied."

"Where exactly do you suggest I go elsewhere for shelter?"

"I'm not certain ma'am."

"I see." Her eyes narrowed on the prudish little man before her. He was not striving overly much to conceal his condemnation for her.

In her old world where she existed alongside her father, Ann once believed she experienced freedom. She never realized until she set out on her own just how coddled a life she had lived.

She had always been aware that most women lived with the constrictions society placed upon them, but Ann had always thought it was a choice: One had the choice to live by the rules if one wished to seek and fulfill higher social aspirations. She'd lived in a cage; a large one, but a cage all the same. And if she had remained, she now realized, she would have eventually felt its bars too.

She had been foolish to believe that women had rights to such choices. She herself did not wish to be an aristocrat's wife, nor did she need riches to be content (although admittedly, life was much less inconvenienced when she had funds at her disposal). She just wanted to love, be loved in return, raise a family, and enjoy many adventures with said family.

She had made some dastardly decisions over the past two years and she understood well, now, the consequences of those decisions. She'd mistakenly trusted and fell in love with a man who turned out to be a scoundrel. Ann fervently hoped she was wrong about James. Hoped that he had good reason for what he did. She did not want to regret the decisions that begot her

her daughters. How could she? But the weight of society, an unforgiving voice, whispered in her ear constantly reminding her of her failures.

It didn't matter that she was content with her isolation from society. It did not matter that she sought nothing from them. She hadn't set out to play their games nor follow their rules. But they would punish her for breaking them all the same.

They all judged her: the single woman, the *fallen* woman traveling with her bastard children. And they went out of their way to ensure she paid the price for it. The irony did not escape Ann, that only recently had she learned of her unmarried state.

Not that it mattered. Even if she had not discovered that damning information, society would not, did not in fact, believe her words. They believed only the image she presented. For what woman would travel alone with two babies in this uncivilized country? It infuriated Ann, that she now knew their image of her was partly true.

Society expected her to either whore for her food or remain in poverty somewhere scraping by. It's what she deserves after all, *as punishment* for the choices she has made. If she were alone in the world, she could perhaps abide it or ignore it; the pain and humiliation others tried to bury her under. Perhaps even submit to it; live alone in a leaky cottage somewhere and spend the rest of her life repenting for her sins. If it were only her, perhaps she would take her punishment like the *woman* society intended her to be.

Only she wasn't alone. And she would be damned before she allowed this little rat of a man before her, to force her babies outside to sleep in the dirt like hogs.

Grayson saw her eyes sharpen with a look of murderous intent. He knew well, there were rooms available and so did she, apparently. He wasn't sure what to do next. When he first heard their conversation, he'd thought he was stopping to assist the woman. *Again.* Now he wasn't so certain the innkeeper wouldn't be needing protection.

Grayson shivered, even able to feel the biting chill from her words from where he stood. She delivered them in a becalmed way, but it was deceiving.

Grayson knew what it was; it was the calm before the storm.

Even the ignorant innkeeper could not mistake her fury. Unfortunately for him he had vastly underestimated the woman's determination. Grayson had learned that from his short encounter with her outside. If the man behind the desk hadn't behaved like such a miserable little toad, Grayson might've felt the slightest bit sorry for him.

"Is that. So?" She cocked her head to the side as if she were examining a new species of insect. The man before her visibly paled and she watched his Adam's apple bob with his swallowed fear.

Good. A predatory smile spread slowly across her lips. *He should be afraid.*

Hot blood pulsed through her charged with adrenaline. She pushed herself aggressively from the desk and, holding her daughters to either side of her, marched towards the hall that led to the rooms.

Grayson watched the startled man jump at her unexpected departure from the desk. Both of them left puzzling over her intent.

"Ma'am!" The innkeeper shouted after her, then sputtered, "Wh-where do you think you're going? Y-you have not been permitted access to that area!"

His angry admonishment weakened by the fear that shook his voice, went unheeded as she continued furiously away from him. Grayson didn't for a second think it wise to stop the woman and in fact he found he even shrank against the wall himself as she charged past him.

He couldn't help but feel a prickle of attraction as her skirts pressed against him and her honeyed scent wafted to him as she fitted herself around him and into the hall.

Ann had not been aware that the ill-tempered man from before had been standing in the hall, witnessing her yet again, in a most undignified state. To make matters worse she had to squeeze past him in order to access the hall and she was very aware of the masculine form she pressed against. She was even more mortified when she glimpsed his face. His expression reflected that she appeared nothing short of a crazy woman fit for an asylum.

Well.

She *was* feeling a bit insane in all honesty. She was *incensed* with anger.

She steeled herself with righteous fury and continued past, refusing to feel embarrassed for protecting her children. −Even if her actions were feeling crazier by the second.

She stopped in front of the first door. And knocked.

She paused confidently awaiting a lack of response. The innkeeper recovered from his blatant dismissal and paused then, too, his pursuit of her, with the dawning realization of her objective.

Grayson stared on incredulously and not without a degree of respect.

She looked to the innkeeper and cocked her head to the side, "Hmm. I don't think this room is occupied." She spoke, her elegant brow arched high with condescension.

She stepped to the next door and rapped. Again, as predicted, no response came from within.

"This one does not seem to be occupied either." She looked down her nose at the odious spindly limbed man. "I'm sure I could tour most of the available rooms in this *establishment*," Her tone indicated she felt the place fell far below her standards.

She turned slowly in a circle as if taking measure of the place and let her expression reveal how very unimpressed she was with her surroundings.

"However, I am certain any of them will do for *one* evening. I am, after all, a very accommodating woman," her mouth quirked, "And I am *very* weary from travel."

She blinked innocently at the man gaping like a fish before her. Then as if coming to a decision she said, "Yes, I'll take the first room."

Grayson wanted to applaud her performance. She had turned the tables on the man who had been ready to kick her and her two infants out into the cold. She made it seem as if *she* were the one in control and considering remaining in such a place. It was almost laughable.

Grayson nearly smiled amusedly by the woman's wit and would have done if he'd not seen her hands trembling as they bunched around tight fistfuls of her skirt. The woman who had seemed as unbendable as iron, was actually afraid.

Of course she was, Grayson acknowledged. She had no real power over the situation and was acting purely out of desperation. Grayson's jaw clenched, suddenly angry that she should feel that way and beyond angry with the man causing her distress.

"But madam-" The gangly clerk started to protest. Grayson wasn't about to let the man kick the woman and her two infants out onto the street when there were rooms available and she was willing to pay, but before he could rescue the woman who appeared to be on the verge of breaking, she spoke and interrupted his would be-heroic gesture.

"I *said* I will take the first room. Thank you." Her lips smiled on graciously, but her eyes booked no room for argument. Grayson stared unabashedly at the brilliant woman.

Ann felt Kit stir at her shoulder. It was a blessing they'd remained asleep this long through her tirade. If Livvy awoke, she would no doubt be screaming for her supper. Ann had to hurry this along.

The anger that had carried her to this point was draining and leaving her feeling weakened. She was exhausted, both with the never-ending battle she seemed to have to engage in on a daily basis, but also from the long days of travel. She felt her weakened back muscles spasm painfully under the weight of her daughters.

She didn't dare show weakness now, though. The man was like any other predatory animal. So far, she had stood her ground. If she gave even an inch, he would take her down.

Just then she and her enemy, the innkeeper, heard something like a growl come from behind. Both of their attention turned towards the man from the hall. Ann had forgotten about his presence in the heat of battle. Did the man oppose her staying at the Inn as well? Her eyes flashed to his prepared to match a glare from him.

His eyes bored into hers boldly, not with the scowling look of disapproval she'd expected, but with heated appreciation. It was different than previous looks she'd received from men. It wasn't an appreciation for her body she read in his eyes, but one of respect and admiration. For *her*. Suddenly, it felt as if someone was on *her* side and she wasn't alone. It was unexpected, and the feeling completely disrupted her steeled nerves and she felt her armor begin to deteriorate.

The desk man certainly took it to mean the man towering over him was on her side as well. His voice shook with barely restrained anger when he stated, "Th-the first r-room then." With that, he resentfully jerked the key from its ring and thrust it towards her. He frowned petulantly allowing for his dissension to be known and with a defeated sigh quit the hall and retreated back to his desk.

Ann released the stale air she'd been holding in a heavy sigh. Instinctively, her back found the wall to rest against and she closed her eyes with relief in knowing she and her daughters had a place to stay for the night.

She'd won.

Once more she had won, but she didn't feel the warm sensations that normally accompanied triumph. Fear for the day when she wouldn't claim victory hung over her forlornly. And then what would become of her daughters? She had to find James!

Grayson watched her slump against the wall behind her; depleted, her fists still clenched to her sides. One fist unfurled as if forced and then began to gently and lovingly stroke the soft fuzz atop her baby's head. Grayson had a renewed sense of anger for the man in the other room and perhaps for his own initial treatment of the young mother.

The black crescents of her lashes fluttered against her cheek and her full lips parted on a soft sigh, before she straightened away from the wall with the realization that she was not alone. Her eyes widened at him as she swiveled her head over that of her resting child. Her pink lips remained parted as if in search of words or perhaps... a kiss.

Grayson shook his head. There was no denying that she was a very attractive and intelligent woman, but she was not for him. He needed to extricate himself from her before he became any further involved.

He had planned to wish her luck and be on his way, but when he looked to her she was looking towards the floor abashedly, as if she was now distressed that he had been witness to her denunciation, and for some reason, he instead sought words to soothe her ruffled pride.

"You're something of a lioness aren't you, when your honor is being impugned."

He'd wished for something clever to rouse again her fighting spirit, but instead her eyes saddened.

"Twasn't my honor...," she trailed off as she looked down to the faces of her stirring children resting at each of her shoulders. Grayson swallowed and nodded his understanding. His own mother had raised him alone after the death of his father, only she had been a respected widow in their town. It was clear, that this woman...

She spoke again, her voice hoarse, either from exhaustion or her earlier verbal confrontation with the clerk, "And besides, I'm not sure many would think a woman like me of having any honor to impugn."

She looked to him then, somewhat challengingly as if she expected him to be of similar opinion as the rest of the condemners, but also with pride that she could give a care less about his standing judgment of her.

"Yes, well some people are quick to judge... when they shouldn't be." He searched her eyes to ensure she knew that was his apology. She let a small smile and nod in gracious acceptance.

The children, if that was the correct label to identify them with. They didn't seem of age to really term them children, but they seemed far too large to be called infants either. That's when he realized how heavy of a weight they must be for her small frame to be bearing.

"Well, you should probably claim your room," his eyes twinkled as he motioned to the door behind her.

She smiled back to him and was about to assent, when she blurted, "Oh dear!" She looked to him miserably, "I have to go back out there. To retrieve my luggage."

She allowed for a slight pause to mourn the idea of having to return to the room with the acrimonious desk clerk before starting past him. Impulsively he reached out his arm to stop her. She looked to him affronted and he knew she would accept neither his pity nor his help.

"I have to return as well," he lied, "For my key. I just realized I forgot to get it from him when I entered. It'd be no problem whatsoever for me to deliver your trunks on my way back to my room."

He gestured to the door across the hall, presumably his.

Ann was certain he was lying, and she was shamelessly grateful for the pretense. She was utterly beyond exhaustion and above all things did not want to face that detestable man behind the desk again.

Still, she didn't want to come off too rejoiced over his offer. "Well, if you're sure."

His lips quirked to the side in a quick smile. That was when she noticed how full his bottom lip was. Not full in a feminine way, but not hard either. They were decidedly *un-feminine* as far as lips went, taking on the peachy flesh color mens often did and surrounded by rough stubble that coated the lower half of his strong jaw. Beautiful all the same though. She wondered what they would feel like against her own...

The sound of him clearing his throat brought her to attention. She fervently hoped he didn't know she had been wondering at what his kisses might feel like. Her cheeks colored at the thought. What a dolt! She need not get moon-eyed over a man just because he was kind. And extremely, ruggedly, handsome...

This time Livvy broke the spell, with an ear-splitting wail and reality came, literally, screaming back. The man -she still didn't know his name- all but fled from the hall. She quickly took Kit and Livvy into their room to quiet them so as not to bother the other guests or worse, send the innkeeper flying back with a good excuse to kick them out.

Ann rose from the bed as soon as the sunlight began streaming through the thinly curtained windows. She rushed around her room readying the girls' items for the morning. They had slept so much in the carriage the previous day, she'd feared they wouldn't fall to sleep last night, but after being fed and cleansed, they crawled around on the large rug in the center of the floor exploring their new surroundings and didn't fuss at all when Ann settled them beneath the coverlet to sleep. She was surprised they hadn't yet awakened, but she was glad for it as it gave her time to shake the dust from her own garments and try to press the wrinkles from them. She tried to tell herself she wasn't making any extra effort for her meeting this morning with Mr. Stone.

Upon delivering her luggage last evening, he'd invited her to breakfast with him. It would have been rude to decline the invite after he had so kindly assisted her. She hadn't wanted to accept as it would delay her journey to Missouri. It was, she reiterated to herself once more, merely the polite thing to do and surely it was always necessary to be polite. She didn't want to analyze that reasoning further. Besides, she needed to ready herself for her meet- er, that is, breakfast.

After accepting his courteous invitation to breakfast she pointed out that neither of them had been properly introduced. He smiled and responded he didn't know what she expected a proper introduction to be, but that his name was Grayson Stone.

She refused to believe that the silly smile remaining on her face this morning had anything to do with Grayson Stone.

She rummaged through her case for the special burgundy gown she'd solicitously packed. Then immediately changed her mind.

No. That would never do. He would assuredly think her vying for his attentions if she appeared to breakfast wearing such an extravagant gown. Never mind that it wasn't considered extravagant in England, it would stand out like a sore thumb in this remote village. No. She refolded it and packed it away.

She decided, instead, on a plain frock the color of, well, dead leaves seem to be the only image that came to mind. Most women, indeed, most people from both genders would probably not find the color very attractive. Ann had packed it due to the serviceable material it was made from that allotted the most comfort.

Admittedly, the color did not affect her adversely as it would most. Brown the color of decomposing leaves was a frumpy color by all accounts, but instead of her skin appearing sallow, it spread warmth to it and made her amber eyes stand out all the more.

That's not why she was choosing the gown, though. It happened to be a very practical choice for traveling, that was all.

She was grateful the clerk had begrudgingly delivered fresh water to her room last evening, shortly after Mr. Stone had delivered her luggage and gone. The clerk even informed her that should she become chilled there was log for the fire in the corner of the room. He had been curt, but kind nonetheless and it had been wholly unexpected. She did not want to push her luck with him though, so she intended to use the water sparingly as not to have to request more. They wouldn't be residing there much longer anyway, if she could help it.

She'd had to use most of the water from the pitcher though in order to rinse her hair before bed. She had deemed that quite necessary. She hadn't wanted her face to rest against a pillow her hair had soiled. That was one positive detail in the Olde Mill Inn's favor; it may be small and rustic but at least it was clean and well maintained.

There was no looking glass, however.

Not that it mattered. There was no reason she should need to be appealing to the eye. No reason at all. She wasn't attending a ball. It was simply breakfast. With a man. The man who had looked at her last night as if she had been a fiery goddess descended to earth.

Nonsense, she shook her head and smoothed the wrinkles from the gown around her hips. Goodness, what had gotten into her? She was on a mission to find the father of her children, the man she *loved*.

She paused and tried to conjure an image of James to her mind. The handsome visage of his face or the pale silvery blue eyes that she'd always thought striking against the bronzed shade of his skin, but the image she'd dreamed of so long ago when she had been safe in her bed at Abersty Estate was no longer.

She felt confident the distance was not to blame. Despite her better efforts, bitterness and resentment for James had built within her heart. The closer she came to finding him the more she believed he had used and abandoned her. She was resolved to see her mission through though. She would find him and at the very least inform him that he had fathered the most beautiful daughters on two continents and allow for him to make a decision. Even if he did not deserve that opportunity; her daughters did.

She smoothed out the skirts of the warm brown gown for the last time and plaited her thick hair into a single braid down her back. It served best for keeping her hair cleaner longer, even though she felt it did nothing by way of improving her appearance. Oh well, she supposed she looked as good as she possibly could under the circumstances.

She heard Livvy coo from the bed and rushed to the little termagant's side before she felt the need to remove herself from the bed on her own by means of toppling to the floor. And as was the case with twins, Kit awoke then and needed rescuing from the bed as well. Ann was familiar with the saying that toddlers were a handful, but honestly twins brought a whole new enlightenment to the word!

Ann hurried their feedings along and dressed them in their cleanest garments and prayed they wouldn't soil their nappies before she could return to the room again. She strapped her girls to her side and packed the middle compartments with items that may be needed to placate them. Livvy was certainly a temperamental little thing. Kit was rarely bothersome.

Ann often felt guilty over Livvy garnering most of the attention. Sometimes after they both fell to sleep Ann would gently pick Kit back up, nestle her close to her chest and softly rock her a while.

They were both conducting themselves in an agreeable manner in this moment, however, so Ann picked up her pace.

It seemed silly, what did she intend to do? It wasn't as if she could arrive to breakfast faster than they could begin fussing. It wasn't a race, she reasoned. Although she logically explained the implausible action, her steps didn't seem to slow.

She smiled to the desk clerk as she passed him. It was the same man from the evening before. She hoped if she comported herself graciously, he would do the same. He did not smile but he did nod, and she took that to be a good sign.

She pushed through the door and stepped onto the walkway where she was momentarily blinded by the brilliant morning sun. Even Kit and Livvy jerked against her at the assault to their eyes.

Oh. That reminded her, she reached into one of the pockets that lined her midsection and retrieved forth their bonnets. Some mother, she reproached herself. It seems all her years of running wild and discarding her own bonnet had ill prepared her for her adult life after all. *I suppose you were right, mother* she smiled to herself. Now, to find the dining tavern Mr. Stone had directed her to.

It was the first Inn she had rested that did not afford its own dining area. Apparently a new Olde Mill Inn (she laughed at the oxymoron and wondered if that's what the owner would rename it to) was being constructed nearby.

She cupped her hand into a visor for her eyes in order to peer through the glaring rays of the sun. Mr. Stone had informed her the tavern was past the area of construction, and so set off in that direction. The girls seemed content looking about them in wide-eyed wonder.

Ann breathed in the day's fresh air feeling happier than she had since setting off on this wild goose chase. She was certain it had to do with the new-found company. Not the company specifically, she told herself, but company in general. She didn't feel quite so alone.

It was absurd, it's not as if Grayson Stone would be traveling with her the rest of the journey.

But for now, she could enjoy conversation with another human being. Livvy chose that moment to coo and gurgle as if offended by Ann's thoughts. Okay, okay, she amended silently, conversation with another *adult* human being. She'd had too many one-sided conversations with herself and was certain that couldn't be healthy and therefore found herself giddy with anticipation when she spied Gap's Tavern.

She entered through the door, exiting from the bright sun into the dimly lit enclosure and waited for her eyes to adjust so she could search out Mr. Stone. There was an older couple at one of the tables already enjoying their breakfast.

Mmm, *bacon*, her belly rumbled.

A man and boy occupied a table and two older gentlemen another. The room wasn't overly large, although larger than

Ann had expected; it sported nearly a dozen tables. Only three had people seated at them, where could Mr. Stone be?

"Good morning miss," A feminine voice chirped near her ear. She swiveled to face the cheerful serving maid. "Where would you like to sit? Oh, and aren't these faces just darling?"

The buxom blonde giggled and preened over Kit and Livvy. Livvy cued a big gummy smile and earned another delighted squeal from the server; a squeal with which Livvy returned. Ann felt this little show could go on a while, so she twisted the future stage princess away from her adoring fan in hopes of recapturing the maid's attention.

"I'm supposed to be meeting a Mr. Stone here, have you seen him?"

"Oh, of course," she bobbed in response, but failed to confirm whether or not he was present. Before Ann could reform her question, the serving maid asked, "You be a part of the wagons he's leading west?"

Ann was left speechlessly surprised by the question.

"He's sitting right over there with his son."

With that, the serving girl's lightly freckled cheeks spread into a cheery smile and she pranced back to the counter.

The driver of the coach that brought her here had informed Ann that most people crossed through the mountains by way of mules and wagon and that many people waited to travel in a large group.

He also informed her that not many would be willing to share a group with a woman, like her, alone...

The many confrontations with hotel managers she'd encountered thus far left her with little doubt that she'd be fighting for a place amongst the travelers.

Mr. Stone must be leading such a group, though. Perhaps, she thought hopefully, her acquaintance with him would endow his assent to joining *his* group.

And he had a son? Well, that hadn't come up in their short conversation the night before. Where was his wife she wondered?

123

Chapter 8

Grayson had directed Luke to stay in their room after they'd arrived and remain there while Grayson met with the other men set out to leave in two days' time. He'd been shocked himself last night when he'd invited the temptingly lovely *Mrs. Morgan* to breakfast with them in the morning.

He didn't believe she was a widow though, for one thing she wasn't wearing mourning colors and surely her infants were too young for her supposed husband to have been deceased for the duration of time acceptable to shed said mourning colors.

He wasn't sure what had caused him to impulsively extend the lady an invitation though. He expressly vowed not to become involved with another woman again and ever since he spied this particular one, that was all he managed to do.

Well, after this, he would politely and gently extricate himself from any future meetings with the woman. He brought Luke along to ensure he kept, what must be his body's longing for female companionship, in check.

Grayson had to question that very ability though in the next instance when she appeared around the table in front of them. She was a sight to behold and Grayson felt his mouth slacken. She stood with the only window in the place positioned behind her and the yet rising sun shone through, its brilliant light casting her aglow like Hestia herself.

He regained his senses, what was his prerogative to compare this woman to the goddesses of Greek? He best not forget that for all she had an inner fire to match her golden beauty, she was only a flesh and blood woman.

"Mr. Stone", she said by way of greeting, "And...young Mr. Stone." She tipped her head to Luke and smiled warmly.

"This is my son, Luke." Grayson gestured to Luke indicating he should make an introduction.

"How d'ya do ma'am?" Luke nodded, politely.

"I'm fairing very well this morning, thank you." She smiled beatifically and seated herself.

Damn. Had it really been so long since sharing a table with a lady that he'd forgotten to assist her with her chair? And this particular woman with the heavy loads strapped to each of her sides? He mentally kicked himself. He didn't want to continue an association with her, but while he was in her company he could do well to behave as a gentleman and set an example for his son.

"Two babies! Are they both yours?" Luke was at that pre-adolescent stage and his mouth was as unpredictable as the weather. Before Grayson could admonish him for the boy's oblivious rudeness, Ann chuckled.

"Yes. Apparently, I am doubly good at bringing forth life into this world." Teasing twinkled in her eyes.

"You talk strange."

"Luke!" His son had to have known the extent of rudeness that statement had been. Grayson truly needed to pay closer attention to his own manners around the boy. He had been alone for so long and learned straight and direct was more efficient. Manners did nothing for your survival in the wilderness. He was learning quickly though they were still required. He expelled a frustrated sigh.

"Is my accent strange to you?" Ann answered in good humor, not at all offended by the young boy's curious questions. "I'm English. Before I sailed to Carolina, I lived in Somerset. All the way across the grand Atlantic, in England."

"Wow. You've traveled a long way."

"Indeed, I have." Her smile faded and eyes lost focus as if she were reliving memories elsewhere. It was plain to see she missed England very much.

Grayson broke the disconsolate moment, "What brings you all the way to Wilderness Road?"

Before she could respond, they were interrupted by the bouncy overly-cheerful serving girl who Ann couldn't help for noticing, bestowed a sugary sweet smile on Grayson before addressing the rest of the table. Ann managed, with not a little effort, to refrain from rolling her eyes. Could the girl be more obvious?

Ann was peeved still further when Grayson returned to her a charming smile of his own, one he hadn't deemed to give Ann yet. Apparently, he saved all of his charm for serving maids. Well, that was no matter to her. Honestly, in front of his son though? Ann felt compelled, to remind Grayson of his manners. For his son's sake.

She coughed delicately and gave Grayson a wide–eyed innocent look when he returned his attention to her. She then turned to the serving maid, giving her a somewhat frostier smile than she had intended and began placing her order even though she hadn't yet been prompted to do so.

The serving maid's smile teetered somewhat, and she took the rest of their orders with a more businesslike manner.

Good. That is the attitude she should adopt around handsome male customers- er, customers, Ann sniffed.

After the serving girl left, Grayson raised his eyebrows mockingly to Ann, "Problem with Mary-Beth?"

"Of course not." She responded curtly and made great work of folding her napkin just so. She couldn't help wondering how it became that he was on a first name basis with the serving maid, but again, that was none of her business.

"Right. So, what were you saying before? Where is it you are headed?" Grayson returned the conversation to neutral ground.

She responded in kind, "I'm on my way to St. Louis."

"St. Louis!" Both Grayson and Luke exclaimed together. Luke looked at her with pleased surprise, but Grayson looked furious. She wasn't certain what to make of his reaction...

Luke spoke next, "That's where we are headed. My pa is leading the wagon train north on Wilderness Road."

Ann smiled to Luke and cast an intuitive look to Grayson, "Is he now?"

Luke chattered on, oblivious to the hostile glare his father directed towards her.

Grayson interrupted his son, "Who exactly are you traveling *with*?" He questioned with an intent look in his eyes.

"Well, previous to the start of my travels I had not realized I would need ought else but to hire a coach to get me there. It is my understanding now, however, that most travel by means of wagons and in groups..."

She confirmed what his notion had been; she was behaving recklessly setting out to who knows where and with two babies in tow. He couldn't fathom why any mother-any *good* mother- would do that.

She ignored the growl he seemed accustomed to making in her presence and descended upon her next question, "Well, now that I am acquainted with the appointed guide, perhaps we can make a deal with one another."

"It's not wise for a woman to travel alone in these parts. This country is hardly the civilized England you're accustomed to." He attempted to talk some sense into her.

They were interrupted again by the serving maid-*Mary-Beth*-returning with their meals.

Ann's stomach rumbled again and loudly when she smelled the heavenly aroma of bacon. Luke and Mary-Beth stifled giggles behind their hands. Her cheeks flamed with embarrassment. The blush only intensified when she dared to raise her eyes and found Grayson smiling broadly at her as well. Drat her undignified stomach.

Surprisingly, Mary-Beth regained her composure first. "Will this be all for you?" She swept a gaze around the table.

"I don't know, we may be in need of a bit more sustenance for Mrs. Morgan, here." The joke caused Mary-Beth to giggle once more.

Ann cleared her throat and adjusted to a more regal-like position in her chair, if one could manage to do so under such circumstances, "No, thank you. I'm sure this will more than carry me through to the next meal."

Everyone then looked dubiously to her small plate of bacon accompanied by a miserable looking bowl of porridge. Not that porridge was capable of procuring an expression, but honestly, did porridge ever appear as anything but miserable?

They looked to her questioningly. They all seemed to be of the opinion that her meal was lacking. She wasn't about to admit that she had limited funds and that the paltry meal shared between her and her daughters would *have* to carry her through to her next meal. She also didn't feel obliged to divulge that her next meal may not be until the following morning. Of course, she would purchase food for her daughters, but they seemed to enjoy miserable porridge and that was least costly and staved off hunger the longest.

Hmm, she thought, she would have to amend her consideration of porridge after all; it seemed it was rather more deserving of slightly higher praise than the 'miserable' title she had previously afforded it.

Mary-Beth tired of gawking at her food left them to their meals.

Ann didn't exactly ignore the other members at the table, precisely; it was more that the bacon held her undivided attention. At least for that first mouthwatering blissful taste.

She may have even sighed. Yes, she was fairly certain that must have occurred because when she opened her eyes-Oh, she had closed her eyes *and* sighed. Over *bacon*.-Grayson and his son Luke were both staring at her. Luke appeared ready to erupt into another fit of giggles. Grayson was looking on her like... well, the way she had been looking at her bacon.

That would never do. Although, it didn't escape her that he hadn't looked at Mary-Beth in quite the same manner, she allowed, satisfactorily. Then silently berated herself; how absurd to think he had been looking at her with the similar rapture she had savored her bacon. He had probably been looking on in fright, horrified by a lady devouring her food so ineloquently. Perhaps even afraid she might extend her fork over to his plate and come after his food!

She cleared her head of her foolish diverted thoughts, "Well, where were we?"

That however had been the entirely wrong question to ask. Grayson's face went from happily gazing upon her to scowling again. Oh, yes, they had been arguing.

Grayson's pewter eyes went steely, "I will not welcome a widow among us."

"Well," she sniped back, "It is fortunate I am not a widow then, isn't it?"

His head all but snapped to attention and she blanched a little in fright at the sudden intensity of his gaze. He almost caused her to drop her bacon.

"You're what?"

She chewed her bacon, before answering him enjoying his impatient fidgeting. Then she replied calmly, "I am *not* a *widow*."

She was even worse than he had anticipated. Not only was she a reckless mother, she was a little harlot as well.

"Where," his words biting, "Is your husband then?"

"In St. Louis." *Hopefully*, she added silently.

Grayson nearly exploded. What kind of man- "And he is allowing you to travel, with his children, alone?" His voice grew louder, seemingly unable to hold his outrage in check. Funny, he had arrived here thinking he would need to keep his *lust* in check and here he was feeling very little attraction for the lady across from him and very much in want of throttling her.

She let her eyes flick about, indicating that he was causing a scene. He exhaled and regained his composure.

"Perhaps we should discuss this in a more private setting?" she volunteered.

His grimacing features never lessened, but he nodded his agreement all the same. She finished spooning the last bits of porridge to Kit and Livvy who wasted precious little time when it came to eating. Grayson waited patiently. Luke looked a bit unsettled, poor boy. It must be difficult living with such a disagreeable father, she thought petulantly. Afterwards they settled their tabs and left the tavern.

Once outside, Grayson spoke gruffly, "Follow me. I need to check on my horse. We can talk more at the stables."

Internally she balked at his dictating bark, but outwardly she nodded her assent and followed suit. It wouldn't do to irritate him more. She spared a smile for Luke who was looking more uneasy by the second. It wasn't his fault his father was such a tyrant.

Once at the stables, Luke disappeared into the stall that she assumed housed his own horse. Grayson picked up a brush and entered a stall with a muscled little gray dappled mare. He did not oppose when she joined him.

The familiar ache for her own horse stirred again and she instinctively reached her hand out to touch the mare's glossy neck. She inhaled the glorious scent of sweat and leather that had always brought her such pleasure and her insides knotted with the unhinged desire to be even nearer to the gentle beast. She might've sidled closer to her, if not for Livvy and Kit at her sides.

"Her name is Dove."

He didn't say more just took to brushing down the mare's back vigorously; still Ann took that to be the peace offering.

Then he said, "Can't they walk yet?"

She realized he was indicating the girls.

She chuckled, "Hardly, they're not even an entire year old. They scoot along like baby sea turtles, though. Into everything."

She sounded prouder of the fact than aggrieved.

He paused in his brushing. "Will they eat straw?"

She looked to him perplexed, "I should say not!"

She watched him put the brush down and exit the stall. She followed after wondering what he was about. She watched him first lay some empty burlap onto the ground in close proximity to Dove's stall. He then proceeded to line the border with bales of straw forming a small enclosure. He stepped back and looked to her proudly.

"There. Let them get some exercise and give yourself a break. You're making my back ache just looking at you holding them up all day."

She very much doubted that. Likely he could sustain a lot more weight on a daily basis than she. She looked at the straw pen with uncertainty.

"Just put them in there? Like dogs?"

"Well, like puppies." He smiled rakishly to her.

The overwhelming desire to walk around without fifty extra pounds strapped to her for a duration won out against the guilt of practically caging her own children. She removed first Livvy, then Kit and placed them in the center. She then tossed in the little trinkets Nancy had sewn them (goodness, she thought, *chew toys*, she truly was a terrible mother), which they ignored, eager to explore their new straw-built world. It seemed safe enough.

She half moaned half sighed her relief and swiveled her shoulders around in newfound freedom. She must have exuded her exuberance a bit too animatedly, for Grayson was wearing a large grin on his face and his eyes danced with laughter *at her*.

"Feel good?"

"Glorious!" She didn't see the need to refrain her enthusiasm.

He chuckled again and threw a brush to her, which she caught readily. They stepped back into the stall with Dove and began working away at her coat. Ann could see the twins easily atop the low stall door and they could see her. Livvy permitted delighted squeals as she discovered she could pull handfuls of straw out of the wall confines. Of course, Kit took a quieter approach and studied her surroundings with more diligence.

The rich timbre of Grayson's voice sounded, "You seem to know your way around a horse."

It was more statement than question, but he raised his brow to her in hopes of an elaboration from her.

"Mmm," she sighed happily, "I certainly do." Then with an impish grin she added arrogantly, "Probably a mite more than yourself."

Grayson just huffed a short laugh at her conceitedness and rolled his eyes.

"Although," she stated forlornly, "I haven't ridden since leaving England."

She tipped her head back tossing the strands of hair, that had already fallen loose of her braid, from her face as she remembered her lovely gelding. She closed her eyes seeing the luscious green grounds of her country estate. Knight's neck stretched out in front of her as they soared over brooks and hedges, flying against the wind.

In moments like this she was so beautiful, Grayson could nearly forget his plans and walk another path, one that included a wife at his side. The thought turned bitter though, that path was all too familiar and for the most part, pure hell. Besides, she claimed she wasn't a widow.

Fresh anger rose within him, "Why is it so necessary that you travel to St. Louis?"

Ann was caught off guard by his sudden cross tone. Of course, the friendly banter couldn't last. They had in fact designated this spot to row with one another. Alright, she sighed, pushing away her beloved memories from home and joining his sour mood.

"I told you. My husband is there." She began brushing with vigor again to avoid Grayson's perceptive eyes on her.

His breath pushed out his next words with each strong thrust of his brush, "So. He. Sent for you?"

"Not exactly."

She glanced in the direction of Kit and Livvy. Reassured they were still safe and happy she stepped around to Doves other side and began currying her cinch area.

Grayson stopped brushing while he asked, "Does he even know you're coming?"

She flicked her wrist swiftly in a way that more speedily and effectively removed the dust from Dove's hide. At least Dove was enjoying the interlude.

She completed a few more thorough flicks before saying, "Not exactly."

This time Grayson threw his brush down into the tack box and raised his hand in frustration, "Damn it, Lady. You brought me out here to convince me to offer my protection to you on the trail. But you've not provided me with one good reason."

Her nostrils flared at the affront, "Excuse me, but you led me here, if I recollect correctly. And pleading for your protection was *not* my intent."

She stepped around the front of Dove who shifted her feet restlessly, seemingly knowing her time for attention was over. Ann crossed her arms in front of her and stared Grayson down.

Then she lied.

"I-I haven't been able to contact him through letter and he doesn't yet know..."

Grayson assessed accurately what she was saying, "He doesn't know he has daughters? How did he remain ignorant of your pregnancy?"

"We married in England," she swallowed, the half-lie caught in her throat. "He left shortly after. Business, he said." Her eyes trailed off unable to meet his.

Grayson remained silent, studying her. What kind of husband would leave his young bride alone so soon? And for so long? If she had become pregnant...

"You must have had one hell of a wedding night." He suggested harshly.

She blushed but anger took hold and she forced herself to meet his eyes with her own, "No need to be crass."

"Are you even certain they are his children?"

She physically retracted backwards from his cruel accusations. How could this man be so kind one moment and such a brute the next?

She leveled him with another stare, "That does not even dignify a response."

She stepped around Dove and exited the stall. Obviously, the man was not open to discussing new terms. She reached for the girls' pack.

Grayson realized he had spoken unfairly and regretted his words the moment she flinched away from him as if his edged words had been an actual blade to her gut. He didn't truly believe this woman of vindictiveness and lacking moral character. He'd witnessed enough of her actions to know that. Not to mention, he'd been married to the type of woman who had been all those things and he could well now distinguish the difference.

"Wait," He grinded his teeth against calling her *Mrs. Morgan*. For some reason it tasted foul on his tongue. Instead he called out, "Ann, wait."

She stilled her angry fingers fumbling to adjust the pack around her and stood. She kept her back to him, but she appeared to be listening, so he continued, "I'm sorry. I should not have suggested... what I did."

She turned to him then, anger still flashed in her eyes, but she nodded stiffly in acceptance of his apology. She lifted her chin a notch, "I *need* to get to St. Louis. He needs to know that he has a pair of daughters in this world. And regretfully, I know my daughters will struggle mightily anywhere we go if it is believed they were sired illegitimately." Her face stained pink with shame, "And you know as well as I that the accusations you spoke moments ago are what everyone else believes to be true."

133

Because it was the truth, she thought miserably. Because she had been a young fool. And now society thought to punish her daughters for it. Well, she'd fight the whole world or die trying before she would allow that to happen. She was prepared to do what she must. Even if that meant marrying a man she once thought to love and now detested. She blinked back the tears, refusing to give in to weakness.

Grayson saw her tear moistened eyes before she could hide them and felt even more the bastard. He hadn't meant to make her cry.

"Well, their judgment will be their cross to bear. You know the truth and once your husband comes to his senses and realizes he was a fool for leaving you behind, well, their opinions won't mean more than piss on the wind."

She quirked her lips to the side in a half smile even though she felt all the more wretched for lying to Grayson. He was just one more person and it was necessary, but for some reason it had felt more wrong than her lies to people before.

"What do I need to do in order to gain your consent to ride the trail as part of your group?" Before he could interrupt, she continued, "I imagine others are reimbursing you for your services. I too have-have funds in which to pay you."

The truth was she had no idea how much exactly it would cost to get her to St. Louis and then if she failed, she would yet need money to return to Charleston.

"Y-y-you," he sputtered angrily, "don't even have a wagon! Let alone have one loaded with supplies! Even if you had money for all of that," He paused to assess her, and came to the knowing conclusion that she hadn't the funds, "There isn't time to make the arrangements before we depart; which is tomorrow morning."

She raised her chin and asked again, "What. Do. I. Need?"

He stared back and answered spitefully, "A man."

She all but snarled her frustration with the pig-headed beast! 'A man' was exactly what she was trying to *acquire*. In St. Louis! She threw her hands in the air and looked to the ceiling as if imploring the gods for patience.

The gods didn't deliver.

"You are an insufferable, egotistical, cad!" She shouted.

"You are a reckless, ignorant, spoiled, hoyden!"

She gasped in outrage, "How dare you!"

"Oh, I dare," he snapped. "You waltzed into the Inn as if you owned the place and think you can bat your pretty eyelashes and men will fall to your feet biddable slaves. Well, not this one."

What on earth was he talking about? She did not once bat her eyelashes at the innkeeper in order to secure a room; she had to fight for that tooth and nail.

Where did he get the impression she was trying to use her femininely wiles on *him* for that matter? Was it when she was coated with dust and her hair hanging in ungodly knots when she arrived at the Inn? Was it this morning when she was devouring her meager breakfast, shamelessly in front of him, as if it were her last meal? Or was it the two chubby, slobbering, squalling toddlers attached to her at all times? What detail exactly, had he witnessed of her that had him believing she was attempting to be some kind of land siren?

They stood facing one another, both with hands fisted at their own hips. Both of them seething through gritted teeth, equally defensive and infuriated with one another. For a moment, neither spoke, as they stared each other down, chests rising and falling rapidly with each livid breath.

Grayson spoke first. His lips barely moved as he growled the words through his gritted teeth, "You will not be coming with *me*."

Next he barked, "Luke! It's time we head back to the Inn."

She was being dismissed then. She couldn't believe he wouldn't even for a second consider her joining the group. She kicked the toe of her boot in frustration into the wood slab of the stall door. She could barely withhold her exasperation for the man; she wanted to kick him too!

Just then thunder shook the stables. She looked to Grayson in alarm, surely it couldn't be rain? The sun had followed them all the way to the stables, not a cloud in the sky. They both quickened their steps to the entrance to peer outside. Ann's shoulders sagged with the disappointing sight of rain pelting the ground.

Ann hadn't thought to bring a cloak to breakfast and why would she? The day had been brilliant with sunshine when she set out. What was she to do now? She didn't want to spend another second with the obstinate man beside her. She couldn't very well risk the girls catching ague and rush out into the storm with them though either. They remained in the entry way of the barn studying the rain pouring down over its threshold, both lost to their own thoughts of despair.

Great. She would be stuck here, she concluded. At least there was clean straw, she considered, and lovely horseflesh. *And manure*, she added silently and wrinkled her nose. She was all but resigned to waiting out the storm in the barn, but it would seem the annoying dictator beside her had other plans for her. -Apparently, inclined to decide her fate on all matters, she hmphed.

"Give me them." He barked and gestured towards her daughters. *I don't think so!* She thought. As if she would entrust their care to this hard-hearted beast!

Her thoughts must have reflected on her face, because next he said, "I have handled babies before. My own son for crying out loud. I'm capable of getting two infants from here back to the lodgings safely."

Then he added more gently, "This storm could last all night. Unless you have enough supplies in that-contraption (He failed to identify exactly what she was wearing)-I believe I can get you and your girls back more safely than if you were to set out on your own."

She couldn't help but expel a frustrated sigh and remain aggrieved with the man. Yes, she would be safer with him. And so would her daughters. She had a feeling he wouldn't appreciate, then, her decision to continue on to St. Louis without him... Now wasn't the time to declare such intentions though, not when he was kindly offering to assist her in this moment.

"Okay," she relented and then, "Thank you."

He nodded extending the truce.

"Just hand them to me. I'll carry one and you'll carry one, but we'll protect them with these."

He motioned for Luke to hand him a horse blanket that rested on a nearby wall rack. Luke carried one to his father and one to Ann.

Ann realized there were only two blankets, "What about Luke?" she asked concernedly.

Luke smiled reassuringly, "A little rain won't hurt me, ma'am."

She wasn't so certain. She eyed Grayson questioningly.

"He'll be fine, has a strong constitution, he does."

Ann nodded acceptingly. Ann handed Kit to Grayson knowing she would probably give him the least amount of trouble. Kit nestled into his arm obligingly, but Ann felt the need to utter soothing words anyway, more for herself it would seem. It was strange seeing her daughter held by this man. Disconcerting.

Would that Kit's own father will want to hold her that way.

"Shh... Kit. There you go angel." Ann brushed her fingertips along Kit's softly rounded cheek.

"'Kit' is it?" Grayson asked softly.

Ann smiled and nodded, "Yes and this squawker here is Livvy." Livvy was already gumming her chubby fist and making fussing sounds.

"Grayson smiled to her and admittedly looked at ease holding the delicate bundle, for such a big bear of a man. It was a pleasant sight, Ann thought.

Grayson used his free arm to drape the horse blanket over Ann and Livvy. She took over arranging it while he did the same with the other blanket over him and Kit. Luke appeared almost giddy, excited about the prospect of running wildly through the rain.

"Okay," Grayson's deep voice penetrated over the echoing sound of rain pounding on the roof, "Everyone ready?" Ann peered hesitantly at the angry rain falling in sheets before them.

"I suppose," she answered and pulled the blanket further over her head."

Luke took that to be the signal for him to dive out of the barn. He was almost immediately swallowed up by the gray of the pelting rain.

Ann swallowed, hesitant to join the exuberant boy.

"Next you," Grayson prompted.

She couldn't remain in the barn, she thought. So, without further balking, summoned her courage and dashed out into the rain.

It was shockingly cold! But refreshing. The wildness of it swelled her chest with a liberating feeling and she freed the laughter bubbling up inside her.

Grayson couldn't believe it. She was laughing like a mad woman. Next, he heard her hoot and holler excitedly as she continued to kick up her heels in her dash for the Inn. He had a feeling that if she hadn't needed to get her children sheltered immediately, she would have danced around in the storm like a gleeful sprite.

He smiled for the fanciful image.

Ann should have saved her breath instead of laughing like a crazed lunatic. The merciless rain that had firstly felt cool and refreshing was fast becoming a thick curtain to push through. The force of the rain pushed at the blanket, nearly collapsing the tent she'd formed with it.

She could only see about three steps in front of her. She desperately wanted to look back for Grayson and Kit, but feared tripping in the sinking ground. The dusted road she'd arrived on had quickly turned to deep, thick, mud.

Grayson reassured her with his voice, "I'm following right behind you. Keep heading straight." He yelled over the rain.

She continued on as he said and in seconds they reached the Inn. Luke swung the door open and she darted inside. Grayson was right on her heels. She joined Luke's laughter with her own as she slid the blanket from around her and Livvy. Her head and chest had remained dry as well as all of Livvy's little form, but the rest of Ann was dripping with water and mud.

The inn keeper stood staring in bewilderment at the spectacle of bodies flying in from the rain. Three of his guests stood allowing rivulets of water to shed from them onto the entry floor. And they were laughing.

They were making a muddy sopping mess! He was about to tell them so too until he noticed the big burley man's demeanor was not matching of the woman and the boy. Indeed, he looked positively furious. That stayed the inn keeper where he was.

"Here." Grayson's brusque tone caught her off guard and she and Luke both stopped laughing. Grayson was pushing Kit towards her impatiently. Exchanging baby for blanket.

Confused, as she'd thought them once more on friendly terms, she spoke carefully "Thank you."

"Nothing has changed." His words were direct and curt.

She stiffened, feeling her anger with him return, "I hadn't been under the impression they had."

"Do not confront me again on the matter. I will not change my mind. No woman or child allowed on the trail unless accompanied by a guardian. Is that understood?"

"Perfectly." She leveled him with her most imperious stare. Then added impertinently, "And do you own the trail, then?"

His jaw clenched in irritable fashion, fastening her with a menacing glower, "Don't even *think* about following on your own."

"You can't stop me." Her eyes bored into his briefly, her jaw clenched stubbornly causing her pillowed lips to pooch out in defiance and look temptingly kissable. Spinning on her heel suddenly, she left him staring after her in exasperation.

He drew a steadying breath to regain his focus then ticked his head in the direction of their rooms, indicating for his son to head there.

When Grayson looked up, the annoying desk clerk was eyeing him meaningfully. When he was sure he had Grayson's attention he scrunched up his mouth and raised his eyebrows as if to say, *See, we should have never allowed the woman to stay here.*

Grayson narrowed his gaze on the man, letting him know he could bear not one more provocation that day, then hied back off into the rainstorm in search of some solitude. Luke would know to wait for him in their rooms.

Chapter 9

Ann had just made it back to her room after retrieving more porridge mash for the girls from Gap Tavern. She'd splurged and had a drumstick of chicken and chunk of cheese wrapped to take back for her dinner as well. The rain had stopped, thankfully, although that hadn't made the trip any less muddy. She didn't see Grayson around anywhere on her jaunt either, not that she had hoped to.

She was fumbling with the key in attempt to unlock her door whilst balancing the girls and the prepared meals, when the door behind her creaked open.

"Oh, it's you Luke!" She gave a breathless laugh, "You gave me a fright."

"Sorry ma'am," he smiled politely and then asked hopefully, "Have you seen my Father?"

"No, I haven't, I'm afraid." Her teeth worried her bottom lip as she took in the solemn boy. "Have you had dinner yet?"

Luke shook his head from side to side in answer, sending his springy blonde hair to-and-froe. His lonesome look hardly escaped Ann.

"Would you care to join us?" She sighed inwardly; she'd have to give up her chicken dinner. It was worth the sacrifice though, when Luke's upturned face met hers lit with surprise and gratitude.

"Come on in, then," she smiled welcomingly.

He took an eager step then paused, "Oh, but my father-"

"I am certain we shall hear his thundering footsteps in the hall when he arrives," she teased, "Hmm?"

He smiled wide enough to reveal a mouth full of new adult teeth that looked too large for his freckled, child's face.

Once in the room she initiated the seating arrangement by slumping indelicately to the floor. That earned a questioning look from Luke.

"What? Too unladylike for you?"

He must not have recognized the teasing lent to her voice, because he quickly shook his head in disagreement for fear he had offended his new friend.

"I hope you will hurry your rump to the floor as well, so we can get to eating. No need to stand on ceremony with me."

"You mean I can disregard all manners?" He looked to her as if she were a newly discovered specie.

She laughed, "Well, certainly not *all* manners. I am a delicate Lady, you know."

Luke snorted at that, coming around to her teasing.

"What?" She complained in mocked indignation, "You don't believe me to be a Lady?" She said as she unwrapped first the drumstick and then the cheese. She used her leg as a barrier to keep Livvy from climbing over to the food. She watched Luke shake his head no.

"Well, I'm certain I should be offended by that." She watched as his playful smile faltered somewhat with uncertainty. She continued, "Because I am you know. A Lady that is." She passed the drumstick to him and the cheese.

"Thank you." He said ever politely and then concern knit his brow as he asked, "But where's yours?"

"Oh, I ate at the tavern. I merely brought back what was left over as well as the girls' supper as it is difficult to feed them in public," she appeased with a smooth white lie and then to bring back the fun, light hearted tone from before said, "As you'll soon see why. These girls waste precious time on decorum, when it comes to their grub."

That elicited a laugh from him as well as, "Much like their mother."

Her eyes widened, and mouth gaped open, surprised and delighted that he returned her teasing so easily. She laughed, "Well one can hardly argue with that!" But she tossed the formerly discarded crumpled cloth that had been used to wrap the food at him in mock reprimand.

He dodged it easily and spoke around a mouthful of cheese he had bit off, "So you are a real English Lady, huh," It was more observation than question.

"I certainly am," she agreed.

She crisscrossed her legs beneath her skirts and formed a hollow spot between them where she deposited both Kit and Livvy. Like eager little birds they waited with shiny wet lips parted wide and ready for their spoonfuls of mash to be fed them. Ann spoke as she continuously spooned porridge into each waiting mouth.

"I grew up in Somerset. My father is an Earl," she said proudly. Luke afforded her with a gratifying look of respect.

"Did you live in a castle?" he asked wide-eyed.

"Not exactly. But it was an immense home, as grand as you could imagine. Built from red stone that glowed when bathed in the rising or setting light of the sun. We actually owned four different properties, but the one in Somerset was my true home." She sighed with longing.

"You must have been very happy there." Luke noted with the astuteness of a body twice his age.

"Yes, I was." She didn't want to sink their lovely visit into a pit of melancholy, so she smiled brightly and recalled a more entertaining memory, "We had a cook that I used to terrorize as a child." She smiled impishly to Luke.

"I used to sneak into the kitchen when I knew she was preparing honeyed scones and swipe them off the warming bricks," she and Luke shared in a bout of giggles, "Then I would run as fast as my little legs could carry me to the stables to share a bite with Knight."

When he looked to her confusedly, she explained, "Knight is my gelding. He was gifted to me when I was six years old and he's been my best friend ever since. Until I had to leave him behind in England, that is." Luckily, Luke didn't detect the grief that choked those last words.

"The daughter of an Earl and your best friend was a horse?" He sputtered raucously.

"I didn't have any siblings and all of the servant's children were older than me. It would have made for a terribly lonesome childhood had I not had Knight." She smiled, "Who is your best friend then?"

"Well, my horse I suppose," he said and laughed sheepishly.

"And here you are giving me grief!" She tossed back playfully.

"But you're a-you were a *girl*." He said 'girl' as if he were spewing slimy worms from his mouth and she laughed at the disgusted face he made.

"Well, for all that I was a *girrrrl*," she bugged her eyes comically at him, "I was rather boyish."

He continued to look on her disbelievingly.

"Honest. As I grew older, not much older than you are now, my father's friends nick named me: Dunneroy's Little Spitfire. To this day I can out ride, out shoot, and out hunt my father and all of his acquaintances I have competed against." She added smugly.

Luke scoffed, "I doubt you could out race me on Buckshot." Then thoughtfully revised, "Well, perhaps you could. But you could never beat my Pa on Dove." Adoration for his father shined in his eyes.

She thought she probably could, but she had no wish of arguing Grayson's prowess with his biggest supporter. Instead she said, "Is Dove a quick little beast, then?"

He was busy chewing the remaining bits of the chicken from the bone so settled for nodding enthusiastically.

"Yes," she agreed, "She looked a fine mare. Your father has good taste in horse flesh it would seem."

He nodded to her happily while smacking his lips and licking his fingers clean. He looked more little boy in that moment, for all Ann had mostly witnessed him acting the part of a young man. She scraped for the last two bites of porridge to divide amongst the girls and then began cleaning their faces. Livvy, of course not enjoying her face being scrubbed clean, cried out her fury.

"She doesn't much care for that, does she?" Luke looked on in concern.

Ann chuckled, "No she does not."

Once free from her mother's attentions, Livvy crawled to Luke. As Ann wiped Kit's face clean, she saw Luke stretch out onto the floor on his stomach to become face to face with Livvy. Ann observed as they studied one another curiously. Then Livvy swatted her hand out with unexpected speed and grabbed a gob of Luke's hair.

"Ow, ow, ow," Luke cried in alarm.

Ann set Kit aside and sought to untangle her daughter from the boy's head. *Mercy, this girl was trouble!* Livvy squealed her delight as Luke howled in pain.

Ann unwove Livvy's chubby little fingers from his hair and sat her away from him.

"I'm dreadfully sorry. I should have seen that coming and warned you. She has a fondness for pulling hair, the little beast."

Luke rubbed his head and smiled sheepishly, unsure how to act after being harmed by a baby. And a girl baby at that.

Luke resumed his seated posture keeping his hair well away from the little she-devil and eyed her carefully as she crawled directly towards him. Ann watched Luke's face take on one of that with horror as the toddler climbed right into his folded legs, laid her head down on his lap and yawned. It was precious to behold. Luke's face turned from surprise to wonder as he became accustomed to the little girl's attention.

"She likes me, I guess," he declared merrily. "She's not so bad like this."

Ann smiled, "Yes, they are always most dear when they're sleeping."

He nodded to her sincerely, not realizing Ann's comment had been in jest. Well, had somewhat been in jest. She adored her daughters in their conscious state as well, she thought and then realized she appeared to be trying to convince herself and decided not to think on it further. Surely a better mother would never voice something so terrible!

Ann grabbed Kit, feeling that a fine time to snuggle her for a change. She swaddled Kit to her chest swayed back and forth and watched on lovingly as her lashes swept over her cheeks in sleep. When she looked up, Luke was looking toward her forlornly.

"I wonder if my mother ever held me like that." He said in a voice that pierced Ann's heart.

She replied softly, "I'm sure she did."

He sighed, "I don't think she ever liked me."

Ann caught her breath and it swelled with the increasing ache in her chest. How had this turn of conversation occurred? What could she say to this lovely, kind little boy who doubted his own mother's love for him? She tamped down the anger she felt for his mother; a woman she didn't know, but hated in that moment irrationally, for causing this wonderful little boy before her such pain. It was a heinous unforgivable crime.

The words wobbled off Ann's lips, "How could she not love you?" She swallowed the jagged aching mass lodged in her throat and blinked back the tears that threatened to bead out of the corner of her eyes. In a rough whisper, her voice thick with grief she added, "I've only just met you and I find you most loveable." She smiled to him and wished she was close enough to stroke the strands of his hair.

He shrugged stoically as if his heart wasn't broken and forced a smile and lighter tone, "She always looked so beautiful."

Ann's insides tightened more, her airways becoming even more restricted with the force it took to withhold her anguish.

"She used to wear these big poofy dresses that made her look like a princess when she would go out. She loved dressing up and going to balls."

She should have stayed home and loved you, Ann thought, but instead choked out, "Did she?"

He nodded in stoic manly fashion and couldn't possibly have looked smaller to Ann. She had an urge to hug him and keep hugging him until he felt all the love he deserved.

"Did she-" she cleared her throat, "-did she pass away?"

He nodded again in confirmation.

"I'm sorry." She was sorry his mother hadn't realized how precious her son was. She was sorry that Luke suffered under the belief that his mother hadn't loved him. She couldn't let him continue thinking such thoughts.

"Luke, listen to me. As a mother, myself, I can tell you with much authority that motherhood is not easy. Sometimes parents can become preoccupied with other things and not realize-" What? Not realize that they hadn't told their child they loved them? Too busy to hug them? Ann couldn't fathom being so selfish. She continued as best she could, "-not realize those other things weren't nearly as important. I know your mother loved you, because all mother's love their children, Luke. It's a natural force that can't be stopped. When a baby is born, a bond is formed between the mother and her child that can never be broken."

Tears streamed down both of their faces. She tried to hide hers as she laid sleeping Kit into the bed and then scooped Livvy from Luke's lap and laid her next to her sister. Then Ann sat next to Luke and wrapped her arms about him, because she just couldn't refrain from doing so a moment longer. He did not resist and instead rested his head against her and cried softly. She closed her eyes against the blur of her tears as they wet the sides of her face uncontrollably.

"Do you know," she whispered after a time and after Luke's breathing had returned to normal, "I will bet your mother watches down from heaven and smiles proudly upon you every day. I know I certainly would if I were your mother."

He smiled up to her and she allowed her fingers to rake the hair back from his face as she longed to do before. Then a soft knock tapped on the door.

Grayson came back to an empty room and set out immediately in a frantic search for Luke. The innkeeper informed him he had not seen a boy come or go in that time. Grayson then hurried his steps back to the rooming halls with intent of questioning Ann. As he was about to rap on the door, he heard what he thought to be Luke's voice, so he waited and listened more closely.

He heard some of the conversation and knew with a certainty at that point that it was Luke visiting with Ann. The bursts of giggles coming from both parties had him smiling and curiously wanting to hear more. So instead of making his presence known, he had remained silent with his ear pressed to the door.

He thought he had nearly given himself away when he couldn't hold back a chuckle over the picture conjured in his mind of Ann as a scone thieving hellion in her childhood. He almost rushed in, in a fit of panic when he heard Luke cry out in pain. He had his hand on the knob in an instant and nearly pushed through, until he discovered Luke wasn't in any real danger, other than being mauled by babies. Once reassured Luke would survive the toddler, Grayson settled back with his ear to the door again and listened quietly again.

The next discovery caused Grayson's fists to ball up. Had his ex-wife risen from the dead to stand before him just then, he believed he could have committed an act of violence that would have easily sent her right back into the ground.

He had to step away from the door then to regain control of himself. When he heard his son's crying through the door, he nearly came undone with the aching that constricted his chest. If only he could carry the pain for his son, he would gladly do so.

He heard Ann comforting his son and felt a sudden overwhelming gratitude for her presence in their lives and indebtedness for her kindness. When the room quieted, he knocked on the door.

"Oh. I'll bet that is your father." She rose from the floor, wiping the wet tears from her face as she did, to open the door. When she did, Grayson stepped into the room slowly.

"I was just looking for Luke."

He looked then to his son's tear stained face and longed to scoop him up, as he did when he was only a boy of four or five, and hug him close.

When he arrived back to Philadelphia to retrieve Luke from that dreaded life, he'd realized how much he had missed with his son. How wrong he had been about so many things. He had known Vivian to be a viper when it came to *him*; had discovered after their marriage how little she cared for him, but he never would have countenanced her not loving her own son.

Grayson stood, studying his son who fidgeted uncertainly before him. "Am I in trouble, Pa?"

"No, son."

Luke bobbed his head feeling the heavy air in the room still and yet not understanding what it meant. Grayson didn't know what to say. He wanted to comfort his son as well, but Luke didn't know Grayson had overheard his honest talk with Ann, and Grayson didn't want to breach any trust between them.

Ann rescued them both with, "Oh yes. I invited him over for supper as I felt a strong need for some company on this lonely evening. Luke was kind enough to oblige."

She smiled warmly to Luke and Luke returned the smile seemingly happy and reassured that she would keep his secrets.

Ann thought Grayson was behaving strangely when he entered. He was too softly spoken and despondent; vastly different from the man's usual display of agitated bull headedness. That's when she knew he had overheard her with his son. She sensed Grayson's desire to protect his son, but he seemed to not know what to say to bridge them closer together. Ann tried to fill that gap and help them both resume a comfortable air with one another.

"Did you know your son is a little charmer? He certainly doesn't get that quality from his father," she teased and chattered on, "Luke here, had baby Livvy charmed right down to her little toes." She winked to Luke. Luke, embarrassed, tugged his flat shock of bangs off to the side and rolled his eyes at Ann's pronouncement, causing her and Grayson to share in laughter.

"Well, if you don't mind, I think Luke and I had better be getting back to our own rooms for the evening."

She nodded, "Thank you for joining me this evening, Luke. It was most pleasant conversing with someone who is able to do more than drool and coo back to me. Or snipe at me, for that matter." She turned a mocking stare to Grayson. He tossed back his head and blew out a breath in response.

As they were exiting the doorway, Luke turned back and asked Ann, "Did you go to balls when you lived in England?"

"Yes," she answered squarely unprepared to face the gravity of another such question.

"Did you like going to them?" He asked.

The question was important to him; Ann answered honestly, "No. No, Luke, I did not." She offered him a small smile; he returned the same.

Then he said, "I wish you were my mother."

With that he turned around and walked across the hall to his own room leaving Grayson and Ann alone together. Grayson stood framed in the door and their eyes froze on one another. Both of their hearts breaking for this child who had been so deprived of a mother's love. She watched as the hollows beneath Grayson's cheek bones worked painfully.

She traced the bristled outline of his jaw with her eyes and stopped at his lips. She suddenly felt an overwhelming need to kiss him, to comfort him in the absence of the words she couldn't seem to find.

For a brief moment, she thought he might want to kiss her too. That he would kiss her. Then he blinked his eyes and backed away, leaving her feeling foolish and alone. Instead he tipped his head to her and thanked her for being with his son tonight. She responded with kind pleasantries in return and then he was gone.

Alone again behind her door, she closed her eyes, touched her fingers to her lips still tingling with want of the feel of Grayson's lips.

She sighed at her foolishness and turned her key in the door to be sure that it locked, blew out the candles still lighting the room, then undressed down to her shift and climbed into bed next to her daughters in hope of finding sleep easily that night.

Indeed, she would not be kept awake with thoughts of Grayson's lips and how deliciously close they had been to descending on hers, only moments ago. She refused to believe the titillating shivers that cursed down the soft curve of her body had to do with aught but the chill in the room; decidedly *not* from the intense desire for her that had smoldered from his stormy eyes.

She pulled the coverlet around her, a poor substitute for the strong pair of arms she wished it to be, and snuggled in for the night.

Ann sighed her pleasure, bathed in the warmth of the sun, its light shining through the finely veiled window where she stood. She hoped today's sunshine wouldn't be chased away by more unpredictable threatening clouds of rain. She had much to get done this day. With a determined bob of her head she set to readying herself and the girls.

She was about to *cinch up* (oh goodness, there she went again comparing herself to that of a pack mule. How very unflattering), when a knock sounded at the door and caused butterflies to flutter in her stomach.

She set the pack down on the bed, eyed the girls who she noted remained a safe distance from the still warm ash in the fire grate and pulled open the door.

She hoped the gratifying sensation upon seeing his face didn't reveal itself in her eyes or in the foolish smile she beamed at him.

"Grayson," Her voice sounded breathless even to her own ears. *Come now, Ann, he's only a man. Pull yourself together.* "Um, Good morning."

An entire night of sleep lost berating himself over his near reckless actions and convincing himself he could maintain a professional relationship with the woman became laughable when she opened the door wearing a smile that radiated the very tempting appeal of her. His eyes took her in the way his lungs craved for a new breath of fresh mountain air. Her brown hair was plaited back in its usual single braid and tossed over her shoulder carelessly, wisps of her bangs already straying from its hold. She was such a contrast to most of the women of his acquaintance.

He recalled the women of his wife's ilk who had paraded before him years ago in Philadelphia. Nothing on their person had ever been carelessly tended. In fact, every single detail down to the stitching on their hankies had been meticulously planned. Every hair on their heads curled or straightened to perfection, gowns selected to cater an ultimate enhancement of their every feature.

And here was Ann. Dressed in servant's attire, a wrinkled dove gray gown, smiling before him; her rich honey eyes warm and welcoming... and he could not recall a singular sight more beautiful.

It did not matter. He had made his decision and he would honor it.

He smiled awkwardly in return, "Ah, yes, good morning."

He squared himself, forcing the sheepish smile from his face and assumed a more business-like composure. –Best to establish the manner now in which he wished to continue.

"I have reconsidered my decision from yesterday. If we can negotiate on a fair cost and terms, I will consent to escorting you to Missouri."

A surprised breath escaped her, and her pink lips bowed in gratitude. Satisfaction that he was the one to place that look of happy astonishment on her face flicked inside him like fingerlings of flames. And he was quick to extinguish them.

"Would you care to join me for breakfast?"

To his own ears, he sounded like a suitor come to beg for her attentions and that wouldn't do.

"That is, would you like to further discuss the details of such a business arrangement over breakfast?" He amended with enough civil cordiality to create a cool distance between them.

Which she must have felt, because her smile slipped from her face, tactfully replaced with a polite formal line. As if to adhere to the non-intimate space he was trying to create she took a step back from him. He squelched the objections of his body.

"Of course." She nodded her head, "I shall meet you there shortly."

He nodded to her before she closed the door.

Apparently, *he* had not endured a restless night filled with thoughts about *her* lips. Of course not, Ann admonished herself; she was the only one entertaining such foolish thoughts. Well, no longer. She secured Kit and Livvy into the pack strapped around her and made her way to the tavern.

Their talk over breakfast went decidedly more smoothly than the morning before. Now that the stubborn man had finally seen fit to reason with her, she mostly ceded to his superior knowledge of trail life.

Grayson already had a wagon stocked, but she would need to purchase more supplies for her and the girls. It wasn't an overly long journey, thank goodness. All in all, she was making out fairly well and would even be saving money that would no longer be used for room and board along the way.

He spared her the cost of a wagon by allowing her to share his wagon -well, Luke's, rather- as Grayson explained he would rarely be in the company of the wagon. Luke was nearly ecstatic that she and the girls would be traveling with him and she saw him transform from the solemn boy she had first met into a chatty, excitable -rather normal- boy of his years. The arrangement seemed to be pleasing to all parties involved.

Grayson spared her yet more coin, by trading services. In exchange for use of his wagon and "protection" (She kept her irritation to herself over his implication that she needed a man to "protect" her.), she would in turn, care for Luke, cook, clean and keep order amidst the wagon, amongst other duties.

She'd never been averse to hard labor, despite her genteel upbringing and was more than happy to conserve what coin she could, so she accepted the terms happily.

Ann had to return to her rooms momentarily to freshen the girls before she was to meet Grayson and Luke at the stables. She'd just completed the task of changing the girls and was readying the pack once more when she heard a knock at the door.

"Truly, Grayson. I told you it was unnecessary for you to escort me to the barn." She chuckled as she pulled the door open to greet him.

Only, it wasn't Grayson outside her door.

Her smiling lips turned to an 'O' and her knees nearly buckled beneath her as she took in a very different set of gray eyes staring back at her.

Chapter 10

"Ann! Thank, God! I've been searching frantically for you."

"Jonathon?" The shock was stark on her face, his name but a question on her lips.

"Yes. When I went to Dr. Fletcher's to speak with you the next day after we met, you were gone. The woman residing there told me of your plans and I hurried after you as quickly as possible. I endured some unfortunate circumstances along the way that slowed my progress, but I've found you now."

She watched almost from a daze as James' cousin stood before her smiling happily. He was covered in dust, mud, and filth; it was obvious he had ridden hard and fast to find her... but why? The question must have been apparent on her face.

"I want to help you. Find James that is. I-I could never forgive myself if I allowed harm to come to you knowing that I could have protected you."

She resisted rolling her eyes. Yet another man thinking her incapable of handling her own affairs. She reigned in her annoyance. However misguided the gentleman was, he was acting out of kindness and extreme generosity on her behalf.

She shook the fog from her mind as the extent of his *generosity* sunk in.

"I cannot believe you traveled all this way."

She stopped herself before saying: *You needn't have.* That would hardly be a kind thing to say to a man who'd exhausted his time and resources hunting her down.

His lips thinned, and she sensed for the first time from him, an agitation seemingly for her.

"Yes, well, Ann, you must know that it is not safe for a young lady to be traveling alone. An *unmarried* one at that," He whispered. "I wish you had waited for me. You have no idea the terrible thoughts that have haunted my mind over the past week, worrying for your welfare."

She gritted her teeth, "I apologize for any distress you allowed yourself to feel on my behalf." She wasn't sure if she sounded as gracious as she'd intended.

"Yes, well, I am here now."

He smiled as if she should feel gratitude for his efforts, but all she could think about was the complications his arrival would cause.

Ann was not overjoyed to see him as he had imagined she would be. In fact, she appeared frustrated to see him here. *Him*. He who had traveled across an entire state and more to find her! To help her find his worthless cousin when all Jonathon wanted was to make her his own in every way possible. As soon as possible.

He'd never been so happy when he arrived, and the Innkeeper confirmed a woman by the name of Ann Morgan to still be in residence. He had nearly shaken the man's hand with idiotic glee; so overjoyed was he to have found her at last!

The Innkeeper had mentioned something of little ones and that had caused his excitement to fade some, thinking perhaps he hadn't found her after all. But the woman the innkeeper spoke of matched her description in every other way and of course there was the *name*.

He knew that to be the false name she went by. It had to be her. He purchased a room and hurried down the hall. He didn't even bother locating his own room in his urgency to determine that Ann was in fact here. He'd never been more relieved in his life when the door opened to reveal her beautiful smiling face.

Her smile, however, had disappeared quickly in her shock to see him standing before her. He had *thought* it temporary shock anyway. Had rather thought she would be glowing with gratitude for him at this point.

He took in her strained features once more and then something behind her caught his eye.

Two babies sat up alongside one another on the floor staring at him with owlish expressions on their soft round faces. One with the same eyes as her mother, the other with the same silvery haze as her father.

Ann saw Jonathon's eyes travel beyond her to where Kit and Livvy still sat on the floor rug. She watched his eyes round first with shock and then fill with dismay and hurt. She wasn't certain why he appeared so wounded unless he was disappointed to learn of the lie she had been hiding from him.

Her daughters had been really more a secret than a lie, though, she reasoned. He looked back to her beseechingly, searching her face for truth.

Perhaps she should have told him everything the night she spoke with him, but she had thought it unnecessary if she could first locate James. The less people who knew of the girls' existence the better...

Ann cleared her throat. "Well. Now you know."

He couldn't believe what he was seeing. Little silver and gold eyed babies. How could he compete with that? Did he want to? Suddenly he felt cheated. And irrational as it may be, he was angry. Deep down inside he had believed in her innocence, had thought to make her his own.-once she realized for herself how foolish it was to pine after James, of course.

Only... how could she ever be his, now? Those were James' bastard children plain as day. Making an innocent young lady his wife, who had been duped by his rogue of a cousin was one thing, but a woman who had been thoroughly bedded and sired his cousin's offspring... well, that was quite another.

Ann reached out to comfort him, but he backed away from her touch as if burned. He looked on her in horror as if she had sprouted horns.

"Jonathon, please, you must understand why I did not tell you," She implored.

"I-I am sorry. I am exhausted. I think I will retire to my room for a short duration."

His boots shook free of dried mud with each retreating step from her. His hair, loosened from its promenade hold, probably days ago, was flouncing madly about his head as he fumbled for excuses to escape her.

Then he recovered enough to say, "We have much yet to discuss. I would appreciate your company this evening so that we may speak further about your circumstances and... your options."

Her options? Ann tried to loosen her clenched teeth into a smile, "Indeed."

He seemed to take that as compliance to his request, "Well, until this evening then."

He managed to not trip over his own feet as he turned away in search of his room.

Grayson sensed Ann's temper when she arrived, "Something amiss?"

She placed the girls into the straw pen he arranged for them again and then paced. Stopping long enough to bark a nonsensical statement to him, "His cousin has apparently come to *rescue* me."

Grayson stopped harnessing Buckshot to stare at her. *His cousin*, what did that mean? But the hairs went up on the back of his neck in warning.

"My," she coughed and raised her fingers to her throat as if the next words would pain her to say, "*Husband's* cousin *followed* me here!"

Grayson's eyes slit suspiciously. She always seemed most uncomfortable when she spoke of her husband.

Her husband's cousin had come for her, huh? So, she did have a guardian after all. And she'd thwarted the poor bastard. He could have smiled for the woman's spunk and temerity if she hadn't involved him in the middle of her mess.

Then as if she hadn't just walked in and announced something drastic, she waved her hand impatiently to him and said, "Well? Are you about done hitching that wagon, so we can be off?"

He looked to her incredulously, "You still mean to travel to St. Louis with *me*? Wouldn't it make more sense to travel with your cousin-in-law?"

She swallowed guiltily. "Yes, well, if he wants to go to St. Louis, I certainly shan't stop him, but I've already set my course of plans and I intend to see them through." She stomped her foot determinedly.

By god she was beautiful, Grayson thought. And stubborn. She was beautifully stubborn.

"Listen, I know I said I was for hire and we made a deal but fighting off an unwanted relative wasn't part of it."

She rolled her eyes to the ceiling, "Oh, please, it will hardly come to fighting. I'm not his property, the decision is mine." She looked to him heatedly, "Now do we still have a deal or no?"

What had he gotten himself into? He sighed, "Get the girls. Let's load up."

They rode around the majority of the afternoon collecting the necessary supplies and discussing Ann's history. Well the portions she could divulge at any rate.

"You'll need a gun."

He spoke the words casually, but she understood the challenge in them. She'd come rather accustomed to having to prove herself competent with both horse and gun more than once in her past life in England.

"I already have a gun."

He didn't reveal his surprise. "Do you know how to use it?"

After leaving Ann's room last evening, Luke -in the resilient way of children- regained his cheerfulness and had endlessly chattered and regaled Grayson with Ann's stories. Luke (as well as Grayson) had been particularly enthralled with the bit she had delved about being able to out-shoot, out-hunt, and out-ride all of her father's male comrades.

He could picture the impish dimples forming near her lips and the competent gleam in her eye, sharing this with his son. The same look she had given him the other day at the stables when she declared herself to be a better horseman than himself.

"Would I carry it, if I didn't?"

He expected just such a response.

Saucy little minx.

To vex her, he scoffed, "You're going to need something with a higher caliber than a derringer."

He suppressed a smile from forming on his lips and watched her bottom teeth scrape against her upper lip in effort to control her irritation as he knew she would.

"I'll have you know," She spoke slowly and directly, "I am in possession of a deadly accurate set of flintlock pistols."

Impressive, if one were admiring guns in a parlor or having a close-range friendly competition, but hardly what one would need crossing the Allegheny Mountains and beyond.

She accurately assessed his reaction as being less than enthused over her announced choice of weaponry.

Ann straightened defensively and crossed her arms in front of her, which Grayson couldn't help for noticing, pushed the exposed tops of her breasts into two delectable, creamy mounds. And the thought occurred to him, that he was glad she chose to travel with him and leave her *cousin in law* behind.

Ann determined his pleased smirk to be condescension on his part and took exception to it.

"Oh, I see. You think the pistols simply to be an aesthetical piece of art." Then she stuck her pert little nose in the air and continued, "Do not get me wrong, they are indeed that. As well they are a masterfully built tool."

She leveled him with a look that told him she wasn't finished delivering her set down.

"What exactly do you find inferior about a .52 caliber, rifled barrel, pistol that shoots eight hundred feet per second, might I ask?"

He had to look in the opposite direction and stifle his smile. He was taking sick pleasure in raising her ire and it had everything to do with that singular dark brow arched in vexation, those flashing eyes and the warm flush spreading across her cheeks.

His humor quelled when he thought about another activity that would bring her to a flushed state. He shifted a bit uneasily, his pants feeling uncomfortably tighter.

He reminded himself then that the woman was on her way to meet her *husband*! That cooled his ardor effectively.

"Nothing. I am sure it is a fine set of pistols. However, you may want to consider purchasing a rifle. On the trail, we generally don't like our enemies to get close enough to have to use pistols as way of defense. They're not very useful for hunting either, for that matter."

Ann didn't want to allot for any extra expenditures on guns. She'd made it all this way without having to ever use the ones she had, it hardly seemed necessary to purchase more.

"Isn't that what I hired you for?" She smiled to him smartly, "To *protect* me?" She batted her eye lashes over-sweetly.

At that he threw his head back and guffawed. Ann turned in surprise at his unexpected, rich rumbling laughter. The infectious sound caused her to smile giddily in return. Even Luke looked from his father to Ann in surprise, wearing a joyful smile that lifted his sweet freckled cheeks.

Who knew the stern Grayson Stone, hard and dominating presence that he was, was capable of such a boisterous sound? Ann gleaned a certain satisfaction for having been the cause of his delight.

The rest of the supply trip was conducted in a friendly tone. Mostly, Ann thought, because Grayson managed to not insult her for the duration.

She tried to tell him more about her current circumstances, but of course it had been impossible to do so without entirely eschewing lies and omissions. She was able to explain her rather short association with her cousin in law, however, and for some reason that had sent Grayson's teeth on edge.

"Seems strange to me that a man you had known for all of two hours would travel four hundred miles to get you."

"He claims he wants to help me, but I think he may just want to locate James as well. Not that I believe him of deceiving me, only, that I think his plans happen to coincide with mine and his gentlemanly nature influenced his decision to act now with intentions of aiding me in the process."

Grayson grunted surly. He very much doubted this man had any gentlemanly intentions when it came to Ann. What man could? When the woman wasn't vexing and irritating (enough reason for a man to forget gentlemanly manners), she was a golden eyed little temptress. Somehow, she managed to be both at the same time. What was worse, she seemed to have no clue the affect she had on the average man.

After purchasing the supplies and concluding their plans they made their way back to the stables. Grayson unhitched the rented buck board and offered to load the supplies into the Conestoga they would be traveling in tomorrow, while Luke assisted Ann with the girls and gathering supper from the tavern to take back to their rooms.

Grayson made quick work. He didn't like the idea of Jonathon Morgan being in close proximity. He didn't know the man and had no reason to be suspicious of him, but the idea of him following Ann over four hundred miles soured his stomach.

Grayson was extra alert when he returned to the hotel, should he run into Jonathon Morgan. He almost wished he would have, so he could have surmised judgment for himself. He half worried the man would be in Ann's hotel room sharing *his* supper. He was relieved when after knocking, Luke opened the door and no strange man was present.

"Did you get everything squared away, then?" Ann asked as she settled plates of food around the small vase table that served more as décor in the room than furniture. There were two small, hard wooden chairs as well.

"You and Luke may sit here at the table."

He looked around. He hadn't thought ahead to the seating arrangement in their tiny hotel rooms, only the privacy to further discuss their plans.

"No, I think you and I will sit at the table and Luke can seat himself on the floor with the girls."

Already Ann's rapscallion daughters were crawling happily towards Luke. One with a very determined look in her eyes that reminded Grayson of her mother. The girls had spent most of the day in the back of the wagon with Luke and apparently, they now considered him to be their personal pet. Grayson thought Luke might oppose being subjected to more of their smothering, but instead he smiled.

"Suits me. They're just like puppies. Watch."

With that, Luke tossed each girl a hard biscuit. They both stopped in their tracks and thumped back onto their squat little behinds in order to better inspect their new gifts. It didn't take them long to discern the prize in their chubby little fists to be food and they greedily lifted the biscuits to their mouths. Their fine motor skills undeveloped as they were made for a sloppy effort on their part and caused all in the room to erupt in laughter.

Grayson's chuckle was brief and instead admonished, "Luke, don't treat Ann's daughters like dogs."

"Ann's the one who taught me." He quipped back.

That earned a guilty blush from Ann. She really should stop comparing her lovely daughters to spawns of hounds. —Even if they did resemble the frolicking creatures a majority of the time.

In Ann's defense she had much more experience in caring for her and her father's hunting hounds than she did babies. Before delivering her own daughters, in fact, her experience with babies was zilch! She'd learned a great deal from Nancy, bless the woman. Apparently, she'd not learned enough as her parenting skills were being scrutinized by a mountain man.

They'd managed to get through supper easily and because Grayson had purchased the meal on his tab, they had eaten well. Ann had (guiltily) long forgotten her appointment with Jonathon Morgan, until the knock sounded outside her door, which is why she nearly jumped out of her skin at the light rapping.

Ann startled when the fist thudded on her door, which set Grayson's instincts on high alert with unease. He was certain he knew the man that awaited the other side as well his purpose for being there and his teeth gritted with the irrational pangs of jealousy.

"I'm so sorry," she excused herself to Grayson as she rose from her chair. "I completely forgot Jonathon wanted to speak with me this evening." She looked to him apologetically.

She'd thought her last comment had indicated for Grayson to take his leave. Before she turned the knob to allow Jonathon entry she glanced to Grayson assuming the sight would reveal him standing and preparing to depart her company, but instead she saw him relaxed back in the chair he occupied, with his booted heels stretched out before him, one crossed over the other. His arms crossed over his chest and his face set in stubbornly fashion.

She raised her eyebrow at him in silent reproach and as one last effort plea for him to leave, but what she got in return was his arrogant smirk and a tip of his hat to proceed.

Arrrgh, the infuriating man! Ann jutted her chin out and probably resembled a horse barring its teeth, as her only response before plastering a polite smile into place and opening the door.

"Jonathon," she greeted cheerfully, "I apologize for failing to send a note around informing you I would be delayed in our meeting. I'm so sorry to inconvenience you, but I do have guests at this time. Would you mind terribly, joining me later? After your evening meal perhaps?"

She felt terribly guilty for forgetting Jonathon, especially when he presented himself in freshly pressed gentleman's attire and his face sank with affront at her rude lapse. She knew, too, how terribly obscene her invitation had sounded and with Grayson in the room to overhear it she couldn't help but blush. She hadn't intended for the rescheduling of her meeting with Jonathon to appear a late-night assignation!

Grayson watched Ann's face flush becomingly at her faux pas and wondered, not for the first time, how she could possibly be the daughter of an Earl? She failed miserably at most social exchanges, from what he had witnessed. One would think a genteel English lady would be trained better in the social arts.

He didn't like that the man on the other side of the door also witnessed the fetching bloom in her cheeks and he realized, he didn't much care for the way Ann was intentionally keeping the door partially closed in order to hide this *Jonathon Morgan* from his view either.

"It's no bother to me, Ann, if you include another guest." Grayson drawled, daringly.

Ann turned her head to his side of the door, and Grayson had to suppress a chuckle when she looked to him with her eyes bugged, comically, from her head.

Just as he suspected, Ann absolutely did not want Jonathon joining them. Interesting. Why didn't she want him around when she met with her cousin in law?

"Well perhaps, Mr. Morgan does not wish to." She snapped to him in a hushed angry tone.

Jonathon's hackles rose instantly at the sound of the other male's voice coming from within Ann's room. Who exactly was this man and more importantly, who was he to Ann?

Jonathon cut in acidly, "I do, actually. Wish to that is. Seeming as your other *guest* does not mind the intrusion of my presence."

Oh dear. Ann massaged her temples with her fingertips, already feeling an ache coming on. What would one man say to the other? She had too many lies for them to be crisscrossing back and forth; sure to form a noose around her neck! She couldn't find a plausible excuse now, though.

She cleared her throat, "Very well, Jonathon, will not you please join us?"

He stepped into the room with a straightening tug to his jacket, wholly unprepared to find the floor before him littered with children. The masculine posture he'd instinctively adopted when he thought he was entering into a cock ring felt breached.

He looked to Ann uncertainly.

"You are welcome to join Mr. Grayson Stone and seat yourself at the table. Mr. Stone, this is Mr. Jonathon Morgan, my cousin in law, as I'm sure you remember me speaking of this afternoon."

Grayson gave a curt nod of his head. Ann located a stool in the corner and carried it to the small table. She tried to position it between the two men, but the table was rather too small to accomplish that feat entirely.

Jonathon spoke then, "I am at a disadvantage, for I have not heard of you Mr. Stone."

He spoke pleasantly, enough, but Grayson recognized it for the dig it was, implying Jonathon already had an established relationship with Ann and Grayson's presence was an unwelcome one.

Ann adjusted herself on the stool unaware of the tension filled undercurrent in the room and finished making introductions, "The young man on the floor is Luke Stone and of course," She implored Jonathon pleadingly with her eyes, "You've already met Kit and Livvy." She gestured to the toddlers playfully tugging on Luke's shirt."

Jonathon looked intently to Ann, and a little sadly, "Yes. Yes, I have."

163

Ann averted her eyes downward shamefully. She really ought to have told him of James' daughters. They were technically Jonathon's family as well.

Grayson didn't like the sentimental moment they seemed to be sharing. "So, I hear you have come to assist Ann to St. Louis to find your cousin."

"My husband, yes." Ann interjected quickly.

Grayson shifted his slitted gaze to her suspiciously. Until then it hadn't occurred to him that Ann might be lying about having a husband nor meeting said husband. But something wasn't adding up...

He looked back to Jonathon who didn't contradict her words, but also didn't confirm them. He just returned a suspicious glare back to Grayson. Grayson had wondered why Ann's *husband's* own cousin would be chasing after her like a love-sick fool. At first, he'd written the actions off imagining her cousin in law to probably be a young pup with a hopeless crush on his cousin's wife with no intentions to act on it.

After having met Mr. Morgan, however a dandy he appeared to be, he was very much a man. A man of age not to be foolish or desperate enough to chase after something he couldn't have. The possessive gleam in his eye told Grayson, he very much thought Ann to be his.

He'd been suspicious of Ann's behavior concerning talk of her husband at first but had decided she was just hurt for being neglected and perhaps embarrassed about having to track her husband down. The fact that Ann tried to evade all questions pertaining to her husband now struck him as a woman attempting to step around the muddying puddle of lies she was raining down. He turned his attention back to Ann who smiled placidly and not nearly as innocent as she no doubt hoped she appeared. He watched her throat work to swallow.

"I'm leaving tomorrow, you should know." She suddenly blurted out.

Jonathon ceased glaring at Grayson and whipped his head in Ann's direction. She looked away, guiltily again.

"That is why Grayson and his son are here. We were finalizing our business arrangement. I have hired him as my trail guide. Well, he is the entire group's trail guide actually..."

she babbled nervously, "But he has agreed to, ehrm, take me and the girls on personally."

"Oh?" Jonathon's attempt to look anything other than displeased with this revelation failed. "So, essentially, what you are proclaiming is: my assistance is unnecessary as you already have Mr. Stone?" he said icily.

Jonathon's focus narrowed on Grayson. Ann's ire was triggered once more. She didn't understand Jonathon's icy tones. She wanted to expound that his assistance had always been unnecessary, whether for Mr. Stone or not, but she held her tongue in check trying to remember that the poor man had traveled over four hundred miles under the misconception that she needed his aid.

Jonathon was staring stonily at Grayson as if he were to fault for Ann's circumstances. Ann couldn't understand it.

Then she looked to Grayson and saw the irksome man was smiling like an arrogant peacock.

Were they rivaling over who would escort her to St. Louis? That notion was too absurd to fathom. She'd practically had to beg Grayson to take her and now here he was smiling for all the world like a man who had won a game of cards. Her jaw tightened, and her teeth gritted angrily. She was tired of being treated like a child.

"I really don't think that a good idea Ann."

Jonathon turned back to her. He didn't seem to realize the extent of condescension that hung heavily from his words. He truly didn't mean to rake her temper.

Ann breathed deeply exacting a sense of calmness, "And why is that, Jonathon?"

"I don't think the other travelers will think well of you, a married woman traveling with a man who is not your husband nor a relation." He explained.

She didn't care a wit for what the other travelers might think or say. She refrained from rolling her eyes, as if she hadn't been under the harsh judgment of society thus far?

Before she could voice her opinion on the matter, Grayson spoke, "I agree."

"What?!" She nearly exploded from the table.

How dare he! He would sell her out? A few seconds ago he seemed pleased as peaches with her decision to continue her plans of traveling with *him*. She knew in the beginning he had opposed her company, but since then they had made a bargain with one another. It was too late for him to reengage now. She'd already purchased the supplies and they were loaded in his wagon!

The raise of her voice visibly concerned Luke who stood now staring at the table of adults with worry knitting his brow. Grayson saw him too.

Ann smiled reassuringly to him. She should not have allowed her shock and anger to get the best of her. Luke was a sweet, sensitive, little boy, no need to concern him with her troubles.

"But Pa," Luke's voice wobbled, "I thought Ann was going to ride with me? I'm supposed to help her with the rein and the girls."

Grayson smiled to his son and spoke low and calmly, "And she still can if she would like."

Luke breathed his relief.

Ann and Jonathon looked to Grayson in confusion.

Grayson continued, "Hear me out. Mrs. Morgan, I believe, is set on going to Missouri."

"No need to speak as if I'm not here," she glared.

Grayson arched his brow back at her, "Might I continue?"

Ann crossed her arms petulantly.

"Mr. Morgan is not incorrect about how the other wagons will judge you," and then before Ann could interject again, "And since my son will be in your care, I'd prefer him not be subject to that kind of treatment."

Well, she couldn't very well argue with that. Luke's hopeful little face studied them intently waiting for a final decision.

"Of course." Ann whispered solemnly.

"However," Grayson's deep voice penetrated the room once more, "If Mr. Morgan here, would agree to accompany our group as well, I think that would be enough to keep tongues from wagging. He is, after all, a relation."

Luke looked from Jonathon to Ann eagerly.

Jonathon had hoped Grayson's unexpected accordance with his notion that Ann shouldn't travel with them would result in Ann's being unable to proceed to Missouri altogether. He hadn't imagined the man would extend an invitation to him to join the party. If Ann was determined to continue in her pursuit of James, however, he supposed the next best option was to join her.

Perhaps he would be able to convince her that he was a better man for her than his cousin along the way. And hopefully, this Grayson Stone fellow didn't harbor similar plans of his own. Of course, Mr. Stone believed Ann to be married, only Jonathon knew otherwise, so why would he set his cap for *his* lovely Ann?

"Yes, of course. That is why I have made such a great effort to find you, Ann. I am of course agreeable to escorting you to St. Louis. Very generous of you, Mr. Stone, to invite me along."

Grayson hadn't wanted Mr. Morgan to join them and that's exactly why he invited him. He was becoming too involved with Ann Morgan, if that was even her last name. He didn't know her story, but he knew she was trouble. Besides he couldn't forget his vow to never marry again. It was too great a risk. He couldn't afford any more mistakes; he just wanted to be happy and for Luke to be happy.

Jonathon's presence would mean he wouldn't need to be near Ann as often. Hopefully the dandy was competent enough to oversee her care. Suddenly he couldn't wait to get out on the trail and get as much distance from the enchanting woman as possible.

"Well, then. It's settled. We will just need to stock the wagon with additional food rations." Grayson directed his gaze to Jonathon, "I'm assuming you have a horse?"

"Yes."

"And a gun?"

"No, but I'll get one."

"Best do so right away. We leave in the morning."

Grayson looked then to Ann, who was unusually quiet. She looked as if inviting Jonathon along had been a betrayal to her. It was for the best though. She would soon realize that. It would have been more difficult for her on the trail if the other women ostracized her. She would need their help. What did a genteel bred Lady know about life on the trail?

He stood from the table, "Ann."

She lifted her chin slightly and tried to clear her face of any readable emotion.

There wasn't anything Grayson could say with Jonathon in the room. Nothing he should say at all for that matter. So instead, he nodded to her and Jonathon and left with Luke, even though the idea of leaving her alone with Jonathon still rankled beneath his skin.

Chapter 11

They set out four days ago on Wilderness Road and Ann had only spoken with Grayson on three short occasions since the early morning departure. Was he avoiding her or Jonathon? The two men hadn't gotten along very well from the start. At best they were civil to one another.

Of course, Grayson couldn't always be counted upon for good manners. She'd overheard him speaking furiously to Jonathon the same afternoon they'd set off. Jonathon hadn't been able to acquire a gun. It seemed a silly thing to squabble over to Ann. They were traveling in a large group with the majority being armed men; surely no lone highway man or bandit would attempt to rob them.

She knew Grayson had a job to do. He was hired by all of these people to get them safely to Missouri. She understood why he couldn't be near the wagon a lot of the time and he explained as much to her before agreeing to their bargain. But Grayson wasn't the only one leading. There was another man by the name of Jacques Dubois. Apparently, the road would split soon, and Jacques would lead those who wanted to go

North with him, and Grayson would continue west to Harrodsburg.

In fact, she had seen more of Jacques around their wagon than Grayson. Her conversations with the Frenchman had been pleasant, but short as Jonathon would usually appear shortly after his arrival, and in Ann's opinion, bore the poor man to death. Jonathon usually rode near the wagon, but Ann didn't go out of her way to speak with him.

It was grueling work keeping a team of four mules in line. They were skittish animals. Ann would have much preferred handling horses. At least, she thought, she could have taken to the system a lot easier. She hadn't much experience driving a team as she'd always preferred being on the back of a horse rather than staring at the back of one. Horses, she was told, were more likely to encourage Indian attacks, so she was stuck with the dreaded mules. –Apparently, not even the Indians wanted them.

She had scandalously driven a curricle once. Her lips twitched involuntarily at the memory. James had rented one while in London and she convinced him to allow her to drive it. She'd met him early at the park one morning, her maid had accompanied her but remained behind with their horses while Ann went racing recklessly through the morning fog. It had been a heady experience and one of the reasons she had been so certain James shared her affections. She had known no other man who would allow her such liberties. He made her feel his equal.

Looking back on it, perhaps all he had ever wanted was a good time. And in her he'd found easy pleasure. His abandonment of her tainted all of her loving memories of him. She'd long lost the feelings of love in her heart for him, which made this journey all the more arduous.

Despite wearing the deerskin gloves Grayson had urged her to buy, her hands ached and felt raw where the reins slid through her hands all day. The curricle had been light and fast, the horses easy to maneuver. This wagon was heavy and lumbered across the rutted road unmercifully. The mules balked every chance they had so that Ann had to work tirelessly to keep them moving.

Luckily her back and arm muscles were fairly strong from carrying around her young daughters, but different muscles she'd never used before were stinging with pain. She'd never longed to be on the backside of a horse so much as in these past days. Resentment for the men riding along flickered as they passed her. It would seem they had the easy job.

The women controlled the livestock and wagons all whilst overseeing the care of children and the men! She understood now, why Grayson had deemed her assistance payment enough for bringing her along. She had to wash his clothes as well as Jonathon's, the children, and her own. She'd only had to do that once thus far as they wore the same clothes day after dusty day.

Just as Grayson had warned her, she hadn't made very many friends on the journey despite Jonathon playing the role of guardian over her. They tolerated her, however, and weren't disrespectful, so she decided that was already improvement over the beginning part of her travels.

It was Ann's turn tonight, though, to manage the campfire. She was not looking forward to that responsibility. She had assisted cook in the kitchen as a small child, but all Ann could recall was making a powder blast of the flour on occasion and always licking the batter or dough from any sweets made for the day.

She remembered well the lessons her father had relentlessly drilled into her. All the overnight camp outs with him and Uncle Rupie. She'd loved those trips most and she was never so thankful for her unorthodox childhood than in these last days. She knew how to protect herself, Luke, and the girls with her guns, not that she'd had to as of yet. She knew how to be resourceful and was comfortable with outdoor living arrangements.

She just wished she knew how to prepare something other than meager soldier's fare.

Ann doubted the other women and their families would be impressed when she presented to them, baking powder biscuits and jerked meat. She smirked to herself.

Luckily, she needn't prepare a spectacular meal. It appeared to be custom that all the wagons contribute food at mealtimes and then the designated woman to prepare it made it all into an edible stew. All Ann really needed to do was ensure it was edible. Could one burn stew? She hoped not. At least she was confident she wouldn't burn the biscuits.

Her bum was beginning to ache again on the hard seat, and she was glad this part of the trip was half over. The plan for the day was to travel on through and not stop for the noon meal. Ann was happy to munch on hard tack and continue driving. She wanted to reach Hazel Patch as quickly as possible and then quit that hard wagon seat for good this day.

"The girls are asleep."

Luke peeped his head out of the wagon. Ann knew he was restless, for having skipped the midday break. She also knew the question that would follow.

"Do you think I could ride up with pa for a bit?"

Blessed child, Ann thought, even he gets a turn in the saddle.

"Yes, of course."

She tried not to reply too testily. It wasn't his fault she was jailed to the rock-hard seat of the wagon.

Sweat dribbled down her face just then raising her ire with the situation all the more. It wasn't a particularly warm spring day; the labor involved in keeping the mules in line was just that intensive.

She transferred the thick rein in her right hand to join the other rein in her left, so she could swipe the itchy rolling bead of sweat. Of course, the mules took that opportunity to veer off the path, the vexing animals!

"Are you sure you don't need any help?" Luke asked thoughtfully, his eyes hopeful that she wouldn't require his assistance.

The truth was, Luke was more adept at handling the beasts than she was. How that could be she didn't know. He was strong for his age, but not more so than her, she imagined. The irksome beasts just seemed to like him better, that was all Ann could figure.

She knew the little boy enjoyed it about as little as she did though, so she rarely asked the chore of him. Only when she was desperate for a break. Besides, she knew too that he'd made a friend on the trail, a little boy by the name of Owen Rhysdale.

The Rhysdale family would be heading north to Boonesborough at the split once they reached Hazel Patch, while Luke would continue with them to Harrodsburg. Today was his last day to romp with a fellow boy for a while.

"No, I can manage. Thank you for helping with the girls. If you're going to break free from the wagon you best do so now. Don't forget your hat. It's not all that warm, but the sun can still burn those little cheeks of yours."

She smiled to him. He pretended he didn't like it when she fussed over him, but his adoring eyes told her otherwise.

"Yes, ma'am." He drawled with feigned annoyance.

He plopped the wide brimmed beaver hat down on his head and then the lucky boy was off on his horse, giving a little wave as he passed by.

Ann waved back, sighed her weariness and brought the reins down on the stubborn mules who were attempting to stop once more to munch the bits of grass that grew alongside the path.

Two hours could not have passed before the sunshine disappeared behind a building storm of dark clouds and Ann began wishing Grayson would send Luke on back. She wanted him safe in the wagon, not out trouncing about in what was likely to be a lightning storm descending upon them. Her brows furrowed with worry as her eyes searched the trail ahead for sign of Luke or the men returning to the wagon.

The booming of thunder clapped the air followed by Kit and Livvy's awakening cries. She knew lightning was sure to make an appearance alongside it's thundering cousin.

Oh, where was Luke?

With each clap of thunder, the babies' startled screams grew louder, but Ann could do little more to soothe the girls' cries than offer shushing noises.

She couldn't stop the wagon and there was no way to reach them from the seat, without possibly losing control of the reins. And that seemed a definite possibility at the moment. The mules danced wildly every time the clouds boomed, but she managed to keep them driving forward.

A rider was approaching; still too far away to determine who.

It wasn't Grayson, she could tell that much by the color of horse. He was the only one amongst the group riding a gray. The horse nearing her now was brown; she couldn't yet discern if it was Jonathon's red roan or Luke's sorrel, Buckshot.

A low rumbling of thunder escalated and ended on another loud clap. At the same time, the back-left wagon wheel drove into a rut. She managed to get it back out onto the smoother part of the path quickly, but the jarring sent Livvy tumbling backwards from her seated position until she landed belly side down and furious. Ann wanted to right her and check her face, but she couldn't break her focus from the mules.

"Ann."

Oh, drat, it was Jonathon. He'd been kind, but for the most part unhelpful the entire trip. She really needed Luke: to ensure he was safe as well as to enlist his help with the girls.

"Ann, there's a storm coming in."

No kidding, she thought irritably, but didn't voice such.

"What's wrong with the babies?" Jonathon's face filled with concern and fear that he may be required to assist with them.

"They are afraid of the thunder," She answered shortly. "Did you happen to see Luke on your way through?"

"Stone's boy? No."

"He wasn't at the front of the train with the rest of the men?" Unadulterated fear pierced her heart.

"Not that I saw, no." *Not that he saw?* What did that mean? Was he riding around with his eyes closed? How could one fail to notice a couple of rowdy little boys underfoot? Jonathon was getting on her nerves.

"I could use some help." She said testily. It was becoming too difficult to withhold her frustrations with the man.

His eyes widened. "I might be needed at the front with the other men," he balked. "I just came back to check on you and the-the babies."

Unbelievably he began to turn his horse back, as if he'd adequately excused himself. Ann stopped him; her voice shriller than she expected.

"Where are you going? You came to back to inquire whether I needed assistance, did you not?"

The girls' continued cries carried from the back of the wagon.

"Quite. And it's obvious you need the boy. I will go in search of him and send him back to carry on his duties as he ought."

He tipped his yet starchy stiff hat, purchased before they set out all those mornings ago, as if he was in charge and providing a great service. Ann curled her lip in disgust and watched him ride past the wagons ahead of her. Please let him find Luke, she thought.

She switched the heavy reins to one hand, gripping them as tightly as possible, even though her tender hand cramped in protest, and twisted on the bench to see to the girls. She reached her free arm back through the bench slat and groped for one of her daughters, darting her eyes back in forth between the road ahead and the limited view of the back of the wagon. Finally, she felt what must have been one of their gowns. She strained her neck further, risking a glance behind her. It was Kit.

"Shh, shh, shh." She soothed.

She reached around for the rolled blanket they'd been using as padded buffers and looped it around Kit's bottom. Hopefully that would keep her from toppling over.

She hurried her search for Livvy, feeling around the floor of the wagon with her hand while she checked the mules. They were pulling mightily at the reins and Ann's hand ached, but they continued along the path. She twisted further this time and saw Livvy still face down, in the drool pooling around her from her relentless sobbing. Ann nearly dropped the reins in order to leap back and grab her.

"Livvy. Livvy, it's okay dear, mommy has you. Ann thrust as much of her body through the slat as possible to reach her. She was able to tug her a bit closer without scraping her face along the floor, until she was close enough to reach. She just had her sitting next to her sister once more, when the wagon knocked down hard into the ruts again.

Ann tried to untangle her arm from Livvy and slip it through the bench quickly before they ended up in the brush or worse.

"Ann!"

Oh, Grayson, thank God!

By the time she was able to twist her frame back onto the seat properly, Grayson already had a hold of the mules' reins.

"Whoa! Whoa!" The deep sound of his voice was like a balm to her frayed nerves. Unbeknownst to her a small tear trailed from her eye.

"Are you and the girls okay?"

She nodded, still catching her breath.

"Luke's not here!" She cried.

Her heart quickened with fear once more with the realization that Luke had still not returned to the wagon.

Grayson's calm never faltered. "Yes, he is. He's tying Buckshot up in the back.

She sank into the bench with relief. Grayson backed Dove up alongside the wagon, restringing the reins together as he went and handing them off once more to Ann. He looked to her again, his eyes directly on hers.

"You okay?"

That's when she realized how weak she'd appeared. She pulled the remaining strength from her core and squared her body, resolve shining in her eyes, she nodded back to him, then he turned his horse around and disappeared behind the wagon.

She heard Luke speaking to the girls inside the wagon.

"Aw, poor Livvy. Come here sassafras."

Ann smiled; her heart lightened at the sound of Luke comforting her daughter. She ceased noticing the building thunder. The next boom that startled her was Grayson's voice.

"Trade me."

Confused, she remained seated staring at him dazedly.

"Jacques and some of the unmarried men are going to finish leading us to Hazel Patch. It's bound to be one hell of a storm."

She didn't understand. Grayson was one of the unmarried men.

But he'd come back to help her. She choked back a sob, ever grateful for this man.

He relieved her aching hands of the reins and gestured for her to shuffle past him into the wagon bed. No easy task with the bunched skirts tangled around her legs. As she climbed over the seat she stopped and rested her hand on his arm. His eyes found hers and she hoped he understood the thanked words she couldn't speak. She hoped he couldn't see in them the other feelings swirling inside her.

A tingling sensation burned beneath her hand where it rested on the steel of his bicep. His eyes told her he was feeling as stirred as she.

"Best get back there and see to Luke and the girls."

He broke the spell, if there had even been one. Perhaps only she had been foolishly moved. The tingles in her hands no doubt came from the sudden release of pressure of the absent reins.

She finished climbing to the back where Luke already had the girls calmed and resituated. The calm lasted only seconds until the first crack of lightning lit the sky.

She barely found Grayson's slicker and handed it off to him in time before cold rain fell down on them in heavy sheets. She and the children remained dry under the canvas while Grayson took the brunt of the storm from the unsheltered seat. Rain poured down the back of his wide brimmed beaver tanned hat onto the back of his trench coat.

Ann offered whispered thanks for his presence. If he hadn't returned it would have been her soaking on the bench being pelted with rain trying to navigate the surly mules through the storm.

A niggling sense of guilt surfaced as she recalled Jonathon was somewhere out riding in the storm. If he had been Grayson, she could have easily shrugged off his absence having confidence in his competence, but Jonathon wasn't Grayson... She bit her bottom lip in worry for the man, despite his annoying, overwhelming desire to smother her and feign protector over her. He was undoubtedly a kind man-a respectable gentleman even, but his skill set outside of that realm was proving inadequate for this journey. There was little she could do for the man, though, so putting her worry from her mind, she settled onto the floor of the wagon with Luke and the girls.

They arrived at Hazel Patch within three hours' time, despite the mud and the Crandall family's broken axle that the train stopped for to repair.

The rain seemed to have followed them although it had lessened from a down pour into a heavy spraying mist. The sides of the canvas were beginning to bead up and drip down the sides, unable to prevent the full extent of the moisture penetrating its exterior. Ann carefully rocked the heavy sacks full of flour towards the center and laid their accumulated soiled clothes around the edges of the wagon to absorb the droplets. The only good to come from all the rain is the filling of the water barrels attached to the outside of the wagon. At least the water supply would be replenished, thought Ann.

The wagons began to pull around and make for camp. A selfish thought entered Ann's mind; did the rain mean she'd get to forego her turn serving over the cook fire? It wasn't the work she objected, only the embarrassment that would ensue once everyone realized what a terrible cook she was.

She had felt out of place from the start once it was clear that her soldier training as a young girl had properly trained her for the role of a *man*. The fact that she knew little about the typical routines and abilities the other traveling women seemed to possess provided her with a relatively new feeling of self-consciousness.

It left a bitter taste in her mouth, that.

She hadn't been looking forward to giving the snooty women in camp another reason to look down on her. She'd feel as helpless as Jonathon and she just couldn't bear for Grayson to think less of her as well.

Grayson parked the wagon and jumped down from the bench to unhitch the mules.

Ann peeked her head through the wagon's entry, "Surely, you don't think a fire can be started under these wet conditions, do you?" She called to Grayson in feigned concern while hope rose in her chest.

He shook his head no and blew rainwater from his lips, "No, I'm sure everyone will want to stick close to their own wagons tonight."

Well, that was a relief. Still, she would have to confirm that with the other women. The childless Mrs. Potter seemed to be in charge; she wasn't the eldest, but in Ann's opinion she was definitely the surliest. She was probably only nearing her forties, but her face always set in angry lines made her appear much older.

Once the wagons were situated, Ann would have to trudge out into the wet and find the cantankerous woman. A conversation with the woman would be more endurable than presenting her with subpar fare, however.

Just then a knocking at the back of the wagon sounded. It couldn't be Jonathon. He didn't normally knock. Of course, due to the rain he may think one of them indecently exposed.

"We're all decent!" She hollered to him. Then the back flap opened to reveal Karen Potter's beady brown eyes filled with contempt.

"One should hope so." She replied with a tight-lipped frown, judging Ann for a strumpet.

It was difficult to recover from announcing one's state of nudity to your neighbor, but Ann raised her chin (somewhat) proudly anyway.

"I just came to inform you, since you did not feel fit to trek out in the rain and inquire for yourself," she accused, "that camp supper has been canceled. Therefore, we will all be seeing to our own families' dinner fare tonight separately."

Truly, the wagons had only just parked. Mrs. Potter must have leapt from hers to reach Ann so quickly.

Ann remained cordial, "Thank you. I was just preparing to come ask you that very question."

"Hmph. I'm sure you were." She quipped, snidely, deepening the wrinkle lines bracketing her mouth.

Ann's smile nearly slipped. The woman was impossible. Still, Ann kept up her cheery façade.

"Would you like some assistance getting back to your wagon? I'm certain this cold wet air isn't easy for someone of your *advanced years* to be walking around in. Wait just one moment while I fetch my hat and coat and I'll be happy to aid you back to your wagon. We'll want to hurry. Everyone has much to do this evening, isn't that right?" Ann smiled.

"Indeed. No, thank you. I don't require assistance." The woman snapped and began to take her leave.

"I hope you have a lovely evening, Mrs. Potter." Ann called after her.

Once the flap was secured back into place, Ann relaxed her stiff smile. Wretched woman, Ann thought. Thank goodness she was not continuing to Harrodsburg with them on the morrow. Ann directed Luke to one side of the wagon with the girls while she sought out the hard tack and biscuits that would make up their evening meal. Busy preparing a space for all of them to take their supper, she was startled when the wagon flap was brusquely thrust aside once more.

"Oh! Grayson! I mean, Mr. Stone." She stammered, placing her hand over her yet fluttering heart. The brute remained in the entry of the wagon flashing a devilishly handsome, boyish grin. Apparently, her fright had provided him with comical entertainment. *The rotten man*, she thought chidingly, but her quirked lips disagreed. Didn't Grayson know what that smile of his did to her heart?

He climbed into the wagon, shedding his jacket along with all the rain on it to the floor, "I prefer you to call me Grayson."

Their eyes remained locked together for some time before the moment was interrupted by Jonathon entering the wagon.

"Wow. Some storm, isn't it?"

Ann cleared her throat, "Hmm, indeed."

She returned her attention to the placement of the meal. She was still displeased with Jonathon's cowardly actions from earlier.

They settled in and around the food, "We'll have to make do with this for supper." Ann stated as if she hadn't been happily relieved for just such a supper.

She all but waited for Jonathon to whine or snicker at the lean fare, but to his credit he ate it without protest. Grayson, however, protested the company and set out to leave immediately.

"Aren't you going to stay and eat with us?" Ann asked a little too desperately.

"I'll eat as I work." Grayson swung his long coat around him.

"But it's raining. Surely you could take a moment-," Ann bit off any further comment, aware of the desperation in her voice. If he didn't want to remain in her company, then good riddance!

He registered the hurt in her eyes. He just couldn't allow for any more moments like earlier to take place and he couldn't seem to control himself around her. He couldn't stand sharing the space with her cousin-in-law either. Not only because he didn't have a lot of respect for the man, but because he was a constant reminder that Ann was unobtainable. The reminder shouldn't feel like a hornet under his collar. He didn't want to be shackled to another woman. Goodness knows he'd learned his lesson on that score.

Only, he'd never met another woman quite like Ann...

"I'll send Jacques around to check on you all later." He settled the hat on his head.

"No need."

Grayson ignored her biting words, tipped his hat and rode off.

Luke sighed dejectedly, "Looks like we'll be holed up under this tarp for a while."

Ann shared his melancholy sentiment. Twin toddlers, a ten-year-old boy, and a helpless man underfoot; that wasn't Ann's idea of a good time either. Somehow, she suspected it would have been easier to accept with Grayson's presence.

When she had allowed him to become a bright spot in her life, she didn't know. All she knew was she was very confused and lately her plans felt more like a noose tightening around her neck than the salvation she dreamed it would be when she was still that naïve girl crossing the Atlantic.

Luckily the rain relented a couple of hours later. It was too late in the evening for sunlight to reclaim the sky, but at least one could venture forth from the suffocating canvas trap again. Funny how sometimes the wagon felt like safety and other times a jail.

Luke had already escaped to play nearby with the Rhysdale boy; He was staying overnight in his wagon as well that evening. The ground was too wet to allow the girls out of the wagon. She shuffled supplies around and made a pen-like area for them near the back of the wagon where she could keep an eye on them from her stool.

Ann thought it best to take advantage of the water situation and scrub up some of their clothes that were already dampened from the wet canvas. Hopefully the sun planned to return tomorrow and dry the garments, but if not, she was certain the cool breeze would see to it.

Jonathon walked to her, lighting a cigar between his lips. "You know," he exhaled the sweet fragrant smoke, "You should call that boy back to help give you a hand with those chores. You ought not to let him play all the time."

She raised her brow delicately, "Or perhaps you could offer a helping hand, seems as you're not busy at the moment."

"This is the first I've had to relax all day. Riding is hard work for someone who is not accustomed to the long miles."

Her eyes blazed with her incensed anger and she bit her bottom lip until the tangy coppery taste of blood touched her tongue in order to keep from flying into a rage at his ignorant excuse. It was entirely fortunate that Jacques chose that moment to meander into their camp.

"Good evening, Ann."

The Frenchmen smiled to her in his usual charming roguish fashion, causing Jonathon to stiffen at her side.

"It isn't gentlemanly to offend the lady by using familiarities." Jonathon tapped the ash from the end of his cheroot.

"Oh, but I have given Jacques permission to use my first name and already accepted his kindly request to do the same." She fair chirped, happy to contradict Jonathon.

Jacques sauntered over and rested against the side of the wagon, effectively obstructing her from Jonathon's view.

"I thought I should stop by and trouble you for some coffee. But I see no fire has been built yet. Ann, you must be chilled, washing away like that in the night air. Allow me, a true gentleman, to warm you."

He waggled his eyebrows implicitly, causing her to smile.

She wished she could see Jonathon's face in that moment. More than likely, however, instead of shame for his own idleness, he felt relieved someone else would spare him the task of building a fire.

"One of these days, Jacques, a woman may actually fall for that thick charm of yours and then you'll be truly caught." She teased.

He clutched a fist to his heart as if pained, "You shall break my heart with such cruel words, mon belle lionne."

Ann smiled enjoying their banter.

Then he tossed over his shoulder to Jonathon, "You will help me, no, Mr. Morgan?"

Ann nearly choked on a bubble of laughter at the comical expression that crossed Jonathon's face. He had clearly been anticipating a relaxing smoke while Jacques worked, and he was disgruntled to learn otherwise.

Served him right, Ann snorted. He was all that was helpful and kind back in Charleston but put to the test his actions couldn't seem to fulfill his words. Thank goodness she had taken action on her own and left Charleston when she had. She imagined her journey would only have been made more difficult if she'd had to endure him as a traveling companion the *entire* way.

It wasn't long, and the men had a blazing fire roaring; its warmth already seeping into her bones as she worked. She stopped scrubbing, long enough to brew coffee for Jacques.

He took a sip, "Ah, now see the fire was worth it for this, don't you agree Morgan?"

Jonathon smiled tightly his response.

"Well, I had best relieve Stone from his duties so that he may return while the coffee is still warm. It was delightful as always, Ann, mon amour."

He drained the remaining contents of his cup then walked over to her and took her hand, bringing it to his lips where he brushed his lips gently against the delicate skin.

"We break early in the morning to go our separate ways, so we must say our goodbyes now. I will truly miss your radiant smile. Perhaps we will meet again one day, and you will be the woman to entrap me, as you say."

His sincerity was touching because it was Ann's first witness of such an emotion from the flirtatious Frenchman.

"I will miss you as well." She beamed to him.

"Am I interrupting something?" Grayson's granite like voice emerged with him from the shadows.

"Ah, Stone, I see you quit your post early."

Grayson chaffed the cold from his arms with his rough hands, while he led Dove to the side of the wagon. "Mr. Hodges and Dan Rhydall stepped in for me. Thought I'd better see what trouble you'd gotten yourself into. Figured I'd find you here, drinking all my coffee."

The words spoken gruffly were followed by a small twitch of his lips that Ann and Jacques knew to be a smile.

Jacques grinned unabashedly in return, "And trying to convince the lovely Ann here to wait for me."

"She's a married woman," Jonathon inserted.

"That has never deterred me from a woman before." Jacques winked rakishly.

"Well, as flattered as I am by your attentions," Ann jested with mock derision, "You will just have to find another woman to charm." She reached out and laid her hand on his arm, "I will sincerely miss your friendship, however and I do hope our paths cross again one day. Safe travels to you."

He patted her hand and smiled warmly before she proceeded to the confines of the wagon.

Grayson's terse voice halted her, "Where are you going?"

Without bothering to look his direction she replied in equally clipped tones, "I'm retiring for the evening."

She'd already hung the clothes to dry near the fire.

"You can leave the wash water where it is, I'll see to it in the morning."

She closed the flap behind her when she entered the wagon, dismissing any further discussion.

Jacques raised his brow questioningly to Grayson, silently wondering why the gentle Ann was being selectively curt with Grayson alone. Grayson just scowled and looked away.

"I'll meet up with you in a few hours," Grayson dismissed.

Jacques smiled knowingly and nodded his head before taking his leave.

"That man is an inappropriate companion for Ann." Jonathon seethed.

Grayson wasn't in the mood to discuss anything with Jonathon Morgan.

"You should ride up ahead and take a watch turn with Rhydall and Hodges."

"And leave you here alone with Ann?"

The hard glint in Grayson's eyes stopped any further protesting from him. Jonathon broodingly stomped out his cheroot and paced off in the direction of his horse.

Grayson walked to the wagon and knocked lightly, "Ann. I know you aren't sleeping. It's warm by the fire, why don't you join me?"

She opened the flap slightly and peeped her face out, "Do you now deign the pleasure of my company, sir?" She replied caustically.

Grayson chuckled at the imperious look she held through the opening of the tent, "Yes, something like that. Not that I can recall a time your company has ever been very pleasant."

She rolled her eyes and ascended from the wagon, "If you were any sort of gentleman like Mr. Dubois, you would have assisted me down."

Grayson stiffened at the reference to Jacques. He knew the man was a harmless flirt, but he didn't like the idea of him trying to charm Ann. When he'd ridden onto that scene of Jacques with his lips pressed against her hand, he'd felt an irrational rage consume his body. Somehow, he'd remained calm and restrained from his urge to break his friend's pretty nose.

That Ann compared him to Jacques raised his ire once again.

"It's not easy stepping down in one's night clothes, I'll have you know," Ann dropped from the wagon with an indelicate huff.

"I only desist because I know what a self-sufficient woman you are." He drawled.

Ann came to stand beside him at the fire, her eyebrow raised disapprovingly. Her arms crossed beneath her breasts inadvertently thrusting the ivory mounds up gloriously. The dancing flames of the firelight cast her lovely features aglow and the white of her night gown nearly transparent.

"Well," she interrupted his stunned perusal of her, "Did you bring me out here for a reason or shall I return to bed?"

Why had he requested her to join him? It had been to apologize for his rude behavior earlier, but now it seemed unwise indeed. He left abruptly earlier to avoid any more moments like this and now he dragged her out of the wagon in her night rail where all of her charms were being adequately displayed by the fire.

Perspiration beaded at the back of his neck. She was married. He needed to remember that.

He pulled the stool closer and grabbed his capote from the rear of the wagon to wrap around her. "Sorry, if it doesn't smell the finest, but it will keep you warm."

"It smells like you." She smiled shyly in approval.

He should explain that he had been avoiding her because of his deepening feelings for her. She would understand then, why it was necessary for him to keep his distance.

"I've gathered that you are a trapper. Like Mr. Dubois."

Jacques again. Perhaps his friend had worked his way into Ann's affections after all.

"It must be exciting; all the adventures you must have." She wore a dreamy smile and stretched her legs towards the fire.

"It's lonely."

The admission surprised them both. He'd never thought he felt that way before. He loved the mountains. Over the years, life there had been a sanctuary of a sort.

He cleared his throat uncomfortable with the new feeling of vulnerability that came over him.

"Yes, Luke has imparted to me how happy he is to finally be joining you. It seems both of you were a mite lonely."

Her words were soft, discerning.

"You probably think me a terrible husband and father, leaving my wife and son behind to pursue adventures then."

"I have witnessed what a wonderful father you are over the past couple of weeks. I'm not one to pass judgment on your past that I know nothing about."

"My wife, Vivian-," He paused searching for the right words, "She had an angelic exterior that fooled a lot of people. Including me. I tried very hard for a time, to be all that she desired of a husband. She had been born to society life: I knew that. Still, I thought I could make her happy.

My father started a furniture business before I was born, and it prospered. When my father died, I was only thirteen, but I thought to help my mother take over the business. Only, she passed on less than two years after that. From grief I reckon...

The business was really all I had left. I hadn't the artistic hand my father did when it came to wood working. Luckily, I did have the mind of a businessman, so I sought out men who could work wood with the heart and devotion my father always had.

It became even more lucrative after that and grew very quickly. I had never mingled in the society circles of Philadelphia, but suddenly I had money, so the circle grew to include me.

I was naïve to have believed a woman as dazzling as Vivian O'Malley would be interested in an 'upstart' like me for any other reason than to line her coiffeurs.

She feigned exactly that though. For a while."

"I'm sorry," Ann whispered. "How old were you when you married?"

He scoffed, "A whole eighteen years. Just old enough to convince myself of such a foolish decision."

"May I presume she was as equally young and foolish?"

He nodded, "Only, not foolish for her. She was wise to the ways of her kind, the social elite; she'd been raised in that world.

"Perhaps she cared for you though. At least in the beginning."

"No. She never cared for anyone but herself." The words were spoken bitterly.

Regret and sorrow shadowed his next words, "But I never realized... never could have imagined even Vivian O'Malley incapable of loving her own son."

Wetness glistened over his eyes and he swallowed hard. Ann's soft hand covered his and the loneliness that had consumed him for most of the past ten years dissipated. Images of Ann's smile and kind eyes shining with love for him filled his thoughts as he wondered at the life they could share together. Suddenly he wanted to make her his and hold onto her forever. Only, that was impossible.

Reality shattered the brief hope. Ann was married, or at least she claimed to be. She needed him only to get her to her husband. His teeth ground on the knowledge and he released Ann's hand quickly.

"I have my son, now. It may have been a mistake leaving him alone with his mother in the past, but we have each other now."

And me, Ann wanted to say. She felt bereft when Grayson pushed her hand away, shutting her out once again.

As she should him.

Feelings for him only complicated her mission and her duty to her daughters. Her head knew this well, convincing her heart was another battle; a battle Ann was finding little strength left to fight.

She wanted to tell him about James, about her own foolish past, but what would he think of her? How would he judge her if he knew she had born her children, perhaps out of wedlock, to a man she barely knew?

No. The only way to protect her daughters and ensure her shame never poisoned them was to continue this journey to find James. It mattered not, that her heart wanted to follow a different path entirely.

He sensed her drawing away from him. He'd begged her company thinking he could explain and apologize, but instead had only continued to push her away.

Perhaps he could enjoy the remaining time he had with her, so long as he could let her go when the time came. Was it wrong to want the happiness he felt when he was near her, however fleeting it would be? He needed to make a decision; he couldn't keep pulling her in and pushing her away.

Ann stood with the capote still draped around her, "I think I will return to the wagon, now, and sleep." She turned to go.

"Ann," he halted her, "I-thank you for tonight."

It wasn't much in way of an apology as he'd intended, but he hoped it was a start. She nodded to him and disappeared into the wagon.

Words didn't always come easily to him, especially words of the apologetic variety, but he intended to show her with his actions starting on the morrow.

Chapter 12

Once the decision had been made to enjoy his time with Ann, it felt as if a heavy weight had been lifted from his chest. He no longer had to refrain from her company. He was almost giddy for anticipating their evening talks.

Occasionally he would gently remind himself that she would disappear from his life, sooner rather than later, but that only made him more determined to enjoy the time he did have with her.

It took little more than three days' time to reach Harrodsburg. Grayson maneuvered Jonathon out of camp as often as possible during that time in order to get Ann to himself. He made it a regular habit of returning to camp after the children were asleep and issuing Jonathon orders to assist with the guard shift. Jonathon complained at every encounter, but his grumbling was worth dealing with if it meant more time with Ann.

He'd come to know her so well it was as if she'd always been a part of him. He found himself riding alongside their wagon when he should have been up front with the other men, just to be nearer to her.

One day he circled around, telling himself only to check on her from a distance so as not to dally too long from his duties. Oblivious to his spying antics, he was able to get close to the wagon without her realizing his presence and he heard her singing. To his surprise she was reciting a bawdy soldier's hymn, loudly to the blue skies above.

Only a couple of wagons remained on with them to Harrodsburg and they were well ahead of Ann. After hearing her singing voice, it was little wonder why the other wagons were distanced so greatly ahead of her. He believed her goal on one particular note must have been to achieve an operatic pitch. And she nearly did, causing him to wince involuntarily.

He decided then, that it would be best for the entire countryside if he interrupted her before discovering just how soprano she aspired to be.

"I think I've learned why the mules are so contrary towards you."

Ann shrieked and nearly unseated herself from her perch.

"Grayson! You scared the devil out of me!" She placed her hand to her chest still heaving from her fright.

"Is that what that was? Then I think the world would agree I did us all a favor." He grinned, merciless in his teasing.

Twin pink blooms stained her cheeks in evidence of her mortification, then she laughed, "I suppose I should not have skipped all the lessons my mother relentlessly scheduled for me."

"I'm beginning to question the talents you have assured me you do possess. So far on this journey I have discovered, you unable to drive a team well"-

She raised her brow, "Not fair. I never claimed to have experience driving a team of mules! I stated only that I was an advanced equestrian."

"You are no songstress," He eyed her comically and waited for her to argue that statement.

She snorted, "Again, something I never proclaimed to be. You could have spared your ears if you hadn't sneaked up on me like a weasel."

"You might have heard me if you hadn't been caterwauling the poor mules into a frenzy," he countered with a chuckle.

She responded with a typical roll of her eyes heavenward.

Grayson decided to continue, "Let's see, what else have we found you to be abysmally lacking? Oh yes, the ability to produce edible meals."

He cocked her a teasing grin.

Her cheeks ripened once more to the color of cherries.

"Hmmph. Well, forgive me. I had not realized *professional* cutlery skills would be required when dining from the back of a wagon day in and day out."

She wanted to cross her arms over her chest defensively, Grayson knew, but couldn't for the reins gripped in her hands.

The rain had not continued with them after leaving Hazel Patch, and unfortunately Ann's turn at the fire became unavoidable. Everyone had then been enlightened of her terrible lack of "womanly skills".

Apparently, it *was* possible to burn stew. And she had scorched it.

Grayson couldn't stop laughing, enjoying her indignity. Jonathon tried to remain polite but did suggest she seek advice from a more kitchen experienced woman next time. Luke was nearly as embarrassed for her sake as she was and tried to comfort her with a loving pat to the back; which nearly caused her to burst into tears on the spot.

She wanted desperately to run and take refuge in the wagon, but she remained by the foul-smelling cauldron and continued to serve everyone who dared to stomach her fare. Grayson finished his entire bowl, smiling around each spoonful. She wanted to take the heavy kettle lid to his smirking face.

She still wanted to most days.

But it was his teasing that kept her feet from running in cowardly flight back to the wagon. He helped make light of the entire catastrophe and instead of the women scorning her for her ineptness, they laughed and shared stories of their own first failed attempts.

Just like now as he teased her for her wretched singing ability, relieving her of what would have been a terribly more awkward embarrassment.

"Don't you have anything better to do than to go around insulting ladies?" She bantered, even though she was secretly pleased to have his company.

"Now you're a lady? The way my son retells your stories to the men up front, you've never been ladylike a day in your life."

He smiled teasingly. The fact that Luke had been sharing her slightly embellished stories with the camp men and that Grayson had heard them made her blush something fierce.

"Besides," he continued, "I find my day vastly improved after I drop by and trade insults with you."

"Ha, ha," she mocked dryly, "For some reason, it doesn't feel much like a trade."

There was a stirring noise coming from the wagon behind Ann, where the girls had been sleeping. Kit had awakened from her nap and pulled herself to a standing position using the bottom slat of the bench seat; she was wearing a very proud smile on her face for her efforts. Ann thought it probably matched her own. Both girls had been pulling themselves up more and more. Soon, she knew they would be walking.

Both girls had formed a strong attachment to Luke, but Kit appeared remarkably interested in Grayson. Kit was generally the quiet one and shy of strangers, but Ann observed that when Grayson was around, her eyes lit up and she would reach her hands out to him. Just as she did now.

"She must have heard your voice," Ann accused teasingly.

The poor darling, Ann thought. Her daughter it seemed, took after her mother when it came to giving her heart away to men too charming for their own good.

Ann stopped the team in order to pull Kit to her lap. Driving with the girls strapped to her was impossibly difficult, but they tired of the back of the wagon and needed the break occasionally.

Kit rocked back and forth excitedly, making it difficult for Ann to secure her.

"Is that my Kitten?" Grayson called. Ann rolled her eyes at the endearment.

Grayson knew "Kitten" was far too docile a name for either of her girls, both as wild as their mother. It annoyed Ann when he called her daughters by pet names, and annoying Ann was one of his favorite pastimes.

He saw Kit's chubby hand outstretched towards him. It was the biggest compliment Kit could pay to someone. He knew Livvy to be the more outgoing of the two, when she wanted something, she made sure all present knew. Kit on the other

191

hand didn't demand much, so when she reached her hand out to him in silent request, Grayson, felt his heart skip a little beat.

"Hand her to me for a bit."

Ann tried to hide a small look of surprise when Grayson requested her daughter. It wasn't that Grayson never helped with her daughters; he often helped without asking, always seemingly perceptive to everyone's needs. Just as now.

Ann knew Kit wanted for Grayson to hold her, but Ann would not have asked it of him to take her daughter out of anything other than necessity. Grayson's awareness of her daughter's wishes and his catering to them, caused a loving ache in Ann's chest.

Ann handed her daughter across her lap to Grayson's waiting arms. No happy squeals emitted from her as would have Livvy, but Kit's happiness was present in the ever-growing smile on her face.

"There we go, baby girl," Grayson soothed.

They rode along like that for a time, Kit sitting from the saddle with Grayson, happy to look about her at all the green lined earth and horses, cattle, and wagons stretched before her. Grayson and Ann enjoying their contentment in one another's company on the fine sunny afternoon. Perhaps Grayson was lost in thought as well.

Ann's thoughts circulated furiously in her mind as she tried to rationalize the tender ache that continued to grow for the kind, handsome man riding alongside her. -Who was not her husband OR the father of her children she reminded herself.

It was difficult in moments such as these, to remember that she had already pledged her devotion to another.

Jonathon claimed her marriage to James was null and therefore never took place, But Ann couldn't understand why? Why would James go through such lengths just to compromise her? She had wanted to believe that he had a plan for them, for their future. In the beginning that was all she had desired.

Now, her feelings for James were as nonexistent as her marriage.

She pushed on for the sake of her daughters. Surely, once she found James, he would have, at the very least, an acceptable explanation and be overjoyed she had found him. Perhaps then her feelings for him would return.

Although, looking at Grayson holding her daughter, hearing him tell her in his deep, smooth voice about the lands they were traveling, and her daughter looking on him admiringly, Ann couldn't help but wish her circumstances to be different. If only she had met Grayson first, she sighed. He was an honorable man.

It surprised her to think how differently she viewed love.

She'd set out to find a joyous love like her parents had, but instead she -naively, it would seem- fell in love with a man's story of adventures, and lust-stricken glances for her that made her feel as though she were the center of his world.

If only she had recognized and determined the difference then between love and lust in his eyes. If she hadn't been a little fool.

Was she still playing the fool?

Nancy had intimated so, even suggesting to Ann that she look to another man to complete her family. But what man would want to take on her burdens? And even if that man did exist, Ann thought she would never allow herself to become so attached again. It would cause her nothing but heart ache or worse.

She'd already learned that lesson.

No, it would be best for her and her daughters if she found their *true* father and he legitimized their union and gave his daughters his name. She was certain she would never again have any fond feelings for James; therefore, it would be easy to remain unattached.

She cringed inwardly at the depiction of marriage to James she'd conjured in her mind. It was a far cry from the loving marriage she'd always imagined she'd one day have.

She felt Grayson's eyes upon her, studying her, and her recalcitrant heartbeat sped faster, refusing to obey her wishes to no longer care for any man.

But Grayson was not just any man.

He was a loving, doting father to his son. Always ready to help others. And despite all the hardships he'd endured, that he had shared with her during their nightly talks, there still remained a twinkle in his eye and a devilishly handsome smile on his lips.

Ann couldn't trust her foolish heart, however. She was certain she was just feeling the pangs of lust again.

Perhaps she yearned for the closeness of a man. Although it didn't seem to be any man that could make her feel thusly. And she certainly felt closer to Grayson than she ever had James.

With James, she'd felt the same stirrings in her body, the attraction, the heat. She'd found him fun and freeing in her constraints of living amongst and adhering to the rules of London society. Every moment with him had been a liberating adventure and shadowed by a mysterious magnetism pulled to him from deep within her body.

Her wedding night had enlightened her to exactly what those feelings had been about. After the brief shock of pain, the rest of her wedding night - she supposed she could no longer call it that - had been a wondrous sensation. She'd felt loved and cherished in his arms. It was still difficult to believe the night had only been special for her.

Would lovemaking with Grayson be different than it had with James? Sometimes, when she looked at Grayson and he looked back at her in that way of his, she wondered, if they might share something even more magical.

My, what on earth was the matter with her? When had she become such a slattern? Her body's desires were what got her in this mess in the first place.

She had lived so much the past year since becoming a mother and grown wiser to the world. She now knew her body's desires were not to be catered to. Too easily, her body's physical attraction to a man could lead her heart to believe love existed where only lust did.

She shook her head, admonishing herself for her womanly weaknesses. She was a mother now. She would not allow herself to make the same foolish mistakes as before.

Grayson's voice interrupted her thoughts, "I think I heard Liv waking up. Here take Kit, I'll ride up and send Luke back to help with the girls. We should be to Harrodsburg within an hours' time, before the sun hits the top of the trees. We'll make camp for the night there."

His words seemed unusually indifferent, but he smiled and tipped his hat to her all the same after handing Kit back to her ready lap. She wondered if he somehow knew her inner turmoil.

But was it her lusty thoughts for him or her desire to shut them out that drove him away?

They reached Harrodsburg and set up camp in good time. The camp's evening meal would not be served until night fall, however, as the people decided to take the opportunity to celebrate their journey thus far. They were all inclined to break the tedium of the trail. Harrodsburg afforded them the opportunity to do so, and they were loath to pass it up as it would be the last town they would come across until they reached Louisville; another seventy-five miles away.

Grayson wasn't certain he could keep up the thin barrier of distance he'd erected between himself and Ann. He'd thought he could sustain a controlled amount of closeness to the woman. But it was growing increasingly difficult the more he remained in her company.

He'd felt a terribly tender ache within him while holding her daughter and seeing Ann cast moon eyes at him, (that he was certain she'd not intended for him to see). It made him want to be the man in her life, to have her adoring gaze on him like that always.

And he had not countenanced on becoming so attached to her little cherubs. How was he to let them go their separate way once they reached St. Louis? A pain formed in his chest at the thought and it jarred his fears back to the surface.

He had handed Kit back to Ann as carefully, but quickly as possible in order to put the needed physical distance between them again. He hoped it would serve to provide the emotional barrier he needed to remain in place as well.

Ann found herself more than a little jittery in anticipation of the evening. Most of the travelers' opinion on what a town constituted, differed greatly from Ann's. So when they arrived at Harrodsburg, Ann was surprised at its size.

It had actual roads and shops. Impressive compared to the other so-called towns they had passed through. According to the camp stories passed around all week long in anticipation of their arrival, Harrodsburg was one of the oldest towns in Kentucky.

Ann, of course took that with a grain of salt as she knew what Americans considered to be "old" and what she considered "old" were as different as their envisions of town.

Camped along the river behind Harrodsburg were Indians with their own crafts and wares set up to sell. Ann, as well as the other travelers, were weary and intimidated at the sight of the native people. Ann had only ever seen one nude man in her life; James, and as he had been cloaked in darkness, a man's body was still much of a mystery to her.

The Indians -Shawnee, according to Grayson- were nude, in broad daylight, from the waist up. Their smooth coppery skin taut over their muscled torsos and bald heads except for the tail of hair left growing in the center of their scalps, made for a powerful looking specimen of man.

Grayson assured her they were friendly and just wanted to trade for goods, but the knowledge did not ease Ann's discomfort. Other stories shared over the campfires at night since the beginning of their journey were tales of Indian scalpings and an Indian hunter by the name of Daniel Boone. The people in the company spoke his name in awe and praised his deadly skills. The stories of both sides had sent chills racing down Ann's body.

"I thought, you said the Shawnee were the hostile tribes, the ones Mr. Boone chased out of Kentucky?" Ann asked Grayson, nervously eying the strange new people.

"Yes, but there are differing tribes of Shawnee. That was near fifty years ago any way and not all remained hostile. You have nothing to fear from these men and women, Ann."

Ann smiled to the Shawnee woman in the distance who had nodded to her, but she remained skeptical and kept her distance. She hadn't any money to purchase items or anything to trade with anyway. She needed to save as much as possible and Grayson had stocked them well with provisions.

She walked around the town and explored with her girls close to her, wishing, as she did so often, that her circumstances were different.

She sighed when she saw one of the shops had new readymade dresses. All of her dresses now appeared ragged and discolored from dirt, sweat and sun on this long journey. She had managed to save her one tailored gown from London.

She'd not wear it though until she was well on her way back to England.

The dress in the shop window was not as fine as her London made gown, but it wasn't dowdy. It looked similar to what the other women had been wearing on the trip, with its floral pattern and durable construction. Ann wished she could trade in her old servant's rags for it, but she'd have to make do instead.

Ann made her way back to where the party was camped. Looking around her, she had to admit, so far, the land she'd traveled across had been breathtakingly beautiful. Where land hadn't been cleared away for farming, it was all densely forested, rolling hills, filled with rivers and creeks. She inhaled deeply, finding peace in the bountiful beauty of green before her. Well, excluding the town that sat in the distance behind her.

The wagon company had camped north of the town along the river. Ann preferred the quieter accommodations. Had grown used to it in fact. Not that she'd ever been a stranger to sleeping beneath the stars as she'd done many times during her training delivered by her father. It wasn't the same here, though. The stars, although they seemed to shine brighter, brought no sense of security to her as they had done back home in Somerset.

The stars were just beginning to appear in the blue darkening sky when Grayson and Luke returned to camp. Luke was smiling suspiciously large. Even Grayson was wearing a smug grin, although that could indicate any number of things. The man was ridiculously arrogant at times.

He neared her, and she felt her heart begin its irregular rhythm of somersaults that were becoming irritatingly *regular* whenever he drew near to her.

He stopped beside her and presented her with a paper wrapped bundle.

"What is this?" She asked, surprised.

"It's a gift."

Grayson smiled. The light in his eyes caused her breath to hitch a little bit and join the irritating dance of her heart.

"Open it, open it!" Luke urged her excitedly.

Her eyes met Grayson's speakingly, berating him for the inappropriateness of purchasing her a gift while also ungraciously accepting and untying the string with childish fervor.

"Oh!" She inhaled her breath of surprise and delight. "Grayson, how did you know?"

She held the dress, the same calico dress she'd viewed longingly through the shop window earlier, to the length of her body. She was certain her smile couldn't stretch any bigger.

Grayson's smug smile had returned, extremely pleased with himself for having chosen a gift and correctly predicting how joyously she would receive it.

"It's not complete, though, without these."

The next gift Grayson had not been as certain Ann would like, but Luke had informed him that her boots were wore through in the sole, so he made the purchase anyway.

"But it's already too much. I-"

Grayson gestured with a raise of his palm and cut off her protest.

"You'll need these in order to continue to provide the quality of service you were hired to perform and have so far delivered.

Ann didn't buy that lame explanation for a second, but she was too glad and thankful for the items to protest any further.

"I've never seen boots quite like these."

She marveled at the tall topped, soft, leather footwear in her hands, running the decorative fringe along the backs of them through her fingers.

Then she blurted, "They look like yours!"

A blush stole up her cheeks as she realized it sounded as if she had insulted the gift.

She tried to counter her blunder, "That is to say, they are far lovelier-"

Splendid, now she'd insulted *him*. "I mean they are similarly made as yours, but more feminine appearing..."

Grayson was smiling, enjoying her torture, "Yes. They are called moccasins. Once you grow accustomed to them, you will find they are far more comfortable than any modern shoe crafted by white men."

His sure smile slipped a little into uncertainty, "I wasn't sure if you would find them very fashionable, but they are more durable and will protect your legs from the weeds and brush as well, when walking."

Emotions of gratitude and tenderness welled up inside her. She was thankful for the gifts, but she was even more thankful for the man before her. She reacted instinctively by going up on her tip toes and placing a kiss on his cheek.

"Thank you, this is the most thoughtful gift I've ever received. Thank you."

She let her hand cup Luke's cheek and thanked him as well before hurrying herself and the beautiful gifts to the privacy of their wagon, before the tears glazing her eyes could fall.

Ann waited until after the evening meal was over and putting the girls and Luke to bed, before donning her new gown. She could already hear the men out around the fires, warming up their various instruments.

Mr. Harper had boasted the night past that he could outplay Mr. Peterson on their fiddles and Mr. Lewis had offered to play his harmonica. Ann had heard talk over supper that people from the town were even going to join in!

It was bound to be an exciting night and Ann longed to put her troubles to the back of her mind for this one evening and find peace and joy again for at least the remaining hours of the night. She smoothed any wrinkles from the bodice of her new crisp calico and set out towards the sound of laughter and music in the distance.

Grayson noticed Ann's presence immediately when she joined the crowd of women huddling on the outskirts of where the would-be-musicians were beginning to strike up a collaborated tune. The fiddles sprung the little gathering to life and while the women may well have remained shyly on the sidelines, the men were far too eager to allow them that option. The wide smiles the women presented showed they were just as eager to twirl about and make merry. Husbands swooped in for their wives, young bucks for their beaus, widows, town ladies and gents who'd come for sport were all soon laughing and dancing about to the lively tunes.

Grayson watched as Ann, a sight to behold, not due to the new gown Grayson had purchased for her -although he was pleased to see her wearing it- but because of the pure joy in the smile wreathing her face.

He watched as a young boy who'd been traveling with them, though Grayson couldn't recall the young man having ever had words with Ann before during all of their journey, shyly invite Ann to dance. She accepted gleefully and not allowing the lad to stall for his timidity, led him quickly to the dance circle amongst the others. Ann's unreserved excitement quickly drew the boy from his timorous state and Grayson could hear them both laughing as they came together and then apart around others, following the steps of the dance.

And so, the night carried on, with Grayson being content to hang back as a spectator. Except for when the occasional pushy widow could find him and leave him with no recourse other than to permit a dance. Ann hadn't refused a dance yet, to Grayson's knowledge. And although she had thrilled to every offer and every turn about the makeshift ballroom under the stars, he hadn't witnessed her take a personal interest in any of her partners. No, his Ann was all about the dance: the adventure.

He couldn't help but smile as he watched her. She was in one of the rare moments without a dance partner, but she continued to dance on her own. She spun about, her hair flowing around her and smiling for the breeze on her face. Her skirts twirled around her legs exposing her bared ankles and feet.

She danced away from the group some. Or was it that Grayson would ever see only her, whether his eyes were closed to dream or not?

Ann in her bare-feet dancing in the blue grass swells, with fireflies glittering the hills behind her was the most beautiful sight Grayson had ever seen. She raised her skirts a little higher once she was out of view of the other dancers, and he watched her slender legs step rhythmically amongst the tall grasses. His gaze traveled up her swaying skirts to her face; her lips were bowed with contentment and her eyes closed as if she had found peace on earth in this moment.

He watched her slender neck arch back as she turned her face to the stars above, just breathing in the night. As if this would always be the best life would offer and she was greedy to experience every last moment of it. His breath hitched at the sight of her.

He realized that he was moving towards her as if his body was disconnected from his mind and moving of its own volition. He knew he was losing the battle once more to assert a safe wall between them.

Then out of the corner of his eye, he spied a man's form approaching Ann, and a possessiveness burned through him. Only he should have had the pleasure of seeing his spirited Ann dancing freely beneath the stars. Whoever this intruder was, Grayson had every intention of sending him on his way, even if that meant he had to physically remove him!

Worse, Grayson recognized the form: Jonathon. The man had been eying Ann when she wasn't looking since he met up with them in Cumberland. Something wasn't right with their story. It didn't make sense for Jonathon to so adamantly want to escort Ann clear across the country if she was indeed married. Grayson knew there was nothing fraternal in the way Jonathon looked at Ann, for all she was supposedly his own cousin in law.

Ann, though, seemed oblivious to the man's mooning. Perhaps it was only obvious to Grayson because he was similarly struck by Ann's magnetism. He should feel sorry for the dandy. But on all counts, Grayson just couldn't bring himself to feel that charitable. Not when it came to Ann. She was *his*.

The breeze felt deliciously welcome upon Ann's face after the swelteringly humid days of travel. The rain had mercifully brought with it cooling temperatures this eve and it couldn't have been more felicitously timed for the cheery celebration.

Amusingly, Ann had not enjoyed the stuffy ballrooms of her past but had enjoyed herself immensely at this rustic imitation of one. Then again, Ann had never been opposed to the dancing, only to the atmosphere created by the forced company.

Tonight's adventure had proved to uplift her spirits once more and freshen her resolve. She was just basking in that newfound sense of peace when her solitude became interrupted, by Jonathon of all people. The one man sure to send her memories and worries crashing back upon her just by his resemblance to the man responsible for her ruination.

"Hello, Jonathon." She tried to maintain a polite facade.

He was not to blame for her situation, and in fact a better person than she would even say he deserved her expressed gratitude.

Jonathon was looking shyly to his boots, for all he had approached her. He began to stammer something of a greeting when an overbearing presence divided them.

Ann knew, without seeing, exactly who belonged to the dominating force approaching them. *Grayson.*

"Jonathon. How have you been this evening?"

Grayson cut in, and as usual what would have been voiced pleasantries coming from any proper gentleman, sounded like nothing more than a curtly delivered insult, coming from this man's insensitive tongue.

Ann shook her head and rolled her eyes from where she stood sheltered behind him. Indeed, where had the man even materialized from?

Jonathon looked to Grayson with surprise. No doubt he was wondering the same question.

"I admit, I haven't seen you present for most of the evening?" Grayson continued, in his dry way that intimated he had no interest in his own inquiries.

Jonathon seemed to have found his tongue, "Yes, well, I have been sightseeing about the town."

He cleared his throat for punctuation and straightened his dressy collared shirt where it buttoned at the throat.

"A rather intensive exploration of such a small town."

Grayson commented with accusation in his voice. Although for the life of her, Ann could not understand why or what Grayson was finding fault with Jonathon's lack of presence at the party this evening. She knew very well Grayson found the man as irritating as she did.

Goodness, she was a terrible person! She just couldn't seem to find it within her to be gracious to her "would be rescuer".

The men eyed one another with an unspoken understanding, though Ann was unbeknownst to know what it could be.

Grayson spoke again, "Well, you should not miss out on the camp's festivities. It's certain not to happen again anytime soon."

Ann had pushed her way around Grayson to stand next to him. To her surprise, Jonathon gave a disgruntled nod in compliance to what they both knew to be an order Grayson issued.

"Good evening, Ann." Jonathon addressed her, before turning his back to them and preceding back to the party, delivering his own small cut to Grayson. She and Grayson watched him fade into the night before turning to one another.

Ann had thought to berate Grayson on his poor manners, but he beat her quick tongue this time.

"You couldn't possibly be more beautiful."

The words had been utterly unexpected, so sincerely given, and most unlike Grayson, that Ann momentarily lost her ability to speak at all.

"I- Thank you." She responded lamely, still addled by Grayson's sudden change in manner.

And what right did he have? He'd been wonderful to her the past week of travel. She'd thought a connection had formed between them. Definitely an electric undercurrent had been building and she was sure it hadn't been one sided. As inappropriate as it was, she had come to take great pleasure in his company. He had begun filling her thoughts and dreams and perhaps even her heart.

Then for no reason at all that she could discern, he had closed up and ignored her all afternoon. Shutting her out once more. Then he'd shown up and delivered her the most thoughtful gift only to disappear again for the remainder of the evening.

She'd tried all night not to appear to be desperately searching for him amongst the crowd. She'd told herself she didn't want to dance with him, that she'd have a splendid time without his company. And she had. But there had been a steady ache she'd had to keep buried, for want to share the special night with him.

And now here he was again, complimenting her and looking to her as if she was something special to him. As if she meant more to him than a business partner on this trip. As if he felt for her what she'd been trying to deny that she'd begun feeling for him...

Well! He could shove off. She wasn't foolish enough to accept his closeness, knowing he would only pull away again once she began to fall. One of these times she might fall so hard her heart would break. She'd already endured heartbreak and abandonment, thank you very much. She'd no desire to experience it again.

Back to her senses, Ann broke the moment, "Well, thank you for the compliment. Now I must be back to the party. A woman's reputation you know...?" She trailed off sarcastically, using his most revered argument against him.

Then she added out of pure contrariness, "I believe Jonathon was seeking me out for a dance. I think I shall find him and accept his request, after all it wouldn't do to be impolite to my dear cousin in law."

Grayson's temper piqued. He'd made himself vulnerable to her, and she'd stamped over him as if nothing out of the ordinary had taken place.

She thought to saunter off and toss threats over her shoulder. Oh, that was just like his Ann, cantankerous bit of baggage that she was. Well, he wouldn't let her ruin what he had finally absolved to do. She'd not be dancing with anyone else again this night, but him.

He grabbed for her hand and ceased her defiant departure.

"I think not."

Then his determined steps outpaced her, and he was leading her back to the group, "If you want to dance. You'll be dancing with me."

"*I* think not."

Ann dug in her heels so that he would have to drag her if he wanted to get her back to the party.

Grayson wasn't proud of his next words, but he knew it would be the only sway he had in getting her to agree to dance with him.

"You owe me a dance." He clipped, then clarified, "For the dress."

Ann looked to him, her mind thinking over his words, he could tell. By the petulant expression upon her face, he thought She looked as if she may still deny him. Probably show him the acidic end of her tongue he was all too familiar with as she refused him, then follow that refusal up with a kick to the shins.

He certainly wouldn't put it past the saucy minx. He began to feel that threatening Ann with blackmail had been an abysmal idea and started to prepare for his rejection, when instead, she nodded curtly and slipped her arm into his.

The motion surprised him, and so did the shock of heat that spread all through his body at her sudden nearness. He was assured the magic was only felt by him though, when she barbed, "Take me to dance then, you brute."

As he and Ann neared the dancing party, many of which had already imbibed more than they ought to have had and were becoming more boisterous by the second, Grayson spied Jonathon sulking by a makeshift table intended to serve as the beverage station.

Grayson did not mistake the man's glare for another either, when he spotted Ann on his arm. Grayson smiled wolfishly, pleased that he was finally taking Ann into *his* arms this evening after having watched so many others be privileged with the opportunity.

He had the girl, now all he had to do was put her back into the fun-loving mood she'd been in before he acquired her. It looked as if that were going to be a challenge as Ann eyed him daringly.

"Shall we?" He bowed arrogantly but did not allow for her to respond with what was sure to be a sass laden reply. Instead he took her hand to his chest then twirled away with her into the crowd of dancers.

"Don't you step on my toes, Mountain Man."

She wasn't done throwing dirt it would seem.

"Where are your new boots? Not good enough for the party?"

He knew his way around a shovel.

He'd thought himself clever, but he regretted the words when she appeared hurt and offended.

"No, they're lovely. I was wearing them, but some of the gentlemen were accidentally stepping on my toes during the dances and scuffing them. So I slipped back to the wagon and put them away."

Well now he felt like a cad. Still- "You worried for the condition of the boots over your toes?"

Leave it to Grayson to make her feel like a ninny. She'd been ever a competent woman before meeting him.

"Yes, you devil, I didn't want to listen to another scolding from you."

Grayson laughed at Ann's waspish tone, which elicited a smile from her.

"There it is." Grayson teased in regard to her smile. "I thought perhaps I'd broken it."

"Well, you're not particularly funny."

"Is that so?" He raised his brows in mock affront.

"Not to mention, your behavior in general tends to be rather boorish."

She was having fun insulting him.

"The stuffy English Lady in you is making her appearance again, I'm afraid."

"No one knows better how to take a rapscallion to task than a proper blue-blooded English woman," Ann countered proudly; recalling her mother cleverly winning arguments against her father.

"Blue-blooded," Grayson questioned, as if mulling the thought around in his mind for a time. "I'd have thought you too fiery for that."

"I've been told the blue flames burn the hottest."

Her eyes narrowed audaciously, and Grayson thought he may have fallen into and very well be lost to her flame already.

The heated spell was broken when their dance became interrupted by the loud squawking of an incensed guinea hen. The large hen dashed through the crowd with its wings spread, flapping in riled indignant fashion, followed by a burly man by the name of Smith who'd been traveling with them from Cumberland. His wife chased behind him shouting for him to catch the wayward bird. Both husband and wife seemed a bit tipsy chasing after the bird causing quite the spectacle.

When Smith finally got close enough to catch the bird, it turned around and charged him. And so the chase reversed, and the bird chased the man and his wife back through the crowd, eliciting all kinds of laughs and guffaws. The man appeared to finally have caught the enraged hen and was carrying it firmly under his arm, his wife following and berating him for bringing the silly creatures along in the first place.

Pink, whether from over imbibing or from embarrassment, spread across the bridge of his nose.

It turned cherry red though, when someone from the crowd yelled, "Aint no doubt, Smith be hen pecked for sure!"

That sent everyone into uproarious laughter. Even the fiddlers had a difficult time keeping with the tune. Ann and Grayson gave in to their own fits of laughter, unable to escape the contagious mirthful spirit.

She knew not if Grayson's intentions had been to dance them away from the group or if it had happened purely by coincidence. All she knew was one moment they had been breathless with laughter surrounded by frivolous celebrators and now they were isolated, his hands on her hips and she was breathless for an entirely different reason.

Grayson had not intended to act upon his wish to secret Ann away into the night, but apparently his body was wont to disobey him. He'd been watching her all night, beautiful in the firelight, and dancing with all the other men in the company. Of course, all the men had been dancing with all the women, and most of the men and women married, but it had not quelled his growing jealousy and urge to have Ann for himself. The idea of her dancing with the swain Jonathon, whether she knew him to be sweet on her or not, had broken his final restraint.

Now they were alone behind the abandoned wagons. The desire to touch her was too strong and Grayson relented to the pull. His hands a light touch to her waist while dancing, now firmly drew her close. Pressing himself against her heat, his whiskered cheek grazing her neck as his lips found her sensitive pulse therein.

Ann inhaled a sharp take of breath, for the unexpected pleasure of it. Her eyes closed, lips parted with surprise.

Grayson's large hands traveled up the length of her back pulling her closer, his mouth covered hers and she welcomed his plundering of her with teeth and tongue. One of his hands remained at her back holding her to him, while his other flattened down her chest, thumbing her taut nipple through her new calico print fabric.

Ann's arms tightened their hold around Grayson's neck. Her legs seemed to turn to jelly beneath her as the v between them pulsated with need.

Her blood heated and thrummed throughout her body, coming to life beneath Grayson's touch. His need for her as apparent as hers for him. The womanly core of her ached for him to be inside her. She arched against him, moaning into his kisses.

Both of them too intent on taking their pleasure to take care of their surroundings. Beyond them the company still danced to the fiddlers' tune, but it seemed too far off for them to care. They were where both of them could take freely from the other and give to one another what they both so desired.

His hungry mouth broke from hers for breath and found her neck again. Ann exposed the delicate curve, offering it to him freely. Her body hummed, aching for the need of him within her and she pressed that most sensitive part to him where man and woman have joined together since the beginning of time. She could feel the hard length of him through her petticoat and wanted to rip her skirts away. To be skin to skin with this man before her.

They had not been transported to another world, however. And their fantasy land faded with the strains of the fiddle, bringing back with it the stinging reality of where they were and more importantly, who they were.

Ann spoke first, halting Grayson's ravishing kisses along her neck, with a powerful will she didn't know she had.

"It sounds as if the party has come to its end."

Her breathy words signified that so had ended she and Grayson's private interlude.

Grayson's breath was still quick and heavy, struggling to resume its normal pace. His eyes, glazed over with unspent passion, found Ann's searchingly. He wasn't ready for this to end. His hand reached for her loose wavy tendrils of hair and smoothed them away from her flushed cheek. Ann pressed her cheek into the firm welcoming touch of his palm, savoring its comfort.

He reached for her hand and pulled it to his mouth where her fingers were met with the gentle pressure of his lips, before he released her and backed away.

His blue-gray eyes remained locked with hers in unspoken promise that they would resume this particular meeting another time. And without a word, turned away into the night.

He left Ann near the wagons giving her the time she needed to compose herself while he made his presence known to the group, therefore negating any suspicions that may have arisen from their joint disappearances and thusly preserving her reputation, such as it was.

Grayson didn't return to the wagon that night. Jonathon slept below as usual and she and the kids huddled together inside. On the nights Grayson was not on scheduled watch, he slept below the shelter of the wagon with Jonathon. Luke tended to join him on those nights preferring to be included in the men's group.

Ann found she couldn't sleep. Too many emotions were roiling within her. What was transpiring between her and Grayson? It seemed to be this game of hot and cold and she could not afford any more games. Past lessons told her these games were dangerous and she wouldn't win.

She'd been drawn to the flame that was James' wild spirit - a spirit similar to her own- and been burned.

But it was different with Grayson, for it was his *steady* spirit that drew her. It wasn't just the security she felt in his presence, either. She knew him well enough by now to know that when Grayson Stone chose to love someone, he loved with everything he had.

But could he ever choose to love her?

Chapter 13

The seventy-five miles to Louisville met full of hardships.

In the days leaving Harrodsburg, Mr. And Mrs. Peterson became severely ill. Fear spread quickly through the wagons that it was dysentery or cholera. The violent retching could be heard throughout the nights when camped and even during the day on the trail until their wagon continued to fall further and further behind.

It was discussed separately by the men and women of the company; however, it was universally agreed upon, that no one was brave enough or foolish enough to try to help the Peterson's. Grayson had forbidden Ann to go near the wagon until he could be certain they had not been afflicted with something contagious. And although Ann's heart broke for the middle-aged couple, she didn't dare risk bringing any contagion back to her wagon.

Grayson ensured water and food provisions were dropped off to the couple every day. By the third day, Mrs. Peterson had succumbed to the illness, leaving Mr. Peterson in his grief to fight the sickness alone.

It was that time, Grayson could no longer distance himself from the sickness. It was his moral obligation to assist the yet ill Mr. Peterson with digging a grave for his wife. After that duty had been accomplished, Grayson noticed the Peterson's milk cow trembling where it stood tied to the wagon.

After closer inspection he discovered the animal to be sick as well. That's when he knew exactly what had caused Mr. And Mrs. Peterson to become sick. He informed Mr. Peterson and helped move his wagon back within the group that evening with the other wagons.

When the other travelers saw Grayson leading the Peterson's wagon into view, many began squawking their protests. Ann trusted Grayson and knew he would not endanger the rest of the party, but she wondered what was happening as well.

"Just what do you think you're doing bringing that sickness to the rest of us!" The burly Mr. Smith shouted the group's accusations to Grayson as he approached.

Grayson remained calm and rode stoically past the indignant Mr. Smith and the rest of them. Mr. Peterson rode atop his buckboard, appearing weak, but relieved for Grayson's assistance. Grayson turned his wagon around and unhitched his oxen, before addressing the angry and fearful onlookers.

"The Peterson's illness was theirs alone. You can rest assured; it will not spread to any of us."

"How can you know that for certain?" Accused Mrs. Harper.

"It was White Snakeroot." Grayson announced to the gathered protesters.

"The Peterson's milk cow must have eaten some. It is poisonous to the animal. It also contaminates the animal's meat and poisons the milk. It is deadly in most cases and Mrs. Peterson is no longer with us as a result. I put down the cow back yonder as it was clearly suffering."

"How do you know the cow was poisoned by a plant and not some other sickness?" Mrs. Harper whined her fears again.

"I know for certain, because I saw the cow myself. Its breath was putrid, and its body was weak with tremors. There isn't a doubt in my mind as to what caused the sickness. Those are common signs of snakeroot poisoning. The animal took longer to show its sickness, otherwise I would have realized this sooner."

That seemed to satisfy the groups' concern. Mr. Peterson sat hunched, his face gaunt and form bony from days of being unable to keep any food down. Grayson saw where Ann's pitied gaze led.

"Mr. Peterson will need our assistance if he is to survive this. I will expect the single men accompanying wagons to assign themselves to the chore of driving Mr. Peterson's wagon until he has recuperated."

Grayson nodded firmly and assuredly to Mr. Peterson who was obviously relieved and grateful for Grayson's leadership. Everyone else nodded their heads in consent, more eager to assist the sickened man now that they were sure it would not spread to them.

The only other milk cow in the group belonged to the Ackermann's, a German family traveling with them. Grayson assessed their cow before turning in for the night. Later that evening, Grayson explained to Ann, Luke, and Jonathon what white snakeroot was and how to identify it.

Animals generally did not eat it, so long as other forage was obtainable. Either someone had unwittingly hand fed some to the Peterson's cow, or the animal had accidentally eaten some on its own. It had been a fatal accident.

It seemed morbid to think anything positive could have stemmed from the Peterson's tragic circumstances, so Ann tried not to think it, but due to Jonathon's "bachelor status accompanying a wagon" he was often assigned to drive Abe Peterson's wagon. He had been terribly put out by the chore of course. Ann couldn't help but roll her eyes for thinking of Jonathon's uncharitable response to being told he would be trading shifts with two other young men. She should probably have taken pity on him, for the task of driving oxen had not come naturally to the man. But Ann couldn't help but be glad not to have him underfoot so often.

She blushed thinking about other reasons she was glad his presence had gone unmissed. Grayson managed to alter his leading of the wagons rotation so that he could be nearer to Ann and the children when Jonathon was otherwise detained. And Luke, being the adventurous young boy that he was, could be counted upon to be riding near the front of the trail most of the time as well; which meant, Grayson and Ann had plenty of stolen moments alone with one another as well as stolen kisses.

She sighed blissfully thinking of the many times he would surprise her by coming up behind her while she was hanging laundry or bent over the cook fire and wrap his hands around her waist and bury his face to the side of her neck and kiss her shoulder. Sometimes his fingers would graze the back of her neck as he moved dampened tendrils of her hair from her flushed skin and press his lips to the sensitive nape of her neck. It was lucky she didn't swoon into his arms when he did those things.

After her initial pleasure, she'd always immediately look about to ensure no one had witnessed their brazen antics. She needn't though, Grayson was ever protective of her and her daughters.

She'd chosen to no longer think of James and his role in her life while she was with Grayson. She knew she should feel a horrid trollop, but she just couldn't bring herself to care overmuch. James had falsely, deceptively even, married her while he was married to another woman. Then he left with the other woman and moved halfway across the country after promising Ann they would build a life together. She had a difficult time considering her regard for James after all the heart ache he'd caused her. She was set out after him and would do right by her daughters even though it would mean sacrificing her own happiness.

But she had these moments. She had these few weeks with Grayson to treasure and cherish. And she hoped that would be enough to get her through the remaining years of her life.

Just thinking about life without Grayson by her side made her want to be near him in the moments remaining. She vowed she would love him with all of the passion and power within her during the short time she had left with him.

Before they made it to Louisville, however, a storm hit, and it left behind in its wake a tumultuous upheaval on the land as well as her heart. A twister, the likes of which Ann had never seen before, ripped through their camp on the seventh evening, unexpectedly. It came about too rapidly for the group to prepare. They had all been scattered about tending to their mundane routines of the evening when it struck.

Its furious winds decimated the land it powered across on its short path to them. The terror in Ann's heart still thrummed to the beat of the storm's electricity.

Thankfully she'd been tending to chores with the girls strapped to her in their pack and Grayson and Luke had been in camp with them. She'd been frozen with fear, powerless to move as her eyes watched the funnel swallow the land before her. Grayson yelled and pulled them all to a shallow dip in the land and ordered them all to lay flat. His quick thinking would have been the only thing that saved their lives, if the raging, twisting, funnel had not veered in the last seconds, so that only the outer winds and gusts inflicted damage on their little camp.

After the storm had passed, and it was safe to emerge from the varying hiding locations everyone had rushed to, it was discovered the group had been met with yet more tragedy.

Poor, young, virile, Mr. Smith while sheltering his wife beneath their wagon, was hit with splintered wood. A large shaft that had been shorn off by the ravaging winds had been forced through his body piercing his lung. According to the shock and grief-stricken young Emmaline Smith, her husband's last words had been for her, tender and loving and filled with regrets that they would not be able to conquer the world they'd set out for together. Ann's heart clenched and ached as she ran to scoop Emmaline into her arms before she crumpled to the sodden earth.

Grayson and the other men worked long into the night hours to bury Mr. Smith. The Smith's wagon had been to the very outside of the camp and had sustained the most damage, leaving it in irreparable ruins and their belongings strewn about in the flattened grasses around them. Mr. Peterson had graciously offered the use of his wagon, and Ann along with Mrs. Harper, Mrs. Ackermann and Ackermann's oldest daughter, made quick work of preparing a makeshift bed for Emmaline in the back of it.

The woman lay listlessly in it, staring off unresponsively into the shadows of supplies around her. Ann thought, it looked as if Emmaline's soul may have died and been buried with that of her husband's body.

Ann shivered. So many trials one must endure in this country just to survive it. She would be happy once this arduous journey was at its end. Ann felt more than ready to hang adventure and settle down somewhere safe with her girls.

Funny, how little more than a year past, she had been thrilled for a life of adventure. She'd embarked on one, somewhat fearfully, but also filled vigorously with excitement, for her new future. She just hadn't planned on so many things going wrong. She had not truly thought she'd been abandoned when she had set out to retrieve her "husband". And her decisions seemed to continuously be leading her into narrower rocky walled confines. She could only hope persistence would see her through to the other side.

The pain witnessed from Emmaline reminded Ann of the heart break she'd vowed to avoid. It was clear, that when real love was involved, more than just your heart could break. Emmaline had appeared empty inside after the death of her husband, like her very soul had broken. Ann couldn't allow her love for Grayson reach such a degree. She did not think she could endure the kind of pain she was witnessing of Emmaline's suffering. Her heart had already been battered. She was certain it could not take another beating.

Two days of travel after the storm Grayson had had enough of Ann's distance. He knew the tragedy that had occurred for the young couple traveling with them had affected her hard, but he couldn't take another day of mundane conversation with her, nor looking upon her while she was obviously distressed and grieving. He thought she was grieving for the young couple, but perhaps she was withholding emotions over something else entirely. Whatever it was he needed to know. He wanted to comfort her.

He waited until it was Jonathon's shift to assist the, now Peterson and Smith, wagon. Abe Peterson was well on the mend now, and no longer truly required assistance, but Grayson made sure to soak one more day out of it in order to wrangle another private moment with Ann. He knew the girls were asleep and Luke should have been attempting to sleep in the wagon with them as well.

Ann had just returned from refilling the water supply from the stream they were camped near when he decided to approach her. In attempt to be patient for the right words to come to him, he instead met her in silence and assisted her with pouring the pails of water into the side barrels. Neither of them said anything to one another and for all the night around them remaining still and quiet, there was a deafening roar in his ears as his heart raced just from being nearer to her.

He had intended to speak delicately about their circumstances, not demand explanations. He'd intended to be gentle with her, knowing she was hurting. He'd intended to bring back her smile and with it, their short lived interim of unreserved pleasure between them.

But his body did not agree with his mind's plan and all of his intentions deserted him.

Her bodice and skirts were damp from water sloshing out of the buckets she'd carried and clung to the feminine curves of her body enticingly. She shoved some of the loose sweat dampened hair out of her flushed face. Were her cheeks pinkened due to the exertion of carrying the water or from his nearness. She was irritated he knew, for him to be viewing her in such a disheveled state, and he found her adorable for it.

Her amber eyes flashed with peevish indignation when she realized he found her state delectable rather than the mess she believed herself to be. She tried to ignore him and continue to see to tasks. But they'd shared enough passionate embraces over the past week for him to know that she was just as affected by him as he was by her.

He needed their closeness again and he thought perhaps she needed it too.

Words no longer seemed necessary. He reached for her wrist and spun her easily around to face him, her back to the wagon boards. Everyone else was busy tending to their own needs within their wagons, so Grayson needn't worry they would be interrupted, but they did need to continue the quietude so near as they were to the children. He knew a good way to keep Ann quiet too, he smiled as he brought his mouth to hers.

His body responded like a starving man. Two days had been too long. He reached his hands up to shake the remaining pins from her characteristically disarrayed chignon that hung loosely at the base of her neck, allowing the voluminous sun caramelized mane of hers to fall freely to the middle of her back. He brought his hands up in her soft hair knotting his hands in it as he deepened his kiss.

She returned his kisses with equal fervor, standing on the tips of her toes to meet his mouth and match his force. She grabbed the lapels of his shirt to draw him closer.

This. This was what they both needed, to release the emotions they'd been holding back over the past days.

Grayson pressed himself to her against the sturdy boards behind them, sinking into her softness, while his hands undid the tiny annoying buttons up the length of her chest. Once they were unlooped, he slid his hand under the white ruffled fabric beneath until his palm cupped one of her soft rounded mounds. He smiled as she moaned against his lips.

He broke his lips away from hers then to trail hungry kisses along her neck and then down towards the creamy bounty of flesh he cupped towards his mouth with his hand. He felt both of her hands move to his scalp where she raked her fingers and tugged at his thick dark hair, sending sensations of pleasure throughout his body. Tonight, he would make her his.

He surely would have if Ann hadn't stiffened under his touch; if she hadn't ceased him with the tremulous whisper of his name.

"Grayson."

His name along with all her uncertainties whispered off her lips into the night air.

His kisses stopped when he heard his name, but his breathing continued rapid and harsh in his struggle to regain control.

"Grayson. We can't do this anymore."

He pulled away, stunned. Her words pained him, but he was certain he knew what troubled her. He searched her eyes intently, while his fingers trailed along her cheek allowing his palm to rest near the base of her jaw where it joined her neck. His thumb continued to delicately stroke her soft skin there as he looked to her.

"I no longer care if you're married." He spoke sternly.

He cared. She knew he cared. He wasn't the sort of man not too.

She swallowed, "But I do."

"You don't love him." Conviction steeled his voice.

Ann looked down. "You're right."

Then more quietly, as she spoke for the first time a truth, that she'd only just realized she felt, "I hate him."

Grayson pulled back as if surprised to hear her make such a vehement statement.

His eyes sparkled though, "Divorce him. Marry me."

Her features took on that of surprise. Nearly as surprised as Grayson felt. He hadn't planned to ask for marriage, but it had slipped out.

A sad smile formed at the corners of her mouth. "I can't."

The light disappeared from Grayson's eyes. She refused his offer. To be fair, she was still married to another. Still, it hurt.

"You can. You just don't want to."

"I owe it to my daughters to try to make a life with the man who is their father."

"Damn it, Ann!"

Grayson, whispered harshly, wanting to yell, but knowing it could wake the children or the others in the group.

"I wish you would tell me what is actually going on. What's your story? I can't save you, if I don't know what it is to save you from!"

This cooled Ann's ardor more effectively than anything else could have. She pushed away from the wagon and Grayson, then turned to face him, anger flashing in her eyes.

"Well, Mountain Man, I don't need anyone to 'save me'. I can take care of myself. My story is just that: mine. And that's all you really need to know."

The following morning was soaked in a heavy, dreary, mist; matching the mood of the entire group.

The men as well as Luke and a couple older adolescent boys went off in search of one of the Harper's horses that had run off in the storm. In the aftermath that was the death of Mr. Smith, the Harpers had not realized the horse had gone missing until it was too dark to search. They were forced to wait for morning, and the morning hadn't been very kind; covering everything in a gray cloud of mist. The animal would be difficult to find and as they were so close to Louisville, the rest of the teams were eager to be on the road.

Ann and a few others had tried to persuade Emmaline to eat and take water, but she refused both. She requested, instead, to be left in peace. Abe Petersen was agreeable to allowing her to stay where she was in his wagon and felt he was strong enough once more to drive himself. Jonathon would be accompanying Ann's wagon more frequently again, since his services were no longer needed elsewhere.

Well, good. It would deter Grayson from coming around!

To think Ann had thought Grayson had cared for her, when really, he only found her weak and in need of rescuing. Blast the man's honor bound, character anyway! Ann shook the rag she'd been using to wipe the dew from the bench seat with a forceful snap! All the better. She had a job to do, a duty to her daughters. She needed to hold onto this anger. It would buoy her and see her through until she completed her mission.

"Pa says it's time to load up." Luke's voice interrupted her angry, internal tirade and gave her a fright.

"Goodness, Luke! You sneaked up on me!"

He laughed, jovially, "You did jump mighty high!"

Luke was definitely a complication in Ann's plan to remain distant from Grayson. She and Luke had grown very close. She loved him dearly, as a mother to a son. Perhaps she could give up Grayson, but how would she ever walk away from this little boy who'd come to steal so much of her heart? She couldn't imagine a future without him in it. Her breath hitched painfully, and tears burned her eyes at the thought of it.

"Ann?" Luke climbed off his horse quickly and came to her, concern shone in his green eyes.

"Are you okay? Did you get hurt? Are you sick?"

He fired off questions in his worried state over her, which only made her heart ache more, because he was such a sweet, gentle, and kind boy and she was going to miss him so much.

Ann swallowed the painful knot of tears and attempted a reassuring smile. She nodded her head to delay having to speak for fear her words would come out choked. She lovingly brushed his overly long bangs from his eyes-for his hair was ever growing, and put her hand to his cheek, comfortingly.

"I'm fine, I promise."

"I'll bet you're afraid to ride the steamer, aren't you?" Luke believing he had uncovered the cause for Ann's despair, declared.

He patted her hand, "I'll admit, I'm a little afraid myself."

Ann happy for a topic that would stymie her disconsolate thoughts, replied, "Have you never been aboard a boat?"

They naturally took up hands and walked with one another, Luke trailing his gelding behind, towards the back of the wagon.

"This isn't just any boat!" Luke exclaimed with equal amounts of awe for the boat and disbelief Ann didn't seem to understand.

"Well, it will take much to impress me. Don't forget, I sailed all the way across the Atlantic on a clipper."

She winked conspiratorially over her boastful tone.

Luke looked to her as if he pitied her for her ignorance, then took a breath to add, "I heard Mr. Harper and Mr. Lewis say Steamers were right deadly. And they weren't too happy they would have to ride one."

"Deadly?" Ann said, surprised and now a little fearful herself. Still, she tried to disabuse Luke of the notion that he need be afraid. "Well, Luke, many things can be termed deadly. Riding horse for instance can be met with accidents that result in death. Do not let such talk scare you, my sweet."

He shook his head in frustration, "Karl Ackermann said he heard his pa tell that these boats are run by great big boilers and they explode real easy like. He said hundreds of people have died on them!"

Ann stopped, uncertainty now weighing down her steps. Subconsciously, she raised her thumb to her mouth to nibble the side wall around the nail nervously in thought. Could the steamboat pose that great a risk? She couldn't imagine Grayson leading them into danger... Luke was still chatting away oblivious to Ann's consternation.

"...And he said that it used to take a whole month to get to St. Louis! But now it only takes two days! That's why everyone keeps using 'em even though they might explode!"

Gracious! The men need to pay attention to whose ears were listening in when they speak of such things! Although she had to admit, Luke sounded more thrilled than truly fearful. Instead she was the one frightened.

Luke must have finally sensed her fretful state, "Don't worry, I'll protect you."

He looked to her earnestly, engendering a flow of maternal warmth throughout her heart for his sweetness.

She smiled to him lovingly, "Thank you my dear. I shall not worry then, so long as you stay at my side while we're aboard the boat."

His pleased smile for having lessened her fears slipped a little.

"Well If I need to explore the boat, I'll make sure Pa is there to look out for you when I'm not."

He patted her hand reassuringly.

Ann had to keep from emitting a sardonic laugh at Luke's last statement. She'd not bruise the child though, over her private tiff with his father. He was not aware of it and Ann thought that for the best.

"Well, thank you my knight in shining armor," She drolled in good humor, "Not even to the boat yet, and already you're passing the bucket of taking care of me to someone else."

They shared a laugh over her teasing, before she sent him on to play.

She couldn't disregard Luke's words. The fear had crept in and made its home inside her mind. A pity she was no longer speaking to Grayson, she was certain he could have alleviated her of her worries.

It didn't much matter anyway, as he never, not once, sought her out the entire duration it took them to reach Louisville. Apparently, they were communicating solely through Luke and Jonathon. She had hoped he would have ridden back to check on her and the girls at least once. She'd been waiting for a spiteful opportunity to snub him, after all. Instead, he'd kept his distance.

And she hoped he continued to do so, she harrumphed.

Luke had been ordered by his father to ride in the wagon as they neared Louisville. Ann wasn't sure if it was to keep him safe and out of trouble or to help with her and the girls. Either way she was grateful for Luke's nearness.

The town was far grander than she'd been expecting. It was bustling with people everywhere. She couldn't even see the Ohio River they would be booking passage on, for all the buildings in way of the view! She would have worried over Luke knowing he could easily be separated and left navigating through these busy streets alone.

The excitement of such a large city spread through the group and even Ann was touched by its electric fervor. She was so caught up in the excitement, in fact, that she forgot she was no longer speaking to Grayson when he finally appeared.

"Grayson!" She smiled gleefully as she steered the wagon down the street following those ahead of her to their destination. "Look at this place." Her eyes glittered.

Grayson had been prepared for an obstinate Ann, but instead she illuminated the world around her with her smile and flashing eyes. Her zest was contagious. Luke was crying out and pointing at buildings too. The pair of them were acting as if they'd never witnessed civilization before, when Luke had been raised in Philadelphia - a far larger city- and Ann had formerly resided in London. He couldn't help but smile in return for the silliness they displayed. And when Ann looked at him that way, he couldn't help but be pulled in. Her love for life and adventure exuded out of her like a bright shining sun. Her wondrous smile was like an invitation; inviting him in to share her world. Looking into her sparkling honey hued eyes, he could almost forget he was angry with her.

"We won't have time to explore, unfortunately. We have to get right to the Lumber Yard to sell off this wagon and try to trade off or sell any remaining supplies we won't be needing."

"Oh, but I heard there is a theatre here." She looked pleadingly to Grayson.

Would that he could grant her every desire. But apparently that was not to be his pleasure. She had made it perfectly clear she was reserving that particular job for another man. Grayson was only good enough for a few stolen kisses along the way of delivering her to said other man. His stomach soured at the turn of his thoughts and his next words reflected the churlishness he felt.

"Perhaps, your *husband* will see you to the theatre once you find him."

Ann's Valley

The stricken look that dashed all the happiness of moments ago from her face, only infuriated Grayson further. He had every right to be angry with her. His words should not inflict upon him as much pain as it had her.

Only it did, damn it. He didn't want to hurt her. He didn't want to care! He shot her an insolent glare, blaming her for his inner turmoil, then spurred Dove ahead the rest of the party leading the way.

Chapter 14

Ann felt wretched. The first time she boarded a boat, she'd felt much the same. Only the last time she had been alone, and she'd been on a ship cast over a seemingly endless vast ocean. Staring up at the steamboats lining the dirty banks where she stood along the Ohio River, she compared then to now.

Once again, she was hying off to unfamiliar territory after a man. -The same man unfortunately. Only now she had added to her romantic problems and was in even more of a hardship than when she first set sail.

Grayson had been present when selling the wagon. Thank goodness, since her head and heart were still processing the new pain she brought upon herself. She felt adrift in a fog through the business and was happy for once when Grayson had concluded the business transactions without her input. He'd then gallantly split the money between him and herself equally, even though he had been the one taking the brunt of the financial burdens of this expenditure. He told her it included her services. And she could not afford to argue as that would be the only monies she had left to see her to St. Louis and back.

In fact, she was certain she did not possess enough blunt for return travel as it was, and she had not even arrived at St. Louis. She was counting greatly upon James to pay for that trip. But, oh, she was far too tired to think about that journey now. Firstly, she needed to focus on finishing this one.

She looked up at the loud, smoke billowing boat before her. She took it in from its flat bottom hull to its tall twin smokestacks. It boasted two levels of cabins; already seemingly grander accommodations than the ship that sailed her across the Atlantic offered. Her tickets had been costly, but at least bed and meals were included in the price. She'd heard the meals were not second rate either. She would be glad for the reprieve from simple campfire meals for a while.

She had Kit and Livvy strapped to her chest as she peered at the grand river monster that would transport them to the end of their journey. Kit was awake and looking at the noisy iron beast with wide intent eyes. Much to Ann's disbelief, Livvy was managing to sleep through the ruckus. She stroked Kit's outer arm soothingly, bringing more of a comfort to herself, Ann was sure.

Ann's fears threatened to sink her more readily than the explosive passage she'd secured before her. The dangers and risks associated with steamboats turned out to be true. Town was filled with talk of it.

It seemed Ann had no other options though. She hadn't the funds to travel further by wagon; she'd learned of the travails that occurred to one traveling across this wild country and had no wish to endure them alone. She too was ready to end this nightmare and return to her beloved Somerset where she would finally introduce her parents to their granddaughters. She hugged her daughters to her. All would be well. Ann was doing the right thing. *She hoped*.

When it came time to board the steamboat, Ann did so with renewed strength and determination. Some of those they had traveled with from Cumberland Gap had decided to remain in Louisville and take a reprieve from travel while they were in a city that offered so many refreshing entertainments and resting establishments. The poor, recently widowed Emmaline Smith had not wanted to continue on and Abe who'd been seeing to her care the past few days had elected to remain behind with her.

The Ackermann family would be boarding as well as the Harpers and Mr. Lewis. The rest of the party would stay behind, either having had decided to build their lives near to Louisville or to wait for the next boat.

Ann would not have minded to have partaken in the refreshments herself, including a much desired and needed bath! But the boat was scheduled to leave while the waters were high enough to pass over the falls and though she and Grayson were on fragile ground with one another, she still trusted him over all else. If he was boarding, then so would she.

She took a shaky breath and started up the wide wood plank that connected the boat to the riverbank. Workers were busy loading luggage and supplies and passengers rushed past her in their eagerness to board. More than once she was bumped and brushed to the side as people scurried in both directions all around her. Wary of the danger the smoking boat possessed, but also resigned to her decision, she pushed on.

"Wait up Ann!"

It was Jonathon's voice. Oh, lord, she would require more strength in order to hold up conversation with him whilst combating her fears of the voyage ahead. She stretched her lips into a polite smile, nonetheless.

"Hullo, Jonathon."

"I would have assisted you and-and the babies, had you waited."

He had not grown accustomed to the fact that his cousin had children and seemed very reserved almost to the point of being comically fearful of the young toddlers. Ann should be thankful, for their company tended to be what kept Jonathon's away.

And wasn't that just like Jonathon, to condescend to her whilst attempting to play the gentleman to her? She made every effort not to roll her eyes.

"Thank you, but as you can see, I am more than capable of carting along my possessions. I travel light."

She smirked with a feigned cavalier tone, referring to her meager state of finances. The humor was lost on Jonathon.

"Yes, well even so, as a gentleman, I must insist."

"Yes, well as a gentleman, you did."

Ann smiled peevishly. Grayson would have understood the look for what it was, and had been supremely annoyed, much to Ann's satisfaction. Not so Jonathon, who all subtlety was lost.

Just then the other irritating man in her life made his appearance. Ann felt Grayson's presence before she saw him, the fine hairs pricking up along her body in an agitating awareness to his proximity. She wondered if he had come to escort her as well. Perhaps maybe even to apologize finally, so that she could welcome comfort from him once more. She was starting to miss him already and the intimacy that had grown between them.

Without saying anything, however, Grayson unexpectedly, in one smooth motion removed Ann of her luggage and kept walking. Leaving Ann sputtering in his wake. Luke appeared beside her in an instant and took her hand.

"I don't know why, but Pa sure is mad at you."

Externally, Ann tried to cultivate an unaffected appearance. Internally, Ann was struggling yet from the surprise over what had just occurred. The irksome man! Well, he had just cured her of her nostalgic sentiment from only moments ago. She absolutely would not miss that boorish man.

Luke spoke again, "He said you are too stubborn by half."

"Yes, well it takes one to know one," Ann grumbled churlishly.

Luke, accustomed to Ann and his father's petty annoyances with one another, ignored her reply and added, "He also told me that whereas a gentleman may offer assistance to a stubborn lady," Luke interrupted his speech and paused for affect.

Then, in case she was too daft to understand the pointed look directed to her, he explained, "He was referring to you."

"Yes." She responded dryly, then bit off "I am aware of that detail."

Luke smiled slyly, resembling ever much the man who spawned him.

Luke continued unabashedly in his innocent childish fashion with his rendition of what had apparently been a teaching lesson for him, "As I was saying: A gentleman may ask, but a real man just performs whatever task needs done."

"That may be your father's opinion," Jonathon chimed in, clearly unwilling to allow the dig to pass, "However I have found that possessing of manners has been known to more effectively garner a woman's favor."

Ugh, heaven deliver Ann from over-chivalrous men and their egos.

"And when a woman can find both, a man with manners and a spine, then she may give her heart." She smiled to Luke.

"And when she cannot," She tossed over her shoulder to Jonathon, "She walks away."

Ann then increased her pace alongside Luke to leave Jonathon behind.

Luke, and Ann with the girls strapped to her, slowed their pace to gawk at their surroundings once their boots clicked onto the newly lacquered, wood planked deck of the boat. There were crates and supplies being rushed and organized into areas everywhere. People were cascading around the piles and workers in every direction. There didn't seem hardly room for all of them in the small space.

Ann suddenly felt there wasn't enough air to breathe. After being on the wide-open trail and through the isolated expanse of mountains all covered with blue skies, it was difficult to cram into a tiny space shared with so many other bodies; some of which needed a bath even more desperately than Ann did herself.

"There's Dove and Buckshot, over there!" Shouted Luke over the cacophony of noise coming from all the people.

"That's where they keep all the animals."

Luke smiled proudly for having knowledge to impart to Ann who was normally *his* teacher.

"Have you and your father already toured the boat, then?"

"Yep." He nodded enthusiastically.

"Do you know where our rooms are?"

"Yep."

He hopped, unnecessarily, over a small keg that had rolled near them and gestured for Ann to follow. He led them to a narrow set of stairs at the back of the boat behind the boilers. Once they reached the top deck, Luke stopped and pointed over the railing down below.

"Those are the paddles!" He exulted.

"Indeed," Ann responded attentively.

Luke was apparently taken with his new role as tour guide, so Ann went along with it, mustering up all the enthusiasm she could, as any dutiful mother would do; even though she was exhausted and dearly wished only to be in the comforting confines of her room. The boy proved to be a fount of information, however, and Ann was happy to appease and nurture his passionate spirit.

Finally, they entered the next set of cabins. A narrow hall divided them down the middle. Ahead of them she saw Grayson speaking with Mr. Ackermann. It appeared he was showing the family where their room was located. Luke's face took on a concerned expression and he trotted ahead to reach his father.

"What is happening father?"

Grayson smiled down to Luke, "No worries, son. I just thought the Ackermann family need this room more so than you and I. They have small children, like Kit and Livvy."

Grayson explicated in a way Luke could understand and sympathize with.

"We're two men after all, we can handle sleeping out on the deck for a couple of days, can't we?"

Luke nodded respectfully although his face fell dejectedly.

Before Ann fully understood what was transpiring, Grayson tipped his hat to her, pointed to the door behind her and told her that was her room. He then fled the cabins, with Luke in tow, before Ann could interject or raise any questions.

Obviously, Grayson had decided to give up his room to the Ackermann's, but why, she did not understand. She'd seen Mr. Ackermann and Grayson exchanging money, so it appeared the Ackermann's had the blunt to pay for a room. Had Grayson given up he and Luke's room solely to avoid her?

Ann was still standing in the hall outside of her room thinking upon Grayson's reasons for fleeing upon her arrival when Jonathon exited one of the rooms down the hall near the front of the set of cabins.

"Oh, hello, Ann. I was just headed to the balcony to have a gander as we set off. Would you care to join me?"

Ever the gentleman, Ann thought. She smiled to him kindly.

"No, thank you. Perhaps later. I have yet to settle into my room."

She nodded dismissively to him. He returned a polite nod then turned away and quit the hall. Ann hurriedly pushed open her door and ushered her and the girls inside, closing the door behind her with a firm click.

Finally, she was alone to think! Well, as alone as any mother of twin girls could possibly be, she supposed. She set about homing up the tiny space. It was basic sleeping quarters that afforded little more than a bed and wash area. A chest stood near the bed with one small drawer centered in it. Across from the bed was fastened a toiletry table with a shallow bowl to wash in and a cabinet built below it, presumably for hand towelettes.

In the corner was a canvas lined box with a lid secured atop it. Ann knew she would find a necessaries pot located within. She wondered, not without humor, when passengers were expected to dispose of the contents that would indubitably fill the container. Would they announce a dumping schedule and all step out at the same time? Ann chuckled to herself, surely this was an independently performed task.

All joking aside, Ann released the girls from their suspended pack, and they were ever happy to be free of their confines. Ann did not see anything in the room that could pose a threat to them, so she allowed her cherubs free rein of the space while she laid across the bed for a brief moment's reprieve.

Of course, her daughters found themselves fascinated with the lidded box in the corner; the one item in the room they should not explore, the opportunistic little devils.

Ann sighed, "You ladies just do not allow for breaks, do you? Always finding ways to get into things you should not."

She shuffled to them, scooped them up into her arms and deposited them near the bed once more. Ann then set to barricading the offending box with their trunks. Not the most desired of places Ann would have wished her clothes and personal items to be near.

Ann noticed the girls rubbing their eyes and yawning, so once she finished tidying the room to her satisfaction, she laid them both to bed. They'd become rather good at nap and bedtime, thankfully. Of course, their days were fairly exhausting, poor babes. Travel was hard on everyone it seemed.

That reminded Ann of Luke. She wondered if Grayson was being attentive of his needs.

An absurd thought. He was the boy's father and he wasn't known to be negligent. Ann had just grown accustomed to seeing to Luke's care. It was strange not to be near to him drawing close to their evening meal that they'd shared for the past few months.

The girls were already fast asleep. A thought occurred to Ann. She stepped from their room into the hall. She could hear the Ackermann's behind their closed door and knew they were yet present, so she knocked. Mrs. Ackermann answered.

"Hallo."

"Hello," Ann smiled in friendly gesture. She'd been hoping Mr. Ackermann would be present, for he knew English well where Mrs. Ackermann spoke mostly German.

Ann had been learned in some French but had never been interested overmuch in languages. Funny how all of these lessons she had balked at growing up and avoided at all costs were coming around to bite her in the behind, just as her mother had warned.

Ann knew not an iota of German, so she was uncertain how to proceed with her request.

"Hallo, Mrs. Morgan."

Suddenly, The Ackermann's fourteen-year-old daughter appeared in the door next to her mother, wearing a sunny smile.

"Hello. Sara, isn't it?" Ann asked warmly.

Sara nodded affirmatively. Mrs. Ackermann smiled as well and spoke something in German.

"I apologize," Ann began, "I am ignorant of the German language."

"My mother asked if there was something we could do for you?"

Ann sighed with relief. Sara, the daughter spoke English exceedingly well.

"Yes, thank you," Ann beamed, "That is, I did come to beg a favor of you, if I may?"

Mrs. Ackermann spoke, and Sara followed in speech with a translation, "Yes, of course, we would be happy to help."

"Thank you. Well you see, my two daughters," Ann glanced back across the hall to the door to her room and cradled her arms as she did in way of gesturing to what she was speaking.

She continued, "They are sleeping. I was wondering If I could ask you to sit in with them for a short time so that I may find and speak with Mr. Stone?"

Sara translated to Mrs. Ackermann, who then smiled and gestured towards her daughter with a nod.

"Meine mutter says it is fine for me to watch over your daughters until you return, if that is agreeable with you?"

"Yes, tis splendid. Thank you both!" Ann lightly braced Mrs. Ackermann's fingers with her own in gratitude. She and her daughter spoke in German to one another, then Mrs. Ackermann smiled and waved her daughter off to follow Ann.

"Thank you again, Sara. Hopefully they will remain sleeping. I shall return as quickly as possible."

Ann let Sara into the room and after assessing that the twins were still asleep, nodded her thanks once more to Sara then exited in search of Grayson.

The sun was already setting in the sky when Ann stepped out onto the balcony of the deck surrounding the cabins. She traveled along the planks, her soft moccasins not even making a sound atop the fresh wood.

The smell of acrid smoke from the engines burned in her nose and caused her eyes to water as she descended the steps and drew closer to the bottom deck. Once her feet hit the level floor, she roved her eyes in either direction searching which way around the boilers she thought Grayson would be. She expected, near his livestock, she decided, so made her way to that side of the boat.

So many bodies crammed together made it difficult for her to navigate through. Her height, being on the shorter side, put her at a disadvantage, especially as this lower deck mostly seemed to be comprised of tall men.

And not of the *gentleman* variety...

Several of the men she passed leered openly at her; some of them even boldly made lewd comments to her as if she were a common doxy. The narrowing of her contempt-filled eyes effectively warned them and kept them from approaching.

No, she thought, *her little Luke was not going to remain on this floor with these oafs.*

She shuddered. The beads of sweat that had built up along her skin from being in such close proximity to the boilers began to run in little ticklish trails down her neck, further irritating her that she was even in this predicament of having to search Grayson out. If he would deem to not act like such a child and hare off at the sight of her, they could all be enjoying a dinner on the top deck at this very moment!

Ann stopped once more to peer around, but it was no use. There was a wall of bodies and cargo blocking her view. There seemed to be a group huddled in the center of the walkway. None of its occupants seemed incline to move which meant Ann would have to step around them.

The heat and steam intensified towards the center of the boat to her left, so she stepped to her right. She had to push her way through some others trying to get around the staid group going in the opposite direction, causing Ann to be wholly unprepared to find herself on the very edge of the boat. The water practically leapt right up over the side onto her moccasins. She teetered for a few seconds trying to regain her lost balance from the momentum of her plowing through the crowd.

Where was the railing? Her stomach lurched, and all her memories of sea sickness came flooding back. She scooted away from the side on shaky legs, barely cognizant of bumping along against people as she went. She made it towards the center and was able to resume a normal rate of breathing. She wondered how many lives were lost purely from people falling off the boat? Best not to dwell on that question over much she supposed.

Ann finally made it to the front of the boat where a railing was secured, thankfully, but she had yet to sight Grayson or Luke. The number of vulgar stares from some of the rough, unkept men were sending chills down her spine. She needed to find Grayson quickly and get back to the safety of the top deck with the other civilized persons.

She began making her way towards the back of the boat once more down the other side of the deck. It was entirely possible she had missed them early on due to the masses of bodies, cargo, and livestock seemingly scattered about in all directions.

"So, we are going to stay right with our things. And neither one of us is to venture off without the other, understood?"

Grayson explained to a crestfallen Luke. He had not wanted to be separated from Ann, but Grayson could see no other option that he could live with.

Luke nodded in understanding. Grayson had explained to him all the dangers posed in this small space. There were plenty of hard men aboard. Crooks, thieves and murderers, Grayson had no doubt. Grayson happened to look up just then as something caught his eye.

"Christ!" He spit. Then growled, "Ann."

It is no wonder he sighted her so easily. She stuck out like a bright greenhouse orchid amidst the tall, deadened, brown prairie grasses of fall. He threw down his capote that would serve as a blanket to lay on for the night and rushed to her furiously.

"Ann, what in the hell are you doing down here? And where are the girls!" His hands reached for her protectively, noticing at once the greasy smirks and lascivious looks in her direction.

Ann shook her forearms from his angry grasp. "The girls are safe above, never you mind them. I'm here to see why *you* are down here." She accused right back.

"What would you have had me do? Tickets for the cabins sold out before the Ackermann's were able to purchase any. They have seven kids, Ann. Three of them younger than Luke."

Ann looked down ashamedly. She'd thought perhaps Grayson had traded boarding arrangements in order to avoid her. She should have known Grayson would never behave so recklessly with Luke's care.

Love for him melted through her again, not that it had ever truly cooled. In these moments, when he was too damn honorable for his own good, it was difficult to pretend she didn't love him. Grayson had done the right thing, but she still did not want him and Luke remaining on this lower deck.

"Well, Luke certainly is not remaining down here, next to the boilers and, and, this riff-raff."

Ann gestured madly with her hands towards the rough, shady looking characters in the distance around them.

"Gather your things Luke, you'll be staying with the girls and I."

Luke looked nervously from Ann to his father, waiting for his father to contradict Ann and uncertain who to obey, if he did.

Ann continued in what Luke's father termed her "Duchess tone", only this time it was directed towards his father.

"You can bed down with Jonathon. It will be safer, and you will be closer to Luke and," She hesitated, preventing herself from stating Grayson would be closer to her and the girls as well, knowing he did not desire to be. So instead she amended lamely, "well, you'll be closer to Luke."

For a few heartbeats, Ann thought Grayson would object as he stood there looking to her with his jaw clenched. She straightened her spine, letting him know she would absolutely not be returning to the top deck without Luke.

In the end he conceded with a demure nod of his head. Luke visibly sighed his relief.

Feeling ready to deflate as well, Ann smiled to him and assisted him with carrying his belongings. Grayson carried his own with no difficulty and the three of them returned to Ann's room.

The girls were awake when Ann arrived, but Sara had been able to entertain them easily. Ann expressed her gratitude to Sara for her help and then again to Frieda, Sara's mother for allowing her daughter to assist. Ann knew Frieda greatly relied upon Sara's help within their own family, what with Sara being the eldest daughter and having so many siblings to help care for.

Sara said how she enjoyed watching Kit and Livvy in Ann's absence, for her own sisters were close in age to herself with only three very young brothers. After Sara's departure and settling Luke into the shared space, Ann decided Grayson would join she, Luke, and the girls in accompanying them to the dining area.

Grayson did not look pleased with Ann's dogmatic pronouncement, if his stance of glowering at her from the doorway was any indication, but he did not dispute her orders. He trailed them silently, causing Ann every bit of discomfort along the way.

They did not make it from the hall before running into Jonathon who was returning to his room.

"Oh, Jonathon, you're just the man I wanted to see."

Ann beamed to him, shamelessly using her feminine advantage to soften Jonathon to the plans she was about to unload on him; knowing he would surely find them objectionable.

He smiled in return and dipped his head politely saying, "I am at your service as always." But his eyes flashed uncertainly to Grayson.

Of course, Grayson would be of no help in furthering his own cause. No, indeed. Instead of being the slightest bit friendly, he stood with his arms crossed and an indolent smile teasing his lips. It was little wonder Jonathon always took on a defensive stance around the infuriating man. He just exuded dominance and competence in annoying fashion everywhere he went.

Ann managed to keep her smile for Jonathon on her lips through her irritation, however.

"Yes, indeed. We have altered our rooming arrangements. Grayson will now be sharing sleeping quarters with you. Luke of course will remain with me and the girls. Would you care to show Grayson, presently, the room in which you both will be occupying?"

Grayson looked from Jonathon to Ann and back to Jonathon, his amused grin widening exasperatingly so while Jonathon, utterly caught off guard searched desperately for a polite way to refuse Ann's behest.

Before he could do so, however, Ann pretended to interpret his flustered silence as agreement, "Oh, bless you Jonathon. You are ever the gentleman. Now, hurry along boys, the children and I are positively famished."

Ann smiled sweetly and then blinked owlishly as if innocently waiting for the two grown men to jump to do her bidding.

If Grayson didn't want to throttle her so badly, he should want to kiss her in that moment. His bossy, little dictator never appeared so in need of a good ravishing as she did when she was commanding people about her like a fierce little general.

Jonathon wore his displeasure openly but unlocked the door to his room and stepped inside leaving the door open for Grayson to follow.

Ann's Valley

Grayson's eyes glittered with an altogether different kind of hunger and the arrogant smile he flashed to Ann promised he could deliver.

She suddenly felt an unnerved sense of danger. Similarly, she thought, to what prey must feel when it realizes it is too late to escape its predator and about to be eaten.

Unlike prey, however, Ann wasn't entirely sure she didn't want to be eaten...

Chapter 15

As it turned out, Jonathon had already taken his meal for the evening and so excused himself from their company after he and Grayson came to terms with one another within their new living confinements.

Courtesy to Ann for having arranged such a hell, thought Grayson, amusedly. As well as Luke, he *did* want to be near to Ann and the girls, though he'd not admit so to Ann, so the arrangement aligned with his wishes perfectly. He hadn't liked seeing so many disreputable men on one entity and decided he would put up with the dandy, Jonathon's, ill humor in order to be near to Ann and the children to ensure their safety.

He refrained from speaking to Ann aside from polite responses, in order to continue her punishment. Although he was no longer certain whom he was punishing. He'd hoped creating a sound distance, would open her eyes to a future where they were apart from one another. He had hoped she would change her mind and choose him.

But thus far, she appeared unaffected. The thought hurt and angered him considerably. Once they finished their meal and he escorted them back to their room, he too excused himself for the evening. Feeling edgy and itching for a bit of physical activity, he headed back down to the seedy first floor. He was in a foul mood and wanted the company of men who matched it.

After checking on the horses, he made his way to a party of men who had rearranged tables out of luggage in the center of the floor for card playing and gambling. They were a merry, rowdy bunch, already sloshed for the night. He was about to join them, when he heard a familiar voice call out his name.

"I said, 'Stone!"

The obviously, agitated and drunken voice slurred again. Grayson turned around to face the man.

"Jonathon," Grayson tipped his hat to him in acknowledgment. He watched as Jonathon Morgan pushed himself bodily from one of the pillaring posts and swayed toward him. Grayson really wasn't in the mood to babysit the drunk dandy.

"I think you should probably head on up to the room before you pass out down here. Don't you think?"

"*My room*. It's my room," Jonathon slurred while pounding his fist to his chest for emphasis, "but she just gave it away to *you*."

Jonathon looked up to him then, trying to focus on Grayson's face, "What else has she given away to you, I wonder?"

He laughed coldly and swigged from a fresh bottle of cheap booze he probably overpaid for from one of the lowlier first deck passengers.

The hairs on the back of Grayson's neck raised defensively. Drunk or not, no man had better allude to Ann in those terms. His hands fisted instinctively at his sides, itching to connect with the bones in Jonathon's face. He flexed his fingers instead, forcing himself to becalm.

Jonathon decided to test Grayson's will power however and continued, "She's not married, you know? She's no better than a whore. My *cousin's* whore."

"You'd better watch what you say, Morgan. Or else you may find yourself unable to say anything at all ever again."

Grayson delivered the chilled words with a menacing look. He didn't make threats idly.

Jonathon's belligerent stance swayed some and his face, contorted with vindictiveness seconds ago, sagged sorrowfully.

"My cousin always got everything he wanted. No matter that he was never deserving of any good that came to him."

Jonathon slunk down to the floor, leaning on the post behind him.

He continued, "When I saw her, I thought, *there is the most beautiful woman I've ever seen*. Then she said his name and I knew. I knew he had gotten to her first. But I didn't care if she was his leftovers."

Grayson listened, even though his fists still flexed with every insult Morgan spoke against Ann. He decided to hear him out though. It seemed the disoriented man wanted to impart something important to him.

Jonathon looked up. When he ensured Grayson was still listening, he continued, "I called her out on her bluff. Told her I knew her secret. That she couldn't be married to my cousin, for he was already legally married."

He looked up to Grayson again, "I knew this for a fact. I witnessed the whole legal *prosheedings*."

Grayson tried not to let his agitation show when Jonathon stopped talking to roll his tongue around as if he could no longer recall how to use it.

"But she still took off after him. *James*. The one who had ruined her. I thought at first, she was still foolishly in love with him. But I thought, If I help her get to James... Well, that's a lot of time spent with her. I could change her mind, make her love *me* instead."

He looked down, sadly, towards his boots stretched before him.

"James talked of her once before to me. When he came back from England, he did. She's the only one he ever shared about. I knew she was special to him in some way."

Jonathon's voice up to that point had been reflective, but it changed to anger quickly.

"This time, I wasn't going to let James win. It was my turn to get the prize. I was the one always cleaning up *his* messes. I was the one taking care of *his* parents and *his* farm. And why?"

He deplored this question to Grayson.

"He never cared about anyone but himself, the selfish prick."

Grayson continued to listen intently, but inside his blood was pounding furiously. Ann *wasn't* married, yet, she still chose to find this, *James Morgan*. She had no legal ties to him, so why? If what Jonathon was saying was true, this man despoiled Ann and used her, even led her to believe he'd married her. Christ! - He'd impregnated her.

"But then I saw his brats. His *bastards*. I knew it to be so, for the one has his eyes..."

It's a good thing Jonathon didn't look up, because Grayson was certain his look would have frightened the man and shut him up for good. Grayson ground his teeth together hard to refrain from growling over the man's base description of Ann's daughters.

"It shook me it did." He spoke, assuming Grayson sympathized with him, nodding his head.

"But ultimately, I decided I still wanted her."

Grayson interrupted then, "If you wanted her, why did you agree to take her to the man who sired her daughters. Obviously, she was hoping to make their union a legal one."

Jonathon laughed, "Ha! As if James would," he sneered. "No. I thought once we reached James and he made it painfully clear to her, that he would never acknowledge her or his brats, that she would turn to me then. I would be the hero that saved her from ruin."

Then his gaze turned malevolently to Grayson, "And then she met *you*. And you had beaten me to it. I don't know what you did, but she had already painted you her rescuer before I could catch her."

Then he added, sadly, "Only, I realized it too late."

Then he perked up again and laughed, "But she has thwarted you too."

He nursed his bottle a few sips more, then added, somberly, "In the end, James will have it all. His land, his riches, and the woman with the golden eyes..."

For all it had been advertised that steam transport could arrive them to St. Louis in two days' time, the days had numbered nearly to three. The boat got caught on a sand bar and workers and helpful passengers alike had worked at poling the steamer across it. Although larger in size, it wasn't nearly as difficult to maneuver from the sand bar as were the smaller Keel Boats, to which Grayson was accustomed. Still the delay had cost them precious hours. In all that time, Grayson had managed to evade both Jonathon and Ann fairly well.

He kept away during day hours, watching from afar and always waited for Jonathon to retire to bed before entering the shared quarters and sleeping himself. It proved more difficult to avoid Ann, since Luke was usually in her company.

Grayson had been angry upon learning Ann was not, in fact, married. He could not fathom why she would chase a man who despoiled her and left her to rot, all the way across two continents. It angered him for himself, but also for the girls. They deserved a better father. And they deserved better decisions by their mother.

Grayson had mixed feelings too about arriving in St. Louis. Would he meet this, James Morgan there? Or would he do as he should, continue on with his life with Luke and forget about Ann?

He couldn't seem to make up his mind, all the more reason to keep his distance, until he was certain of a decision. He wanted badly to discuss the matter with Ann, but to confront her with the knowledge of her secrets could result in resounding rejection of him, severing their ties permanently. Something deep within him balked at that. He didn't want things between them to come to an end. - At least not yet. Perhaps not ever.

Grayson scuffed the toe of his boot to the deck as he continued to aimlessly meander the base floor, lost in contemplation.

He'd offered her marriage once already and she had refused. If he repeated the gesture, would she accept his suit or reject him again? Did he want her to accept?

Did he love her?

Did he want to spend the rest of his life with her?

Would Ann even want such a life as he had to offer? Isolated in the mountains, just the two of them, and Luke and the girls, of course.

Most women wouldn't, he thought. But if she did, if he could convince her, was that what he wished? For Ann to be with him always?

A vision filled his senses, then, of Ann laying haphazardly tangled in the sheets with the fresh early morning rays of sun sluicing through the small paned window of their room. Him waking next to her to crisp mountain air on his skin and feeling the warmth of her soft body hugging to the hard planes of his...

God, yes. That was what he wanted.

Suddenly he needed to be nearer to her and found his legs already eating the distance between them. He bounded up the narrow staircase in search of her and had no difficulty locating her on such a small boat.

His eyes took in the sight of her. She was standing with Luke at her side and both girls strapped to her in that contraption she insisted on carrying them in; all of them looking out over the water towards the shoreline.

"Look! There's another eagle!" He heard Luke shout and point towards the majestic bird gliding effortlessly through the clear blue sky above.

Then Ann's voice, "You have an impressive infinity for finding them," she laughed. "Absolutely beautiful," she agreed sharing in Luke's awe.

Grayson had thought to let his presence be known then but was interrupted by two short deafening blasts of a horn. It had sounded just as unexpectedly to Ann and the children as it had himself and they leapt from the edge of the balcony with a start. They were nearly equally startled to turn about and see Grayson standing before them.

Ann threw her hand to her chest, "Goodness!"

Kit and Livvy looked undecided if they should ignore the current happenings or wail in fright.

Luke laughed. Grayson, too, smiled at the comical situation, drawing forth a smile from Ann.

Although smiling, Ann was still somewhat irked for having been startled and then embarrassed for Grayson having had witnessed her goosishness.

"I wonder why on earth the captain thought it necessary to deafen all his passengers."

"He's letting all know of our arrival," Grayson pointed back towards the river and the town coming into distance beyond, "Look."

"Oh my!" Ann followed his direction and she and Luke scooted closer to the rail once more to peer out in front of them.

"There it is."

Ann's excitement seemed lessened to Grayson and as he looked to her face, he saw her smile wobble nervously. Perhaps she was not as certain as she believed herself to be concerning her feelings for James Morgan. Hope ignited within him.

Luke giggled, "The people of St. Louis must be zealously devoted to their religions."

At that declaration, Ann and Grayson looked across the town of St. Louis and shared an amused smile as they saw for themselves the many, many steeples in varying locations scattered throughout the town, rising above the other buildings.

Grayson shook his head, "I swear there are at least two new churches built every year in this town. They would be better off building more schools, if you ask me."

Luke gave his father a comically ill look expressing how greatly he disagreed with that sentiment.

Ann's smile faded as her brows knit with concern, "How are we ever to reach port? There must be fifty or more other boats lining the bank, taking up the entire stretch of the town?"

"No worries, most of those are simply cargo carriers being loaded and ready for departure soon. We will land beyond there on Market Street," Grayson explained.

They reached port in good time, even though this bank appeared just as busy as the first, with boats and freight carts crowding the landing. Jonathon joined them, and they all disembarked the boat together. Grayson never left her side. She didn't know what to think about that.

The man was perplexing in his changing attitudes towards her. He was continuously pulling her in only to push her away. The last time, she had absolved not to allow herself to be drawn to him any longer.

She scoffed at that sentiment, as if she hadn't fought that very fight only to lose over and over again already.

But not this time.

She was so close. So very near her victory.

St. Louis. She had arrived! Her feet were wont to outpace her body with urgency as they stepped to the limestone paved bank of her destination, but the dense flow of traffic was rather that of a herd of slow lumbering cows. Everyone was coming or going in a state of wear and exhaustion. Ann rather thought her body should feel as those around her, but she'd ever had an easily renewable spirit in the face of new embarkments.

This was especially titillating as it was an end as well as a new beginning. She desperately wanted to locate the city directories office, but she knew firstly she needed to see to the care of the children.

She felt Grayson's touch at her elbow. "I know of a decent Inn we can recuperate at for a time that is family friendly and fairly priced."

He spoke to her as well as the Ackermann's who Ann only just realized were crowded together with them.

Grayson guided gently with his hand once more for her to step out with him, which she did so, naturally. The rest of the group followed behind.

Jonathon seemed unusually silent the last couple of days. She did not know what had prompted his sudden mood, but she was not about to look a gift horse in the mouth, so she feigned ignorant and remained politely distant.

Grayson worried for Ann and the girls. He had interrupted Ann the day prior in her cabin while seeking Luke. He'd witnessed her counting her pitiful stash of money, with a fearfully serious expression upon her face. She had of course tried to wave off any of her concerns, but He wasn't obtuse enough not to realize Ann was running short on funds.

He had suspected as much all along, as throughout the journey, her penny pinching became obvious as well as comments she interjected in ways that suggested she never required luxuries and only minimal necessities had led him to that very conclusion.

He had covertly tried to assist in that area when he could, knowing she would not accept charity. With their new strained relationship, he worried how he would be able to spin paying for her hotel room.

Technically he had delivered her to St. Louis and that was the extent of their business agreement. However, he had become personally invested in her welfare since that transaction had taken place and an especially divested interest in keeping her nearer to him at this time.

He needed to speak with her before she sought out the man who had fathered her children.

It did not escape Grayson's notice that Ann hung back, her throat working nervously once they reached the front desk of the Inn. He knew she waited to overhear the price the Ackermann's would be charged for a room in order to know if she had enough coin to cover it herself or if she would have to seek less reputable, alternative arrangements.

Not that Grayson would allow that to happen.

He watched her sigh with relief when she heard the fair price of the room and would have stepped up to pay. Grayson was about to step before her and secure their rooms, her wrath be damned, but unexpectedly, Jonathon took the lead.

"I'll need a room for my cousin and myself. Separate rooms, please."

Both Ann and Grayson gaped at Jonathon in surprise. Then further shocking them, Jonathon turned and tipped his hat to Grayson. Ann watched in awe as Grayson and Jonathon seemed to share an unspoken respect for one another in that moment, leaving Ann to wonder what exactly had transpired on the boat in her absence.

Earlier she had not questioned Jonathon's newfound silent reverie, but now she found herself immensely curious, for obviously it involved Grayson as well. Just, what on earth was going on between these men?

Jonathon then held out his arm for her. She was so flabbergasted she absentmindedly looped her arm through his, forgetting entirely to thank him for securing her room. Grayson conceded with a bow of his head to Jonathon and suddenly Ann felt as if she were a beloved family dog being transferred ownership elsewhere.

She gritted her teeth finding ill favor with such a comparison. She continued on Jonathon's arm, albeit more crisply and made it clear she had no wish to dawdle. Her sudden change in pace seemed to have awakened both men to her uncharitable mood. The perplexed expressions on their faces brought her no small amount of satisfaction for having turned the tables on them.

Once arrived at her room, she turned her haughty veneer to Grayson nodding curtly to him in a way that she hoped signaled well her irritation with him.

"Thank you for the escort gentlemen," She waxed in an overly sweet tone that left little doubt of her vexation.

"I think the helpless woman can manage her basic toilette without aid, though, don't you think?" She simpered, affectingly.

Jonathon, as predicted, blushed at her reference to performing intimate female duties, while Grayson recovered from his initial state of perplexity with a return of his usual annoyingly, self-pleased, smirk.

Good. He knew now that she would ill tolerate being treated as a delicate milksop. With that, she turned on her heel and entered her room, shutting the door, and them out, directly.

Hours later after having seen to the care of her daughters, and having freshened herself - as well as having ignored all knocks at her door during that time - she determined it time for her to search out the directory and discover just where that blighter, James, had been hiding.

She needed to act before her nerves got the best of her. Without further consideration she opened the door forcefully, determination set in every bone in her body as it would take that much strength to finally face her fears.

Originally her fear had been that James had forgotten her. After having met Jonathon, she began to fear a greater deception.

In the beginning she had believed deep down that once she confronted James and he learned of his daughters, he would step up and do what was right. For Ann had only ever been surrounded with honorable men in her life, she could not fathom the thought that she could have allowed herself to have fallen in love with a slimy toad of a man.

Jonathon had certainly shaken that belief. But even then, she had hoped to learn that Jonathon was somehow wrong, or at the very least James would offer an explanation that could excuse his abandonment of her.

However, her hopes dissipated with every mile that brought her nearer to her sought redemption.

And the truth of the matter was, her love for James had died a cold death upon the crossing of the icy waves of the Atlantic.

She continued on because her pride demanded she do so. The soldier her father had trained her to be would not accept defeat. But after delivering her daughters, it became less about healing her pride.

They should know who their father was, should not they? Did not they deserve to know the blood that sired them? The doubts that Ann had been able to crush down within her for so long surfaced suddenly, spiraling tormentingly-so about her mind.

She pressed her back to the door. With her eyes closed, she let the solidity of the door lend her strength. When she opened her eyes, however, another surprise greeted her. There Jonathon stood before her, nervously clutching his hat, wearing a pained expression upon his face.

"I-I have some bad news for you. Well, for us," He amended. "I went to the City's directory office in hopes of finding James."

Ann waited, her lips parted to continue drawing breath all the while her stomach did somersaults on the inside.

"I found him."

Her heart pounded rapidly in her chest, but she remained silent, knowing Jonathon had not yet imparted the 'bad news' he'd come to share, leaving her guessing wildly at the possibilities it could pertain. Had the blackguard remarried in yet another legal union? Did he know about Ann's presence in St. Louis and refused to acknowledge her? Was he dead?

Jonathon looked down, as if searching for the words he needed to appear on the floor. Then when she could hardly stand to be patient any longer, he looked back up, straight into her eyes, with what she knew to be an inner strength brought forth to deliver a hard blow. She braced herself.

"He-he is no longer in Missouri. We didn't make it in time. He has moved on to Texas."

Her heart yet thudded like a racing cart in her chest.

"Where did you discern this information? Perhaps, it is incorrect. We need to look into it further…" She rattled off all the incessant thoughts whirring in her mind.

Jonathon shook his head with finality, "I spoke with Lorraina's father-James' late wife's, that is. He had no reason to lie to me, Ann. He said James left here, near on three weeks ago for Santa Fe."

Ann felt her bottom lip tremble with anguish. She would not give in to it. She needed, she knew, a few private moments to process this overwhelming new development. She just needed to lay down, and-and still her spinning world for a few moments. Seek clarity. A bit of rest, she encouraged herself. Then she would know what to do.

She pulled her tremulous lips into a tight line, as was the best smile she could attempt under the circumstances.

"Thank you," She hesitated to clear her throat, "Jonathon. I need a few moments to myself."

She did not wait for a response from him. Somehow her fingers managed to locate the knob of the door and her numb legs beneath her carried her weightlessly through the room to the bed. She ensured Kit and Livvy were set safely to the floor. Then Ann lay atop the coverlet on the bed.

Her eyes, too numb to cry, stared blankly at the ceiling while her mind sorted through the frenzied emotions for an answer. What to do, now?

Not an hour later, Ann heard a soft knock at her door. She had every intention of ignoring it, until she heard the small voice on the other side.

"Ann? I brought us some supper. It's just me. Pa told me I should bring the food up here to you. I wanted to eat with you and the girls. I hope that's okay?"

Tears threatened her eyes. *Luke.* Her precious, Luke. She quickly made her way to the door and opened it for him.

"Of course you may. You are always welcome."

She smiled warmly to him, her heart full for the dear boy. She leaned down and placed a maternal kiss atop his head and hugged him close, knowing he needed reassurance that she was okay. She had to battle the tears off once more. She'd not be very convincing if she allowed for them to fall in his presence. The last thing the child needed was to worry over her.

"Supper smells delicious! What did you bring us?"

She assumed a more gleeful tone, bringing forth an eager smile on his little face.

"Why, a half wheel of cheese of course. I know how much you love it."

He smiled widely, so extremely pleased with his own thoughtfulness, that it choked out a genuine laugh from her as well.

He continued, "And chicken, and biscuits too! It's all still warm!" He finished excitedly.

The girls were already clamoring up to Luke, both out of adoration for Luke as well as the food he carried. Oh, they were shameless, thought Ann, happily.

The camaraderie didn't last, however. As they finished their meal, Luke said, with a hopeful glimmer in his eyes, "I asked Pa if you could come with us tomorrow. He said, yes."

The brevity of the night bore down on Ann suddenly with crushing weight. This was the part Ann had dreaded most for the last months. She didn't know if her heart could take it.

She wiped the food residue from her fingers onto the cotton napkin provided. Then she went to her trunk, where she rummaged through until her fingers clasped the cool, smooth, wooden frame. She brought it over with her and handed it to Luke.

"It is a miniature of me. It's quite recent, my mother had it done of me before I made my debut in London, not two years past. I brought it with me when I left, because it has my horse, Knight, there you see? I thought the artist well captured his gentle spirit in his eyes and the way he would rest his muzzle over my shoulder like so in the picture." Ann smiled.

Luke smiled in return and looked over the picture in awe. Luke's smile faded then and with the keen perceptiveness of someone thrice his age, whispered, "You'll not be coming with us, will you?"

Ann bit her bottom lip in attempt to fight back the pain welling within her. The bitter taste of blood tinged her tongue, and still the pain did not compare to the wrenching in her heart. The realization that she had made her decision only then becoming clear. She swallowed the hard knot of grief then because she knew she had to explain.

"I've wished on all the stars in the sky that I might stay with you, Luke. You are very fortunate, you see. You have a father who loves you very much. You and your father are going to make grand memories together.

Kit and Livvy, they have a father too. Only, they have never had the chance to be loved by him and I don't think it is fair to deny them that chance. Do you?"

Silent tears streamed down Luke's face, "But I'd share mine. My father could be a father to them too."

So many anguished feelings were spoken in those simple words. Luke loved the girls like they were blood brother and sisters. Tearing them apart was breaking more hearts than just her own.

Ann scooped Luke's large boyish form onto her lap and into her arms where she rocked him and tried to soothe his hurt best she could.

"And I, like a mother to you." She said aloud the words he had left unspoken. His pain and heartbreak were evident on his little face and Ann didn't think she could bear it.

"I want you to keep this picture of me. And if ever you miss me or are in need of a hug, just look at my picture and remember how much I love you. Because I do, Luke. I love you just as I love Kit and Livvy."

They clung to one another and cried silently, both striving to find a strength neither felt.

"I don't want you to be sad, though, when you think of me."

Ann smiled through her tears.

"If looking at my picture makes you sad, then I don't want you to look at it. Because I only ever want your happiness."

She stroked his hair some more.

"Okay?"

Luke sniffled and nodded.

"That's my brave boy."

When Grayson came for Luke, he seemed fidgety and unlike himself, usually steadfast with certainty. He opened his mouth to speak a few times, but no words came forth. All of them were struggling with an inner turmoil and none of them seemed to know how to proceed. So instead, Grayson tipped his hat to her awkwardly and ushered Luke from the room after Luke hugged Ann and secured a promise from her that she would not leave on the morrow without telling him goodbye once more.

The next morning, Ann wasted precious little time arranging for her departure. The longer she remained in proximity to Grayson and Luke the more reluctant she would be to perform the duty to her daughters. She made her way to the post office directly and sent off a letter to Nancy and Doc.

They would not be pleased to learn she was continuing her pursuit of James. She hoped her words informing of her and the girls' good health would bring them some comfort though.

Ann wondered if her parents or Uncle Rupie had discovered yet, where she'd secreted away to? Had they made it to Charleston? Perhaps even found Nancy and Howard?

She didn't express those thoughts in her letter to Nancy and Doc, though. She couldn't afford more than one sheet of paper and she filled it with as much information and tender stories of the girls to pass on as she could squeeze into the limited space.

After mailing her letter she conferred briefly with Jonathon, who agreed with her urgency. And they set out with one another to make the necessary purchases to outfit the last course of their journey.

She had assumed Jonathon would continue on with her, but she had conflicting emotions about his company. She was torn between being grateful for his persistent presence, and at the same time irritated.

She realized however that her irritation was mostly directed at the shifting course of her life that seemed to be cruelly demanding her to leave pieces of her heart behind at every turn. She wondered if she would ever feel whole again...

She pushed the ever-drowning doubts from her mind. She and Jonathon had been able to bargain for a used but sturdy wagon and she needed to concentrate on loading it with the necessary supplies. This task was made more difficult when Jonathon admitted, he too was running low on funds.

They would just have to make do. The wagon had been costlier than anticipated. They had hoped renting would negate some of the cost, however that plan had been soundly rejected.

The man selling and trading the various carts and wagons had laughed out right when they requested only to rent a wagon. The man rudely named them for fools for thinking he would rent a wagon to anyone traveling La Jornado.

He then proceeded to list the many reasons why his wagon was unlikely to return. All of which ultimately resulted in their untimely deaths. Ann was wont to shrug off his fear mongering drivel, but the hairs at the nape of her neck refused to relax against the provoking warning.

Back at her hotel room to gather her belongings, she knew it was time for the dreaded goodbyes. She packed and readied her belongings, leaving them within the safety of her room, and stepped into the hall. She made her way to Grayson's room one foreboding step at a time until she came to his door.

The door swung open before she could finish the first knock. Grayson had known it was she and now stood before her, his eyes piercing with hurt and accusation.

As if she wanted this any more than he did.

Luke stepped around him to stand in front, nearer to Ann. His disconsolate gaze found hers. The girls strained in the confines of their pack upon seeing Luke and reached their little arms out towards the boy, who for all intents and purposes, had become their brother.

Livvy gurgled excitedly and swiped her pudgy hand across the air to happily touch his face. Luke stepped into her touch as he knew she wanted and she rested her head upon his, smiling and cooing as she did so.

It was a common interaction between the girls and Luke, for he had cared for them thusly every day for all the past months of their passage to St. Louis. The girls adored Luke; for in him was their play mate, protector, and doting big brother. And he so adored them.

Ann had once thought that the idea of never seeing the faces of her parents again would be the hardest thing for her to bear. But she knew differently, now, as she watched her daughters squeal and kick against her in delight to see their brother, unaware that this could possibly be the last time their eyes ever gazed upon him.

Luke tried to laugh through the obvious anguish he was battling and be strong for his sisters. Ann knelt then and scooped him into her arms, at once maneuvering the girls further to the sides so as not to press upon them. She held Luke's small form tightly, never wanting to let go. He hugged to her just as tightly, ever careful of his baby sisters.

The heart wrenching grief constricted the walls of her chest until it hurt to breathe. She fought through her heart ache to speak past the stinging in her throat.

"You have brought so much love and joy into our lives, Lucas Rhys Stone." She rocked back to her heels in order to look him in the eye, "I will never forget you."

Luke's face crumpled, "But Kit and Livvy will."

Surely this pain was too great.

She felt near to bursting with it, yet seeing it reflected in Luke's eyes, she knew she would take more if it meant relieving him of his. She hugged him to her again, wishing that it were possible for her to do so; to take the pain from him.

"Listen, listen," She hushed, comfortingly, "That will never happen, I will not allow it. I will speak of you every day and always remind them of their big brother."

She tightened her arms around him, "I made a promise to Kit and Livvy that I would find their father and although I have endured many hardships, I have not yet given up on that promise. Have I?"

She looked into his face once more. "Just as I will not quit this vow I make to you: After this business that I have sworn to do is complete, I vow I will do everything in my power to find you."

Luke bobbed his head up and down against her chest where she cradled his head.

"Be my brave, strong, boy," She continued, "And take care of your father. Don't let him turn too sour. You know he needs to be reminded, often, that he is human like the rest of us."

Ann teased, and her heart soared a little when the corners of Luke's lips lifted in smile, as she had intended.

She was too cowardly to meet Grayson's gaze. Not because she feared admonition from him for her jest, but because she could feel his eyes intently upon her and she knew that though her attempt to lessen the heart ache of their good-byes had thinly worked on Luke, it did little to defuse the tension between them.

"I must go." She placed a last tender kiss upon Luke's head and then hurried from the room.

Safely back within the confines of her room, the urge to throw herself onto the bed and give in to the anguished dam of tears threatening to burst through the cracks of her tormented soul was overwhelming. Thankfully, the girls strapped to her sides prevented her from partaking in such weakness, although the pain pulsating within, did not abate.

She peered out her open window below, where Jonathon awaited her near their cart, in the street. She blew out a strained breath and closed her eyes fighting for the strength to carry herself downstairs away from the people she loved and would be leaving behind.

A breeze carried in from the window, but even it could not provide Ann the air her lungs craved. She wondered if it would always hurt so to breathe?

She placed the girls on the floor. They should get as much exercise as possible before they were forced to return to the cramped quarters of a traveling cart.

The cart she and Jonathon were able to afford was not nearly as large as the wagon Ann had driven from Cumberland to Louisville.

Ann removed the pack as well in hopes of feeling less sting with her every inhale and exhale. The bed still looked inviting, she thought, but of course, she could not indulge in such childish antics.

Her eyes wandered to her daughters: her responsibility and reason to keep fighting.

She watched Kit and Livvy pull themselves to standing positions. No doubt they would be walking soon.

How strong and resilient babies were, she thought. *Their instincts drove them forward. They didn't understand failure: it wasn't an option. They would learn to crawl, and they would learn to walk, never deterred by how many times they would fall trying.*

Isn't it funny how people lose that as they age?

The outside world latches onto a body like an invasive English Ivy; spreading tendrils of fear and self-doubt like a poison throughout, until one is no longer certain of anything.

The click of a latch closing startled her from her contemplation. She abruptly turned around to find Grayson filling the space between her and the door.

His chest rose and fell swiftly as if he'd run a marathon, but Ann knew it was instead because of the fighting war within; the pain and anger whirling around inside of him. She could see it in his eyes.

"Please, don't." She pleaded softly. *Don't hurt me more than I already am hurting.*

"Don't tell me how foolish you believe me to be for the decisions I have made. I decided upon this course long before I met you, damn it!" Angry tears choked any more words from spilling forth.

Grayson's stance seemed to yield some, the angry lines pinching his face, softened, defeated.

"I-," Grayson stopped.

He had come for precisely those reasons. To shake sense into her if need be. She was his. He was hers, how could she abandon him?

But when she looked to him with her wide, amber jeweled eyes sparkling with unshed tears, and her body trembling all he wanted was to take all her hurt away.

The fighting words he'd come in with dissipated and in an instant, he was at her side. She collapsed into his embrace as he reached her. They stood then, her head tucked under his chin and face pressed against the hard planes of his chest, each clinging to one another in hopeless desperation.

Then his mouth was on hers. She tilted her head back opening to him freely, taking all he could give her and returning it with the same clawing urgency. His hands began touching her everywhere. his body was ravenous for her, taking over in an uncontrolled entity; wanting to imprint her form, her scent, the very taste of her into memories that would last him a lifetime.

"I only want you. I only want you..." She wept.

"Don't leave me."

It was his breathless words, as he trailed kisses along her neck, that repelled her away from him once more.

She stared back listlessly, her spirit broken. "I have to."

Grayson's hurt and anger returned. *Vow to her daughters, or no, couldn't she see the destruction and havoc she was wreaking on everyone's lives wasn't worth it?*

The fire licking in his eyes reflected the pain burning through him, "Do you really think this man will be the father Kit and Livvy deserve? He's a scoundrel! A vagabond!"

Ann averted her eyes to the floor.

"I love you, Ann, but I don't understand. I love those girls-" Grayson's voice hitched.

Ann lifted her eyes to his intently and said, "If they were your daughters, wouldn't you want to know of them? Can you honestly say that keeping a man's daughters from him is honorable?"

Grayson remained silent.

"You don't know James like I do," Ann continued while Grayson still chewed on her question.

"I admit that the illustrious visage of adventure that cloaked him, blinded me to his faults; faults that have become painfully obvious over the past year."

Ann struggled to find the words that would open Grayson's heart to her reasoning. How to make him understand? No longer fooled by her own imaginings, and able to dissect her memories of James, she felt strongly that keeping his daughters secret from him unfair punishment.

"I no longer hold affection for James, tis true. And I have no illusions that he ever loved me. But that does not mean he would not love *them*." She pointed to the girls still, playing on the floor, oblivious to the tension in the room.

Grayson's eyes softened as he followed her direction to the dearly loved girls. But when he returned his gaze to Ann, his eyes were hard once more.

"The question is irrelevant, because you see, Ann, there is no way I would ever sire children into this world and not know of it. I would never, *have* never, left procreation to chance. Simply put, I would never be so careless as to bed a woman without taking precautions to prevent an undesired pregnancy. And I would *never* feign marriage to a vulnerable young girl in order to satisfy lusts and shallow fancies."

It was true, she knew. Grayson would never be so reckless or so careless. But he was a cad to think himself above human imperfections.

"I know all I need to of him," Grayson spat, "And he doesn't deserve *the honor* and privilege of being a father to *them*." His face was twisted in disgust.

Silence filled the room, with seemingly no way to breach the divide in their hearts. Air swirled in from the window, sending a chill throughout the room to match the cold stare of Grayson's eyes upon her.

"You are not their father. He is," She said simply. "If I could go back in time and change it, well, honestly, I don't know that I would."

The breeze swished her skirts around her ankles and her hair across her face, emphasizing the tangled feelings within.

"I'd not give up my daughters for the world."

She sniffled back the sting of tears.

"If I could have you both..."

Her voice hitched.

"I wish they were yours and Luke was mine, and they were ours. I wish-I wish..."

She moved the blowing strands of hair from her face and lifted her eyes to Grayson's grimly.

"But wishing won't make it so. These are our lives. We have to live them. And all the mistakes -mistakes we've both made- Well, we have to live with those too." She trailed off woefully.

"Yes." He agreed with a hard look glinting his eyes, "Mistakes have been made. I vowed never to trust another woman after Vivian. I broke that vow. I'll not do so again."

His words were meant to cut, and they did so like tiny shards of ice piercing her heart.

She saw through the cold steel of his eyes, though, to the raw pain beneath.

Pain she'd caused.

And it nearly broke her.

Chapter 16

They hadn't been able to afford tickets to ferry from St. Louis to Independence so were forced to travel the more painstakingly slow mode by wagon. Of course, they had not been able to afford the bigger Conestoga wagon and team either.

It made for a grueling trip with the smaller enclosed wagon, more of a cart in Ann's opinion. She, Jonathon, and the girls could not all fit with the supplies. They'd even had to suffer it partially stocked and hope they would be able to replenish at stops along the way.

The first week of travel, Jonathon had kindly kept the talking to a minimum. She supposed she hadn't made it difficult for him to sense her irritable state of melancholy. The girls, too, had become increasingly agitated once it became clear their brother would not be appearing to occupy their interests. They'd lost their caregiver as well as playmate.

Ann had dwelled upon that loss, as well as her painful parting with Grayson, for the entire 250 miles to Independence. She recalled over and over, the slamming of her hotel door behind him as he fled furiously from the room.

Was there something different she could have said? Something more she should have said?

She reenacted the scene in her mind continuously, searching for that answer, until she'd exhausted all avenues of thought on the matter.

Kit and Livvy were impatient and irritable and Ann decided they required her full attention. Perhaps if she concentrated on them and let go of her own frustrations, they would feel comforted.

Ann was right. Once she decided to let go of her anger, while unable to forget her pain, but at least bury it deep down inside where it couldn't be seen, her daughters began to smile again. Their ornery cantankerous attitudes faded along with her own. And the next length of their journey passed more smoothly.

Jonathon eventually sensed the shift in her as well and began to brave conversation with her. Their conversations never ran very deep; mostly he spoke of the childhood he shared with James.

Although Jonathon never proclaimed to harbor any jealousies, Ann could sense it in the hostile tone of his voice when he spoke of James. She was not certain how she felt about that. If everything Jonathon described was true, she could understand why Jonathon would feel some antipathy over the man.

She'd grown tired of hearing all of James' faults, however, and tried to politely direct conversation away from such sour topics when she could. Guilt for having treated Jonathon rather poorly in the beginning of their travels spurred her to be extra kind and considerate of his sensibilities.

She tried to keep that in mind now.

His incessant whining, and the desert heat since passing Council Grove, were both getting on her nerves, though. Her irritation grew with every itchy bead of sweat until she was ready to curse and swear off all men the worldwide.

Nearly five days had passed since they'd left the Arkansas River behind. The men stationed there had informed them it would be the last stop for water for sixty miles until they reached the Cimarron River.

Ann had heeded their warning well, but she'd only had so many barrels and canteens she could fill with water and they were empty and dry as the grit seeded air they breathed.

They had gone through the last of the barrels yesterday morning, forced to rely solely on their personal canteens. The horses had to suffer without.

The heat of the full fiery sun blazing down upon them only exacerbated matters. Ann tried to lick her chapped lips, but her tongue was like sawdust in her mouth.

She had nearly a fourth of her canteen left, but she daren't use it on herself. Luckily the girls were sleeping through the miserable midday heat, but when they awoke, Ann knew they would need the water.

She fervently hoped they would reach the river soon. Even Jonathon appeared ready to topple from his seat.

"Here, let me drive, a bit," she managed to croak out.

Jonathon gladly conceded the reins over to her expert hands. The horses were far easier to maneuver than the mules she'd had to drive to Louisville, but her strength was waning with her growing thirst.

She hadn't driven long when she spied it. A divinely glowing, glimmering, blue swath of ribbon amidst the deadened earth: the Cimarron River. Like a celestial light, it beckoned her.

The horses were drawn to it as well, for they nearly pulled the reins from her hands in their effort to reach it.

She pulled the cart off the trail nearer to the embankment. She hopped down to unhitch the horses and hobble them beside the cart. She couldn't allow them access to the stream yet, for she feared they would gulp down the water too fast and colic. She instead grabbed for a pail from the back of the cart.

The girls were still napping, so she made her way to the water. Jonathon was already knelt in the wet sand, greedily cupping water to his face and splashing it unto his hair. Ann sank to the earth as well, allowing the frigid water from the sparkling stream to soak through her skirts and cool the sun's burning heat from her body.

She quickly splashed some water up both sides of her arms, onto her face, and rubbed some of its blissful coolness on to the back of her neck, then forced herself to stand and carry the full pail to the horses. She alternated between them, allowing only for a few sips in each turn until she felt they were cooled enough to receive more.

Luckily, Jonathon returned to the wagon just as she heard the girls stirring from within.

"Here," She stretched the bucket in Jonathon's direction and politely commanded, "You take over this chore, while I see to the girls, will you."

He did as she bid, albeit slowly.

Too slowly, in Ann's opinion. She preferred tasks performed speedily and efficiently. She tried to ignore her soldier training, however, and refrain from snappish impatience. It would do her well to keep in mind that Jonathon had never had to see to physical duties that did not revolve around himself prior to this trip and he was managing as best he was able.

Never mind that nine-year-old Luke had better adapted to trail life and seen fit to carry responsibilities of a man's proportion.

She kicked the toe of her boot into the wagon wheel in frustration. She sighed; she wasn't doing a very good job of maintaining a tolerant attitude.

The girls were soaked through with sweat when she pulled them from the wagon. She decided to take them directly to the stream and bathe them in it to cool them off. As she suspected, the poor dears had heat rash spread across their dimply, little, bottoms. It was no wonder they'd been so crabby of late. This tiring heat was difficult on all of them, including the animals.

They were very near to Santa Fe, so Ann did not wish to tarry long; even though the spring was a welcome respite from the heat and traveling on in this dreary desert land was almost too punishing of a thought.

Ann decided she'd endured enough miserable hours trussed up in layers of skirt beneath the baking sizzle of the desert sun. She took the girls back to the wagon where she let them crawl around on a blanket bare bottomed in hopes the air would dry their posterior and heal the rash faster.

She then sought out Jonathon, who by this time was finished watering the horses. She tried to ignore the fact that he had not taken the initiative to replenish the water barrels as of yet, although she couldn't resist a roll of her eyes and issuing of complaints in her mind.

"Jonathon," she barked, snappier than she had intended.

She cleared her throat and sought patience, "I need a pair of your trousers and one of those linen shirts you're wearing, please."

Honestly? She thought to snipe at the man whilst asking a favor of him? How ill-mannered of her.

Jonathon looked from her down at his pants and back to her again.

"Good heavens, not the ones you are wearing," It was all she could do not to look as entirely exasperated as she felt.

"You have extras, I know, as I've done your laundry as well as mine for over the past six months."

"You-you want my trousers?"

"Please. I cannot stand to sweat in this heavy mass of fabric another day. Also, it's quite dripping wet and I'd like to quickly wash my, ahem, unmentionables as well."

Jonathon's cheeks burned with mortification on her behalf and barely managed to stumble and stutter out a simple, "Y-yes," before dashing for the wagon and his bag of personal belongings.

After having retrieved the requested articles of clothing from Jonathon she made her way back to the stream, leaving Jonathon to watch over the girls and promising she would wash up quickly. She would have liked to have taken her time disrobing and savoring the cool licking current, but the stream was not deep enough to bathe adequately in and they didn't have enough supplies nor time, to waste on frivolities.

She dried off and hurried into the borrowed trousers, pulling them up over the prominent bones at her waist. She guessed she lost well over two stone on this trip. Luckily, much of that had been excess weight from her post birth of the twins, but even so, she was thinner than she'd ever been before her pregnancy. She couldn't help but think she looked a starving street urchin, especially clothed now in Jonathon's larger, baggier, attire.

She tightened the black cord tie as well as she could. At least the yet, slight swell of her hips would prevent them from falling down. She tucked the long length of the white linen shirt into the waist of the pants which helped fit them more closely to her as well. She then rolled the sleeves to her elbows. She should probably have buttoned the blouse to the neck, but damn if it wasn't hotter than the devil's own oven in this blasted country! She buttoned just one past where the valley of cleavage began.

Jonathon could hang propriety!

She gathered her damp belongings, already partially dried from having laid out on the embankment in the searing sun while Ann donned her new set of britches and scrambled up the slight hill to the wagon.

Jonathon's eyes bugged at the sight of her, with obvious male appreciation. She hadn't thought her form all that enticing, rail thin as it was and packaged in the ill-fitting attire she was in.

Oh, botheration. Men could be such imbeciles.

"Jonathon," Her clipped, assertive tone effectively seized his attention away from her person, "We need to fill the barrels quickly and be on our way. We should get in some distance before dark yet."

He nodded and took to transporting the kegs to the stream. Ann took the time to hang her clothes from the wheel of the wagon in hopes they dried the rest of the way in the little time it would take to pack the filled barrels of water and hitch the horses.

Inside, the girls squealed. Ann joined them in the wagon and found a hard biscuit for them to snack on. It wouldn't nearly be enough, but Ann thought it would get them through until they made camp for the night and could fry up some of the salted pork they still had meager supply of. Ann hoped they made it to Santa Fe quickly from here.

She helped Jonathon latch the barrels back to the sides of the cart, then re-hitch the horses. They crossed the stream easily and climbed the hill on the other side of it.

When they crested the hill, the sight before them sent bone chilling shivers down her spine.

Two Comanche warriors sitting astride painted horses stood calmly blocking the path, directing their stony gazes at them. Ann's heart began pounding in her chest. Her mind raced with horrid thoughts and fear tingled through her extremities for her daughters playing behind her in the wagon. They were partially sheltered, and Ann hoped out of view of the natives. Their stop at the Arkansas River had been quite informative on the ways of the Comanche. Ann had hoped since they'd made it to the Lower Springs unscathed, that they had avoided any run ins with them.

She'd been wrong.

Jonathon tipped his hat to the intimidating, copper skinned men, and tried to maneuver the cart politely around them. For his part he remained calm and in control, something Ann may not have believed of him if not for witnessing it with her own eyes.

She was grateful for his clear and decisive thinking in this moment, for her head was a swirling muddle of graphic, horrifying, imaginings.

She heard the Braves speaking in their native tongue. They seemed to be in discord over something. The larger one of the two, whose hair was sectioned into two equal parts, the bottoms of each section twisted through with some sort of red bands, spoke first.

He spoke the same word, repeating it twice and pointed to Ann excitedly. The leaner man next to him who's satiny black hair fell loose to just past his shoulders, and who wore a band that wrapped around his crown decorated with two feathers, shook his head vehemently and backed his horse a step. He pointed to Ann and then to his own eyes. Something about his posture and wide eyes made Ann think he feared her or their wagon for some reason.

She feared once Jonathon directed the wagon back to the path, that they would see the girls through the opening in the back. Ann wouldn't take any chances. She slipped over the bench, smoothly thanks to the freedom allowed by the borrowed trousers she wore. Jonathon tried to stop her with a tug to her shirt.

He grumbled something under his breath as well, that sounded like, "Don't, you'll draw more attention."

But there was no way Ann was leaving her girls back there unprotected. Besides, her pistols were back there. She thought it high time she reacquainted herself with them.

To her surprise though, the Comanche did not attack, seemingly content to follow; keeping all the tiny hairs on Ann's body raised with unease. They followed at such a distance, it appeared they had ceased trailing them altogether.

The horses could not continue on without rest and water, but Ann was loathed to stop.

"We cannot make it to Santa Fe tonight."

Jonathon's hoarse voice whispered to her into the dark of the enclosed wagon behind him.

"I know."

Ann's babies were asleep. The sun had gone down nearly an hour ago and it was fully dark, now.

"What do we do?"

So often she relished being in charge and in control. This time Ann wished she had someone else to defer too. Ann closed her eyes to see Grayson's assertive figure flash in her mind. *Oh, how I wish you were here...*

Jonathon spoke again, "I think, perhaps they moved on upon realizing we did not have much to offer."

They had plenty to offer. Their scalps for one, if Ann was to believe the couple soldiers stationed back on the Arkansas River crossing. Apparently more and more white settlers were arriving to the Texas land and pushing the Comanche out of their way in the process; brutally killing them, and worse, to drive them from their land.

That seemed incentive enough to Ann for the Comanche men to continue after them. What she didn't understand is why they hadn't attacked right away. Why keep their distance and follow? As the night sky descended upon them, Ann feared their absence was deceptively beguiling. She wouldn't allow herself and the girls to be easy pickings though.

"We make camp." Ann spoke decisively.

"You think they're gone then?"

"No." She replied softly.

Jonathon looked frustrated.

"We'll water the horses and take shifts during the night, with guns at the ready just in case."

There was little light within the wagon, but Ann could still see Jonathon's throat muscles work as he swallowed. He gave her a curt nod, though, despite his doubts.

"No fire. If you eat, let it be only hard tack. The girls and I ate earlier while you were driving."

Truthfully, with her stomach in knots and her constant eye out the rear of the wagon on their unwanted company, she'd not been able to eat. But as her stomach was still sick with apprehension, she knew better not to bother with even a light repast.

"Let's move quickly and keep the horses hitched to the wagon. It's cloudy as of now, but if the sky clears, we may yet travel on tonight. I'll stand guard while you see to the horses."

Even on Jonathon's shift, Ann found she couldn't sleep entirely. The clouds remained, casting the night in a near inky blackness, so they were forced to stay put. Feeling a sitting duck, Ann knew she would never find sleep and finally traded places with Jonathon for good.

He was wise enough to her moods not to dispute the matter with her. As soon as the dawn cracked its first meager light above the stubbly terrain that was the desert floor, Ann prepared the horses once more for travel and woke Jonathon to drive.

After an hour or so of travel, Jonathon spoke, "Well, I take it we're safe now. Surely if they were to attack it would have been sometime in the night."

His statement held a hint of question in it though.

Kit and Livvy were crawling about her feet and she was serving them breakfast via more stale, crusty biscuits.

They found it great fun to have mommy serving as their personal climbing tree for the time being. Ann wished she could afford them the attention they so obviously yearned for. Her heart skipped painfully with the reminder of Luke. How she missed him...

Just then she heard Jonathon yell, "Ann!"

Before he could say more, an arrow whizzed, seemingly from nowhere, and pierced Jonathon in the chest. He groaned and fell from his perched seat on the bench to the ground. Ann in an unthinking state of shock, dived for the reins.

She wanted to slap the reins against the horses and run. She couldn't leave Jonathon behind though. The arrow had hit at an angle somewhat in the right side of his ribs. There was a chance he could survive. Ann quickly hit the parking brake and tied off the reins. Then she grabbed the rifle off the seat and promptly aimed for the first strange body she sighted.

Only, there was no one in sight. Ann's ears tuned in finely to the eerie silence. Her breathing was harsh and heavy, coming in as rapidly as her heartbeat. The pounding in her ears and noisy breath made it difficult to hear. She jumped from the bench seat, rifle still fitted snugly to her shoulder and took light, slow steps towards the rear of the wagon.

She spied Jonathon on the ground only a short distance away. He was wriggling in slow, agonized movements.

Next, clunking noises of wood and harness sounded. They were unhitching the horses! She turned to run back towards the horses when she spied a partially nude, copper hued body appear at the back of the wagon. *The girls!*

From that angle, she'd not get a shot. She raced alongside the wagon to the back with the hammer pulled back on the rifle ready to fire in an instant. The rifle barrel reached the rear of the wagon first. Before she could turn to aim, a muscled arm swung down hard, knocking the rifle from her grasp entirely.

The Comanche sneered at her with a promising glint in his eye. In one easy hop, he was down from the wagon, towering over her. She knew the other Indian was at the front of the wagon near the horses, she prayed his interests remained averted from the girls while she dealt with this one. She recognized him as the larger of the two who'd followed them from the springs.

His eyes roved over her person, leaving little doubt the plans he had for her. She knew she would have to act quickly. Though she'd practiced different fighting strategies alongside her father and uncle, she'd never had to implement them in actuality. She was glad for the knife Grayson insisted she keep on her at all times.

Since switching from her voluptuous skirts where concealing a weapon was made vastly easier, and into trousers, she'd not had an area of which to secure even one of her pistols. But she'd found room for the knife tucked into her folded pant cuff inside her boot.

She'd have to reach down for it and remove it from her boot and its sheath with speed enough to impart a deadly blow to the Comanche before he reached her... And time was of the essence.

Just as she was about to drop down to retrieve her knife, she saw the other Comanche hop into the wagon. She could hear both Kit and Livvy's fearful wails from within. Her immediate concern shifted to her daughters, distracting her from the threatening man nearest her.

"Leave them!" She roared and lunged for the wagon, only to be intercepted by the solid wall of man she'd forgotten in her haste for her daughters' imminent safety.

The large Comanche with the braids crushed her body to his but her wild eyes crazed with panic were latched on the man in the wagon, now holding Livvy away from him as if scrutinizing whether the babe was worth his energy. Every motherly instinct came together in Ann's body in an astonishing rush of adrenaline.

With speed she hadn't known she possessed she slipped her body, like an eel, down the Indian form that held her, dropping to the ground in one languid movement. In the same instant, grabbing the hilt of her knife and dragging it up along her leg with enough pressure to release it and slide it from the confines of its sheath.

The Comanche made unsuccessful swiping motions with his arms on her descent to the ground in effort to prevent her maneuver and before he realized what she was about reached down for her again. That was when she drove herself back up with the ferocity and desperation of a lioness springing onto the only meal that would ensure her survival for another day and plunged the knife into the demon's chest. She felt the knife blade glance off bone before gliding easily between two ribbed slits to the beating muscle within.

The Comanche's eyes widened with shock. He opened his mouth to utter something, but instead blood gurgled and sputtered forth, sprinkling its ruby spray across Ann's face. Ann showed no mercy for the villain that shot Jonathon and would have performed unthinkable acts of violence on her. The Indian fell to his knees before her, eyes already glazed over with the passing of death. Ann kicked him onto his back on the ground, then stepped upon him to offer resistance as she pulled her knife from his chest.

She did not allow for her mind to ruminate over the fact that she had just killed a man. Out of the corner of her eye she saw the other Comanche swing easily up onto his horse with Livvy hooked under his arm. Ann's heart thundered and roared in her ears; the only sound Ann's world emitted her to hear in that moment. It was as if all the rest of the world deafened into nonexistence.

Boom! Boom! Boom! Her heart thudded in her chest and ears. She felt its furious pulsing course in the very marrow of her bones. Her instincts propelled her forward in a race for the other horse that was no longer in the possession of the dead Comanche currently saturating the thirsty desert floor with his life's blood.

She swung up onto the back of the stallion with as much ease as the Indian who'd made off with Livvy seconds ago. Ann, no stranger to riding bare back or at breakneck speed, dashed off after the perpetrator who'd captured her daughter. Her muscles recalled the practiced skills automatically, as if she had not been absent from a horse's back for over a year.

She kicked her heels into her mount, squeezing from it all its spirit could give in a race for her daughter's life. The surrounding world became a dizzying blur as she and the horse cut through the air, flying at a pace Ann had never been before. She observed the Comanche struggling to keep hold of her daughter and remain balanced at such speeds.

Please let me reach her in time. Ann sent a rare prayer up to the heavens.

Her senses riveted to the sight of the horse's hooves suddenly slowing in front of her and the Indian turning towards her with the reins in his teeth, instead of his hand. A flash of shine glinting off something metal caught her attention and Ann knew the Indian was aiming a gun at her.

She swung her legs wide bringing them to meet the sides of the horse in repetitive abandon. The horse sped faster and faster as if it too, sensed the peril.

Ann reacted quickly. She wrapped her legs around her mount tightly. Then as the gun fired, swung herself so that her entire body was nearly, wholly on one side of her racing horse. She pulled herself quickly back up into place on the horse's back once more, with a victorious grin, knowing she had cost the Comanche his shot. He'd not be able to reload with Livvy beneath one of his arms, nor without powder. She glimpsed a metallic shine fall to the earth as the Indian discarded the gun in order to focus once more on his escape. Within a second's time, she was parallel with him. His failed attempt to shoot her cost him a wasted shot as well as wasted time.

She tried to pull Livvy from his grasp, but with the reins clenched firmly in his teeth once more, he used his other arm to inhibit her actions. His arms were longer and stronger.

But Ann's love for her daughter was greater.

Her horse coughed, and she knew it had given all it could. The time to get Livvy was now or she would never see her daughter again. Fear filled her with an adrenaline induced rage.

A barbaric cry tore from her lips and she lunged with all the strength and will she possessed, plunging the knife grasped tightly in her pale, desperate fingers into the back of the sinewed shoulder that held Livvy. The Comanche howled in pain from the unexpected attack and slackened his arm as Ann anticipated. She grabbed her daughter in that moment and pulled her to her chest in one fierce movement.

She cradled her wailing daughter to her chest tightly. She pulled back on the reins sending her horse sliding to a halt, but before the animal came to a full stop, Ann already had it rolled onto its haunches and pivoted in the opposite direction, riding away. She glanced back and saw the Indian continued in the other direction at full speed. Ann slowed her mount to a gallop, the poor animal continued hacking from its over exerted run.

I'm sorry, you beautiful animal. Ann squeezed her eyes tight in silent respect for the horse. She would never have condoned such cruelty to an animal under other circumstances, but when it came to the life of the horse or that of her daughter, she knew she would make the same choice again.

Ann would always choose her daughters lives over anything or anyone: including herself.

She glanced over her shoulder once more. The wounded Comanche was nothing more than a vanishing speck on the empty horizon. Ann expelled what she believed had to be her first breath since the attack. She wanted to slow the horse more, but it was imperative she get back to the wagon to check Kit as well as Jonathon.

Kit was squalling when she arrived at the wagon, pinned between a trunk and a one-hundred-pound sack of flour, with a barrel lid atop her like a small shelter. It had kept her from sight of the Comanche, Ann assumed, and protected her. She settled the girls best she could in quick time; they were distressed, but uninjured, so Ann hastily constructed a pen and was forced to leave them in their state of tribulation. Ann would see to their comfort, but firstly she had to get to Jonathon.

Ann left the wagon-and her daughters-warily. She neither saw, nor heard anyone approaching, still she made her steps quick to Jonathon's prone body. He appeared dead. Blood dribbled from his lips, his skin stark white against the dusty brown stained collar of his shirt. Her discerning eye detected a slight rise and fall of his chest. She dropped to her knees at his side.

"Jonathon?" She spoke tentatively.

His eyes fluttered open.

"Ann," He called out to her, pleasure evident in his tone, "You're alive." His body erupted into a fit of coughing.

"Shh, shh, shh," she soothed, "Yes, the girls and I are safe."

"I failed. I failed to protect you," Jonathon's face twisted in grimacing pain, "Stone. -He made me promise. He outfitted me with more weapons. I didn't believe him."

His breaths were coming far more rapidly and shallow, preventing him from speaking more.

"No, no. You did. You saw them and yelled to me, even though you'd been wounded. You still bravely warned me and gave me time to protect myself and the girls."

"The Indians we met before, they'd been gentle, kind. I didn't believe him." His eyes were wide, terrified with shock remembering the attack.

While he'd been speaking, Ann had removed his shirt and tied it tautly around him to staunch the blood flowing from his wound.

"Yes. Shh, no more talking, "she crooned.

"I'm afraid I cannot drag you back the distance to the wagon. I'm sure that would not improve your wound either. You shall have to wait here a few moments more. I shall hitch the horses and circle back. Won't take long, I promise."

Jonathon's hand shot out and clasped around her wrist with surprising strength in his wounded state.

"No, Ann, I must tell you-," his words were cut off with another fit of coughing. A thick swell of blood streamed from his mouth.

"No, Jonathon, you mustn't speak. Please, let me bring the wagon back. We'll get you to Santa Fe. There must be a doctor in Santa Fe."

She tried unsuccessfully to hide the panic rising in her voice.

Jonathon used much of his waning strength to pull himself into a sitting position, his grip on Ann's wrist, not lessening.

"I have documents, in my trunk."

Ann could tell this was important to him, so she ceased arguing and allowed him to continue.

"I purchased a marriage license. It's all very legal."

A few more sputtering coughs escaped him. Ann's lips tightened to prevent her from stopping him again.

"All you need to do is sign it. Then you will be protected by my name. I-I loved you as soon as I saw you."

He coughed again. It seemed to drain his remaining strength from him, and he lowered himself back to the ground. He brought his other hand around, though, and covered hers with it, while continuing to hold her hand in place over his heart with the other.

Sweat accumulated in beads along his mustache and across the rest of his pale face. Before Ann could respond to his surprising revelation, he smiled up to the sky and with glazed eyes spoke once more. His words sounded as if he were dreaming aloud, as he said, "My Ann with the golden eyes..."

Ann watched in horror as his head lolled to the side on those parting words, his eyes now glassy and lifeless.

"No! No, Jonathon. I'm going to bring the wagon. You'll be fine! I'm going to bring the wagon!"

Dear God. He was dead.

Thoughts bombarded her mind from every angle. First processing that this man she'd come to know fairly well had just died before her eyes. Her strongest ally, whom she'd apparently underestimated just how much she'd meant to him. Guilt for not having realized Jonathon had harbored tender feelings for her, while at the same time she had felt little more

273

than friendship at best and oft times worse and severely agitated with the man.

She didn't know how to sort through the overwhelming chaos of emotions, and she didn't have time. The wounded Comanche more than likely returned to his people and would undoubtedly be back with more friends for vengeance.

Although unhitched, the horses remained near to the wagon. They could probably smell the water in the barrels, thankfully.

Ann shut her eyes tightly out of respect for Jonathon. He'd paid the ultimate price for this journey and now she realized it had been for her sake rather than for the shared goal of locating his cousin as he'd led her to believe. This was a new burden on her heart. She couldn't even give the poor soul a proper burial. There was not time enough to dig a shallow grave.

She could not keep his body in the wagon with her daughters, nor did she have the resources to build a stretcher of any sort to pull behind. Not to mention, any way of transporting the body would only slow her, and she wasn't fool enough to chance that the Comanche she'd wounded wasn't gathering reinforcements to come back to slake his revenge on her. She needed to get her and her babies away from here as quickly as possible.

I'm so sorry Jonathon.

Ann worked to wrap his body in a sheet she had stowed away in the wagon. It would have to do. She then used some precious ink to write his name on the linen so that he may be identified if other travelers happened to come across his body. Then she issued a silent prayer over his form.

Ann's nimble fingers made short work of re-hitching her two-team of horses, then tied the, yet lathered, Indian pony behind the wagon. After settling the girls and placing them within the safety of the wagon, she reloaded her guns, then drove to the area where the Comanche had fired upon her and dropped the gun he'd stolen from her. She quickly checked its barrel and pan, clearing them of all dust and dirt particles as she drove. With the guns within reach of her readied hands she picked up the pace sending the team into a gallop for the better part of the way to Santa Fe.

Ann's Valley

She'd stopped only briefly in the night to water the horses and allow them to graze on some of the short buffalo grass. Ann herself, though exhausted to the point of near collapse, did not permit herself to sleep. Instead she kept the team moving at a brisk but safe walk throughout the night, returning to a gallop once more by the light of day.

She rode into Santa Fe on the dust cloud she carried with her.

She'd made it.

Chapter 17

Ann pulled up her lathered team; she would begin with seeing to their care while she deliberated on how to find James. Some curious onlookers paused briefly to stare at her as she made her way to find a livery. She couldn't fault them for it, she must appear quite the spectacle. A woman in man's clothes riding as if chased by the hounds of hell. -Not to mention said clothes were soiled with accumulated dust, sweat, and blood.

Too much blood, Ann reflected morosely.

Most people about the town continued on as if newcomers like *her* were a regular occurrence. An unsettling notion, that. Just what sort of town was Santa Fe if the people were accustomed to such dramatics? She'd thought the town marked her safety from the Comanches. Ann shivered - judging by the lack of reaction from passersby, perhaps not. She needed to find James quickly.

The town was nothing more than a few pueblo constructed buildings and store fronts.

And Dust.

Ann recalled the lush green Allegheny mountains she'd traveled through and the grassy hills of Kentucky. A faint memory transpired of the forested Exmoors she'd romped in as a child and she wondered if she'd ever see and smell such wholesome land again?

Thinking of *home* in *England* at this time would break her, and she needed to remain strong. She managed to choke down the memory along with the dust coating her dry mouth.

A young woman appeared before her. Her thick, dark, braided hair hung over her shoulder, contrasting sharply with the crisp white of her loose blouse. Her wide brown eyes took Ann in.

Ann tried to smile, but her dry, cracked lips split painfully and it came across more as a grimace. Her voice was little more than a croak when she tried to speak.

"Hello," She attempted to swallow against the dryness and tried again, "Hello. I'm looking for a livery or stables to put my team up for the night?"

The young lady's face looked on her pityingly, but Ann also read kindness there.

She tipped her head in greeting, "Si."

She pointed a slender, copper toned arm in the direction Ann was heading. Ann could make out a corral next to a building towards the end of the street. The buildings were few but spread apart, making the street unnecessarily longer than it ought to be, in Ann's opinion.

Then again, every bone in Ann's body was weary with exhaustion. Perhaps she was just contrary due to sleep deprivation as well as from the fear riding her all the way from the Cimarron Springs.

Ann was about to dip her head in thanks, when the small woman spoke again.

"After you see to the horses. Come. Mi madre has rooms. Clean beds. We shall fix you a good Mexican meal." She smiled, "And a bath."

Ann smiled then too and some of the tension in her body eased. "Thank you."

The young woman gestured down the dirt ally, where some pueblo style homes, and some other scattered businesses resided. Ann watched her turn into the first block-like structure, longer than the others. Square cut windows lined the long front, but no glass panes resided within them.

It must be this town's idea of an Inn, thought Ann. But she'd take it and gladly. A real bed after sleeping in the cramped wagon with the girls for months was too comforting a thought to turn her nose up at.

It hadn't taken Ann long to deal with the owner of the livery, although the man did not speak English. -Not even broken English as the young lady she'd spoken with earlier had. She'd traded Jonathon's saddle for one night's board for her horses and cart. Or at least, that was Ann's understanding of their arrangement.

She felt a small measure of guilt for having bartered Jonathon's belongings, but she could see no reason in hanging onto the items either. If James decided he wanted them for sentimental value, then he would have to see about purchasing them back, she decided.

Ann carted the girls in the sling around her chest and her two bags of luggage at her side. The rest she'd have to chance leaving with the cart. She hoped the people of Santa Fe were honest people.

If the young lady she'd spoken with earlier was surprised to see Ann with two large babies strapped to her, she did not show it. Instead she gestured kindly for her to enter the establishment.

A more aged and robust woman bearing the same features as the young lady stopped wiping down one of the four tables to offer a friendly smile.

"Bienvenido a Rosa's."

Then, surprised by the sight of two babies strapped to Ann, the woman held up two fingers and exclaimed with a toothy smile, "¡Dios mío! Dos niñas."

Then the woman's skirts billowed into quick sashaying movements. Her purposeful strides bringing her closer to Ann and the girls to make their acquaintance.

"Bonitas niñas."

She smiled again after peeking at both Kit and Livvy and fussing over them both with delight. Next, the woman spoke to the young lady, who Ann presumed to be her daughter, in more of the foreign tongue. The younger nodded her head to her mother before turning to Ann.

"Mi madre say you have beautiful girls."

Ann smiled congenially, "Thank you."

"She also say you are welcome to a room and she will start food for you, no?"

"Yes, I would be ever so grateful. I thank you both for your kindness."

The young lady dipped her chin in returned complementary.

"My name is Elena. Mi madre es Señora Rosa Valenzuela Espinosa."

Elena's eyes crinkled teasingly, and a smile again brightened her features,

"But you may simply call her Rosa."

"Tis a pleasure to meet you Rosa and Elena. My name is Ann, and these are my daughters: Catherine and Lavinia."

She faced each daughter to their audience as she introduced them. It had been so long since Ann had called them by their formal names, it sounded strange even to her ears.

"Follow me and I will show you to your room, so you and the little ones may freshen up before supper is readied."

Just as Ann turned to follow, she caught a glimpse of a familiar form walk past across the street.

"Wait!" Ann shouted. She swiveled back to the startled Elena, "I'm sorry. I know that man. I must speak to him!"

"Mr. Morgan?"

"Yes! Yes, James Morgan."

Elatedness and anxiousness came to a head and bubbled within her. *Mr. Morgan.* She'd been right, it was him!

Both women watched, Elena with concern and Ann with renewed determination and hope, as the man they discussed walked into a saloon across the street.

"It appears you must wait to speak with him, now," Elena spoke reasonably.

Women did not enter saloons in America just as ladies did not enter such establishments in England.

But Ann wasn't inclined to follow gender restricting dictates.

Half afraid James would vanish again before she could get to him, Ann glanced between the view of the saloon and towards the hall that led to her rooms, uncertain how best to proceed.

Ann nodded, trying to force a state of calm over her body even while her heart continued to race in her chest.

Elena proceeded forth and continued the lead to the room Ann would be staying in for the night. Ann did not spare even a glance at the accommodations. She just hurriedly placed her bags onto the brightly hued, quilt covered mattress. Then turned on booted heel to make her exit.

Elena of course yet stood in the doorway.

"Thank you, the room is lovely." Ann felt compelled to compliment the quarters even though she had not actually observed whether the room was "lovely" or not, due to her hasty retreat and what could be misinterpreted for dissatisfaction with the space.

She then added in explanation, "I must speak to Mr. Morgan right away. It is urgent business that concerns him."

Elena's eyes were wide with shock and disbelief, but she recovered quickly and said politely, "Of course."

Ann stepped around Elena into the hall with intent of marching to the saloon, but instead Elena stayed her with her hand gently grasped to Ann's elbow.

"Please! Please. You should not go in there. Bad men are there."

Ann replied simply, "I must."

The two women studied one another; Ann searching for understanding, Elena searching for logic in what appeared to be a mad woman.

Elena surrendered, stating patiently, "If you must, at least allow me to care for las niñas. Do not take them to that place."

Ann swallowed. She did not want to take her daughters into a saloon. Nor for them to be present for her first confrontation with James. But to trust strangers with her daughters seemed equally risky.

Elena could see Ann thinking over the offer. "We will remain here, within sight of the saloon. I will feed the girls." Elena reached her arms for Kit and Livvy, kindly.

Elena and her mother seemed to be very generous people and openly kind and genuine. Her gut told her they could be trusted. She handed over Kit and Livvy. The girls were becoming accustomed to seeing many new faces, however, were still reluctant to leave Ann's side.

Ann kissed each of them on the forehead, "It's okay my dears. Mummy will be back as quickly as possible."

Of course, they could not understand Ann's words to them, but she hoped her tone would mollify any fears on their part. Elena was gentle with them and with each under her arm followed Ann back into the dining area where Rosa was busy behind the counter.

Elena called to her mother, "Madre. Mira, tenemos que cuidar a las chicas por un tiempo."

Rosa turned wearing a smile, although confusion knit her delicate brows together. She took in the scene before her: Elena holding the twin girls and Ann near the door and surmised quickly Ann's intentions. From one mother to another, an understanding passed between them.

Rosa nodded her head in a small assertive manner indicating her accord with Ann's plans. She was a woman and a mother herself and knew well the harsh realities and limited choices afforded women in this world.

With that Ann charged across in wide purposeful strides, not allowing for speculation and doubt to cause hesitation. Although admittedly, she had not as of yet formulated a plan. All the speeches and deliveries of said speeches practiced repeatedly in her mind over the changing courses of the past year seemed but a blurred, unfocused, whirring storm.

She could hear only the soles of her boots crunching into the packed dirt as she made her way across rutted road and the sound of her heart thundering loudly in anticipation of finally confronting the man who had changed her life so drastically. Her stomach felt like she was at sea again, being tossed around like a cork in the violent waves of the angry Atlantic.

Subconsciously she swiped her sweated palms down her grimy trousers before her anxious fingers sought out the wooded handle of the pistol at her waistband. Its wood warmed in her hand bringing with it familiarity and comfort.

She took a breath.

And pushed forcefully through the swinging doors.

Her perceptive gaze took in her surroundings in an instant: the bartender stood still, in shock, behind the bar in mid swirl of a rag to the inside of a glass mug, his eyes fixed upon her. One man stood at the bar with his back to Ann, and three men sat at a table in the corner playing a hand of cards. The three men at the table stilled and stared curiously at the bedraggled woman interrupting their space. The man at the bar sensing the tension in the room slowly turned around. As he did, their eyes met.

James' silver gaze piercing her as it did nearly two years ago across a crowded ballroom. Only this time, instead of making her heart throb with delicious thrilling possibilities, it brought a bitter acid taste to her mouth. The future she'd once dreamed of them had shattered for the delusional fantasy it had been, long ago.

His face was still handsome as ever; more bronzed from the sun than last she'd seen him, making his silver hued gaze all the more striking beneath his bold, dark arching brows. His short-cropped hair dark at the sides faded into a burnished, sun streaked gold on top, just as she remembered.

His jaw always clean shaven during the time she'd known him in London, was now shadowed with stubble, darkening the dimpled groove in his cheek. Lines that hadn't been there before crinkled at the corner of his eyes only adding more charm to his familiar boyish smile.

And, oh how that smile had once melted her to a puddle like fine German chocolate on a summer's day.

But no longer.

Ann had to keep her lip from curling in disgust. He stood there, smiling flirtatiously to her from where he stood. She remembered well, that look in his eyes.

But he *did not* remember *her*.

She ground her teeth together, thoroughly annoyed. *He'd married her for God's sake!* A sham wedding it may have been, but a small ceremony had still been performed. And of course, there had been the *wedding night*. Surely, he hadn't forgotten *that*.

Through gritted teeth she seethed, "James Morgan, I implore you to wipe that grin from your face before I remove it for you."

She was unaware she'd aimed her gun at the center of his chest until she heard the click of its hammer.

The men in the corner scooted their chairs around to the far side, either in fear of being targeted or to have a face on

282

view of the show, Ann wasn't sure. But as men were wont to underestimate her, she fully suspected the latter.

"Don't you remember me?" She asked in a deceptively coy manner. Her eyes turned cold, "The *wife* you left behind in England?"

She saw his eyes alight with dawning recognition.

"Yes. I followed you across the great Atlantic and then further yet, across this wild country. You see James, I wasn't the only one you'd left behind in England."

She fixed him with a pointed look. His eyes passed down her body until they rested at her midriff.

"Congratulations," she said dryly, "You're a father."

He brought his eyes back up to meet hers.

He licked his lips somewhat wearily, eying the gun she yet held in her hand. Although she'd since directed it to the floor between them, he didn't think she'd hesitate much to draw it back to chest level once more on his person.

"I'm sorry, Ann. You should know, our wedding was fabricated."

Before he could continue, Ann cut in, "Yes. YOU fabricated it."

Surprise rose his brows higher above his eyes.

"You figured it out."

It was more statement than question, since it was obvious she had discovered his deceit.

"And yet you followed me anyway..." He squinted his eyes questioningly

"I had little choice in the matter. You were a father and I thought you should know."

She averted her eyes unable to speak the rest of her naive goals she'd begun her journey with. How she'd thought she'd find James and he'd be overjoyed and live out the rest of their lives together a happy family.

So much had change since then: her entire world. She may as well have entered an alternate universe with her first step onto the *Clara Stella.*

James must've perceived her original hopes anyway.

"I see." He spoke pityingly, "You came seeking a last name for the babe."

Plenty of men had been willing to give up a last name for Ann. She may have been used goods, but in America, she was still a *woman* and there weren't enough eligible ones to go around.

She thought of poor Jonathon.

Of Grayson. She closed her eyes as if to stop the image of him from procuring in her mind.

No. She had not sought *a* last name. She'd foolishly sought *his* last name. Because he had the right to be a father to his children.

James held up his hand to display a silver band. "I'm sorry, I can't help you. I'm married. -And legally." He rushed to say.

"That's not what your former father-in-law said back in St. Louis." Ann said smartly.

James shook his head, "That's not the marriage I speak of."

He'd married again? In the short time since he'd left St. Louis? Ann felt the air slowly expel from her lungs, leaving her deflated. She'd given up everything to find this man. To allow him the honor of raising his children. *Everything*.

Anger filled her once more, quickly displacing any feelings of hopelessness.

"Oh," she scoffed, "Well you can see where lie-in the confusion. How DO you keep track of all your brides?"

She managed to quip out.

His eyes flashed momentarily with regret.

"You're bitter I see."

That was an understatement.

"I wanted to marry you, legitimately, of course. For many reasons. To spite my parents and father-in-law, for one. To line my pockets with some of your father's riches, for two."

James looked to her then, his smile crooking in a half fashion that deepened the dimple in his cheek. A smile that had once greatly appealed to her.

"And because you were the most beautiful woman I'd ever seen."

He continued, "So much fire in those flashing ember golden eyes."

He said the last as if he believed himself charming. As if his words could ever again seduce her.

He further explained, "But when I returned home to America, I was unable to null my marriage to Lorraina as planned. I'd been smart to stage our wedding," he added referring to his and Ann's. "Two wives would have been immoral: a sin in the eyes of God."

"Indeed." Sarcasm dripped venomously from her tongue.

"So you can understand why," He carried on, "I didn't return to England for you. Of course, I didn't know you'd gotten with child." He added tactlessly.

"Yes! You got me with child. *Your child*!"

"Well, I don't know what you expect me to do about it at this point. I have a new wife. And her father owns most of the land around these parts. I plan to make a smart go of it this time around. Of course, Maria's beauty doesn't compare to yours and her father doesn't have an English title, but I daresay, his coffers are just as plump as your father's."

"Remind me to congratulate your current wife on what a catch she's made." She sneered dryly.

"I can't help you right now. It's too early to set up a mistress, only been married a week after all. But once enough time has passed, I could set you up well. And your bastard."

Ann's blood boiled. She steadily raised the gun once more. "You bastard," she spit.

"Well, if it is mine, which still remains to be seen, I'll throw in a little extra of course. Proper gentleman's schooling and all that."

Rage nearly consumed her.

"I left my home and country, the very people who raised and loved me. I crossed an ocean, scared, pregnant, and alone. To find *you*. So we could be a family."

She did not allow him to interrupt.

"Even after I discovered the despicable act you'd committed. I continued my search for you, believing you loved me and would want to make our marriage legal since you were widowed and thereby released from your forced vows. I crossed mountains and rivers, survived tornadoes, and risked my life countless times to find you.

Even though along the way my heart lost all love for you.

I continued on, because it was the honorable thing to do. I foolishly thought you'd want to know your-" She stopped herself from disclosing that he had two daughters. He didn't deserve to know the beautiful girls he'd sired. She finished instead with, "ch-child."

"I do! I'm so glad you followed me. I will be the luckiest of all men to be married to a rich land-owning wife and have the world's most beautiful mistress sharing my bed."

Ann shook her head in disgust, nearly choking on the bile that rose from her nauseated stomach. Her temper flared to massive proportions.

"Say, *how did* you track me down, anyway?" James tilted his head questioningly.

The answer to that question doused some of the volcanic fires ready to erupt within her.

"Your cousin. Jonathon."

Poor, sweet, guileless Jonathon. She averted her eyes, guiltily.

"Jonathon? You don't say. How is the paragon of the family, anyway?" he asked casually, wrapping his hand once more around a mug of cheap swill.

"He's dead." She answered blatantly.

"Between here and the Lower Springs, we were attacked by Comanche."

That's when James seemed to take in her appearance fully for the first time since she'd swung through the double doors.

Her torn blouse-a man's blouse. Ripped, soiled with days of trail grime and dust, as well as her own sweat. And of course, the stale brown stain of blood covering a goodly portion of the collar and middle area.

Her trousers were caked with grease from her sweaty, dirty palms, dust from the trail, and of course: more blood.

For once, she didn't think the stares elicited her way were due to the curiosity of a woman in breeches, but instead due to the state of her attire in general: battle worn, as they were.

"I see." James said after a time. "Well. That changes everything."

He turned back towards the bar and sipped from his mug.

Ann thought perhaps he was shaken some by the news of Jonathon's death. His last statement made little sense, however. -At least so far as it concerned her. She stood there puzzled for a moment. The other men who'd been watching avidly from the corner returned to their card playing, no longer interested in the little drama unfolding before them. One of the men shook his head pityingly.

"Jonathon died... And you managed to escape?"

"Yes. I killed one, but only wounded the other."

She answered reflectively. She should have placed a better hit on the second, but her only concern at the time had been about getting Livvy back.

A sad smile played at his lips before he muttered, "'Dunneroy's Little Spitfire', that's what they called you."

Ann swallowed. It was painful to be reminded of her past; it seemed an entire lifetime ago. Perhaps even a life having belonged to someone else. She was no longer that naive young girl. She was no longer a beloved and doted upon daughter with protected, limited freedoms.

No, now she was a woman grown. Harder and stronger than when she set out. Experiencing real freedom.

Real freedom wasn't all it was cracked up to be... Full of hard choices and harsher consequences...

His voice pulled her from her musings.

"...So vibrant you were. You would have been a real trophy. As it is, you're not even good enough to be used as a whore, now that you've been touched by savages."

His words, although callous, had not been spoken maliciously. He'd not stated them intending to sting, just matter of fact like.

But the words shocked her all the same.

The other men who'd until then been pretending to ignore the act, shook their heads now in piteous agreement. As if her circumstances were tragic, but, of course, of little consequence to them.

Her lip curled again with disgust.

"The only savage I've ever been defiled by is you." She spat venomously at James.

For an instant her finger feathered the trigger of her gun. Burning a hole through the center of the scoundrel procured a desirable image. Instead she clicked the safety back into place. She'd destroyed her, and her daughters' lives enough over this fool.

She saw little point in remaining and wasting any more of her life on the scum before her. She turned on her heel and fled back to her babies.

She'd left the town of Santa Fe at dawn the next day.

Rosa had pleaded for her to stay and rest a few days more. Ann knew she should, if only for the girls' comfort, but she just couldn't bring herself to do it. She didn't want to take the chance of running into James again. She wanted only to be free of him. At last.

She'd also heard a group of men had left that night for St. Louis. Fur traders.

Grayson's face surfaced in her mind again.

It worked well for Ann. She thought to follow a ways behind the men, close enough for safety against another Indian attack, but not so close as to endanger her or her daughters. Not all fur traders were like Jacques and Grayson... Most tended to be a rough group, as she'd discovered during her time aboard the steamboat.

They'd traveled past the Lower Springs without a hitch, much to Ann's relief. It was there she'd seen where another traveler must have taken the time to dig a shallow grave for Jonathon's body. She'd closed her eyes in another rare offering of a prayer, silently thanking the anonymous person for their kindness. Whoever had taken the time to bury his body had also ensured his name was marked correctly onto a simple wood cross made of two crudely planked branches from a Mesquite tree.

The caravan was encamped only about two miles ahead of Ann near the Upper Springs. Ann waited on the nights she planned to secret out information, a good while after the men made camp, before sneaking up closer to listen to their chatter and discern what their plans were for travel. She also listened for talk of any dangers or concerns they addressed such as if they may have noticed signs of Indians Ann may have missed.

Ann shuddered at the thought of another Indian attack.

Last night she'd heard some of the men speak of that precise possibility. Apparently, a band had been keeping to the north east and traveling parallel with the caravan, making the men uneasy. Ann waited until she heard them confirm they planned to cross the upper springs just before dawn, then she scurried quickly back to her own camp.

Ann had barely slept the entire duration of the trail, for having to stay alert both day and night in order to protect herself and her daughters. She had to set up camp far enough off the trail to keep her presence unknown to the rough men ahead of her, leaving her more vulnerable to the various deadly creatures roaming the wilderness. Most nights she'd been unable even to make a fire for the land had been too flat and she hadn't wanted to risk alerting the trappers of her presence. The girls were not shy about letting Ann know they were sick of eating hard tack and crusty biscuits.

Ann hadn't a choice, however. If she'd remained in Santa Fe, she would have run out of the last of her funds to see her back to St. Louis. Ann knew one of the forts ahead housed wives of a few of the soldiers, for she'd met them when she and Jonathon had traveled through south. She fervently hoped she would find them charitable towards her and perhaps they may even offer to share a meal or two along with a safe place to rest.

That would be a ways off though and Ann needed to keep her mind clear and focused on her current surroundings. She sensed something was wrong. Gray light began to glow, lightening where a once black night sky had met the earth.

The caravan should have already crossed the river, yet Ann could see in the meager light, the men still standing on the south bank. Their mounts were saddled, but most of the men had yet to seat their saddles. They were quiet, yet restless. They appeared to be waiting for a sign of some sort.

Ann grew weary in the unnatural silence.

Livvy began to grunt and whine in the cart and Ann knew it would turn into wails if she didn't get the cart moving soon. The girls remained relatively content if the cart was in motion, but as soon as it stopped, they believed it indicated mealtime. Ann had to stay put, though. As it was, she was scarcely hidden from view of the caravan by the small grove of sparsely shaded trees. Ann spied only low shrubbery beyond her to the men's encampment. She was on high ground looking out across the land from above their camp set up on the riverbank. Scattered trees sheltered them as well, growing more thickly near the water's edge. Ann hoped the trees the men were standing in added to her cover as well.

"Shhh…" Ann stretched her hand behind her and smoothed Livvy's wispy blond hairs away from her forehead, soothingly. All the while keeping her eyes narrowed in on the fur traders camp in the distance.

In the next instant, the eerie calm of the morning turned to chaos.

Ann saw a man with a back full of arrows stagger into the fur traders camp, his agonizing screams pierced the forced quietude of the group. Ann realized then they had been waiting word back from a scout they must have sent ahead.

Well, the message was clear.

She watched as men scurried to their saddled mounts, hastily drawing rifles from their sleeves. Some of the company raced to the supply and goods wagons they were transporting, in hopes of fleeing. Ann saw the band of Comanche race into the camp and she knew the men driving the wagons' attempts to escape were futile.

Ann cracked the reins turning her wheels north-west, nearly the opposite direction she'd been traveling. She wasn't about to stick around and watch the arrows start flying. She closed her eyes to the image of the massacre she was certain was taking place below. Out of the corner of her eye she thought she saw a Comanche look in her direction and shout waving a long lance in the air. Fear sharpened in her heart and she forced her small conveyance over the rough terrain at break-neck speed.

She was forced to slow when she reached the foothills. For all they were termed hills, Ann couldn't help thinking they appeared nearly as large as the mountains in the distance. She chose her path carefully, for fear of her horses stumbling or her cart overturning. She paused only once, long enough to don the chest pack and strap Kit and Livvy to her. They made driving more difficult, but Ann knew if their escape came down to abandoning the wagon and running on foot, she'd have no time to gather the girls at such a point.

The Indian pony secured to the back of her wagon followed along demurely. She hoped that was a good sign. If the Comanche were closing in on her, surely the horse would be nickering to its old comrades. She knew the horse was "buddy sour" because it had whinnied frantically after the horse it had ridden with, when the Comanche Ann had wounded while saving Livvy, had ridden off. The horse would hear and smell the other horses approaching before Ann would. She hoped she was well ahead of them.

Most likely the Comanche Warriors had been after the traded goods in the wagons. She had an uneasy feeling in the pit of her stomach, however, that the Indian that had raised the lance and shouted in her direction was the one she'd winged. She'd also killed his friend, perhaps even brother. That he saw her and would want to seek revenge was a definite possibility.

Ann pushed the horses into a faster pace once more. She knew there were two paths to Independence; The one she'd traveled on south to Santa Fe and had planned to travel back north-east on, and the mountain path that went mostly directly north before cutting east. She'd been told the mountain path was longer and more of a trial if traveling with wagon or cart.

Ann feared going straight north would pose greater risk of running into the Comanche, though. Her only hope would be to go northwest further into the mountains until she felt it was safe to turn back and search for the mountain route.

Once she was safe from the Comanche, she would head once more in the direction of north east and continue on in that direction until she came across the path that would lead her to Bent's Fort. That was precisely what she would do, she assured herself.

Ann pushed the horses all day stopping briefly, only once, at a cool trickling spring. Ann let the horses drink while she filled only her canteen. The terrain had grown so steep, some of the supplies began to roll towards the back of the wagon, forcing Ann to maneuver the wagon at an angle. She'd held her breath in those moments wishing with all her might for the wagon to remain upright and her horses to be sure footed.

The daylight was fading fast and Ann knew she needed to find a safe place to bed down for the night. She couldn't risk riding the steep rocky land in darkness. She could easily drive off a cliff or bust one of her horses' legs.

She hoped she'd managed to put enough distance between her and the Comanche. They had probably never ventured after her in the first place. They were after the supply wagons and trade goods, she told herself once again. The image of the warrior with the lance flashed in her mind, but she willed it away.

She needed to find a place to make camp quickly. She could barely see now in the fading gray light offered from the overcast sky. A bitter, cold wind had grown stronger as the day went on and now it was whipping so fiercely as to sting Ann's eyes. Ann tucked her head and reached back for one of the quilts to wrap around her and the girls. She slowed the pace and allowed the horses to pick their own footing.

A familiar scent hung in the autumn air and Ann knew, with certain dread, that snow would begin falling soon. From stories Grayson had shared with her on the trail, Ann knew snow in the mountains wasn't a good thing. She needed to find shelter fast. She hoped the impending snow remained only a threat this night. Surely, she could find her way back to the route that would lead her to Bent's Fort on the morrow. If the snow held...

Little time had passed when Ann came to what appeared to be a dead end. A steep rising cliff she'd seen from afar was suddenly before her and more imposing than she'd imagined, for there didn't seem an easy route around the fortified wall. She was loathed to turn east so soon in fear of crossing paths with the Indians, and yet, it felt just as dangerous to travel west further from the trail. The rock structure before her stretching to the clouds above left her little choice, however, as she could hardly climb it or go through it.

The horses harnessed to the wagon had pricked ears and Ann felt them tugging at the reins eager to head east along the wall. Ann listened closely, and she heard what the horses had picked up on; a babbling brook. The sound of rushing, gurgling water over smooth rock. Ann's eyes followed the sound, studying the land distant her until she saw it. A steady stream of water sloping southeast lazily down the mountain side. Which meant it was coming from the north. It appeared to be streaming as if magically from the stone wall. But Ann didn't believe in magic.

She loosened her grip on the reins giving the team their head and let them make their way to the stream. As they neared, Ann observed that the rocky cliff walls bent inward; a break in its barrier as she'd hoped. The stream did not come from that fold; however, it instead ran along the border of the wall and where it should have run east downhill, it was instead trapped between the wall and a naturally carved out ravine that ran lengthwise along the wall.

Some distance back, Ann saw the water flowed from a small cut out spot in the wall. A hole roughly the size of her wagon wheel. Small enough for critters to travel perhaps, but not she. The horses eagerly tossed their heads once they made it to the side of the shallow brook, in attempt to strip the reins from Ann's hands and get to the water faster.

Ann relinquished the reins and tied the break, jumping down from the wagon seat. Both girls were quiet, but bright eyed, strapped in their pack on Ann's chest. They peered about silently as if taking in their new surroundings. Ann was still in awe herself. This was a new wilderness, one far vaster than she had yet sojourned.

Her muscles were sore as she stiffly made her way around to the back of the wagon to lead the Comanche horse to drink. Leading the horse further upstream she saw that the bend in the rock wall might lead to a cave. After a quick drink, she hobbled all the horses. She had no choice than to take the girls with her.

She kept both pistols loaded and holstered to her side. She slid Kit to her back and positioned Livvy to the center of her chest so that Ann could get to her pistols with more ease and speed if necessary. She walked the narrow path between the curving walls. Ann judged her cart would barely fit through between the walls. It was open above her yet and the remaining light allowed her to see that the walls curved back yet again further ahead, like a maze. If it had been any later in the day when darker, it would have appeared another dead end.

Ann walked steadily, placing each step with caution. She pulled her pistols as she cornered the bend. She'd assessed correctly. The short winding path had led to a cave entrance. Ann wished she'd thought to bring her candle tin along.

Her breath shallowed in fear-quickened breaths as she entered the darkness. She let her eyes adjust to the blackness before moving forward. The mouth widened out, but narrowed as it furthered into the darkness. It was deep, but Ann thought she could see all the way to the back wall, and it appeared to be empty. No animal dwelled here, nor man. Ann expelled the breath she'd been holding in heavy sigh of relief. She could make camp here for the night.

Riders. She recognized the sound of horses being ridden even through the thick rock walls. Thank goodness a heavy, sleeting rain had fallen in the night. The violent pelting of the downpour surely washed away all sign of her tracks. In the night, when the rain had begun, Ann had not been as thankful for it, for it meant she couldn't hear the sounds of the outside world as well.

She blinked her eyes in effort to rid them of the burning sleep still plaguing her. She'd not allowed herself to sleep for more than minutes at a time since leaving Santa Fe and her body was rebelling greatly. It was yet dark in the cave. Of course, not much light could enter centered between a wrapping of maze-like walls, as it was.

Ann had maneuvered the cart and horses into the cave safely, although with much difficulty. It had nearly proved disastrous rounding the two bends with the cart in the narrow passages. The task had taken her far longer than she'd anticipated, but once they'd arrived into the cave and settled, Ann had made yet another discovery.

The back of the cave was not a solid wall as she'd thought initially; it had an exit path similar to its entry.

Ann listened intently. She could discern the faint sounds of a horse pawing into the stream she knew was on the other side of this thick chasm. She cast a furtive glance to where her horses stood yet resting in the cave. Both team horses stood, heads down, and back hoof resting. They cared little for whatever activity was going on outside. The Comanche horse stood to attention, ears pricked, but remained silent as of yet. Ann knew not who the riders were, but only that danger could befall her if she remained to find out.

Quickly and quietly as possible, Ann hitched the team and ponied the other horse to the wagon once more. She shushed Kit and Livvy soothingly when they woke as she placed them into their leather harness and secured them once more to her side. Ann was anxious to put more distance between them and the unknown riders. It sounded as if they had already passed on, but Ann couldn't take the risk that they wouldn't circle back. She turned the wagon inwards towards the back of the cave and the other exit she had not traveled yet.

Exiting the cave proved easier than entering it. The naturally carved rock walls were wider allowing more room for the cart to pass. It was also only one bend and the walls began to shrink lower and lower to the ground until they were nothing more than crumbling white boulders that led back to the main cliff walls Ann had traveled along before she'd discovered the mazed cavern. Only, she was now on the other side of it.

The landscape beyond the wall was saturated from the night's rain. All was gray and brown and slick with water. Puddles pooled in every shallow dip of the floor. The cold weather had already robbed the trees of life, only the pine remained tall and strong.

Ann felt safe to continue east along the inner cliff wall, so she let the horses have their head. It would have to break again at some point she reasoned.

Ann jerked awake. Somehow, she was still seated and the team moving forward. The panicked realization that she'd nodded off while driving the team, sent her heart pounding and her eyes in a frantic search for Kit and Livvy in the wagon.

The thick, impenetrable wall separating her from the danger in which she'd fled gave her a sense of security. That combined with utter exhaustion must have lulled Ann to sleep. Ann had heard of that happening; a body becoming so fatigued it would just shut down.

Her heart resumed regular pace again when her eyes fell upon both her daughters attempting to crawl in the small allotted space on the floor, falling and laughing with each bump sustained by the wagon. Ann couldn't help but smile wanly at her playful cherubs. Somehow, Ann needed to remain fortified against the despair constantly ebbing its way deeper and deeper into her soul.

She would find her way to Bent's Fort and from there, onto Independence and St. Louis where civilization bloomed and hopefully she could make contact with...someone...eventually. Her situation was not entirely as desperate as it seemed.

She winced, unwilling to accept her hopefulness for the lies they were.

She turned her attention forward again and stifled an involuntary yawn as she determined what position the sun was in the sky and what direction they were heading.

The white cliff wall she had been following when she started out this morning had transformed into the browns and greens of the wooded mountains she had traveled yesterday. Still all surrounding her was too steep to climb. She looked back in the direction she'd come, only she could not see the white bluffs in the distance behind her where they should have been.

The sky was overcast again, gray, and the air crisp with sign of impending snow. Ann wondered, if flakes would fall today or if the sky would release another torrential pouring of rain; either way, she needed to find or make some sort of shelter.

She felt sure she was turned around somehow. Heading west once more. The mountain walls had seemingly formed a solid barricade, wrapping around this vast valley Ann had chanced upon. She was uncertain how long she had slept. That she could no longer see the tall stark cliffs where she had begun this morning, had her believe she'd traveled far. Perhaps half a day of travel. If only the sun would show itself, so she could gauge what time of day it was presently!

Just then a fat, fluffy, snowflake floated down from the heavens and landed on the tip of her nose. When she tipped her head back to peer once more at the gray, glowing clouds, she saw the sky filled with soft falling flakes. Fear gripped her. She had not prepared for the snow, had hoped to be halfway to independence and following the mapped trail before winter descended.

Already the white fuzz that had been falling lazily from the sky moments ago had thickened before her eyes; now flurrying down around her, dusting the land in a thin coat of white. Her heart beat thunderously in her chest. The horses shifted restlessly, sawing the reins through her calloused fingers.

If the wall circled all the way around, perhaps continuing forward would reach her to the cave again and more quickly than turning back. Prior to the snow falling, she'd contemplated cutting across the land, but now that she could barely see five meters in front of the horses, she deemed it safer to continue on along the mountainous wall.

She must have dozed again. Irritated with her weakness and body's inability to remain awake, she shook her head to clear her senses.

It was irrational to be angry with herself. Her body was exhausted beyond its limits. But their survival depended upon Ann to remain sharply attentive to their surroundings at all times. And, blast, she didn't have time for sleep!

She knew not how far they'd traveled, but the sky was far darker than had been before. The bordering path of the mountains must have shifted, too, and turned her yet again, for the wind now blew directly into her face. She snuggled Kit and Livvy together in a wrapped quilt in the wagon. They were low enough to the floor; she hoped the biting wind missed them as it whipped around Ann through the canvas opening.

The snow was midway to the horses' knees deep now. Luckily the flakes weren't the heavy wet, dense variety, but more of a dry airy fluff, allowing for the cart's wheels to yet slice through the accumulating mass.

Ann was astonished at the amount and rate of which the snow fell. Her hands were chapped red and cold to the bone as she struggled to keep the hard leather in her stiff fingers. She could no longer keep her gaze focused ahead of her. The wind bit at her fiercely, forcing her to bow her head to block its sting. She had to trust the horses not to stray from the wall.

She hoped the cave from the night before was near or that she may stumble upon another such crevice that could shelter her and the girls for the night.

The smoke hued sky quickly darkened to starless black night, seemingly before her eyes. Kit and Livvy stirred behind her and began to make whining mewling sounds, indicating their hunger. Ann knew they needed to find a shelter of some sort, and fast!

The wagon jerked to a stop. The horses stepped backwards a few inches and pulled forth again. The wheels rocked forward slightly then stopped and turned backwards again into the impressed snow made from their tracks. Ann flicked the reins down against the backs of the team urging them forward once more. The horses' haunches doubled under them as they tried to power through the rising snow. The wheels churned over the hump of the piled snow only to fall prey to another swell.

Travel continued this way for a while. Ann's muscles strained against the stiffness in her neck and shoulders from tensing against the cold and the burning ache in her torso and arms from the exertion of keeping the team moving forward.

"Come now! Move along!" She yelled, encouraging the beasts, though her voice rang with desperation and fear.

Then an unnatural structure, a darker shadow against the night sky, caught her eye through the snow flurrying gusts of wind. She blinked the frozen crystal flakes from her lashes and looked again. This time she was certain of what she was seeing.

A Cabin.

Chapter 18

Grayson's anger sustained him halfway to Independence, before it dissipated and left him feeling merely defeated. He'd endured Luke's pathetic sighs and sorrowful looks in the week after Ann left them. During their travel to Independence by steamboat, Luke's doleful looks turned resentful.

"Just what did you expect me to do, Luke?" He shouted, irritably.

"I asked her to marry me. I asked her to come with us. It was she who refused!"

He knew his words would inflict more pain upon his son, but he couldn't stand the thought of Luke blaming him for Ann's decisions. Was he supposed to spend the rest of his life being punished for her doing?

Luke, still leaning against the rail of the Steamboat, looking out across the water, growled and turned his angry face from Grayson. At the last second before Luke had shaken his head with exasperation, Grayson glimpsed disappointment flash bitterly in his eyes.

Disappointment that should have been aimed at Ann, surely.

Grayson snarled and joined his son at the rail where he rested his forearms. Silently, he wished Ann to the devil. And then in the same breath wished for her presence beside him.

She would know how to communicate to Luke. She would offer the words that could bridge them together.

Grayson growled again. She was the one tearing them apart now, wasn't she? Her and her fool hardy, honorable, intentions!

For a time both father and son perched restlessly against the rail of the boat, both wallowing in their own hurt and anger; neither one knowing how to express to the other exactly what they were feeling or how to soothe one another.

Only, perhaps Luke did. Perhaps Ann had imprinted on him in that way.

Luke whirled towards Grayson to face him like a man and the words exploded from his mouth, "You should have gone with her! You knew she was ill equipped to travel that distance. And you left her with that dandy! Who is going to keep her safe? Who is going to keep the girls safe?!"

Luke's fury and anger disintegrated into tears. Showing true to the scared little boy beneath.

Grayson wanted to reach out to him and pull him close, but through the sheen of tears in Luke's eyes still laid angry accusation. Grayson unknowing how to close the chasm between them, bristled.

"I made sure they had the essentials. What she wouldn't accept I sneaked into their wagon or relinquished into Mr. Morgan's care. Mr. Morgan, the "dandy" by the way, is her cousin in law and has every right to travel with her!"

Whereas Grayson *didn't*.

Luke glared at him, even as he wiped the dripping tears from his nose down the length of his arm.

"I heard what the merchants were saying in St. Louis. About La Jornado. About what happens to women and children traveling that path to Santa Fe..."

Luke had looked down as he voiced the fears in his last sentence, but looked up once more, sharply, "We. Should. Have. Went. With her!" He ground out.

And it hit Grayson then, that his son, this young boy before him was absolutely right. And a wave of sickness rolled in his stomach. What had he done? He'd been angry and hurt. She told him they had to go separate ways and he allowed his pride to listen to her words and ignore his heart.

His mountains, that had been his respite all these years, where he'd worked steadfastly and made irreversible sacrifices, to make into his retiring paradise to share and build a home with Luke, now seemed unappealing... He no longer wanted to build that life; not a life without her. He refused to.

A steely glint hardened his eyes, "You're right, Luke."

Luke's scowling eyebrows shot up with surprise.

"As soon as this boat docks, we're going after her."

"But she has nearly a two week start on us."

Luke's giddy enthusiasm showed he didn't care if she'd had a two-month start, he was just as determined to fetch her back.

"What are you going to say? When we catch her that is?"

Grayson grinned down at his son's excited questions, "Well, words didn't work too well the last time. I think we will just spirit her away until she agrees to marry us this time."

"Keep her, captive?"

His words were spoken in equal parts shocked disbelief and approval. Which probably should have worried Grayson. Luke looked up to determine his father's sincerity in executing such a plan. Grayson wasn't sure what he read from his expression since he himself wasn't entirely certain he wouldn't go to such extreme measures to keep Ann with them this time.

They didn't have a lot of time before cooler temps moved in. Grayson didn't figure on returning to his isolated paradise this winter. By time he found Ann and could convince her she needed him as much as he needed her, the mountain passes would be too filled in with snow. He wouldn't risk Luke, Ann and the babes in such perilous conditions.

They would travel back to St. Louis and winter in town where it was safe and wait for spring. That would give Ann plenty of time to purchase new clothes, and small furniture items they would need to cart with them to their new home. Grayson smiled to himself, thinking of the happy future they would have together.

Of course, he had to *find* the stubborn woman first. And hopefully she didn't already marry the scoundrel who'd fathered the girls. That could prove tricky to maneuver around. One way or another though, he'd make her see reason. He looked down into Luke's smiling face. He hadn't any other choice.

Grayson and Luke decided against purchasing a wagon. Hopefully Santa Fe would have some for the trip back with Ann and the girls, once they reunited with them. Instead, Grayson and Luke had purchased two pack mules, so they could travel lighter and faster.

Grayson had traveled the Santa Fe trail twice before in the past, but never going as far as Santa Fe. Both times he'd come from Bent's Fort and headed towards Independence. He packed extra canteens knowing the weather that way could be bringing drought this time of year the nearer they got to Mexico.

Most of the traveling had been uneventful although grueling for the fast pace they kept. He and Luke stopped at Fort Larned and rested a night. They were lucky to find that a group of soldiers were preparing to take off for Santa Fe as well. Grayson spoke to them and while they were wary of taking a boy along with them, agreed to allow Luke and Grayson to accompany them.

They explained that there'd been trouble recently with Comanche Indians in the area between Santa Fe and the Cimarron Springs. Apparently, a company of fur traders with loaded wagons had been attacked and all the goods stolen. Grayson grimaced sympathetically, knowing any men who survived the attack had lost their livelihood, just the same. It would be tough to survive the winter without anything to trade for supplies.

Grayson described Ann to the soldiers hoping someone had recognized her outfit traveling through. One of the men did indeed recall a woman fitting of Ann's description. Two babies and a gent traveling with her, he'd detailed, confirming that it was she, and Grayson's tight muscles relaxed in relief. *She'd made it this far.*

The fear was always niggling at the back of his mind, but he kept pushing it away. Luke, ever astute for a young boy, had been right. If Ann or the girls came to harm, he would blame himself. Grayson shook off his guilt and doubts. He needed to believe she was safe and focus on finding her.

The soldiers would travel fast and light and it would be far safer for him and Luke to ride with them. Especially if it were true that the Comanche were hostile and making trouble for travelers.

The soldiers did not disappoint and together they covered a lot of ground in just a few days. Not too far after crossing the lower springs, they came upon a crudely constructed cross marking a grave. Grayson took the time to read it just as he had the other grave markers they'd crossed along the trail.

As always, Grayson's heart pounded in his ears and his blood pulsed with the anxious fear that the name he would read across it would be Ann, Kit, or Livvy's. All the other crosses and markers he'd read along the way always proved to be a name he didn't recognize, and the air would rush out of him with relief.

Not this time, however.

Scratched across the wood, read: *Jonathon Morgan.*

Grayson swore. By god, something had happened to them. And he hadn't been there to protect them. *Were Ann and the girls safe? Was it possible Ann managed to escape with the girls?*

It was entirely possible Jonathon had contracted a sickness and died from illness. Perhaps his death hadn't been caused by an attack. Although, the thought of Ann and the girls being exposed to a sickness wasn't comforting either.

Luke came closer and after reading the cross for himself, leaped from his horse and joined Grayson in the dirt.

"That's- That's!"

He looked grievously to Grayson, unable to say Jonathon's name. Grayson knew Luke's mind went right to fear for Ann and the girls, just as his mind had done. Grayson's jaw ticked as determination steeled him.

He nodded sternly to Luke, "We're going to find them."

Santa Fe had proved inauspicious. Grayson gleaned little information other than learning Ann and the girls had made it to Santa Fe alive. According to the owner of the little bed and breakfast, Rosa, and her daughter; neither Ann nor the girls had been ill, making it more likely Jonathon's demise had been caused by Indian attack rather than sickness.

Grayson winced and wondered if Ann could have survived such an encounter unscathed. The women assured him they were hale and hearty, however, so he had to believe Ann had managed to keep herself and the girls safe.

The two women confirmed that Ann had confronted a man by the name of James Morgan, the day she arrived. They had little more to offer, other than to say Ann and the girls had stayed the night at their establishment and then set off the next day alone. The two women imparted Ann's plans to trail behind a company of fur traders, but that when news came the company had been attacked, Rosa and her daughter had assumed Ann and the girls to be dead... or worse...

Grayson knew Ann had not traveled back to St. Louis by way of the Cimarron route or they would have crossed paths. He swallowed back the nauseating wave that swelled from his stomach. Could it be she'd been attacked that day as well? The soldiers shared nothing of a woman or child's body in their report. And surely, they would have said so to Grayson when he'd questioned them of Ann's outfit passing through.

He was anxious to set out for Ann, but first he asked more questions of the townspeople. He started with the saloon across from Rosa's, where, as she'd informed him, Ann had met Mr. Morgan. The saloon owner recalled Ann with ease and shared of the incredulous encounter.

In fact, it seemed Ann had gained herself some notorious fame within the town for her bold antics. Two men having drinks, explained as they were there that day as well. All told and chuckled as how they'd feared for their lives when the crazy, ill-tempered woman, had pulled her gun.

It was just like his Ann to let her temper get the best of her and pull a stunt like that. Grayson's amused grin hearing of Ann storming the place, pistols drawn, turned down into a seething snarl upon learning of the cruel treatment and words exchanged by the girls' father to her. The more he learned, the more he wished she'd shot the bounder. James Morgan wasn't fit to breathe the same air as Ann.

None of the men in the saloon had heard of a woman and babes being found after the attack on the fur traders. No ransom had been rumored either.

That was a good sign, thought Grayson. Perhaps she'd been far enough behind that she'd been able to hide or flee undetected. Grayson thought, perhaps in escaping the attack, she'd been forced to take Raton Pass instead. Raton Pass this time of year, though, was perilous indeed.

Still if anyone could make it through, it was he. Luke being with him couldn't be helped. Luke had learned how to survive on the trail; together, Grayson was sure they could make it. Besides, even if Grayson could leave Luke safely behind somewhere, he knew nothing short of chains and a cage would stop that boy from searching for Ann and the girls.

Overall, it had taken them three days to gather all the information they could pertaining Ann and the girls, restock supplies, and rest their mounts and mules. They were at the livery, all saddled and ready to ride off when a man on horseback came racing through town towards them, riding hell-bent for leather.

The whirring dust around the man was as dizzying as his presence. He slid the horse to a stop right up alongside Grayson astride his mount, dismounting recklessly before his horse had even come to a complete stop. The act was so startlingly quick and unexpected, Grayson could only remain frozen in shock as the man darted around to grab Grayson's reins.

"Are you Grayson Stone?" The man confronted.

Grayson took in his grimy appearance in an instant. He was accustomed to taking the measure of a man in that amount of time. Often times, life or death depended upon his quick judgment.

He took in the man's slim frame and gaunt features covered in trail dust. Old, dried blood, and tattered clothing bespoke hard and fast traveling for months on end. Soot hued shadows filled the slight hollows below his eyes; eyes the color of a wolf's.

Eyes he'd only ever seen once before... Ann's eyes.

If the similar coloring wasn't enough to clue Grayson in, the distinct, commanding, British accent left little doubt, that this man was a relation of sorts to Ann.

Still, Grayson couldn't help but chaff at the man's commanding tone and belligerent stance. He continued to eye him suspiciously.

"Damn it. I know you are he. The soldiers at Fort Larned told me a man and boy traveling together, befitting your description, had been through recently searching for a woman with twin daughters. A woman by the name of Ann. Where is she? And why the bloody hell are you looking for her?"

The British man demanded, shaking with barely controlled fury, despite appearing that he could collapse at any moment.

Grayson stared at him coolly before responding, "Just who are you to Ann and why should I tell you a damn thing?"

The man's hard eyes softened, and weakness chased away all the fight he'd begun with.

"Please," he entreated, "I'm her uncle. Rupert Dunneroy. Although, I've been informed my niece has been traveling under the name of Ann Morgan. Her father, Edmond Dunneroy, Earl of Abersty, -and my brother- hired men to track her down as soon as they discovered her missing. Of course, I came along to oversee the search and ensure she is found and returned home safely."

Dunneroy closed his weary eyes and used his thumb opposite his fingers to smooth out the lines on his forehead, as if the entire debacle was serving his very death sentence. Grayson could sympathize. His search for Ann had only begun and was already proving to cause him near heart failure with worry over her.

Grayson held out his hand to the trail-tired man before him, "I am Grayson Stone. This is my son, Luke. We traveled with Ann and her cousin-in-law, Jonathon Morgan from Cumberland Gap to St. Louis, Missouri."

"That's where I nearly lost her trail. I was lucky enough to intercept a letter from her to her friends back in Charleston."

He eyed Grayson, speculatively. "I knew she was after her-" Dunneroy coughed -a cough that was clearly contrived-before continuing, "-her husband. I was also informed that her-" Dunneroy coughed uncomfortably again, "- husband's cousin chased after her and caught up with her in Cumberland."

Dunneroy's eyes narrowed in on Grayson, "What I don't understand is where you fit into this blasted nightmare."

"You can cease the theatrical hacking. It's clear you know as well as I, Ann was never truly married to that scalawag. Although she gave her every effort to be, despite my opposition to her foolhardy plans."

Grayson ground his teeth together.

"In fact, she should be marrying me."

That announcement grabbed Dunneroy's attention.

"And when I find her, I'll not be giving her the chance to turn down my offer again."

Dunneroy studied him shrewdly, raking his eyes from Grayson's face and rigid demeanor, taking in the boy's face as well, at his side. Then he stated plainly, "You love her."

The boy, Luke, with assertiveness, spoke for the first time, "We both do."

Dunneroy smiled, "Well, that makes three of us then."

Although Dunneroy and his horse clearly needed rest, he refused, insisting on traveling with Grayson and Luke. They rode slow the first day, mostly at a walk and camped early. The whole while they shared facts and pieces of the puzzle that was Ann until they were both comprised of all the details of one another's accounts of Ann's journey and past. Of course, Grayson left off sharing any intimate moments between himself and Ann.

Grayson had come to know Ann as a survivor and intelligent woman, and he was doubly reassured by her uncle's assertion that Ann had ample skill and knowledge to take care of herself.

Grayson negated explaining how the far more tamed land of England Ann had been trained to survive in wasn't nearly the deadly threat the vast wild mountains of the west posed... He much rather preferred to believe she was traveling along the Raton Pass and would meet up with her at Bent's Fort. It was all he could afford his heart and mind to believe. Anything else was too painful to contemplate.

Chapter 19

The cabin Ann had stumbled across in the night during the blizzard, turned out to be little more than a shack. It was small, one room, and constructed from crudely cut timber, but it had allotted them safety from the storm. It appeared abandoned. Other than a lumpy, mouse bitten, horsehair mattress in the corner, there were no furnishings to be seen. Ann had shivered as she contemplated sleeping with the vermin that no doubt took up residence within.

As the team neared the run-down shack, Ann had spied a lean-to shanty built off the back side. It wasn't large enough to house her rig, but the three horses fit inside and there was even a rail that slid into place to lock them in. Any bedding the lean-to may have had at one time, had long since rotted away, revealing that it hadn't sheltered livestock of any kind in recent months, perhaps even years, Ann thought.

The cabin had the same neglected and abandoned feel to it. After shutting the horses up, Ann grabbed the girls and as many quilts and bags she could carry, including a tin pail filled with stored buffalo chips, in hopes of starting a fire.

She kept the girls strapped to her chest in their pack and got to work using her flint and hook to spark her only, and quickly dwindling, candle within its lantern. Once she had some light, she was able to assess her surroundings a little more. At least the mud held over the cracks in the logs, she breathed some relief. It would block the biting wind if nothing else. She was chilled to her bones, despite the warmth from the girls clinging to her, and Grayson's thick fur lined capote draped over them.

Bless the man for having sneaked supplies into her wagon. After setting off from Independence, she'd discovered his capote and wrapped within, a sharp hunting knife, extra flint and hooks, as well as lead and moulder. Despite his anger, he'd still cared.

She surveyed the tiny room with the candlelight and breathed a sigh of relief when shadows cleared revealing a cooking hearth in the corner. There was no stove, but it was, obviously designed to house a fire. No wood lay stacked within the structure, but Ann had come prepared.

Grayson had taught her to pick up and store as much fire fuel she could find during their travels. She'd made an effort to search every time they stopped to rest and had banked up quite a bit.

Since she already had the candle lit, the fire was easy to start. She'd have to find more kindling in the next few days, as the supply she kept safe in a kit was depleting. She grimaced, thinking of the blanket of snow dampening everything outside. It could prove difficult to find anything dry enough to burn.

The fire was slow to fill the room with heat despite its cramped quarters. Once feeling came back to her fingertips and her muscles began to unstiffen and relax against the curling heat, Ann bravely stepped towards the mattress. She toed it with her boot first, half expecting vermin to explode from the lumpy mass. When none came forth, she pressed her foot into it, pushing its edge to its center. Still no mice darted from its folds. Did she dare risk sleeping with hungry little teeth and claws?

In the end, exhaustion had won out. She dressed the old, soiled, looking mattress with her own bedding and after releasing the girls from the confines of the pack, snuggled closely to them and fell into a much-needed sleep, never even removing the harness from her person.

She felt safe, for the first time since leaving Santa Fe.

309

The feeling of safety was brief lasting, for it snowed endlessly for the next three days. Ann had never witnessed so much snow in her life. It was up to her waist and the horses' bellies. Ann watched them attempt to leap through the mass in search of food, but they didn't get far. Travel was impossible under such conditions and Ann shivered with the realization that she and her girls may be stranded in this valley until spring.

Already their meager supplies dwindled. Her wagon being smaller in size than those commonly used for long distance travel, due to the necessity of economizing, allowed room for only so many provisions. Ann had planned to restock at the various forts along the way. The problem was, she wasn't certain where she was at all at the moment, let alone how far she was yet from Bent's.

She would give it a few days more. Perhaps the snow would cease falling and melt away. After all, Ann had seen weather perform plenty of unbelievable feats since her journey initiated.

In the meantime, she would hunt. Perhaps she would even bring in enough meat to fortify them on however long their journey may be to the nearest fort. If weather and game were on her side, they may yet make it to the fort within the month.

Ann knew her thoughts were merely empty hopes, but she refused to acknowledge the sinking feeling in her stomach. Instead she brushed her fears aside as nothing so much as hunger. Which reminded her again that she should load the remaining ammunition and set about restocking their meat supply.

She recalled stories told from Jacques and Grayson earlier in the year on the trail about some of their experiences in the wintry mountains. They had claimed to have constructed special footwear that allowed them to walk atop the snow.

Ann searched the confines of the cabin for any such shoes or resources of which to craft her own but spied nothing useful. It appeared she'd have to wade through the waist-high snow in order to locate materials. The horses needed feeding anyway, and she could bring in the last of the supplies as well.

The wind blew up flurries from the ground and sprayed the icy wetness into her face as she made her way to the horses. They remained in the shelter not wanting to battle the elements either. The grain sack was nearing empty and she'd already been rationing them for days. The fear and doubts prickled over her skin. She set her chin and told herself the cold had caused the goose flesh. She gave them each a cup full of grain that they ate up in seconds.

"I know how you feel," Ann spoke to the dissatisfied horses.

As if to validate her emphatic remark, her stomach growled loudly. She rubbed the nearest horse's smooth muscled neck, stealing warmth from under its course heavy mane. Then she buried her nose there as well and inhaled deeply the scent of sweat and horse; a scent that always calmed and contented her. She drew strength from the memories that arose with the familiar scent.

She carried back to the shack the last few sacks of food and satchels of clothing and other items. A path had begun to form through the snow from her many trips. She only had so much time before the girls awoke from their nap to get much work done, so she had to move quickly.

Two more days passed. Ann's attempts to procure snowshoes failed. She hadn't the leather to spare and other materials didn't hold up under her weight. The snow had blown around so much, though, that she was able to ride out yesterday on Comanche (as she'd begun calling the dun pinto horse she'd claimed from her Indian attackers) so long as she steered him through the dips between the swells of snow.

She'd felt safer astride. Some of the bone chilling stories shared by Jacques and Grayson about this wild land had frightened her into extreme caution. She'd listened to them speak of mountain lions, wolves, and bears nearly as tall as a house -if they could be believed. She didn't want to be on foot in the deep snow alone if she encountered an animal such as that, even if she was renowned a crack shot.

The shack was built higher up in the tree line into the side of the mountain. In fact, the back wall of the shack and horse lean-to was protected and sheltered by a jutted-out formation of massive rock wall. Spread before the shack on all other sides was the valley and it appeared more densely forested towards its center. Ann hadn't the time to explore the valley in its entirety, but from what she'd seen, the valley was completely enclosed with hard, sharp, mountainous cliffs all the way around with the only way in or out through the maze of rock formed cave of which Ann had entered.

She and Comanche had ridden towards the center where she knew more game would be present. She hadn't figured on seeing so little life. It was as if every living thing had been buried with snow. She had not counted on not being able to hunt for her food.

Then just as she was about to give up and head back, for surely, her girls were near to awakening form their daily nap, she spied movement. Comanche balked and made it clear that whatever it was, they shouldn't be getting any nearer to it. Ann pressed him forward anyway, all of her senses on alert.

She heard again the muted growling and gnawing noises. She drew in a short, panicked breath and felt the adrenaline flow through her veins, her body readying itself for survival. Her ears finally picked up where the threatening sounds were coming from and thankfully the animal, a large looking cat with a short inky black tail in the air, was hovered over a kill with its back turned towards Ann. She knew from story descriptions it wasn't a mountain lion, but she couldn't identify the animal either.

It knew she was there, but it didn't fear a confrontation with her. The cat seemed to be daring her by keeping its back to her all the while issuing its threatening low throated growls between gulps of food. She raised the rifle stock to her shoulder and looked down the barrel.

You shouldn't fear me taking your meal, kitty; You should fear me making you mine.

It paused when Ann cocked the hammer back, but quickly resumed its eating. Ann waited for it to raise its head once more then gently squeezed the trigger.

The sound was deafening as the booming echoed through the tall pine. Ann knew she'd felled the cat as she'd never taken her eye from the target.

It was a beautiful animal. Its plush grayish-brown fur was thick and soft and would make excellent mittens for herself and the girls. At this point, she knew any fresh meat would taste delicious, so she feared not on that score.

She saw all the tracks around the dead deer the cat had been feasting on and knew it was not fresh, but she packed as much of it up as she could anyway and slung the cat over the rump of the horse to carry back to the shack.

Grayson, Luke and Rupert hadn't had any luck in finding Ann and the girls. They reached Bent's Fort, but the stationing soldiers reported no women and children had come across them. The fort, unfortunately, was lacking in provisions for the winter, so Grayson was kindly informed he would have to be responsible for his own party. He, Luke and Rupert camped within the fort walls for a few days, riding out every day to search for Ann as well as game.

Grayson's own little homestead wasn't all that far, northwest of the fort. One of the days while searching for Ann, they traveled to the cabin he'd built for him and Luke. Ironic, that. His goal had been to reach that very destination not all that long ago. Now he planned to bring Ann and the girls here as well, when he found them.

Grayson was filled with excited anticipation as they grew closer to its location. He hoped Luke wouldn't be disappointed when he saw it. Luke was meant to live a very extravagant lifestyle back east where he had been raised. Grayson hoped the warmer, loving atmosphere between them would offer *more* somehow.

When they arrived at the clearing, however, Grayson was shocked to find that where his newly cut cabin had once stood proudly, was now nothing more than a black charred stain upon the land. At first Grayson could only stare in shock.

Luke looked to his father questioningly, concern shining brightly in his eyes. Rupert's mouth thinned into a grim line and shook his head sympathetically.

"Indians." Grayson said simply. Then explained, "Most of the tribes in these parts were friendly when fur traders and trappers first came to the area. It's only been in the last few years they've really come to resent our presence here."

Grayson surveyed the ruins stoically. The black ash was faded from months of weather and washed away by rain. Some was buried under a light dusting of snow. All that remained was some of the stone foundation and charred support beams laying a top the rubble.

"I knew it was a risk, leaving it unattended."

Grayson kept his eyes averted from the others lest they read the grief written in the hard lines on his face. The shadowed destruction resembled, in this moment, all of his hopes and dreams for his future with Ann and their children. And his mood blackened like the ash pitted earth before him.

When they arrived back to the fort, the Commandant Officer made it clear they were unwelcome guests. Grayson had to shake his morose thoughts from his mind and concentrate on forming an alternative plan. Rupert was disgruntled, but Grayson well understood the soldier's plight.

In the winter months, game moved plenty, migrating to wherever food could be found; which meant food near the fort was often scarce. Grayson knew the soldiers had some hogs butchered and game stored up, but weather and food rations were always unpredictable. He and Rupert had little choice but to move on.

They decided to make their way back to St. Louis. Perhaps Ann had sent contact information ahead from Santa Fe that they had missed. Also, Rupert departed the rather surprising information that he had a woman and children waiting there for him. It was a safe place to wait and make plans for a renewed search for Ann in the spring when the mountains and paths were more passable.

Everything in Grayson's core wanted him to push on and keep searching. Cover these mountains high and low through blizzard and hunger until he found Ann or died trying. But he wasn't alone. He had his own son to look out for. God knew, Luke was willing to make the ultimate sacrifice as well, in order to find Ann and the girls, but Grayson wouldn't allow him to.

Luke didn't hide the fact that he wasn't happy to be moving on without her. None of them were. It felt an awful lot like leaving her and the girls to die, or worse. The daunting thought invaded his mind every moment that passed without finding Ann. His stomach sickened and twisted with every mile further from the fort, knowing they would probably never see her or the girls again. If she hadn't made it to the fort by now...

The ends of that sentence were too painful to contemplate. Ann was a determined and resourceful woman. If any woman could make it in the rough mountain wilds, it was she. Those were the words he encouraged Luke with. He would have felt more confident of such an outcome if she didn't have two little ones depending on her as well.

He always omitted such logic when talking to Luke, but he sensed the boy knew. The two little girls ever seemed to be his main concern. Grayson always kept his voice hopeful and reminded Luke that he had personally, secretly stocked extra supplies in her wagon and Ann would use them to see her through.

He'd placed in her wagon; extra rope, a sharp hunting knife, a hatchet, more lead, powder, and a moulding ladle. He'd also left behind his own capote, a wood canister filled with punk in case she ran out of fuel and findings to make a fire, as well as an extra flint and steel hook, and a sewing needle. Now he wished he would have packed more. Of course, her cart hadn't been large enough.

He should have seen her outfitted properly. No, he amended, he wished more than anything that he would have went with her, and pride be damned!

It was too late now. All he could do was hope and pray she would make it. In the meantime, he needed to get his son back to the safety of St. Louis before all the streams and rivers became too blocked with ice to travel through.

Ann wasn't certain how many weeks had gone by. All she knew was, they were out of food and game had moved on to another area. Ann couldn't travel further for hunting because she couldn't leave the girls behind, alone in the shanty, for any greater periods of time than she had already risked.

Ann had learned that lesson the hard way. The one time she had dared to venture further away into the more densely forested center of the valley in hopes of finding more game - a successful hunt that had resulted in bagging two rabbits - she returned to the shack to find that both girls had awoken from their naps in the amount of time she had been gone.

Kit had managed to climb over the barricade of trunks and belongings Ann had constructed as a divider to prevent the girls from getting close to the fire. Livvy had been caught still in the attempt to follow her sister over, so Ann didn't think Kit had been on the other side of the room, near the hearth, long, but it had still given her a fright.

She knew then she could no longer leave them unattended with a fire and yet, she couldn't allow the fire to extinguish, either: they would freeze.

That's when she decided it necessary to shoot one of the cart horses.

An entire horse, even half-starved such as hers were, could probably feed herself and the girls for a month at least.

Only, the next morning when Ann set out to fulfill the daunting task, another blizzard had hit during the night and the horses were nowhere to be found. Even Comanche whom she had come to rely upon and had developed a strong affection for, had disappeared. She knew they had fled in search of food. The very real threat of starvation hovered over Ann and her daughters, and yet, Ann felt a small, guilty, glimmer of relief: she hadn't wanted to shoot her horse.

God, could she have sentenced herself and her children to die a painful death because she hadn't wanted to take the life of her horse? She had known the horses would eventually have to leave in search of food. She should have killed them sooner.

She had thought she would have plenty to hunt, though. And she had harbored hope in the beginning that they still had a chance of continuing on towards the fort and would need horses for that purpose. She had told herself she would shoot the cart horses when and if necessary and use Comanche to haul them away in the spring.

Now she didn't have any horses. And her daughters would starve to death.

No.

No.

Ann couldn't allow that.

She'd strapped the girls to her that instant; determined to hunt and find food for her babies. She gathered any extra supplies she thought she would need, attached them to her belt, and set out on foot. A most difficult task. Wading through the waist deep snow was made nearly impossible with the added weight of the girls.

But it was either that or starve.

Ann had tried to shelter them from the harsh wind as best she could. Once Ann made it to the trees, the snow became less deep and thus enabled her to travel slightly easier. She had not had to travel far. Luck had it that another animal had made a fresh kill of an elk and left most of it behind. Ann scouted the perimeter to ensure the predator was gone before she moved in towards the felled beast.

On closer inspection, Ann realized the elk must have perished from natural causes as there were no lacerations, wounds, or blood to be found. It was small, less than a year old she guessed. Perhaps it had been sick.

Would that cause the meat to be bad?

She would have to risk it she decided. She quickly made a litter from a few sweeps of pine branches and begun dragging the carcass back to the shack. She hoped the sweat and heat radiating from her body was keeping the girls' body temperature from dropping too low.

They were successfully nearing the more sparsely populated area of woods that stretched about a mile, leading to the shack, when she heard it.

The low growl of a hungry animal.

She turned slowly. She had both girls strapped to either side of her. She tried to slow the raging beat of her heart and ignore the drumming pulse in her ears. She was shortly relieved to learn she had not been trailed by a pack of wolves. She had not feared the possibility as much when she'd had Comanche. But on foot it was a different story. A one-shot pistol would not prove very effective in such a circumstance.

The big cat stepped boldly closer. It wasn't as large as the other cat Ann had shot, and its fur was lighter in color and spotted. Ann had little doubt, however, that its claws and fangs were just as lethal.

317

It growled menacingly and eyed Ann but kept its main focus on the elk to which Ann was tied to the branches pulling its weight. The cat suddenly abandoned its cautious perusal and sprang towards the elk, digging into it immediately.

It seemed content to eat its meal right there. Ann watched as it shredded and tore into the hide of the elk, making a sloppy butcher of the animal. Occasionally the cat sent warning looks her way and growled through its teeth as it ate away at Ann's food.

That's when Ann had had enough.

That food belonged to *her*.

Her grip tightened around solid curve of the gun handle and the wood warmed against her hand, reminding her she wasn't entirely defenseless. She thanked herself in that moment for always keeping one of the pistols loaded and in hand. Drawing her arms up was made difficult due to the position of the girls beneath her, but Ann pursed her lips and exhaled slowly as she steadied her aim.

At the precise moment she released the hammer and the ball fired, Livvy squirmed in rebellion to the cramped position she was made to be in and sent the ball wide.

She missed!

The sound cracked through the air. Kit and Livvy both wailed instantly and simultaneously. The cat darted away from Ann and the elk and ran nearly fifty yards to a large tree that it leapt into.

She had missed, but the sound of the shot had frightened the beast. Ann wasn't foolish to believe the cat would remain frightened for long. Ann tugged on the rope, but remained facing backwards towards the elk, and the cat in the distance. Sure enough, the cat hopped down from the tree in one effortless motion as soon as she began pulling the elk away.

Quickly she ran towards the elk, dropped to her knees and reached around Kit for her knife. Sweat beaded up on her face and dripped off the end of her nose; in part due to the sawing and working of her knife through muscle and bone, but also because she could sense the cat stalking closer and closer. Sweat dripped in rivulets between her breasts, beneath the layers of fabric and fur, and itched terribly, but Ann ignored the discomfort.

She heard herself panting, from the effort and from fear, for the cat was nearly upon her. Just as she sawed the rest of the front shoulder loose, severing it from the elk's body, the cat leapt towards her. She fell back onto her heels in a stumbled reflex to flee the attacking predator. The cat was two arm lengths from her then.

Ann quickly threw the severed limb at the cat as she jumped to her feet and ran back around to the front of the elk.

The spotted, bobtailed cat emitted an angry scream, and hopped forward, but didn't give chase. Ann began backing away, dragging the elk, slowly. The cat hissed and swiped angrily in the air towards her with one of its large paws, before circling back towards the more easily accessible meat lying near its feet.

Ann exhaled slowly and continued backing away. She watched it take the bulk of the shoulder into its mouth, effortlessly, and turn and run in the opposite direction of Ann and the rest of the elk. Ann exhaled a gusty breath of relief and wasted precious little time getting back to the shelter.

That was the day everything changed for her. *On the inside...*

She reached the confines of the shack, safely. Methodically, numbly, she saw to her tasks. If she allowed herself time to think about what might have happened if that disaster had occurred any differently, she would break down. And she couldn't afford to lose control. Her girls needed her to keep a steady head.

She freed the girls from the harness and hung the harness near the door. Next she checked the fire. The coals were still glowing, so she added small strips of dried bark. Once those blew to life with flames, she added some thicker lengths of broken deadwood. Every couple of days she took the short-handled ax and chopped wood. It took her most of the day. Especially as she had to regularly see to the girls' needs. It was physically grueling work and she dreaded the chore.

The first few attempts, the ax had rung in her hands and sent tremulous waves of shooting pains up her arms. She had eventually learned to grip better and to swing with her body to absorb the shock of the blow. Even with adapting her technique, it still took her far longer to hack away at a tree than she remembered it taking the men to perform the same task along the eastern trail. In the beginning even smaller trees, barely as round at the base as her thigh, took her hours to fell.

Much of the firewood she used was found and so dead she could split it easily by cracking it against something hard. That method seemed to be faster, however the broken pieces always burned far more quickly than the hardwood she split with the ax.

She noted the low supply stacked near the hearth. She would have to chop wood on the morrow. Firstly, however, she had to see to the meat. She had worked out a pulley system in the horse lean-to where she could hang any game she shot. It made it easier to strip the hides and cut the meat from the bone.

Once she finished cutting the meat, she packed most of it in a dirt cellar of a sorts she had dug, using the lid of a camp kettle, before the ground had frozen. She only made it deep enough and wide enough for the wooden keg from the wagon that had housed the salt pork. She made the hole a little wider and kept snow packed all around the keg. She didn't cover the lid with dirt. Instead, she found two heavy rocks to place on either side of the handle. Thus far it had worked against keeping animals from finding her food.

The sun had already sunk down below the cliff border casting the valley into shadows by the time she returned with supper's meat rations. It wasn't until she had fed the girls and put them to sleep for the night that Ann had allowed herself to feel. She had pressed herself up against the cold wall and slunk to the floor in utter exhaustion.

Similarly, to how she was ending this day. Again, she tried to recall how many weeks it had been since she ran out of the elk meat? That had been the last successful hunt, for she hadn't dared venture far into the wood with the girls strapped to her again. It had been a close call that day. Too close. Not only had they been lucky to survive the bobtailed cat, but they had returned with red chapped faces. Luckily their skin hadn't been permanently damaged by a worse degree of frostbite, as the tips of Ann's fingers had already suffered.

Ann's Valley

It had been days, perhaps over a week since they'd had anything to eat. Ann had cooked everything she could think of. She'd tried to hunt nearby, but there no longer seemed to be any game. She even tore apart some of the hides from the kills. Most of them were being used to protect them from the cold. Ann had unskillfully sewed boots and hats for the girls. A challenging feat since Ann didn't know how to tan a hide. She knew only how to flesh it resulting in rawhide.

She learned to shape them over the ends of posts for hats, one fur side down, another fur side up, cut to shape, and stack them upon one another. Because she dried them and shaped them oppositely, it resulted in a hat that was fur lined on the inside as well as the out, although, still quite stiff. Once they dried stiff in that shape, she sewed them together. They weren't the most comfortable, but they kept the girls' heads and faces warm. The elk hide she had fleshed and used as a stiff rug on the floor for the girls to have a soft warm area to play.

It was that hide she boiled first. She'd had to have something to feed her daughters and they were desperate. But now they had nothing. It had been days and they were all so weak, Ann didn't have the strength to go in search of game, not that she believed she'd find any. Everything had moved on.

The sound of her daughters' hungry wails had even died down to sleepy, soft sobbing. Ann's heart clenched; it was as if she could visually see life being extinguished from their bodies.

She still had one ball left in her gun.

She only had so much firewood left. She was so weak... She needed to hunt. She had to, or they would starve. She had to get more wood, or they would freeze to death.

She wrapped her arms around herself and thought of her youth. She had loved her soldier training. She remembered the pride she felt in developing her skills and how she reveled in besting her father and uncle in sporting competition. She remembered the laughter they would share in, surrounded by the campfire.

The taste of salt from her tears trickled into the corners of her mouth, as she recalled her father's smiling face and her uncle Rupert's teasing eyes.

Angrily, she brought herself back to the present and surveyed the crude quarters around her. The wind outside howled against the logs at her back. *This*, she thought, was real survival. She wasn't camping. All of her training; shooting, building ravines, fires, and meals from little resources: none of it had prepared her for *this*. It was too hard. She was powerless against the force of mother nature. It would win, she thought.

She looked to her daughters; frail and weak, laying on the bed, softly whimpering even in their sleep due to pain from the hunger they felt. They needed her. She closed her eyes and conjured memories of them along the trail from Cumberland. How they smiled and laughed and learned. They discovered so many new strengths. They learned how to sit on their own, then stand, and then to walk. They were never slowed down by the hardships of trail life. They just continued on growing.

Ann remembered how it felt when they would giggle and reach for her. Even if the day had been particularly draining, their warm, trusting embrace as they snuggled into her, always had the power to uplift and renew her spirits. Their ability to not only persevere but prosper despite the challenging lifestyle Ann had committed them to, always restored Ann's resolve to keep fighting.

One after another, flashing memories of her daughters, happy and thriving, filled her mind. Their chubby cheeks uplifted with wide gummy smiles. Their sparkling eyes. Their peals of laughter that rang out and filled the wagon and brought life to the tediousness of the endless travels. Especially whenever Luke was near them.

Her heart squeezed again. *Luke. Oh, Luke.* She'd not forgotten his sweet face. And Grayson. He'd loved her. He had loved her daughters. And they had loved him. She'd been such a fool!

And now her foolish decision would take the lives of the two most precious beings in the world to her.

She wanted to hate James. She did in fact. But she could not lay blame to him; it was not he who was responsible for putting their daughters lives in danger. Ann had done that all on her own. What sick irony, that her every decision had been made to protect them, but instead had led them to what was sure to be a miserable, death.

Ann's Valley

One more ball loaded in the pistol.

The thought kept recurring in her brain. Her body wracked with silent sobs, and tears streamed down her face in defeat.

She couldn't do it!

She cried harder, her body shaking violently in her fight to silent the excruciating anguish spreading through her soul.

She couldn't aim that gun at her babies. And she would not leave them behind on this earth to suffer while she found peace. She wanted to throw the gun. *Useless!* Only the anger, she knew, was truly directed at herself. *She* was useless. They were depending upon her. And she was useless.

Suddenly she was exhausted. She realized she was stretched out with her cheek pressed to the cold planks of the floor. She closed her eyes and pretended Grayson was beside her, sharing his warmth with her. She pretended she could feel his strong heavy arm draped around her, holding her near to him. Could feel his warm breath at her neck. Feel his bristled jaw nestled there as well. She sighed contentedly, succumbing to the dream that was removing her from the hell of reality.

Perhaps it would be her last dream.

She and her daughters would sleep this night and never see another sunrise. And all of their suffering would be over.

Chapter 20

It was not to be. Ann awoke to the biting chill of the morning. She was still weak from hunger, and her muscles were stiff from having fallen to sleep on the hard floor. She lifted her face, lined she was sure, from the cracks in the planks. No crackling or popping sounds came from the hearth. No heat permeated the room either. Ann, determinedly, pushed herself to a near sitting position and looked at the gray ash where the fire should be, absent even of any glowing embers.

No, no, no.

She pulled, and half dragged herself closer. Her hand felt a thin, broken off piece of log and she used it to stir the ashes. A small fleck of glow gave her hope. Her weakening state made the simple task of restarting the fire an exerting one. She could hear her heavy breath and feel her chest rise and fall in fast shallow pants.

Ann did not accept weakness well. Irritated with herself and her self-derived circumstances, she angrily swiped the flint and steel together, emitting a shower of sparks. The small pile of hair-like strips of bark flamed readily and Ann quickly blew the flames to life and added larger pieces of bark until the fire steadied.

She laid her head to the floor intending to rest her weakened body, but she heard whimpering sounds coming from the bed and knew she had to get to her daughters. She gave a silent prayer for they, too, had made it through the night.

She scooted along the floor, determined to get to them. To see their faces. To offer what comfort to them she could. In her eagerness to comfort them, she hurried, but not out of worry they would fall from the bed before she reached them.

They had been too weak to do much more than sleep the last few days.

The low murmuring sounds were different from the mewling cries from yesterday. That piqued Ann's haste the most. Did the fact that they had stopped crying mean their bodies had given up hope for food?

Ann reached the side of the bed and looked to her daughters. Livvy was nearest her and reached her fingers out to touch Ann's face. Her tiny fingers brushed down Ann's nose to her dry, cracked lips.

"Mmm ahmma."

Ann stared incredulously.

Livvy had spoken the word "Mama." It had been faint and weak, but Ann had heard it all the same.

"Ahmma." Livvy babbled the word again with more strength this time and Ann couldn't help but look on with surprised delight. Livvy followed the word with a big smile and Ann's heart swelled, fit to burst, with joy.

Ann smiled against Livvy's fingertips where they rested against Ann's mouth, then pressed a kiss to those same little fingers.

She saw movement behind Livvy and knew Kit was stirring as well. Ann pulled herself up onto the bed and crawled up beside her babies. She lay on her side, snuggled up against Kit and draped her arm over both girls.

Both girls lay, looking up and smiling to their mother. Ann smiled back and gazed upon them adoringly. A tear escaped the corner of Ann's eye.

They hadn't given up.

And neither would she.

A thought occurred to Ann. She decided she would search south of the cabin, a direction she had not yet ventured. She would head out in the direction of the entry caves to the valley, for she remembered the wide stream that had led her there.

She would never make it to the cave she knew, but she hoped the stream had come from this direction and perhaps she would find it meandering this way. Perhaps deer or other game had made their way to the stream as well.

She debated briefly whether she should bring the girls along. She feared something dire happening to herself while she hunted; that she should collapse and not make it back, or perhaps become attacked and unable to prevail... Thoughts of the girls remaining behind by themselves, waiting for their mother to return to them and expecting to see her face, made her ache.

If death were to take them, she would have it take them all together; Ann holding them tight in her arms, allotting them as much comfort as possible as they passed into their next life together. If she couldn't make it back to them... Well, she couldn't bear thinking of them frightened and calling out for her...

The alternative was that she try to carry them. The risks seemed greater with that path. Ann could barely hold herself up, how was she to carry the added weight of two toddlers?

She was left with little choice. She would have to leave them behind.

She spent much of her energy placing the barricade back into place. She believed the girls too weak to walk, much less climb, despite them showing some renewed strength this morning, but felt it better to be safe than sorry.

She fed the fire again and ensured the girls had access to water by placing snow in a pot near to them. Ann felt some strength return, herself, after eating some snow. The pretense of chewing the ice crystals seemed to satisfy her stomach as well, although she knew the feeling would only be temporary.

She found the strength to stand and attach the harness to herself. She thought to use the girls' harness to help carry pieces of firewood back that she collected along the hunt. Panting and still weak, she stepped outside into the cold and immediately sought out a long branch to use as a walking staff to aid in keeping her in an upright position. Once she found one suitable, she set out with her crutch, around the back side of the cabin in the direction of where she hoped was the source of the water. And with it, game to kill.

Ann's Valley

This may well be her last chance to save her daughters.

After walking little more than a mile, she found it. She had been correct. The stream had originated on the side of the valley southwest of the shack, but in a way Ann had not imagined. It was a remarkable sight; one Ann believed would be even more spectacular in spring or summer when the valley was in bloom and lush with green.

Overhanging the cliff side wall of the valley was a falling pane of twisted ice. In the spring it would be a glorious waterfall. Some water yet trickled forth and mingled into a steady path in the center of the stream. The outer edges of the wide brook were shrouded in thick jagged ice and deep snow. Ann didn't dare approach further. The water meandered away from the cliff perimeters some and trees spotted the bank line.

The growing density of brush as Ann walked following alongside the stream, forced Ann to edge nearer to the icy path. She'd had to stop several times along the way to rest and catch her breath. When she felt particularly weary, she would eat snow and it would revitalize her once more.

The snow was no longer as deep in the area she walked, as the denser tree population and brush prevented the snow from accumulating as much. It was still a strenuous effort stepping over twisted vines, tree roots, and pickery bushes that appeared to be growing in abundance along the bank!

Ann carefully placed each foot so as not to lose her balance or step onto the thick shards of broken ice along the edge. She had no desire to fall through and get an icy soaking. No doubt such a mistake could easily be the death of her.

Even as Ann made every effort to tread as carefully as possible, she still managed to misstep. Something unnatural seemed to take hold of her ankle as she was bringing her back leg forward and immobilized her mid step. The sudden action sent her sprawling face first into the snow.

"What the devil!"

Ann shouted aloud to the quiet of the snowy wood around her. Her vulnerability due to the surprise attack, made her fear instincts kick in immediately. She quickly assessed her surroundings. No Indians. No predators of any kind that she could see. The quick shallow breaths squeezing her lungs faded slowly back to normal rhythm. Must be then, she had tripped over something.

She started to rise, only to find herself shackled in place. Ann sat down on her rump in the snow and angled herself so she could see her foot. A rusty steel chain was taught over the ankle of her boot. Curiously, Ann grabbed the chain and lifted it from the snow. One end was tied to a wooden stake Ann now saw protruding at an angle out of the ground. It had been placed there intentionally by a man. Ann tugged the chain in the other direction, and it led to the water. Ann, now standing, pulled the chain along the heavy bulk it was attached to, from the water.

It was a trap!

A steel trap used to catch beavers and other small critters that stayed near water. A jittery excitement welled up inside Ann. She closed her eyes, tipped her face to the sky and inhaled a hearty breath of fresh, frosty, air. And she felt it for the first time in months: *hope.*

Her nerves were making her restless as she was anxious to check her traps. It had been three days since she'd stumbled upon the steel blessing.

Many fortunate developments had occurred that day. Ann still could not prevent the feeling of wonder that floated up within her just thinking of how quickly her luck had turned around. After tripping over the chain and discovering the rusty, albeit intact, trap, Ann had hurried back to the shack with her find. Along the way she discovered another treasure: Woodlouse.

The trees near to the shack had not produced any of the crunchy little bugs, but apparently, the trees near the water bank, did. Ann found them while breaking down dead branches and pushing over stumps as she retrieved firewood on her way back to the shack. She first discovered them in an old rotted stump she kicked over. As she picked up the pieces, bark crumbled off and revealed the little shelled bugs scurrying beneath.

After that she checked many other trees near the water and found more and more until she had a small pocket on the harness filled. She'd had to keep her arm over the pocket in order to keep it tightly closed and prevent the tiny bugs from escaping.

Ann came back that day with dinner that tasted relatively like shrimp, a trap, and newfound hope for their future.

There hadn't been enough bugs to make a great meal, but it put something in their bellies at the very least and sustained them until the following day when she could collect more. She'd spent all the rest of that day studying the Beaver trap until at last she felt she understood how it worked.

She used the remaining grease from the hole in the stock of the rifle for bait. She and the girls had been forced to consume the bear grease Grayson had given her to use as mosquito repellent on their travels through Kentucky. Luckily, she had forgotten about the grease hole on the rifle for it was that which she used to bait the trap. She set out at first light the next morning to set it and prayed it worked.

After setting the trap by tying the chain back to the anchored stake where she had found it, she pressed the jaws open. It was difficult and took a lot of strength, so she had to press them against the slant of her leg to open them all the way.

Upon studying it in the shack she learned where its triggers were, so she gently placed it in the shallow water near the cold, muddied bank. She'd had to break much of the ice away in order to do so. There was a bayed-out area where the stream ran into and out of, making for a little pond-like area. Ann figured the traps had been set near this location for that specific feature and Ann took to calling it "the beaver pond".

After Ann felt she accomplished that, she prayed to all the Gods-or any God that would listen-in hopes one might feel generous enough to answer her prayers by sending a big fat animal to her trap. Her stomach growled just thinking of real meat. She would eat anything that sizzled in a pan, she thought.

Next, she'd hunted up more woodlouse and even some stinkbugs. She wished she had hunted for the stream sooner; she may have saved her daughters some suffering. She still hadn't come across any game to shoot, however. All her hopes were set in the jaws of her one steel trap.

As she scouted for plenty of bugs and firewood to take back, she had stumbled across yet another trap! It was exactly as the first one she had found. She cleaned it off, set it and trimmed the rag with the grease from her first trap in order to split it between the two traps. She hoped it would work well enough for a lure.

Her stomach twisted, the sickening anxiousness swirling around inside her like a tornado. Today was the third day. Yesterday she had set the traps. Today she would check the traps for food. Today would determine whether she and her daughters would live or die, for they couldn't survive the winter on the paltry supply of bugs she'd been finding.

Ann had left the girls sitting up on the bed. They were still weak, but the fact that they were no longer sleeping or crying most of the day away was a sign their meager meals of woodlouse was sustaining them for the time being.

Ann tried to be alert, despite her frazzled nerves and the endless thoughts firing off in her mind. All the *what ifs* were sure to drown her, but she couldn't seem to stop them from filling her head with worry and doubt. She had to consciously check herself every few steps and make herself attend to her surroundings. Especially, now, as she neared her traps. If she had been fortunate enough to catch anything, it was very likely another hungry predator may find it before she did.

Finally, she spied the wooden stake pointing up out of the ground. She stopped, stared at the bank and issued out a slow frayed breath.

Well, this is it, she thought.

She stood shaking, fearful her trap would be empty; for surely, she hadn't had enough grease for bait. And surely the grease was too old to attract anything. Such thoughts had repeated over and over in her mind all night nearly preventing her from sleeping at all.

Just, check it. She told herself. *Delaying the process won't change whether or not you were successful.*

She neared the water's edge on bended knee, giving little care to the damp mud seeping through the triple layer of breeches she wore.

At first her breath shot out of her with a start. The trap was gone!

But, no, her eyes located the chain still attached to the stake and followed it deeper into the water. It was too dark for her to see the trap at the end, so she tugged on the chain and began pulling it towards her.

Was it her imagination, or did the trap feel heavier? Or could it be that it felt heavier because it was dragging back with it, mud and rot at the bottom of the creek? Finally, it surfaced.

And there, wedged between the steel jaws, was a fat beaver!

Ann continued pulling the lifeless, drenched, beast to the water's edge. She freed it from the trap. And wept.

She wept tears of joy. She turned her face to the heavens and thanked anyone who was listening up there. She was so happy, she reached to hug the dripping, sodding carcass. But then thought better of it.

That would be rather disgusting, after all. Plus, she didn't relish the idea of wetting her fur capote.

The other trap had not met with success, but Ann couldn't manage to feel anything other than elation; still reeling over the blessed bounty from the first trap.

The beaver was extremely heavy. Far heavier than she ever imagined one to be. She skinned the hide from its body right there, being sure not to damage the castors and oil glands near its tail. She'd need those bits for making more lure.

Once she had them safely removed and all membrane scraped away, she cut the tail from the pelt and tied it to her waist belt. She decided to prepare a makeshift travois for the rest.

She didn't want to be caught in another situation like the bobtailed cat incident. If she kept the meat divided, she stood better chance of fleeing a predator and still having a meal to take home.

She made certain the hide was laid out carefully in a way that the fur wouldn't be damaged, then set off for home where more work awaited her. She grinned cheerfully at the thought of fresh meat for dinner.

Two weeks passed. Ann was catching critters quite regularly. Mostly, raccoons and muskrat though. Ann had only caught one other beaver, and that had been with the second trap she'd found and scantily baited with the bear grease. Ann wondered why the new lure she'd made from the castor oil, wasn't attracting the beavers. But she couldn't complain, since she was still trapping an abundant number of other critters.

She and the girls had recovered well from the brink of starvation and Ann was confident now she could get them through to spring, so long as she had the traps.

The girls seemed to have regained their former health more quickly than Ann. Although the traps were successful two to three times of the week, Ann allowed herself only small portions, for fear the day may come when her traps became ineffective either through damage, or lack of game.

She tried to push the doubts and fears from her mind as she set out to chop trees for firewood; another skill she was becoming quite adept at.

She had crafted a small sleigh for the girls by using two strips of green ash, bending them into a U shape using heat from the fire, and more wood used as crossbars to hold them in place. She created a seated platform up top and the bottom served as runners. The sleigh made it vastly easier to transport the girls from area to area where Ann worked.

Even so, Ann never traveled far from the shack when she cut wood with the girls in tow, less chance of running into predators that way. She only had one ball left for her pistol and she hoped she never had to use it.

As she trekked out this sunny morning, trailing the lively girls behind her on the sleigh, Ann spotted a movement in the distance. It darted behind a copse of cottonwood trees and disappeared as quickly as a shadow to darkness.

Ann's skin prickled with apprehension. She'd already felled two cats, but she knew the largest cat in the mountains she had not yet met. She shivered and prayed she would not be introduced today.

She needed firewood but feared going further. In fact, she much rather felt like running full speed for the shack.

To retreat is defeat.

She could almost hear her father's warm voice and see him dressed in his soldier's uniform as he delivered these words of wisdom.

As she debated in her mind, what was best, the moving shadow in the distance moved into the light once more. Ann studied the shape trying to make out what animal it was and what sort of threat it posed.

The warmth of her breath hit her cool lips as she stood, mouth agape, and eyes fixated on the shape. One thing was for certain, it was definitely coming her direction and at a confident pace. Ann licked her dried lips, getting a rude taste of the foul balm she'd concocted from animal grease in order to protect her skin from the winter elements.

She wanted to turn back for the shack but didn't dare turn her back on the ever-approaching form. She leveled her gun at it and kept it steady, waiting for it to come into range.

As it grew closer, however, Ann realized, it was another human!

A young boy.

Ann quickly lowered her gun. She kept her eyes directed at the child while her mind wracked for an explanation as to why or *how* a small boy came to be out in this wilderness *alone*. That was what made her remain uneasy. A boy *wouldn't* be alone.

As he neared, she took in his attire. He was Indian. Instantly fear rooted itself once more in her gut.

He was a diversion. He was sent to make her lower her guard and then the rest of the tribe would attack!

Ann turned and ran as fast as she could with the girls sliding after her atop the snow in the safety of the sled. They shrieked and filled the valley with echoes of giggles and laughter, completely oblivious to the danger they were in. Ann pulled the sled right into the shack when she arrived as to waste little time barring the door.

Once inside she quickly pressed her face to the wall to peer through any crack she could find, for there were no windows. She ignored the girls' squirming and impatient squawking from the sled. She focused instead on finding the rise where she had been standing when she had spotted the Indian boy.

There was nothing. She could see no sign of the boy. Ann swallowed nervously. Perhaps he was back with his tribe and they were surrounding the shack. She knew the idea sounded ludicrous, grown out of fear and paranoia.

If only it were simple paranoia. Unfortunately, she had reason to believe such an incredible occurrence could take place. She had heard stories in her travels from St. Louis to Santa Fe, about the Native Americans' hatred towards white people, that drove them to perform particularly heathenish acts.

While Ann understood the root of their hatred, and knew white men returned the demonic acts of hatred with equal fervor, she couldn't countenance it; from either side. Her discountenance of such cruelty did not, however, dispute the fact that such hideous crimes existed.

An hour had to have passed and still no disturbance. Ann remained vigilant. However, after a time even she had to admit, she had been wrong.

Now she wondered other possibilities for the boy's presence. Did he need help? Had he been looking for aid and Ann had abandoned him to the snowy hills?

Ann looked around. They still needed firewood and there was plenty light left of the day. She packed the girls into the sled again and stepped out into the brilliant sun. She made a visor of her hand to shield her eyes from the sun and gaze out at her surroundings. All was quiet except for the occasional call of a bird or gust of a light breeze. Nothing but trees dotted the hilly landscape before her.

Well, that was that, Ann reasoned to herself. She straightened her spine and trudged a new path towards a different copse of trees. She spent the rest of the day chopping trees and carting the girls, as well as firewood, back to the shack. It took multiple trips and the sun was near to setting by the time Ann finished. She'd remained alert for any sign of the boy during that time but there had been no reappearance of him.

She slept that night with the child on her mind as well as her conscience.

Two days later, she still had not seen the boy, so she decided he had moved on and went about her day as she had before the unusual occurrence. Of course, it was then, when she let her guard down that she saw him again.

She was carrying cut logs into the shack to resupply the short stack she kept near the hearth. She'd been humming an amusing, bawdy, soldiers tune to herself, almost subconsciously, and looking towards the ground. When she glanced up again, she stopped dead in her tracks. There was the boy standing only the length of the shack from her. He had cracked open the door and seemed to be shyly, peering inside.

She'd left the girls in there.

Her gasp upon seeing him, drew his attention to her, though he did not seem startled. -As Ann had been at the sight of him. She stood gaping like a fish and blinking her eyes for a few moments before she found her tongue again.

"Y-you," Her tongue decided upon a short supply of words it seemed.

The boy was small, young. Ann judged him to be seven, perhaps eight years old. And he was filthy! His black hair hung in greasy locks around his grungy, browned skin. His wide, black-brown eyes made a slow, innocent, curious study of her.

Ann spoke again, determined to help the poor child. "Hello. My name is Ann. I saw you the other day. I am sorry for having run from you. I had thought - well, I had a lapse in judgment, I suppose."

His face held no expression and revealed not whether he understood her words at all. He was thin. Far too thin. Ann felt certain he must have somehow become separated from his tribe and was in need of help. She didn't know how she could possibly take on another mouth to feed, but she couldn't turn her back on the child. He was just a little boy.

"You are welcome to stay, if you like. I-I have some food." She tried again.

The boy nodded to her, then much to Ann's surprise, abruptly turned on his heel and began walking away.

Ann dropped the firewood in astonishment and called out, "Wait! Where are you going? You can stay and get warm in the house."

The boy turned towards her once more, but only shook his head.

Frustrated that he didn't seem to understand, she desperately tried to gesture with her hands.

Then he spoke, "Too small. I hunt."

Her initial reaction was surprise. He did speak English! Then, perplexity, as she registered his words. What was too small? Her home?

Suddenly, she felt defensive and rather miffed. This small boy, out in the world alone and starving just judged her accommodations to be inadequate?

"Well, pardon me. I had only thought to be friendly."

She wished to turn on her heel, return to collecting the firewood and escape into her cabin with her irritation in check, however, she couldn't bring herself to abandon the boy.

"Where are your parents? Your mother or father?"

"None."

He answered simply and unemphatically. He was orphaned, just as Ann had suspected.

"Please, you can't possibly survive out here on your own. You may stay with me."

She humbly issued the invitation, once more.

This time the boy scoffed at her. -Actually scoffed!

"You think you can do better than this? You have a grander abode than this somewhere with a full larder?"

Ann held her arms wide gesturing towards the shack and horse lean to that she considered hers.

Lone Wolf shook his head in disgust. He didn't know much about people, especially women folk, but her voice rang with insult as if he had somehow offended her. And here he was helping the woman!

He repeated once more, "I hunt."

Then when the woman stood staring at him with mild confusion, he added, "You go back. Make a fire."

Surely, those simple instructions would not further confuse her.

Ann's eyes widened at the absurdity of the boy's remarks. Had a small eight-year-old boy just attempted to order her about? Well, then, he could high off for all she cared. He obviously thought he was better off without her.

Without further comment, Ann clamped her mouth shut tight and turned back towards the shack.

She was going to see to the fire. Because it required tending to, though, *not* because some small scamp of a boy had ordered her to do so.

The boy returned before sundown, dragging behind him a small doe through the snow.

He tapped on the door and Ann answered cautiously, showing surprise when she saw him standing before her with the heavy doe at his feet.

Lone Wolf smiled, arrogantly.

"I hunt," He said as if in explanation to her questioning look.

Ann crossed her arms over her chest. *Well,* she thought and shook her head in exasperation.

Then the boy asked, less confidently, "I stay?"

Ann uncrossed her arms and smiled warmly. "First, we'll see to this deer. And, I'll need your name."

"I am Lone Wolf."

Ann pityingly felt his name very fitting.

"I suppose you are." Ann stated softly.

Quietly in her mind, she added, *But no longer*.

Chapter 21

Over the course of the next few weeks, Ann and Lone Wolf taught each other many things. Ann learned Lone Wolf's true name to be Logan Williams. He had been born to the white man's world and been raised to speak English. He hadn't had anyone with whom to speak for so long, he had grown unaccustomed to speaking altogether.

The more he and Ann spoke, the more his vocabulary came back to him. Even so, he had only the articulation of a seven-year-old boy, despite, Ann discovering he was actually ten years of age. -Far older, than she had initially judged him to be. He was quite a bit shorter and slimmer than Luke had been last she saw him, and Luke was of similar age.

His story was not a happy one. One might presume as much, knowing he was an orphan, but his tale was far more tragic than Ann could have imagined...

"My father was a white Man, an American fur trader. My mother was Indian. She was of the Crow Villages near Wind River. That's where they met." Lone Wolf explained.

He still preferred to go by the Indian name he had given himself, for he felt he was more Indian than white man.

He continued on, "My father was there on business. He worked for the American Fur Company. The Crow Indians, my mother's people, allowed for the men from the company to trap beaver in their territory in exchange for other goods. They fell in love and married. He took her to live with him in the White Man's world.

I've seen some white men take squaws for wives and not treat them good. My father and mother truly loved one another. I remember, they were always smiling and laughing. Whenever my father would return from checking traps - sometimes he would be gone weeks, if all the beaver from the nearby ponds were trapped out - He and my mother would embrace, and they would be nearly inseparable during the time father was with us."

Lone Wolf smiled to himself as he shared about his happy home life.

He and Ann were sitting on the floor of the shack. It was late evening and a particularly chilly night, so they had the fire stoked hot. Kit and Livvy crawled, climbed, and toddled between them and he and Ann took turns redirecting them away from the fire.

He looked to the fire then, solemnly, grief for his parents heavy in his heart.

Ann asked softly, "What happened to them?"

A bitter expression twisted his features as he answered, "The other white men in my father's company were cruel and full of hatred for Indians. All Indians. It did not matter that my mother had acclimated to their ways; she dressed like them; she spoke like them."

Lone Wolf nearly shouted his exasperation with the ignorance of humankind.

"And it was the same, for my mother's people. A couple years after she and my father married and after I was born, my mother's people banded together with other Indian villages, in hatred, against the white man. They no longer wanted them moving into their territory. So, they planned an attack against the company."

The fire crackled and popped as a log burned through. Lone Wolf imparted with disgust, how his mother's family burned all the white men's homes with women and children still inside.

Lone Wolf stared off into the distance as he recounted the vivid memories from his mind.

Cayt Lawson

"They didn't burn ours, though. I remember, my father went out to try to talk peace with my mother's father: the chief. He begged him to show mercy on behalf of his daughter and... his grandson. My father, in a show of peace and trust, handed his gun over to one of the warriors riding on either side of the chief.

And they shot him. Right there, with his own gun.

My mother ran to my father's aide, crying and screaming in her native tongue."

Lone Wolf looked back to Ann.

"I remember feeling very frightened. I knew my father was dead when my mother stood up away from his body which remained unnatural like and unmoving on the ground. She rose from him and spit at the chief, her father. I thought, he would kill us then for the disrespectful display. But he didn't."

He looked away guiltily and sorrowfully added, "Sometimes I wish they had."

Ann hesitantly, reached for his hand. Her natural mothering instincts longed to comfort him. But Lone Wolf, although kind, considerate, and eager to please and be helpful to her and the girls, was not as easily accepting of the same compassion in return. Ann knew he was holding back.

From the outside, anyone looking in at them these past weeks would think they were looking at a happy family. From an outside perspective, their little home would appear to be a completed puzzle.

But Ann knew, sensed, Lone Wolf always holding back some of the pieces that would allow them to truly fit together as a family. She hoped in time, he would heal. His wounds were deep, and he'd suffered much in his short years of life.

Ann loved easily, she had a compassionate soul by nature, but she had known a far happier childhood built upon love and trust. Lone Wolf's, thus far, had been wretched. His childhood wasn't over yet, however, and Ann was determined to shower the boy with love and fill the cracks in his heart until there was no more room for the pain.

As Ann expected, he shifted in order to draw his hand away, but he continued with his story:

"I never learned my mother's native tongue as well as my father's English, although my mother insisted I practice both. But I heard the chief that day and I understood what he said.

He told my mother, that after this day, he would no longer consider her his daughter and blood. Then he rode away, his head held high as if he had bestowed a very honorable gift. As if he hadn't just ordered my father shot to death right before my and my mother's eyes."

A muscle ticked in the boy's jaw. Ann recognized anger and resentment in his rigid features. She wished she could place her fingertips to his face and smooth away the tense wrinkle between his brows; and with it, the hurt.

Ann was left unprepared for the next part of his story.

"A few days later, some of the white men from the company, who had been away trapping, returned and found their homes burned to the ground. Along with the remains of the wives and children of the few men who had had them.

All the homes in the area had been burned: except ours."

Ann's stomach churned, with dread, knowing the story was about to take a turn for the worse.

Lone Wolf continued, nearly in a daze, as if he needed to separate himself from the event in order to recite what had happened aloud.

"Their horses hooves thundered up the path to our house. My mother leaped from her chair, sensing the danger we were in. She told me to hide.

I climbed into a trunk that had once held many of my father's belongings. My mother had buried him with most of the items, so the trunk had enough space for me to climb inside.

I heard the angry men pound at the door. They accused my mother of the fires. Said she was one of them, therefore she was just as much to blame. My mother held her ground. She told them we, too, were attacked and were grieving with them.

The men wouldn't listen. They broke down our door. My mother shot one of them. But she didn't have time to reload and there were too many to defend herself from."

Lone Wolf paused. If Ann had not been watching his face so intently, she would have missed the brief moment his wall crumbled, and tears moistened his eyes. He viewed his grief as a weakness that he had to fight against in order to survive. Ann was familiar with the feeling.

He recovered quickly, and once again his face was unreadable. He kept his eyes averted to the fire as if entranced by the dancing flames therein.

"She fought them, but they held her down."

His voice cracked. Ann couldn't stop herself from scooting closer until her arm touched against his. Tears streamed down her face, but she remained silent as he continued relieving himself of the haunting memories. At least, she hoped his sharing of his tortured past would help unburden some of the pain from his heart.

He closed his eyes tight, in his continued fight against his grief, but tears leaked from the corners of his eyes and made wet paths down his face.

"I can still hear her screams."

Ann could no longer hold back. She brought her arms around him and pulled him to her. She fought to silence her tears, but her body wracked with the restrained sobs. He did not pull away. In his giving way he probably sensed Ann's need to comfort and so allotted her that. He too began crying, finally releasing all the years of pent up fury and anguish.

"I ran to her. I wanted to kill them! I tried. I tried to take one of their small guns, but the man was faster than I. He hit me hard over the head with it and knocked me unconscious.

When I awoke, there was blood all around my face from my skull where they had hit me with the gun. There was so much blood, I think they must have thought I was dead. Perhaps they did not care, because what had finally awakened me was the smell of smoke.

It wasn't long before I could see the fire. It was already consuming the front of the house from where they had entered. I saw a blood trail leading to the back of the house. I followed it to my parent's bedroom.

She was there. Her eyes already had that glass look. Her body - her body had been cut to bits! Blood was everywhere."

Lone Wolf was crying fiercely then. Ann's stomach wanted to heave for the injustice and torments this little boy had endured, her heart ached as if being squeezed together with spikes.

Kit and Livvy, grew worried with the emotional tension they could not understand filling the room. They toddled over and climbed into her and Lone Wolf's laps trustingly, sensing something was wrong and wanting to feel safe and secure. Lone Wolf, calmed then, and pulled out of Ann's embrace, aware that Livvy sat in his lap. He did not hug the little girl as Ann did Kit, but he let Livvy hug and cling to him.

"I escaped the fire."

That was all the more he said. Ann could tell he was drained.

"I'm glad you did."

Ann squeezed his hand and hoped it was enough to convey all in her heart; that his life had meaning and purpose; and that he was loved.

Ann's relationship with Lone Wolf continued to grow. Just as Lone Wolf had shared his soul with her, Ann reciprocated in kind. She explained where she had come from, and how on earth she had found herself alone in the wilderness. Lone Wolf expressed indignation on her and the girls' part of course, over James' rejection of them; which Ann had found sweet and endearing.

They had made a comfortable team right from the beginning, but time turned it into a stronger maternal bond. Life fell into happy routines, and laughter came easily to them once again. Both were healing and lending strength to the other. They performed all the daily tasks and chores together.

Lone Wolf was eager to take on a man's role and made every effort to take on equal work loads. Ann, however, tried to prevent him from taking on too much; as he was, in her eyes, still just a child.

Ann had to admit, though, his knowledge of surviving in this land surpassed her own. He was also very strong and agile for his youth, like a monkey, always climbing. Once his eyes began to spark with happiness and trust again, his energies seemed to double, and he never seemed to still.

Even in the evenings after a long day of work, when Ann was completely exhausted, he continued jabbering away, with story after story; often using his entire body to bring his tale to life. Ann wasn't so certain all of his stories were strictly factual, however she enjoyed them, nonetheless.

Ann recalled the day she proudly introduced him to her beaver traps. He had laughed at her, when she admitted she caught more muskrat, than beaver. He guffawed, when she explained to him her technique.

"That's what you're doing wrong," he said. "You can't make lure from beavers from the same pond!"

He taught her better places to set the traps. He even showed her how to tan hides; which was a blessing, because with the softened hides, she could finally stitch more clothes for them all. Then of course, one evening when she was doing just that, Lone Wolf shook his head, wearing an amused grin on his face.

"I would have thought you could stitch better than that, you being a woman and all."

Ann gave him a pointed, dry look.

"I'll have you know; I am far more capable at other pursuits. Tisn't my fault men assigned boring entertainments to women. I never much understood following men's foolish sense of dictates anyway."

He laughed then, "Perhaps you should just stick with hunting."

Ann held up the warm one-piece suit she was making for one of the girls, for inspection.

"I think it is turning out rather good."

It had a decidedly human form to it, from her perspective.

Lone Wolf came over to her and kneeled beside where she sat. He draped the legs portion of the suit out over his raised knee and pointed to her line of stitches.

"Look here. They are not evenly spaced. Also, they aren't quite in a straight line, either."

"Well they are supposed to be curved there. See?"

He obviously was making a great effort not to laugh aloud again.

"But your stitches aren't following the cut of the fabric."

Ann looked again, more attentively.

"It will feel uncomfortable to wear," He said, docilely, with more consideration for her feelings.

"Well, it isn't *unwearable*, I daresay. And don't forget the girls will grow out of it quickly. Then you may sew the next one!" She barked back, teasingly, causing him to smile.

Ann was able to continue Lone Wolf's education when time permitted. Nancy and the doctor had gifted her, or rather her girls, with a simple primer book, not long after the girls were born. She had that as well as one other book she had carried with her from her father's home in England.

She was glad for having taken it, now, for it felt like a part of him she had near with her. *Ivanhoe* by Sir Walter Scott, had been one of her father's favorite books to read to her when she was a young girl. And, she smiled, she hoped it would soon become a fond pastime spent with Lone Wolf and her daughters.

Ann silently thanked her parents for ensuring her education. -The very one, Ann had griped about having to endure while growing up.

She had wanted to be outdoors and preferred physical activity to intellectual studies. Although, she had applied herself vigorously to the subjects of mathematics. She had taken pleasure in knowing she'd been permitted to learn a subject commonly restricted to women. More than that though; she seemed to be naturally inclined in that area of study and so thoroughly enjoyed the lessons.

She was thankful more than ever now for her mother's interference mandating she be tutored in many areas, including art and refinement; her mother's favorite lessons for Ann. Due to her education, she was more than qualified to instruct young pupils.

Lone Wolf excelled quickly with his reading and writing. He seemed to relish the challenge and Ann felt pride in his attitude and accomplishments. As he studied and became more familiar with the English letter, he one day surprised Ann with the revelation, that he wished to revert back to using his English given name.

He had felt anger towards all mankind after what had happened to his parents, however he had felt at the time that he had identified more with his Indian ancestry.

After his mother's brutal death, he had sought out his grandfather, the Indian chief, despite his grandfather's involvement in his father's murder. He had no other relatives to turn to.

He had hoped to be accepted by his grandfather, but although Lone Wolf had done all he could to earn his grandfather's approval, he had never been accepted by his tribe.

Lone Wolf realized it would never be so and set out on his own once more. That was when he had discovered Ann, he explained.

Lone Wolf, once again known as Logan, also explained, that he wanted Kit and Livvy to see him as a brother and so he too, should have an English name. Ann had assured him she and the girls would love and accept him, no matter what name or life he chose, but he had chosen, for now, his English name.

Logan surprised Ann again one day, when he presented to her a bow he had crafted for her. He also taught her how to hunt with it, that way they could take turns seeing to the girls and hunting. She had not had much practice at archery due to her father being a soldier and preferring guns. She took to it quickly, however, as Ann seemed to acclimate easily to most athletic endeavors.

Ann did not like the idea of Logan hunting alone. He protested, bringing up the very valid point that he had been hunting alone and done everything alone for the past three years and survived just fine. Even so, Ann worried. Because she worried, she saw to it that they often went together. It made for an awkward hunting party of one hunter, one guard, and two restless toddlers. Ann felt confident though that it was safest to remain together.

They didn't need to hunt often, anyway. She and Logan had discovered more traps and with his knowledge and new methods applied, they were catching beaver on a daily basis, as well as anything else that managed to find its way into their traps.

Logan had proved to be a veritable fount of information. He related that much of his past had been spent shadowing other groups of people.

He told her about how he attempted to earn acceptance with his grandfather's tribe, despite his anger, out of sheer fear and desperateness when he first found himself alone. He had learned much of his survival skills from his grandfather's tribe, but he had never been welcomed there. The children and adults alike, were cruel to him, often punishing him for being half white and trying to make a slave of him.

He finally made the decision to part ways with his grandfather and set off alone once more. That is when he discovered the very useful skill of becoming a shadow.

He would follow behind groups of men he came across and listen and learn their ways. He followed French trappers early on, but they did not tend to migrate as far, so he moved on.

He followed American trappers who worked for the big companies. Sometimes he trailed behind smaller groups of independent trappers. He listened and learned, but never approached the men or engaged with them. He learned many things.

For instance, he knew when and where they met for the spring and fall rendezvous. And the location happened to be just a week's travel north of their valley.

Together, they made grand plans of selling their beaver pelts at the Rendezvous in the spring near Bent's Fort. She was hopeful they would make enough money to travel to St. Louis. Having already told Logan of the events in her life that led her to the valley where they now lived, he understood her desire to return to St. Louis to search for Grayson and Luke. She could send word to Dr. Fletcher and Nancy while there as well.

It seemed over night the valley had thawed and melted all the powdery, white hills of snow, leaving everything bathed in splashes of cool water. The sun shone brilliantly that morning, sending the entire valley glistening like the magnificent chandeliers Ann remembered from London ballrooms where she'd danced; seemingly a lifetime ago.

Kit and Livvy wanted to run and romp along beside her and Logan on their way to check the traps; however, if allowed to do so, would surely take them until night fall just to reach the river. The sled Ann had constructed was useless in the soft sludge the ground had become since the snow melt, and the girls were far too large, now, for Ann to carry both harnessed to her. Instead she and Logan made up a quick travois of two sticks and a stretch of elk hide, then took turns dragging them along.

The contraption proved to be not much better than the sled in the mud, but they trudged forth. Sometimes they walked along in silence, enjoying the breathtaking scenery before them. Sometimes, it was just too cold or blustery to make conversation. But on this sunny, cheery, day, Ann was filled with a revitalized energy.

The spring air affected Logan as well, for even he was partaking in the merriment and far more chatty than usual. - Not that he was found to be in a nonchalant or morose mood prior to this day, but after so many years of being alone, despite progressing rapidly with relearning the English language, he was still accustomed to speaking very selectively.

They had spotted Ann's horse Comanche - she was certain of it - in the distance the other day. Logan was confident he could recapture the horse or lure it back to them, now that the valley was quickly replacing the snow with lush, green, life. They were laughing as Ann teased reprimands if she caught him stealing her horse.

"If you try to coax my horse away from me, I'll not make you my famous blueberry pie, I've been telling you about."

He rolled his eyes, "Bragging about, you mean."

"Dreaming about, more like!" Ann sighed a hungry sound, comically.

"I'll believe this pie when I see it. Before I took over most of the cooking, your meals were practically boiled to leather!"

"Well, I fear cooking has never been a strength of mine," she grumbled. "Baking however, is entirely different from cooking."

"Is that so?" Logan eyed her skeptically with as much derision as a ten-year-old could muster.

Ann chuckled, "well, I can't claim to be entirely proficient on the subject. The only thing I ever learned to bake well was blueberry pie."

They were both still laughing when Ann noticed the change in the trees.

"Look, there, at those pole-pines," she pointed, "And that one. And there as well." Ann saw at least five trees before her where the large base had been robbed of its bark.

"They look bald," she laughed, "What on earth happened to them?"

She looked then to Logan, only to see his face had gone pale, his worried gaze taking in the sight before them.

He explained quietly, "Those are Grizzly rubs."

Ann had never seen a bear before, but she'd heard countless stories of them during her travels; always about the fearsome, and deadly, brown grizzly.

"We need to get the girls back to the cabin," Logan stated.

"We need to check the traps," Ann countered, practically, "The rubs seem to veer off away from the direction of the river. Clearly, it has moved on. Don't you think?"

Logan shook his head.

"This valley is enclosed almost all the way around. He probably had a cave somewhere high above and was able to get down when there was yet snow. He, or worse, she, may not be leaving for a while."

"This valley is huge, though. We may never even come across it. We can't hide in the cabin all the rest of our days."

"You don't understand!"

Ann got the impression; Logan would have shouted at her if he hadn't been trying so carefully to keep his voice quiet.

"Grizzlies are like nothing else you've ever hunted. They can be nearly twice *your* height when they stand up. I've seen one's claws strike through a man's head like a melon. And this time of year... well, they are hungry. If it's a sow bear with cubs, they are particularly aggressive. It's not an opponent to underestimate."

Ann laid her hand on Logan's shoulder to calm him, for he was nearly shaking with fear.

"Alright," she looked him in the eye and vowed, "I'll not take the threat of one lightly."

He seemed to visibly relax some.

"You're right, the girls should not be out here. You and I have weapons, but they are defenseless."

Then she added, "But we still need to check the traps."

He looked to her ready to argue. Ann held her hand up gesturing for him to be silent, "You take the girls back. I will check the traps. If we harvested anything, I will gather however much I can carry and follow quickly behind you."

"But you didn't bring your bow."

"I still have one shot left in my gun."

Logan looked distressed at the thought of leaving Ann behind with what he considered inadequate protection, but before he could argue, Ann insisted, "Take the girls now. I'll not tarry. I'll be back to the cabin safely with you as quickly as possible."

The girls who had fought the restraints of being strapped onto the travois, were now sleepy from the excursion and blessedly docile therefore Ann knew Logan could get back quickly.

With a small irritated groan, Logan grabbed the poles of the travois and hurried back in the direction they'd come. Ann walked swiftly along the swollen river to their traps.

It had been disappointing to discover their traps had been swallowed up by the river. The snow melt had widened the stretch of water so much, Ann could no longer see the ground where her anchoring sticks should have protruded from.

She'd not run into any grizzlies at least. And due to no harvest to gather, she had been able to head back for the cabin with haste.

As the cabin came into sight however, Ann saw one of the old cart horses near the edge of the woods! They sorely needed the horses. She wanted Comanche returned most, but she'd gladly take her cart horses as well.

She was certain, the girls were napping. Logan was probably bored. Amend that, she thought, he was probably pacing with worry for her. She chewed at her bottom lip for a second. This was too great an opportunity, surely Logan would understand. It wouldn't be too much to let him fret a little longer, if it meant capturing back one of the horses.

She'd tracked quite a distance out around and behind the horse, but as she neared it, it spooked and took off at a gallop. Apparently, it was reveling in its new-found freedom. Or perhaps, it knew she had planned to eat him over the winter and still held a grudge, Ann remarked amusingly to herself.

She decided to head back for the cabin. She'd never catch the flighty animal at any rate.

As she topped the slight incline of the trail she'd followed back to the shack countless times on her return from hunts, an eerie sensation prickled at her spine. She thought she heard a raucous coming from the shack. The sun was peaked high in the sky causing Ann's eyes to squint in order to look any great distance from her. She made a visor of her hand to allow her better to see.

The door to their home was pushed inward, opened. Ann frantically scanned the area surrounding the cabin. Surely Logan was nearby. He wouldn't leave the door open, he must be entering or exiting.

The boy was not outside in sight of the cabin. She held her breath hopefully, but neither did Logan exit the cabin. Then she saw it.

What must be an enormous, Grizzly bear, backed partially out of the cabin door in order to turn and adjust its size in the diminutive space of the cabin. Ann's knees nearly buckled. Why were the girls not crying? Or Logan? Were they in there with the bear?

Ann searched with her eyes again. The travois Logan had hauled the girls home on was propped against the shack to the right of the door.

She froze with fear, unable to move, unable to breathe as she watched the bear rummaging and destroying the inside of her makeshift home. She could hear its grunts and groans as it searched meticulously for food.

Neither Livvy nor Kit were crying...

Oh, God! Oh God, oh God, oh God, no!

They were dead already.

For how could they not wake when a Grizzly was tearing their home apart all around them. And how could it be possible the bear would not have made a meal of them as soon as it entered the small dwelling?

These were not questions she would allow herself to contemplate further. Her brain whirled out of control not knowing what to do.

Then she heard it.

The cry of one of her daughters. They were yet alive!

The bear heard them too and roared; a deafening sound in such close range. Ann reacted without thinking. She called out to the bear. It turned as she'd hoped and peered it's head out the doorway. Next, she saw its shoulders emerge.

Fear and anger filled her with mind numbing strength. Anger that they would have survived the winter only to die now by a bear.

The bear's weight crushed the wood planks that made up the entryway, sending wood splintering about with mighty cracking sounds. Her daughters cried once more, and the bear stopped. Ann wasted no time. She fired the last shot of her pistol, knowing she was out of range of hitting her target. It worked effectively, however, in returning the bear's attention to her.

Provoked, the animal lunged out of the cabin. Ann had never known fear for her own life like this before. The bear stopped long enough to stand on its hind legs and roar again, shaking the timbres throughout the Valley. Its size dwarfed the cabin in comparison. Its head was level with the roof!

Ann knew she wouldn't be able to outrun it.

This would be the day she died, she thought. But she would fight until her last breath.

The bear charged toward her. Ann raced madly in the direction of the bear to the large boulder that lay just to the right of the path that led up to their door. She climbed it in three quick movements. It wouldn't be tall enough to hide from the monster Grizzly, but Ann didn't intend to hide.

The last pull brought her to her feet at the top of the boulder just in time to see the brown expanse of fur fill her vision. She leaped with as much force as her weightless legs could push with. The adrenaline may as well have severed her limbs from her body for she could no longer feel them.

Somehow, she landed atop the beast's back and was able to lock herself into pace. The animal, crazed with fury, threw all of its weight to its front paws as if stomping the ground over and over again. The knife was already in Ann's hand, though she could not recall having pulled it from her waistband. In one swift movement She plunged it into the bear's neck with all her might and buried it to the hilt. But when she instinctively attempted to withdraw, the knife would not budge. The bear roared with pain and Ann felt it begin to roll.

It planned to crush her.

She dove from its back and barely rolled out of the way before the bear thrashed around from its back to its side, already returning to its feet to come after Ann again.

Only this time, Ann had no knife.

Even if by some miracle she survived this bear, she knew she would not survive in these harsh mountains without her knife. Grayson's words echoed in her mind: *"Always keep your knife close to you. It will be your lifeline once you run out of ammo. And you will run out of Ammo."* His words had been harsh, still angry with her for leaving.

The bear's grunts were nearly as loud as his roar as it pounded the earth and ate up the distance between it and Ann. Ann braced herself for the attack, in hopes that somehow, she would be able to reach the handle of her knife and find the strength to pull it from the bear's hide before she was torn apart.

She dived to the side of the bear her arms reaching. It's fur and thick skin on the underside of its neck filled one of her hands. The other hand had found the shaft of her knife, but she wasn't quick enough. A paw bigger than her face, with razor sharp claws, double the length of her longest finger, struck her with full force.

The claws sheared the side of her face as the paw pinned her shoulder. She cried out in agony as the crushing weight sank her into the sodden earth below. Somehow, through the pain induced fog, her body mindlessly and instinctively reacted again. And when the bear raised its front body up, intending to bring both paws down in a fatal blow, she rolled once more inches away from where the paws slammed the muddied ground. She rolled again and again. Unable to stand and acting purely on instinct.

She heard the bear groan in pain. Her eyes located the beast again, it was no longer coming after her, but standing on its hind legs. Its deafening roar filled the valley once more; that's when Ann saw two arrows in the bear's side and another fly past her and pierce the expanse of its chest in the heart. The bear jerked when the spear head entered its body.

From the ground, where she lay, Ann watched the bear tilt back and forth, as it swayed on its hind legs. It gave one last pain wrenched moan as it crashed limply to the ground. And Ann knew it was dead.

Logan. He'd saved her. Saved them all.

She closed her eyes. During her life or death battle with the bear it had felt as if she had left her body entirely. And now, it felt as if she was flooding back into it. Her spirit, once again, filling her physical form and becoming one. And with it, the searing pain in her shoulder.

Air whooshed back into her lungs. She hadn't been holding her breath, she simply hadn't been aware of her breathing during those fighting moments and now it was as if it was her first breath. She couldn't seem to push herself from the ground, the pain was too great.

She was coated in sticky, red blood. But was it hers or the bears? Her mind seemed muddled, and the world around her seemed to be fading in and out. Roughly, she managed to croak, "The girls. Check the girls..."

She thought she heard both girls crying from within the cabin and heard Logan shout their names. Then he was at her side. His voice more fearful and anguished than she'd ever before heard it.

"I'm so sorry!" He cried, "I shouldn't have left them alone!"

Ann couldn't quite make sense of what he was saying, but she felt she needed to reassure him he was not to be blamed for the surprise of the bear. If anyone was to be blamed, it was she. She should have listened to Logan and returned with them. She should not have hied off after the horse and left them alone even longer.

She focused intently on righting herself. She managed to make it partially to her knees, with her good arm extended in attempt to push herself up, when Logan flung himself into her.

"I saw your horse, Comanche again. He was so close. I just wanted to surprise you. I thought the girls would be fine with the door shut. I wasn't going to be far away."

He was sobbing and holding her tightly as to not let go. She managed to use the ground as leverage and push them into a sitting position with the boy on her lap and brought her good arm around him and hugged him back just as fiercely.

She did not know where her tears were, because her heart ached mightily. Her eyes though were still widened and dry with shock from the ordeal. She attempted to soothe Logan. Her mind still denied her to focus upon the event that had just occurred.

"You're okay? The girls are okay?" She managed.

The child nodded affirmatively. Once his sobs subsided, he spoke between gasps and gulps of air, "You fought a bear."

Ann could only manage a nod of her head.

"You jumped onto it's back and stabbed it with your knife."

Again, she nodded.

He pulled out of her arms then and looked up to her face with hurt and anger in his eyes and said, "That was not a smart thing you did."

She shook her head no, agreeing with him, her eyes still glassy with shock and body still trembling, not processing yet what had happened.

He looked into her eyes again to be sure she was focused on him and then spoke firmly, "Do not ever do that again."

Although still racing, she could feel her blood going to her limbs once more, and her mind began to clear. She took in the look of desperation on Logan's face and knew in that moment that he loved her as a son did a mother. He may not call her mother as she had given him leave to do, but he did return the maternal feelings.

"I cannot promise that."

He looked to her incredulously and not without anger.

She stopped him before he could accuse her of more foolishness. "I would always sacrifice myself for those I love: Kit, Livvy... and you."

She grabbed his hand and squeezed affectionately. Or rather, that had been her intention, but her hand didn't seem to be responding to the command. The pain in her shoulder flooded her again, and it was all she could do not to cry out.

"Hurry."

Logan tugged on her, not realizing her arm was the reason for her agony.

"We have to clean the gash. I'm sorry, but it will require stitching. It will be painful."

Gash? What Gash was he referring to, she wondered? She looked to her shoulder, there was no open wound. It was internal. It did not even appear to be disfigured, for all that her arm hung limply at her side.

It felt better if she cradled it.

"It's my shoulder." She told him when he tugged her again. "It hurts like the very devil."

"Your shoulder? Oh, it does appear to be pulled out of place. But I'm more concerned about your face. Please hurry inside so I can clean it."

Dawning realization hit Ann. She released her hurt arm to reach up and touch the side of her face. When she pulled her fingers back, they were covered in blood tinged with mud. For some reason she could not feel pain from it. Perhaps that is why she was still in a half state of shock and perhaps, her body knew she needed to be...

Somehow, she and Logan pulled herself into the house and onto the bed. She saw the shapes of her daughters crowding closer to the bed; no longer crying, but curious and a little frightened. They were too young, yet, to comprehend that their mother had been injured, but the break in routine, alerted them that not all was well.

Her vision blurred the room around her. She knew she was losing too much blood. Head wounds always seemed to bleed the worst, she told herself, encouragingly.

They had little supplies left. Ann had used sinew to sew with mostly; she did not relish the thought of it being woven through the flesh of her face.

It came as a surprise when Logan informed her, with a smile, that he had horsehair.

He explained how he had successfully caught her horse, Comanche. He'd been locking him into the horse shed, when he'd heard the gun shot and the bear.

Ann smiled. She wanted to pat his hand but was too weak.

He gathered the horsehair and returned. After carefully washing the blood and debris away from the cut, he threaded the needle then looked to her apprehensively.

She nodded to him, encouragingly. He brought the needle to her face with trembling hands and looked as if he would be ill.

Ann was feeling ill herself at the thought of a needle piercing her skin and possibly leaving a horrendous scar in its wake, but she needed to be strong for Logan. It needed to be done and he was the only one who could do it. Ann could barely lift her arms. Not to mention, they were not in possession of a looking glass.

Ann smiled reassuringly and made an attempt at humor to ease his fear, "This is your punishment for laughing at my horrid stitch job on the girls' garments."

His lips tried to form a smile but quavered slightly instead.

"What if I don't do a good job and it scars? What if it becomes infected?"

"Don't worry about that now, dearling. Just do your best. The important thing, presently, is to stop the bleeding. It will not be easy. I admit to never having done this sort of thing myself..."

Her breathing seemed to slow. She was so tired. Her body kept trying to send her into sleep, but she fought through the fog to speak more encouraging words to him, "I have every confidence in you."

Then she added, in another attempt to bring a sense of levity to the atmosphere and ease Logan's spirit, "And when I wake up, perhaps it will be my turn to laugh at your stitch work, no?"

His eyes remained solemn, but the corners of his mouth did turn up some. Then she heard him take a fortifying breath and bring the needle to the burning flesh to the outer edge of her right eye.

That was the last she remembered before drifting into unconsciousness.

Chapter 22

"Are we loaded up and ready?"

"I don't know about this."

"Logan, we have repetitively discussed this. We need the money and the supplies. It's the only way."

"I wish you would let me do it."

Ann paused hitching up the cart reins to the horses and blew out a puff of exasperated air. Comanche, seemingly as exasperated as she, snorted as well. Ann patted the horse's muscled shoulder.

After the bear attack, and despite her and Logan's best efforts at cleansing and patching her wound, the strike across her face had turned putrid and a fever put her into a forced sleep for days. When the fever broke, and she finally woke, Logan had nearly crushed the remaining mere existence from her with an exuberant hug filled with unbridled joy.

He shared the gruesome details from when she had been unconscious, about how he had to reopen the wound and pour boiling water over it. How he often worried to the point of actual sickness with the dread that he had not done a good enough job and she would die because of him.

"If I had died, it would have been because of me and my decisions. I'm alive because of you," she had told him.

It was the truth. He had kept her alive and she was inexplicably grateful for his efforts.

Self-consciously, she touched the raised hardened skin behind her right eye and followed the line to the underside of her jaw. It had scarred terribly. Not only the area that had been stitched, but the surrounding flesh as well from the boiled water. One day she had dared to peek at her reflection in the river, even with the ripples from the moving current distorting the image, she could tell how ghastly her face truly looked.

She was alive though, and if the skin often pulled and pinched from its leather-like toughness when she smiled or squinted from the sun, it was consolingly a better price to pay than death or even losing a limb. She could survive these mountains with a roughened face, but she needed full mobility of her extremities.

She smiled to Logan, who stood trying to appear as if he were not fretting terribly over their current situation.

Yes, she thought, she owed her very life to the boy. And she hoped to have a lifetime to repay him.

After Ann's fever had broken, Ann had finally begun healing steadily, but was still too weak for the first few days to leave the bed. During that time, Logan had been busy and seen to wood chores and meals by himself. She was able to get him to wait for her to return to a more recovered state before checking traps again.

But as Ann was on the mend, and after he had been cooped up in the shack for days with the daunting task of saving her life weighing on his shoulders, he was finally able to seek a measure of freedom. He stayed gone most of the days. Ann couldn't fault him. She worried when he was away, but she understood, stuck as she was, within the confining walls of the cabin.

One day, after he had been gone a particularly long while without checking in, he bounded through the door with barely contained excitement lighting his eyes and announced he now had two horses corralled. Due to Ann's shock after the attack, she had forgotten Logan had captured Comanche. He now had one of the cart horses returned. The boy amazed her endlessly.

Ann finally regained her strength and returned to assisting with the daily chores. She and Logan were always extra vigilant, of course, studying their surroundings and discerning for any signs of grizzlies in the area. They never saw any more tracks or other signs, leading them to believe, perhaps their valley was free of the beasts once more and they were able to check their traps in relative peace. That was, of course, after Logan dived down to find the sunken traps.

The last two months seemed to disappear rapidly as they prepared for their travel to the rendezvous site. They discussed and argued endlessly in that time, the details of their plan. Logan did not want Ann to travel alone nor to enter the camp alone. He feared for her safety, being surrounded by all those rough men.

Ann, however, was abhorrent to the idea of sending a small boy alone. - No matter that the boy in question, considered himself a man.

"Practically a man, is not the same as *a man*." Ann stated matter of factly.

Logan then pouted, much like the boy he was, rather than the *man* he claimed to be.

Ann was also uncomfortable sending Logan due to his heritage; she feared the white fur traders may ill treat him based on the sole fact that his appearance resembled that of an Indian. And, of course, he was part Indian.

Ann trailed her hand down Comanche's back to his rump and neared the front of the cart. She felt the stallion's muscles quiver beneath her touch. The horse had spirit to match his beauty. Ann had never seen a more well put together horse. His coloring, alone, was eye catching; mostly solid, dark dun, with white only up to his knees in front and his hocks in the back. A splash of white over his neck above his withers, another splash of white on his back near his hips and a star centered on his forehead tallied up all the white markings he possessed. She patted him lovingly once more before returning her attention to her task.

Logan was already finishing up with his side. She heard him mumbling to the old horse they had begun, with morbid humor, calling "Buzzard Bait".

The old bay horse had survived the winter, but the sparse food and climate conditions had taken its toll on the poor thing. He would fatten up though, Ann knew, with all the fresh green growing all around. Time would tell if he would be able to adapt to the new conditions.

Logan met her eyes from the other side of the cart steps. "You should see if you can trade him for something a little younger and not half starved."

Ann nodded, still gazing sympathetically on the bony horse. "He's not so old you know. I looked at his teeth. I would say he's not much older than fifteen years. He'll fatten up in no time on this rich valley grass."

Then as an afterthought added, "Can't say it will do much for his confirmation however."

Logan smiled and shook his head.

Ann quipped again, "Perhaps we should switch to calling him, 'Homely Homer' instead."

That remark garnered a short laugh from the boy followed by a roll of his eyes. - His typical response to her witticisms; or rather, as he liked to remind her, her failed attempt at them.

She met him near the back of the wagon, where he plead once more, "At least let the girls and I go with you."

"Absolutely not. If it is too dangerous for me to go, it is certainly too dangerous for those bit of cherubs to be brought along."

Ann checked over the supplies once more, not that there was much.

"Listen, I don't like the situation we are in either, but it's the best we can arrange at this time, and the task must be done. We need the seed and grain to get us through. By fall, or perhaps next spring, we shall have a bountiful harvest that will ensure more lucrative tradings and a ticket out of here. For all of us."

He nodded, grimly, accepting their truth.

Now it was Ann's turn to worry. She abhorred the thought of leaving the children behind with so little protection. Logan was an excellent shot with his bow, she did not doubt his prowess with the weapon. Toddlers were so unpredictable though. So many tragic circumstances swamped her mind.

They could catch a cold. Something as simple as a cold could be lethal for little ones. They could fall and break a bone, which could lead to infection and death. They could fall into the river when Logan checked traps. There could be another bear! Ann shivered at the thought.

She needed to be brave. They all needed to be brave. In order to enrich one's life, one must take risks. Ann exhaled slowly, and regained control of her nerves.

Logan seemed to sense the churning of her thoughts. He directed his eyes to the two girls who were stomping and giggling in the shallow puddle.

"I will keep them safe; I'd never let anything harm them."

Ann lovingly cupped his cheek with her hand and brought his attention to her. With conviction, she stated, "I know."

She smiled and brushed some of his wild black strands of hair from his face. "And in order to keep them safe, you must also keep yourself safe."

It was her reminder to him to care for himself as well and also, that she loved and worried for his life as much as she did her girls'.

He nodded stoically and straightened his spine to appear taller. Ann took the opportunity to hug his rigid frame and kiss the stubborn boy on his forehead. He was yet uncomfortable with receiving affection, but Ann was relentless to love it out of him.

She then made her way to her daughters. They had their thick leather leggings soaked with the cool spring mud. Ann shook her head at their silly antics, then worried her lip with her teeth thinking of them catching a cold.

"Come here, my giggle monsters!"

Ann crouched and splayed her arms wide preparing for their trotting, toddler bodies to throw themselves into her arms for a hug. She kissed both their sweet, chubby, faces dozens of times, while tickling them until they cried out with laughter.

Ann wished she could rid her chest of the tight ache building within as easily as she could hide her tears.

"I love you."

She said softly to each and hugged them tightly. She then kissed the springy, fine hair atop their heads before steadying their feet to the ground once more and rose away from them.

She turned to Logan about to instruct him, but he cut her off.

"I know, I know. I will change them into dry warm clothes before we set out for wood."

Ann smiled proudly at him.

"I had best get going, then. The sooner I depart, the sooner I may return," she smiled.

Logan followed her to the front of the wagon as she climbed to take her seat. She took the reins in hand and bent to release the break lever. She adjusted the straps once more, the reins familiar in her roughened hands.

Comanche tugged, expressing his eagerness to move forth. Ann held him in place. He was unaccustomed to being hitched, but Ann and Logan had worked with him and he was learning quickly.

"Take care while I'm gone," Ann said earnestly.

Logan gave a small nod of his head indicating he would uphold his duties.

"And Logan, I love you too."

Logan swallowed and nodded again. He didn't need to return the spoken words. Ann's maternal heart knew he returned the sentiment.

With all the goodbyes said, Ann flicked her wrist and set the pair off at a somewhat uneven, but brisk, pace towards the secret passage Logan had discovered to the North. It measured just wide enough to fit their small vehicle. And with little else on the drive to distract her mind, the worries returned with abundance.

Ann followed the river as Logan had instructed her to and encountered no problems whatsoever. A rare luck that, Ann lamented to herself.

After nearly a week of travel, she saw the smoke from the traders' fires above the trees on the other side of the river and knew she neared the rendezvous camp. She crossed the river and as she grew closer, she could hear the unmistakable sound of meaty fists pounding flesh beyond the thick trees. Knuckles, along with bones, cracking. She heard men cheering well before she entered the clearing and saw the madness with her own eyes.

More than one fight ensued. White men donned in thick buckskin outer wear and furs littered the valley clearing before her, as well as what Ann estimated to be hundreds of Indians sporting native designs unique to separate tribes. Ann had not expected so large a number of men. And rough men they were.

Cayt Lawson

A shiver of apprehension prickled her skin. Self-consciously, Ann checked to ensure her braided hair was tucked securely beneath her hat and pulled the brim down lower to cover her face.

Ann gazed out at the temporary "town". Logan had used the term "camp". However, as Ann looked around, she determined that to be entirely inadequate. True, there were no permanent structures or storefronts. But men along with their tents and hastily built lodges scattered about encompassing all the land this side of the river making it appear as heavily populated as some of the smaller towns she'd passed through on her travels.

Ann looked on in disgust. The tents were set up in an unorganized fashion that would have made her precise soldier minded father's teeth grind. Men were brawling in huddles as others swarmed to cheer, and probably wager on the ensuing fights, blocking the main muddied and trenched path that divided the sloppy set up of dwellings.

A sea of loud, angry, men as far as Ann could see and blocking the only clear route. Ann was wont to take her whip to their foolishness but daren't draw any unwanted attention to herself.

She turned her rig instead up the grassy knoll and rolled and bumped along the uneven terrain behind the mass of tents in search of a secluded spot a safe distance from the raucous affair.

The river winded back and forth like a slithering snake and she debated whether to cross back and camp just on the other side as a precaution. Then she would have to ride Comanche back and forth across the river though. She sighed and instead followed the river to where the woods deepened once more and used the trees for cover. She didn't unpack. She planned to remain only long enough to make good her trades then be off.

Deciding there was yet plenty of daylight left to conduct business, Ann wasted little time and set off. She hobbled Comanche behind the wagon in the wooded area and hoped he remained out of sight. Ann didn't want to risk him being stolen. She hobbled Homer closer to the wagon, she needn't worry over him being stolen. One would have to be even more

364

desperate than she to risk being hung for thieving such a miserable looking beast.

She set off for the trading tents, weaving her way through the clutter. Clusters of men were everywhere, some groups making merry music with varying instruments. Ann heard strings being plucked and wooden spoons click-clacking together in a harmonious upbeat tune. That's when Ann first noticed other women in the camp. Their colorful dress hems swirled around in the dirt as they kicked up their booted feet in dance with some of the men. They appeared in good spirits, but Ann knew such women were often paid to appear that way. The rouge on their worn faces indicated they were just such women. Ann tried to avoid eye contact with both the men and the women and moved along swiftly.

There were tables set up in front of the tents with all sorts of goods and wares to trade. She passed an eager hat seller. Ann declined his many offers and tried to continue past his tent, but the pushy fellow then had the audacity to attempt to replace Ann's hat with one of his own. As he grabbed for her hat to remove it, Ann reacted with the speed she had adopted in her recent years of struggle and survival and pulled her knife.

"Remove your fingers from my hat or lose them." She growled menacingly.

The man jerked his hand back in surprise, then held both arms up as if in surrender.

"I meant no harm. Just thought I could interest you in a better hat, that's all."

Ann nodded to him in manner of a truce, then moved along peacefully. She stopped in front of a tent that had powder and weapon supplies.

"Hi, I have quality beaver pelts to trade."

Ann held up the one pelt she had pulled from one of her bales in order to prove she had currency.

The top of the man's greasy, dark, head never even turned up, but remained focused on whittling a hunk of wood in his hands.

"What caravan?"

Ann hesitated, "I'm not with a caravan."

He looked up then and studied her face, then spat brown gritty tobacco juice out of the side of his mouth. His lip curled with disdain, "You're a woman."

Damn. She had forgotten to lower her voice. Her disguise was blown on her very first attempt to trade. -Not, that it had been a good disguise, but she had hoped being bulked up with men's clothes and her disfigured face would aid in her attempt to look like a man.

She narrowed her eyes and repeated, "I have quality beaver pelts to trade for some powder and load."

"I don't trade with no women."

His dirt stained face wrinkled up near one side of his mouth as his mouth twisted with arrogant condescension. Ann resisted the urge to break the big beak of a nose protruding crookedly from the center of his face. By the looks of it, the man's rudeness had resulted in his nose already being broken a few times in his life.

Instead, Ann smiled winningly and turned her back on the greasy mopped, scare-crow shaped man. Surely someone would want fine beaver pelts. They were as good as money and Ann didn't know many men who would turn down money, even if it came from a talking rock.

She winded her way through the crowd and passed more tents. Some Indian women were selling beaded jewelry. They would probably trade with her, she thought. Unfortunately, she didn't have any use for the pretty body decor. Ann shared a small smile in passing with them. Finally, she came across another tent selling rifles and weapon supplies.

Just as she was about to approach the man's table to inquire, a body bowled into her from behind, sending her crashing to the ground. Her hat fell from her head in the process and her long, thick chestnut colored hair spilled out, partially unbraided over her shoulder. She scrambled to her feet in quick succession, thinking it was probably an accident. Lots of drunken men, and women as Ann had noticed, were clumsily picking their way through camp as well.

She reached for her hat, assuming the drunk had already moved on, and started to place it back onto her head when it was ripped right out of her hands!

What the devil?! Ann looked up into the cold blue eyes of a ruddy faced man holding her hat back out of her reach, like a school yard bully taunting another child.

Anger spiraled through her and every nerve in Ann's body went into defense mode.

"Joe was right. There is a lass walkin' round in men's clothes."

The Ruddy faced man announced, sending his group of chums around him chortling.

Then, eyeing Ann lasciviously, asked, "Just what kind o' wares you be selling?"

Once again, the man and his cronies crowed with laughter, believing their mate quite the clever one, indeed.

Ann glared at the group of insolent sods, gritting her teeth. The hat wasn't worth spending another second dealing with these fools.

"Keep the hat."

Ann spat then dismissed them with the turn of her heel to walk away.

Ann heard the big oaf's boots grind in the dirt as he stepped after her, just before she felt his big paw crudely pat her backside.

"Come now darlin'. Tell ya what. I'll give you back this fine hat if you give me some of that fine arse! Sound like a fair trade, boys?"

The crowd behind her hooted and hollered in agreement.

Ann remained standing fixedly, refusing to turn around. Then she felt his hand roughly grab her shoulder in attempt to force her to face him. The anger pooled within her and spread like a wildfire in her veins.

The man stepped closer behind her nearly pressing his form against her backside. Ann could smell the man's rank sweat from his body and feel his rancid breath against the back of her neck. In a blind fury, Ann instinctively brought her elbow up and back delivering a forceful blow to the man's throat. Then before he had time to double over and make good his gasp for air, Ann caught his hand at her shoulder, and pulled him forward, using her body to effectively flip him onto his backside.

He quickly scrambled to his feet. With a growl, he lunged for Ann. She anticipated his rash attack however and kicked him in the groin with intent to maim. It sent him sinking on his knees to the ground. She didn't wait for him to recover but drew her pistol. In an instant she had the hammer back with a click and the tip of the barrel inches from the point of the man's face between his eyes, where a bead of sweat trickled, leaving behind a dirt stained trail.

Neither he nor the little group that had been behind him were laughing now.

"I'm disinclined to blowing your brains everywhere and making a bloody mess all over this fine establishment," Ann drawled. "But I find being accosted once more even less appealing. You had best keep your pecker in your breeches or find a woman who is willing. Less I decide to decorate the two tents behind you with bits of your ugly mug," She seethed.

A gruff voice ahead of her from behind one of the seller's tables chuckled, "You'd best do as the lady says, Niall. I don't fancy having to clean 'bits of your ugly mug' from my tent none either."

Another man making his way through the crowd towards her, spoke next, "I witnessed this lady use her gun back in Santa Fe. Trust me, men don't fare well on the other end of her smoking barrels."

Ann didn't recognize the voice. She turned her head wondering who the man was claiming to have witnessed her kill a man in Santa Fe. The implication was preposterous. Ann had only ever *thought* of killing a man in Sant Fe -her lying, supposed husband. She had, somewhat regrettably, left the deed undone.

The man grew closer and she could see the teasing glint in his eyes. Brown eyes, set in a bronzed face, neither of which she recognized, but she sensed he was no enemy to her. Indeed, he seemed to be coming to her aid.

The trader in the tent spoke again, "What say you Niall? Give the lady back her hat?"

The ruddy faced and newly sobered Niall shook his head affirmatively and said to Ann, "Yes ma'am. No harm done, right?"

Then one of his chums came forward offering back her hat. Ann took the hat and positioned it onto her head with one hand, never taking her steely eyes off of Niall, allowing him to sweat her decision a few seconds more.

Then with a crisp nod she tipped her gun up and set the safety back into place, freeing the loathsome whoremonger. Ann didn't see the contemptuous glance he sent her over his shoulder as he stood and passed by. She did hear him mumble, in face saving fashion to his crowd, "Wouldn't want to dip into her sour pot anyway. She's apt to pickle a man's prick, she is."

Ann drew out the process of strapping her pistol back to her side, seemingly ignorant of the man's lewd comments as well as he and his cronies' laughter as they meandered off into the crowd.

When she looked up, the brown eyed man who claimed to know her from Santa Fe and the trader in the tent both stood smiling conspiratorially at her.

The trader's smile never wavered as he asked, "So you killed a man in Santa Fe, did ya?"

The brown eyed man barked a short laugh and a small smile in kind formed on Ann's face.

The brown-eyed man clapped her on the back, and with a wink responded to the trader, "No, but she ought to have had."

Ann smiled less reservedly then at the man's comment and leaving all polite conversational etiquette aside, asked directly, "Do I know you?"

The man slapped his chest in feigned gesture as if wounded, "I suppose I can forgive you. Even a visage as handsome as mine, cannot be expected to be remembered by a lady when in the process of breathing fire and facing down a blackguard."

When Ann yet looked to him puzzled, he further explained, "I was one of the unfortunate wretches caught in the saloon when you-er-barreled in and made us all fear for our lives."

Ann blushed, realizing the man had been present to witness her mortifying revelations with James in Santa Fe.

"Is this a habit of yours? Or are you some sort of avenging angel sent to ensure all the scoundrels of the world repent?"

Ann laughed then, "Hardly. Although I do seem to be rather good at the position."

"My name is Antonio García. It is a pleasure to be near-but not a recipient of-your ire, once more."

Ann laughed again, "My name is Ann-er-Dunneroy," she nearly replied Morgan, but at last second decided upon her maiden name instead. Morgan was dead to her. She did not need him or his name.

This time the man named Antonio swept her hand to his lips and brushed a kiss along her knuckles, smoothly.

"Again, it is an honor."

The man's eyes sparkled flirtatiously.

She responded with what she hoped was the right amount of levity. She was out of practice for "ballroom etiquette". -Not that she had ever mastered the craft. This man seemed a replica of the rogues that frequented such places in her long ago past, however. She hoped she did not let on how uncomfortable she was with his flirtation, if indeed, that's what it was.

He hadn't rescued her, but he had stepped in and aided in resolving that bit of ugliness far more smoothly than she would have been able to accomplish on her own.

Even now the man seemed to be helping her. *But why?* She hoped he wasn't anticipating being rewarded with a form of *payment* she would never agree to...

Goodness, but she had turned into a jaded, suspicious creature, hadn't she?

His words drifted into her thoughts, "I think this senorita is in need of some trade, Cooper. What say you? Surely you are not so stiff rumped as the rest of these hypocrites, eh?"

"No, indeed. She surely showed she can hold her own any-a-ways."

Then the man called Cooper turned his attention to her, "I'd be happy to trade with such a braw lass. What can I do for you Miss?

The rest of the afternoon went smoothly. Word got around, good and bad, but thanks to Antonio and Cooper, most of the tents traded with her without remonstrance and treated her respectfully.

One man convinced her to trade for a lamb, though she ill had room for one. She could tie it to the wagon, she supposed, and hope it kept up. It was difficult to turn the man down. He shared he was a widower and became quite emotional talking about his late wife, Sal.

"You remind me of her," he said, "It takes a special kind of woman with moxie and mettle to survive these parts. And I can see that you've got 'em. All the same," The bewhiskered man continued, rubbing his bristly jaw, "You ought to have some protection in these parts. Wait right here, Missy."

He went around back behind his tent and came back holding a little ball of fur.

"Oh, I thank you sir, but I can ill afford to purchase another animal." She started to decline his offering.

"No, no. It's a gift. My Sal would want you to have it." The old man's eyed twinkled with warmth and kindness as he held the unusual pup up then for her to see.

Once she saw it, she couldn't turn it away, no matter how impractical. It was like no other dog she'd ever seen, with a blue speckled coat, copper legs and a stark white breast and collar. She had the sweetest face with the same copper coloring brushed on her cheeks and white strip coming down the center to her nose. And most brilliantly, the pup's eyes were a striking shade of ice blue.

The man assured her she wasn't blind. He explained as how it was a new breed, bred specifically for a certain sheep being imported from Australia to be worked in the mountainous climates.

So perhaps, it *was practical* to take on the pup, she weakly justified. She gathered the soft, fluffy, bundle into her arms. Thank you, Sir."

"The name's Gene."

"Well thank you Gene," She smiled graciously, "I think I will name this beauty," she looked down to the quiet, intelligent looking pup in her arms, "Sal. After your late wife, if that is agreeable with you."

A tear formed in Gene's eye, "Right it is, Miss. Aint no better name, that's fo' sure."

He smiled and nodded his farewell back to her, and she made her way back to her camp for the night. The day had gone fairly well, and she was loaded with flour, sugar, and seeds for planting as well as other supplies that would see them through.

She penned a letter to Dr. Fletcher and Nancy on a torn sheet of foolscap she'd managed to haggle in with some other items she traded for. She would use the remaining coin she had to ensure the letter got posted and made its way back to St. Louis and then onto Charleston.

She sighed. It would take months for Fletcher and Nancy to receive it, and she may never hear from them in return, but at least they would know she and the girls were safe.

The next morning, all packed up she made her way to the main encampment, built from sturdy logs. She was told the man in charge of distributing and carrying mail could be found within. After questioning a few men, she was finally directed to the man named Shaw. He was a wiry fellow, from his frame to his blond curly hair. He was a loquacious fellow, too, but seemingly pleasant and jovial. He took her letter and assured her it was in safe keeping and he would ensure all mail made it back to St. Louis.

With much relief Ann was finally able to leave the raucous embodiment of the camp and be on her way back home.

Grayson unsaddled Dove and tied her to the wagon Luke and Rupert Dunneroy had just disembarked from.

"Why don't you set up camp," He directed to them, "I'm going to head over to the main lodge in search of a post boy. There's bound to be someone riding back to St. Louis with mail. Seems like the most promising place to start."

All three of them had been pacing the hotel floors in St. Louis for months, itching to get back to their search for Ann and the girls. Actually, Dunneroy had been pacing the floors of his own town house he had purchased out right for his new wife and family.

They decided to stop at the Spring Rendezvous on their way to Bent's Fort to ask around. They'd finally made it and Grayson was impatient for answers or at the very least a lead to go on.

Dunneroy and Luke nodded to him and so he left the horses and wagon in their care while he set off with his questions.

Grayson recognized a lot of faces. Longtime friends and acquaintances came to welcome him with jovial pats on the back and boisterous greetings.

Talk of the camp centered around a shocking woman in buckskins, walking around like a man and transacting business and trades with her own beaver pelts. A kernel of suspicion tugged at his heart, but when he questioned about the appearance of the woman, the ready descriptions offered by those around him never seemed to match Ann.

"Fierce like an amazon she was!"

An amazon? Not his Ann, she was a petite, tiny frame of a woman.

"Didn't take bull from no man here. Pulled a gun and threatened to blow the ballocks off of 'em at wasn't gonna trade wit' 'er, she did."

"Why, you see her flip Niall Meeks right over her back? Laid him out in the dirt like. Best entertainment all week!"

It seemed almost a competition between the rowdy men to learn who had witnessed her most daring act. Tales were being bandied about like wildfire. Most of the men seemed in awe of the woman, respect for her shown in the sparkle of their eye as they reminisced about their experience with her. Not all were so. Grayson heard faint grumblings as well about women acting like men "weren't right."

No one seemed to be able to place a name with her, although bestowed nick names, respectful and lurid alike were aplenty. Grayson came upon an older man. He recalled seeing him in the past at other rendezvous.

"Howdy Gene. It's been a long time. You and Sal still makin' a go of it out in these parts, eh? I'd have thought your rickety bones too old to be this side of the Mississippi anymore."

Grayson flashed a teasing grin to the grizzled old man.

The man tried to share in his humor, but grief clouded his eyes, restraining him from partaking in the banter as he normally would have.

"My Sal passed away. Last spring she did." Grayson grew sincere, "I'm sorry to hear that Gene. She was a good woman."

"That she was." The old man smiled to himself, as he reflected on past memories.

"Hey, Gene, I was wondering if you had by any chance run into this 'brawny, buckskin-clad, gun-slinging, miss' all the men are yarnin' about 'round camp?"

Gene gave a rough, rusty chortle, "That what they're sayin'?"

"You disagree?" Grayson fixed a shrewd gaze on the elder man, prepared to analyze his response.

"A woman approached me fer some tradin'. And she was right wearin' buckskin breeches I's suppose. She wasn't no brawny thing though and never pulled no guns on me."

The gnarled old man chuckled and stroked his whiskered chin. The amusement glinting his eyes faded into a revered earnestness, "She was a tiny thing. Sweet lass."

Grayson's heart drummed in his ears as its pace quickened, "Was she English? Would you have considered her a beauty? Rare features? Like golden eyes and gold streaked hair?"

Gene thought reflectively on that before replying, "She was English, deed she was. Perhaps once she may have been considered a beauty. Her face was mangled like. Big scar slashed one whole side of it. Can't say as I remember the color of her eyes. Her hair was dark though, I'm fair certain. Of course, she had it tucked under a hat..." He trailed off.

Grayson wasn't sure. Perhaps he wanted to find Ann so much, he was twisting details to fit the picture he wanted to make. Just then a Spaniard looking gentleman joined them.

"I was passing by and couldn't help but overhear you discussing the woman who passed through here not long ago."

The man leaned up against Gene's tent pole, casually, and lit a cigar.

"The lady did have golden eyes as a matter of fact. What do you know about her and why are you looking for her?"

The man blew out a slow trail of smoke.

Grayson's eyes squinted with interest at the man. He was astute-and direct. Equally suspicious of one another, Grayson tried to gauge whether or not to offer more details to the man. '*The lady did have golden eyes as a matter of fact.*' It had to be Ann. And this man knew something. That decided it.

"I am searching for a woman, although I can't be certain she is the same that passed through here."

"What do you want with her?" The man countered, measuring Grayson with a level gaze.

Grayson decided to take a cautious approach. Since he was neither married nor affianced to Ann, his tie to her may seem precarious to an outsider. Instead of explaining his complicated relationship with Ann, he went with another truth.

"I was hired to lead a group from back east to Missouri. The woman I'm looking for was traveling in that group under my charge. Her uncle -" Grayson hesitated, unsure of how many details to divulge to the stranger. While throwing the weight of Ann's father's title around may intimidate a man into talking, he wasn't certain revealing Ann to be a daughter of an Earl wouldn't make her a target. Then again, titles didn't carry a whole lot of weight here, anyway. He decided to disclose information somewhere in the middle "- Lord Dunneroy located me in his search of her."

Grayson didn't imagine it when he announced her uncle's name; the man's eyes lit up with recognition. Grayson's blood fairly drummed. Ann was close, he could feel it! Still, he needed to remain calm and garner as much information as he could.

The man sucked on his cheroot again, "Dunneroy, huh?"

Grayson remained silent.

The man's brown gaze eyed him speculatively, "That doesn't explain why *you* are looking for her. Why are you aiding her uncle in his search? And are you sure she wants to be found?"

It took all of Grayson's control not to ball his fists and beat the information from the man. He made a conscious effort to unclench his jaw, "Her family has reason to believe she may have been duped by a man claiming to be her husband. She may be in danger. I take my duties very seriously and as she may have come to harm under my care, I feel partly responsible and am offering my assistance."

"Stone!"

Dunneroy's haughty command interrupted. It seemed ingrained in the Englishman to bark orders, but Grayson had grown accustomed to his stodgy manner and come to respect the man greatly. Just now he trudged hurriedly up the slope to where they were standing, appearing uncharacteristically impatient.

"I've been looking everywhere for you. After we set camp, I headed to the main lodge and found the post boy. He said he hadn't spoken with you yet."

"I discovered some information along the way."

Grayson looked pointedly to the Spaniard taking the exchange all in.

Dunneroy turned and leveled a gaze on the man casually leaning against the tent smoking a cheroot. Grayson knew the instant the Spaniard recognized the familial similarity between Ann and her uncle.

"You must be the uncle."

The man extended his hand to Dunneroy, a far more friendly gesture than Grayson had received from the man.

"Indeed. And who might you be?"

Before another stare down could take place, Luke came jogging over to them, talking excitedly, "Did you tell him?" and then to Grayson, "There was a letter! She sent a letter back to the doctor in Charleston!"

Grayson wasn't sure if it was seeing the joy on the boy's face or seeing the proof of Ann's familial connection, but the Spaniard finally blew out a breath.

"The name of the woman in the stories on every man's lips here in camp is indeed Ann Dunneroy. I spoke to her myself and she introduced herself to me."

"Garcìa!"

Another man made his way to where they had begun to form a small group. Grayson recognized the burly man. As he neared, he recognized Grayson with a startled surprise.

"Grayson Stone! As I live and breathe. You made it after all."

He extended his hand in greeting.

Grayson clasped his hand back, "Cooper."

Cooper took in the strange atmosphere of the group with a cautious manner. "You met García?"

"Only just."

A heartbeat of silence. Then, apparently Cooper felt the need to smooth over whatever the bother was, "He can be a might surly somedays!" Cooper laughed and clapped García on the back.

García spoke, "These gentlemen are inquiring about Miss Dunneroy."

A surprised expression came over Cooper's face. "That's what I came to tell ya. Larkins saw Niall and Scarecrow Joe light outta here in the same direction Miss Dunneroy did earlier this morning. I don't think it a coincidence."

Something in Cooper's voice set Grayson on edge.

García met his eyes and confirmed the fear sidling up inside.

García and Cooper explained why the men may pose a threat to Ann and told all they could recall of the direction Ann was headed.

They still needed supplies, so it was decided Grayson would set out immediately and Dunneroy would follow behind with Luke after loading and restocking the wagon. Cooper had to remain to man his tent, but García offered his assistance. Grayson didn't much like the inkling feeling that the tall handsome Spaniard seemed to have such an interest in Ann, but he could ill afford to turn down the help. García, too, needed to make preparations before he set out, and so agreed to travel with Dunneroy and Luke.

Grayson was saddled and ready to go within half an hour.

Ann was alive. And by God he would find her.

There was no way he would fail her again.

Chapter 23

Ann was four days into her sojourn back home when she felt the prickles of unease raise the hairs on her neck. A feeling that something, or rather, someone was following her.

She was forced to travel slowly what with all of her supplies and the animals, so whomever was behind her was staying there, deliberately. That alone caused a suspicious unease to settle through her. The only reasons she could contemplate for someone wanting to remain near, but unseen all concluded badly for her.

It wouldn't be difficult for anyone to have located her, she grumbled to herself and directed a curt glare to what appeared at the moment to be a sweet, cute, docile lamb, but was truly a devil renegade! At the moment, it was sleeping peacefully near her lap seated on the driving bench. And making Ann's job all the more difficult, for she had to repetitively catch the lamb and keep her from falling off at every unexpected jostle.

Luckily, Sal, the pup, took to trail life with ease and seemed capable of managing herself for the most part. And to think, Ann had originally wanted only the sheep and attempted to decline the offering of the pup!

Ann shivered again. If someone was following her, she wouldn't be able to lose them. The deceivingly docile lamb, turned into a loud, bleating, alarm near dusk, no matter how Ann tried to comfort the senseless beast. The first few nights Sal was so upset by the squalling lamb, that she began barking as well. Ann felt more and more like a traveling circus, everyday!

Even If she weren't traveling with the loudest pair of animals since the dawn of time, there was no road and Ann didn't trust her ability to find her way back home if she didn't stay near to the river.

She continued on as normal, not breaking any of her heretofore routines so as not to give away that she was aware of whomever was out there. Her shadow fiend, as she'd taken to calling the person (or persons, for at one point she thought she heard more than one horse nickering back and forth to another in the distance) following her, could have easily ridden up on her by now. Ann couldn't understand what the plan or motive could be to wait.

Then, unexpectedly, on her last day of travel, the shadow seemed to have disappeared. She no longer heard horses nickering in the distance. She no longer felt the anticipation of danger rising like a turbulent wave of acid in her guts. Perhaps, they had been travelers and as suspicious as she herself was, decided to stay a distance away as not to invite trouble? Or perhaps they met with an ill demise?

Ann couldn't be sure, but she would take no risks. It pained her to see the brush that marked the secret passage to her valley, and be unable to pass through it, when she desperately wanted to get home to her children.

She wanted to ensure her 'Shadow Fiend' was truly gone though. So she traveled a distance past her opening in the opposite direction and made camp, resigned to wait out the evening at the ready. If she did not encounter her Shadow Fiend this night, she would hurry to the entrance in the early morning before the sun could begin to chase the moon from the sky and be sure to cover her tracks well.

Ann had made it within the confines of her cave walls safely the next morning. Once the walls opened up into the grandeur of her valley, she hid and waited for a time as an extra precaution. When no one else entered behind her, she decided she was safe and continued quickly to home.

Tears glistened like shiny pools in her eyes when she spied the children outside of the cabin on the hilltop. Logan appeared to be stacking firewood and both girls appeared to be unstacking it. A choked laugh riddled out of her of its own accord; all the tension, fear, and worry shaking out of her with it. At last she was home!

Logan spied her and grabbed the girls to keep them from rushing the wagon. Ann leaped from the wagon, not even bothering with the parking brake, as she trusted Comanche and Homer were too well trained and too tired to bolt away.

Once Ann's feet were securely on the ground, the children ran for her gleefully.

To Grayson's surprise, the men he tracked seemed to know what they were doing and had made it difficult to find their trail. They weren't following closely behind Ann. Despite her load of supplies, she was traveling at a swift pace and was probably a half a day ahead of him yet. Grayson's pace was slowed too, due to hunting for the hoof prints of the two riders. Grayson discovered another trick the men were using to sneak up on Ann, was to travel separately from one another. They kept in the denser woods, far to the left and right of the path Ann had left behind.

Grayson figured they neared a veering off of Ann's path or else the men may have lost sign of her direction, because after a few days of riding the tracks finally came together. Then signs from the men as well as of Ann disappeared entirely.

He had to be close. Which meant he needed to proceed with acute caution. He needed to know the placement of everyone to ensure he didn't put Ann in danger, or himself for that matter. He wouldn't be of any help to Ann if the trackers discovered him first and got the advantage of him.

Luck changed when night fell. He smelled the faintest hint of smoke. Someone had foolishly made a fire. He couldn't see it burning, but he had to be within a mile or so from it, by his estimation. The trees, in full leaf, blocked any light of the moon from penetrating the forest floor and made traveling devilishly tricky. He couldn't risk injuring his horse, so he climbed from

Dove's back and led her, ever slowly. The fire wouldn't burn all night. He needed to follow the smoke trail while he could still smell it.

It was a gruelingly slow pace; picking along for the safest and quietest footing amidst fallen trees, roots, and holes. But necessary. About thirty minutes in, he lost scent of the smoke. He was close though; he could feel it. There was little else he could do to progress his search tonight without risking discovery.

He allowed himself no more than three hours of sleep as he wanted to be awake before Ann if she was still near, or her trackers. He woke well before dawn and was rewarded by the sound of wood wheels crunching over crumbled rock.

The sound seemed to come from south of him. It was still dark, the sun hadn't yet begun to rise, but the sky had that lightened shade to it. The black velvety blanket behind the remaining glittering stars had softened to an ashen gray that faded into a violet blue; a promise that the glow of morning was on its way. It was still difficult to see, however, and he'd have to continue leading Dove, when it would be faster to ride if he had better light to see by. But he was able to tread a somewhat quicker pace than he had in the ink black of night. Or perhaps his body thrumming with the awareness that wagon wheels meant Ann was near, had him taking risky, brisker steps.

He came to a wall of rock that extended far above him into the sky. A dead end. He traveled west first, but when he didn't come across any tracks, doubled back east.

And there she was.

He couldn't see her well, draped in layers of buckskin obscuring her form, and a floppy hat pulled low over her face, but he knew it was she. She seemed to be cutting or clearing branches away. But why? Behind lay the steep incline of rock that jutted from the ground to tower above them. The cliff wall seemed to extend out in both directions as far as the eye could see. What was her purpose for clearing a path there? He watched, wanting to call out, but being unsure of where the two trackers were, didn't dare. They could be nearby watching her just as he was.

He saw her clear some more brush away. It looked as if much of it were dead and just resting along the wall. She didn't seem to be struggling or hacking away at it either.

Then he watched Ann drive her cart and disappear through a clearing where the brush had been. What in tarnation was she up to? She reappeared at the opening and replaced the tall stalky bundles and branches, obscuring sight of the clearing once more. Grayson continued to wait. God, how he had wanted to rush to her now that he was so close. But his gut told him to remain hidden to make sure the men following her hadn't seen her enter through the wall as well.

Nearly fifteen minutes had passed, and Grayson was starting to think the men had lost Ann's trail.

Suddenly, pain exploded across his back! Something solid and heavy hit him from behind with enough force that it knocked him from his horse. He landed near Dove's dancing hooves but managed to keep a hand on the reins to steady her, despite the throbbing pain tearing across his shoulder blades.

He'd been so intent on watching the wall and path beyond that he had not seen the man approach from behind with a thick branch. The swing of the branch had connected mostly across his upper back and right shoulder, not his head, thankfully.

He jumped to his feet in time to block the next attack from the man, who had switched out his branch for a bowie knife. The man managed to get the blade to Grayson's throat, but although tall, the man was lean and weak.

The struggle did not last long. Grayson thrust the man from him with a solid kick, drew in a lusty breath of air, and readied for another advance.

Everything about the man was lanky, from his long, greasy black strands of hair, to his tall, scarecrow like frame: Scarecrow Joe, he presumed. Grayson knew he could overpower the man, so his goal was to not kill him. Not before he could glean from him the information concerning his missing traveling companion. But the man left Grayson little choice when he came at him again armed with two blades, one in each hand.

One of the blades caught Grayson along the outer side of his right bicep as Grayson reached out and twisted the man's arm holding the other blade and plunged it deep, back in towards the man's own body.

The man's eyes shot around frantically, wild with the knowledge that death was taking him. Grayson released the handle of the knife and lowered the man's body to the ground.

"Are you Scarecrow Joe? What's your name?" Grayson demanded, "Where's your friend? Why were you after the woman?"

But the life was draining from the man swiftly and no answers came forth before the last pump of his heart gave.

Grayson swore, then led his mare to where the loose brush had been positioned at the rocky wall. Only, when Grayson reached it, the brush was no longer covering the space Ann had pulled her cart through; it was shoved off to the side.

As if another had passed through and not bothered to hide the opening.

Goosebumps shivered down Grayson's body. The other man.

Grayson hurriedly walked his horse through the narrow mouth of the cave-like entrance; it wasn't tall enough for him to ride. The rocky path was narrow and curved like a maze. Before long the walls crumbled away and opened into a vast green valley. The white cliff walls seemed to go out forever and then turn and follow the swells as if barricading the lush land for its own safe keeping.

Grayson hadn't time to admire the beauty of the land though; he had to get to Ann.

The sun was nearly fully above him when he finally cleared the dense woods and was able to take in the sight before him: Ann -even from such distance he knew it was she- had her arms wrapped around a small child. One of the girls!

A boy and another small child stood near. Sounds of laughter from the group danced merrily on the wind; a faded tinkling echo. Grayson barely had time to take it all in.

A movement, halfway between him and Ann, caught his eye. A man stalking on foot appeared in front of him, oblivious to Grayson's presence, and stepped from behind the shelter of two large pines with a long rifle aimed in the direction of Ann and the children.

Cayt Lawson

The boy in front of Ann must have discovered the threat in that instant as well, for he raced forward as if to shield Ann's body with his own.

Without a second's thought, in one smooth motion, Grayson raised his cut down smoothbore at the ready in his hand, aimed and fired. Only the sound of a single shot rent the air, but Grayson's breath didn't release from his tightened lungs until the gun fell from the man's grip in front of him and Grayson watched him sink to his knees in the tall, lush, valley grass.

Tears of joy were streaming down Ann's face as she hugged each of her children. Logan was firing off questions about the rendezvous, about the sheep bleating from the wagon, and the supplies, and why on earth would she spend their money on a dog? But the last, question, or rather accusation, was slung at her with a happy smile picking up the corners of his mouth.

"It sure is a cute little fur ball." He looked on the pup, failing to maintain his stoic stance. The girls abandoned their mother's arms to maul the puppy, who soaked up their attention quite greedily. Ann had thought she and Sal had bonded quite thoroughly on their trip home, but it quite appeared Ann would be losing her little companion to her children. And quickly at that! She chuckled to herself.

"You will be happy to know we will be eating fare other than just meat for a while!" Ann beamed to Logan. But her teasing glint faded from her eyes when she saw his fear-stricken face.

Before Ann could gather her thoughts to ask a question or turn to see what he was seeing, Logan dashed around her.

Ann realized he was acting as cover for her when the explosion of a gun sounded. A terrified scream tore through Ann's throat at the same moment.

Quickly Ann spun towards Logan, her eyes scanning everywhere, taking all in at once. A man in the distance falling to his knees in an unsteady wave that marked him as good as dead. The girls were crying holding Sal but looked fine. Logan was still standing before her, patting at his torso in bewildered shock.

"Logan! Oh, Logan! Are you hit? Are you okay?"

"I'm not hit." He replied, with awe.

"Oh, thank God!" Ann searched his body anyway just in case. When she was satisfactorily relieved, she returned her gaze back to the clearing where the body had fallen, and beyond. For, had someone else fired a shot or had the man's gun backfired?

She stood and walked closer, Logan at her side, until they could better see the body. Though they were yet some distance from it, they could see the blood trickling from his mouth and his lifeless stare. Ann recognized him as Niall from the rendezvous, the man who had tried to assault her and whom she had publicly humiliated for it. So, he had been the one following her. She shivered looking on his lifeless form.

A realization came to her suddenly; part of the man's scalp was missing. A backfiring rifle would have exploded in his face. The top part of his head missing, indicated he had been shot by someone else.

Just as she snapped her gaze up, Logan tightened a hold on her arm protectively. Some distance behind Niall's body sat another man on horseback. His horse stood unmoving as the man stared forward in their direction.

The stormy blue gaze bore into her, as if she moved she may disappear.

Grayson.

Her hand cupped her mouth muffling the sob that wretched from her throat.

Logan looked from the man, to her confused. Ann placed her hand to his chest to stay him as she took a tentative step towards the still form beyond.

He came for her.

It was Grayson! He'd come for her!

Stop letting your heart get all fluttery. He has a homestead in these mountains, somewhere. Perhaps he is headed toward his own and this is coincidence.

Coincidence, that he trailed you to the middle of nowhere?

That did seem unlikely. She continued to stand there breathlessly, considering the surreal moment.

It was Grayson: the man she loved. What else was there to contemplate? She took a confident step towards him, then faltered again.

She was no longer the same woman. She was scarred inside and out. Who's to say he would even want her now?

Self-consciously, she trailed her fingers down the familiar path they trekked so often, along the thick puckered seam disfiguring her face. Naturally, shyly, she turned her face to the side, keeping her scar hidden from his view. She averted her gaze downward to the sprigs of grass between her feet, unsure of how to proceed after so much time and so many events had altered their paths from one another.

Grayson's heart pounded in his chest. He couldn't believe how close he had been to losing her all over again. Only this time he would have seen her death with certainty in front of his very eyes. His stomach suddenly felt the inclination to purge. If he'd had anything to eat that day it probably would have been cast up. Grayson, queasy and weak with the fear for Ann's life still pulsing through him, miraculously remained seated in the saddle. He took some deep breaths to recover. She was safe.

He drank in the sight of her. The sun shined brightly in the sky now, casting its brilliance over the world. But it seemed to spear a special beam of light over just Ann, setting her aglow like a goddess come to save him. Much like the first time he'd ever laid eyes on her.

Something had changed inside her though. He could see it in her shy countenance, her hesitancy. Surely she recognized him? Was she not happy to see him? The Ann he knew formerly was a hell cat; she would never have stood demurely as she was doing now. Had this life broken her as he'd feared it could? And if so, could he help her put back the pieces? Would she let him try?

She watched his horse come to a stop some distance from her yet, as Grayson swung his leg over the saddle and swiftly dismounted. She couldn't help a small intake of breath; lord, but he was beautiful.

He wore a new Stetson hat. She recognized the brand from the ones being sold at the rendezvous. He pulled it low, businesslike. A movement she well remembered, and the familiarity panged in her heart. Grayson was ever strong, rational, vigilant, and dutiful.

Another familiarity came to her as she watched him stalk towards her. His long-muscled legs eating up the ground between them in a purposeful stride that was all his own. He was magnificent. She shivered even as warmth spread throughout her body as she took in his broad shoulders that tapered to the hard, trim waist she remembered being pressed up against all too well.

As he neared, she braved to tip her face upwards and meet his eyes. What she saw in them nearly shattered her. His stormy blue eyes looked on her hungrily as if he were aware of her sinful thoughts and was as thirsty for her as she for him.

But he was holding back, treating her like a nervous young filly that was likely to spook or bolt.

She understood how her new reticent and mindful nature might cause him to approach her thusly. She was no longer the rash and reckless young woman she'd been at the beginning of this journey. No longer filled with a false sense of certainty.

The world had worn her down and shaped her as sure as the wind and rain carved the hard mountains she now called home.

She came to have a new respect for nature and learned there is no such thing as certainty. But more importantly, she had learned to accept it. Change would always occur, good and bad. Resisting the change invited trouble, would hold one down, could trap someone in darkness. Adapting and growing was the only way one could win. She learned that was the key to happiness. And not least of all, she learned when to take advantage of opportunities when they arose.

Like this moment.

Grayson was here before her, trying to read her as she was him. Searching her soul, her heart, to see if he was still a part of it; if she would welcome him back into her life. His compassionate and considerate innateness, often shielded by walls he put in place, was made vulnerable to her. For her. It showed more than anything how much he loved her, and it made her ache for him even more.

The tip of his tough, capable finger gently wiped a silent tear from her eye, then tentatively brushed smoothly along her skin to trace the path of her scar.

His throat worked painfully, but his eyes did not show disgust. They expressed pain, and guilt that shouldn't be his to carry, and love as tender as his touch.

Ann choked a tear ragged breath, her chest tight and full. She smiled and looked up into his eyes.

Grayson knew now why his confident Ann had seemed broken and insecure. He felt along the toughened skin that began just below the outset of sooty lashes underlining her honey hued eyes. God, what had she had to endure? He should have been there with her.

Finally, her golden gaze tipped up to meet his eyes. He could see the love and need for him reflecting within.

She took another ragged breath and a slow small smile tugged up the corners of her pink lips. The strength that he remembered, the vital core of her, shined in her eyes once more.

"What took you so long?"

Her strong husky voice uttered words that were so completely Ann. His Ann, with the teasing glint in her eye. His source of relentless exasperation.

He released any of the worried tension in his body and pulled her to him wild for her touch. To again kiss the only woman who could melt through his frosty demeanor and spark him out of his cool tempered world and fill it with warmth and light. The only woman for him.

He was raining kisses all over her face. He kissed her scar. Her impertinent nose, the lines that grooved between her brows born of hardship and the strength to pull through. Her lush lips that he'd missed so much and began to think he'd never taste again. Then lower along the sensitive flesh of her neck.

He was wild with hunger for her. And he swore he'd never let her go. Because they had already lost so much time together and he didn't plan to waste another second.

He cupped her face and spoke earnestly, "Just so you know. I plan to marry you. You're never leaving me again."

He may have stated the words, but Ann knew the questioning uncertainty within them.

"Absolutely you are going to marry me," she smiled putting all his fears to rest, "And I'll never be so foolish as to leave my heart behind again."

Then Ann kissed him back as fiercely as he'd kissed her.

A sound of a throat clearing was heard behind them. He felt Ann shaking lightly with laughter in his arms and looked down into her gaze beaming with joy. He wanted to kiss her again, but another throat clearing sound from behind her made him pause.

The sound came from the cabin behind her. And Grayson remembered the children. He peered over Ann's head to see their audience: a young Indian boy he didn't know, holding the hands of two little girls.

Ann took Grayson's hand and led him back to the cabin where Logan had retreated and stood protectively with the girls.

Grayson's heart clenched as he stared down into the two precious faces he'd only seen in his dreams for the past several months. The heartache of fearing for their safety and wondering whether or not he'd ever see them again choked him now.

He couldn't believe how they'd grown! Livvy's corn silk hair sat about her shoulders in little wispy curls. She looked to him curiously with her mother's golden eyes. Her soft round cheeks curved into a smile showing a fine row of pearly white teeth. A smile that had been mostly gums last he'd seen.

And then his Kit, serious and observant about her world and cautious much like Grayson himself; those shared qualities had bonded them from the start. Her chocolate brown hair had grown long too. Her cheeks weren't turned up into a big unreserved smile. Kit always smiled with her eyes. Her silver eyes sparkled, and he knew she remembered him.

He pulled from Ann, intent to embrace the little girls that had found their way into his life and owned their own pieces of his heart. But the Indian boy protectively stepped forward blocking Grayson from them.

"It's okay, Logan," Ann said, "This is Mr. Stone. Grayson."

She said his name as if she still couldn't believe he was here with her.

Logan's eyes looked on Grayson cautiously, but his evident trust and love for Ann shone more brightly and he stepped to the side.

Grayson sensed the boy's stance and gauged him to be somewhere in proximity to Luke's age. Which meant he was a young man. So, Grayson approached him as such and held out his hand.

Logan accepted and shook his hand firmly. The gesture welded them together with mutual respect for one another's place in Ann's life.

"Hi. Nice to meet you. My name is Grayson."

Logan nodded his own greeting and responded, "Logan Williams. Ann has told me much about you."

Grayson tried to smile reassuringly. Then turned his attention back to the girls. When he crouched onto his haunches in order to get to their level, Livvy rushed him with a hug. He hugged her little frame close. He looked to Kit who stood patiently awaiting her turn, with arms outstretched towards him, telling him in her subtle way how much she wanted to be hugged too. So he scooped her towards him and hugged both girls.

It was then they heard the other riders.

"Who could they be?" Ann asked warily.

She and Logan both tensed with readiness. Ann looked to Grayson with alertness. He was standing now with one of the girls in each arm, looking out across the hills in the direction of the two approaching riders and one wagon driver. A knowing smile grew across his face, settling the growing wave of nerves in Ann's stomach.

"Who are they Grayson? Is it Luke?" Ann nearly cried.

She had been overwhelmed with joy to have Grayson back in her life but a niggling sense of worry for Luke's absence had remained in her heart and mind. Her spirit buoyed now seeing Grayson's answering smile confirming her hopeful cry.

But who could the other riders Be? Surely Grayson must know them well to entrust them riding with Luke. Ann relaxed in the sense of safety once more and took Logan's hand to reassure him.

The man driving the wagon stopped near the dead body while the two horses and riders raced towards the cabin. Both came sliding to a stop a safe distance before them. Ann recognized Luke's sandy hair and youthful form as his feet hit the ground at a run after leaping from his horse.

"Ann!"

Luke raced to her and threw himself into her embrace nearly sending them both to the ground laughing and crying.

"Luke! Oh, Luke, how you've grown!" Ann held him back from her. "Look at you. A fine young man you are."

He was already taking on the lean muscular form of an adolescent boy. He beamed back at her with emotion filled eyes. She was glad to see he had not reverted into his shell. He was still the winning boy she'd left.

Never again though.

She was never letting him, or Grayson go again. She held him tightly to her once more then pulled away and sniffled away her tears to introduce him to Logan.

"Luke, this is Logan. Logan, meet Luke."

They looked to one another with uncertainty. A competitive flicker of jealousy licked through them both as they wondered which of them Ann loved most. They stood taking each other's measure.

Ann's voice broke their perusal of one another, "Logan, Luke," she took each by the hand, "I love you both so dearly. I hope you will come to feel the same for one another. Just as I know you do for your sisters, because now, you are brothers."

She let that resonate with them. Luke reached out his hand first, Logan accepted and joined his hand with his in a manly shake. Ann smiled a sigh; it was a beginning.

Then Livvy's squeals filled the air bringing everyone's attention to her, kicking and squirming against Grayson in attempt to get to Luke.

Luke choked back a cry and ran to her. Grayson released her into Luke's hold.

"My precious, wild Livvy!"

Luke held her tight and Livvy pulled on his sunny locks as if she had never been parted from him for several months.

Luke reached up and pet Kits arm lovingly, "And my sweet Kit."

Ann moved to Luke and Livvy's side, who were between she and Grayson still holding Kit. Ann pulled Logan close to her other side. Her happy tear stained face still wreathed in smiles met Grayson's equally joyous face as They embraced their new family and the beginning of a glorious life together.

The moment was interrupted when the man who had accompanied Luke came forward. He took off his hat and wrung it in his hands almost nervously. Ann's eyes traveled up to his face and she was hit with pure shock and another wave of joy.

"Uncle Rupie!" She stepped -or more aptly, leapt- into his embrace.

She looked up to his face, "How? Why? How?" She was so dismayed by his presence, she couldn't string a complete thought together.

"Believe it. I'm here. I've been chasing you all over this blasted country. Luckily I ran into this Grayson chap who was as intent on tracking you down as I."

He and Grayson shared a look of camaraderie with one another.

"It's good to see you again, lass." Uncle Rupert, ever the Englishman, wasn't one to let his emotions surface, but Ann felt every bit of the depth of his feelings in his steely embrace and the sheen of unshed tears in his eyes.

The man with the wagon drove up then to join them, surprising Ann again.

"Señor Garcìa!" Ann blurted.

He gave her a rogue smile and tipped his hat to her, causing a faint blush to stain her cheeks. Grayson emitted a low growl and stepped closer to her side.

Uncle Rupie diplomatically inserted himself into the conversation then. "I presume the other corpse belonged to Niall Meeks?"

"Sì, it did." Antonio García climbed down from the bench.

"Other corpse?" Ann asked.

"Two scoundrels followed you from the rendezvous, with ill intent I'm afraid," Her uncle supplied.

"Yes, I recognized Niall." She shivered and immediately felt Grayson's arm wrap around her comfortingly.

"The other was a man who went by the nick name of Scarecrow Joe," Garcìa added. "I'm not certain if they were hombres or just shared a loathing for you, but they set out together. Luckily, Mr. Stone arrived in time."

Grayson's heart clenched painfully at the reminder that Ann had nearly been killed today.

Garcìa continued, "If you can spare the hospitality and do not mind, I could use a refreshment. Then I'd like to collect the bodies and get them back to the rendezvous as quickly as possible."

Ann could hardly wrap her head around all that had happened this day, but she nodded and said, "Of course."

Logan had had to serve their guests for he had been the one collecting and storing the water while she had been gone. If Garcìa had been insulted to be served with their primitive utensils, he did not let on. Ann could hardly be embarrassed over a lack of such social etiquette, however; it wasn't as if her home was very established yet.

And out here, her home would probably always be considered too rustic by most gentlemen and ladies' standards.

It wasn't long before the men had both wagons unloaded and assisted Garcìa on his way.

The cabin was crowded that night and heard more laughter and held more love within it than it probably ever had before. It was positively filled to the rafters with familial chaos as everyone tried to tell their tales and fill one another in on their lives.

Ann discovered Uncle Rupert had married Cora, her friend, and Dr Fletcher's medicine supplier! The confirmed bachelor was now a husband as well as a stepfather to six children! According to Uncle Rupert, Dr. Fletcher and Nancy were doing well, albeit worried for Ann and the girls. Uncle Rupert dropped another shocking surprise into her lap when he told her, her mother and father were residing in the states with Nancy and Fletcher and awaiting word from him.

"Your mother and father are most eager to see you again. As well are your friends. I daresay your mother and father are anxious to meet their grandchildren, too."

Ann smiled happily knowing her parents finally knew of their granddaughters and to learn that they were awaiting her and them with open arms.

Rupert's eyes perused her tiny home as if searching for answers before coming back to rest on her.

"Of course, they had thought you would be returning to them and traveling back home to England."

Ann swallowed. That had always been her plan. Well, partly. She had begun with the idea that she would be returning to England with her children and their father. She thought of Somerset now and recalled the fond memories of her childhood in what had once been her home.

She felt Grayson's presence behind her. Felt the warmth of his body and the steadiness of his arm as he linked it with hers.

"I will go wherever you go. My home is with you."

His husky voice, although hushed softly against her ear, was laden with steel.

The decision was hers.

Ann surveyed her cabin. The walls that had been both her prison and her liberation at times. The bed where she snuggled her daughters each night and where Livvy spoke her first word. The wood planked walls and floor she often rested against while dreaming of her future.

She recalled the salvation this shelter offered when she had most desperately been in need. The security the cliff walls afforded her when she had fled from danger and didn't know how she would keep herself and her daughters safe.

She thought of Logan. He'd essentially raised himself in this wild land. Even if he consented to returning to England with her, the land, it was a part of him. He would never feel whole in England. Would, even Ann now?

British society was ever unforgiving of human mistakes and flaws. The people there would never welcome her pieced together family. She smiled to herself thinking of her new family; Grayson and Luke, her fatherless daughters, and Logan. -Patched together like a warm quilt, they were.

England would never be accepting of Ann's plans and the aspirations she had for her life, either. Here in these rugged mountains, one could carve any life one dared, if one possessed the courage to do so. If one could survive and thrive, the possibilities for life were endless.

She looked to Grayson, "Would you mind terribly, then, if I decided we should remain here?"

A smile broadened across Grayson's face. Before he became too enthralled with her decision, she continued.

"I don't mean just here in the states. And I know you mentioned that you have been building your own homestead somewhere in these mountains. But I mean to stay here, in this valley. Would you leave all you've worked for to join me here?"

Her eyes looked around the meager confines of her home, somewhat anxiously, knowing it was being judged and most likely comparing poorly to whatever Grayson had built.

"In this hovel?" She finished.

If possible, Grayson's smile grew even more as he shared, briefly, a wink with her Uncle, who chuckled.

"Ann, darlin', I would love nothing more than to stay here with you."

"Truly?" She looked to him eagerly and then glanced back around her humble abode in askance, as if to ensure he was seeing the sparse lodgings she was seeing.

The corners of his mouth were still crinkled up in a charming grin when he said, "And I'm not just saying that, because I'm recently homeless, either."

Ann's eyes widened, and she heard her Uncle Rupert guffaw behind her. She swatted at Grayson, playfully.

"Do be serious."

His soft laughter faded, "I am. My house was burned over the winter. I was serious before, too. My home is wherever you are. This Valley has evidently come to be your home, so it will be mine as well."

Ann gazed adoringly into his eyes and smiled, "Ours. All of ours."

Her uncle remained with them for nearly a week before he lit out for St. Louis where his new family awaited him. In that time, though, they made all kinds of plans.

He agreed to meeting again at the fall rendezvous and to Grayson's request that he bring glass panes along from St. Louis. He and Grayson, along with Luke and Logan, discussed the many building plans they had for the cabin. Ann laughed at Grayson's ambitious prospects to expand their home. Uncle Rupert looked around at all the children and commiserated with Grayson that it was no laughing matter.

Uncle Rupert would write to her parents and Nancy and Howard to let them know of Ann's welfare once he returned to St. Louis. He promised her, her mother and father would not be leaving the states until they saw Ann again in person and to plan to receive them as soon as they could make their way west. Perhaps they would even yet make it to St. Louis in time to travel with Rupert to the fall rendezvous.

Ann wrapped her arms around herself at that revelation. She would see her parent's loving faces again. She couldn't believe the turn of events her life had taken. The path that had seemed impossible not so long ago had led her to the most beautiful hope filled days of her life as well as to all those whom she loved. The rafters of her small cabin had never before been so filled with love and laughter as it was now.

And Ann Knew her valley would never be lonely again.

Epilogue

Ann's Valley
June 12, 1834

"So, what do you think?" She asked.

They had been residing in Ann's Valley for little over a month. The first project Grayson began, was building an addition on to the cabin that included a separate room for him and Ann's bedchamber. Next, he assured Luke and Logan, they would begin constructing a room for them, and lastly a room for the girls.

Other than awaiting the glass panes from Rupert, the addition was complete. For now, he and Ann used a deer hide to cover the window; luckily, the early summer nights were not unbearably chilly with a fire lit. Rupert promised in a recent, and very unexpected letter delivered to them by Antonio García, that he would not forget the windows. Also in his letter, he informed Ann that her mother and father, along with Dr. Howard and Nancy Fletcher were all on their way to St. Louis and expected to travel to the fall rendezvous with him. He teased Grayson in the letter, stating Grayson had better get to work on those additions for he would be housing his bride's parents, friends, as well as his brother-in-law's extremely large and growing family for a time.

Grayson had grumbled and then barked orders to Luke and Logan that they would need to work night and day in order to complete the mansion Rupert expected them to have built by fall. Ann laughed, delightfully, joyously happy with life. Her entire world was brighter now, and she could hardly fathom how lucky she was.

She was especially happy to learn her parents would be present at the fall rendezvous in time to witness her marriage to Grayson. -Her official marriage that is. They spoke their own set of vows to one another beneath the stars one night, with only trees as witnesses, after the children had gone to sleep. They had had to serve as their own minister, which didn't bother Ann in the least. In her and Grayson's eyes, they were married.

Even so, knowing her parents would be present to witness the official *legal* ceremony performed by the soldiers of the fort who would be present at the rendezvous, brought her great contentment.

Grayson and the boys worked every day from sunup to sundown on the construction of their new home and Ann and the girls continued trapping and working hides into useful attire and household accessories. The full workdays didn't leave Ann and Grayson much time together. Even with the new bed chamber built, knowing the children were on the other side of the wall, made it seem not so very private. So she and Grayson had made a habit of waiting until the children fell to sleep before sneaking out of the house and secreting away for some intimate seclusion.

As of yet they had not consummated their marriage. Ann admittedly, was hesitant. Grayson's every touch was only loving towards her and the man did know how to ignite her to flames with that touch. She feared, however, that perhaps she was not as adept at the art of lovemaking. The last time she had consummated a marriage, the groom had fled to another continent, after all. It hardly bolstered her confidence that she would be able to please her husband now. Her love for Grayson was so much deeper than she now realized her love for James had been.

If he found her lacking, the cut to her heart would be that much deeper, too.

This night, as many of the nights past, she and Grayson escaped into the night. They walked hand in hand along the hill's ridge, limed in the light of the moon, and spoke softly of the plans for their future.

They had stopped along the crest of the hill when Ann had posed the question. She nudged him and asked again, "Well? What do you think?"

Grayson knew as to what she referred. He surveyed the land before him with an assessing gaze. Taking in the rolling forested scape before them.

The way she spoke of it, he knew her love for this land ran deep and it was important to her that he love it too.

He stood at her side and pulled her close, rubbing the night chill from her arms as they gazed upon their own little valley.

"I think," his gruff voice finally scraped the air, "That we're finally home."

Ann tightened her hold around him, happily, and he placed a tender kiss upon her tucked head against his chest.

She looked up to him alight with glittering eyes. She looked so kissable in that moment and he desired nothing more than to pull her to him and bring his mouth crashing to hers.

Unfortunately, before he could bring about such action, her mouth started to chatter in rapid succession about her plans for their valley. His body's eagerness to join hers left his brain in a fog as he worked to catch up to all she was detailing.

"We are going to catch some more wild horses and breed them to Comanche. -He's the strongest and fastest stallion I've ever come across. All we need is a mare to match him and we'll have the finest horse ranch on either side of the Rocky Mountains. -Maybe even on both sides of the Atlantic!" Her eyes gleamed with enthusiasm for her ideas and plans.

She broke away from him then and started pacing, "Of course, we'll need some more sheep as well. A lot of profit in that I predict. Plus, I gained an excellent shepherd, born and bred specifically for herding the new sheep brought here from Australia. Perfect pup, good for shepherding *and* hardily built for the mountains. I know she doesn't look like much now, but you'll see. Also, a milk cow would not be remiss."

Grayson tried to focus on what she was saying, but her animated countenance only stirred his fires for her. Before she could say another word, he pressed his fingers to her lips. She looked to him at first with laughing eyes at his bold action, but slowly, they softened with desire.

His caresses intoxicated her to the point she could barely manage to think clearly. The past month she grew more and more desperate to experience the pleasures Grayson promised her and yet, her fear that she could not return such a gift held her back.

She could not allow her insecurities to rule her any longer. She vowed to herself, this night she would become Grayson's wife in more than just name.

Grayson's passion-laded voice grated huskily into the night air, "We'll explore all these plans another night. Right now, all I want to explore is you."

Ann's eyes burned with arousal at his words. And she moved her lips against his fingers. He felt her tongue in the small kiss she placed against them. Next, she grabbed his hand and led him down the hill into the forest sheltered darkness of the valley.

She pulled him down to the soft bed of grass with her and wrapped herself in his arms. She was unsure how to proceed. She hoped Grayson would show her. Perhaps if she followed his lead, she wouldn't bungle it so terribly.

For all she had mothered twin daughters and engaged in heated embraces with Grayson often on their secluded evening walks, Grayson knew she didn't have a lot of knowledge or experience in lovemaking. In the past her innocence had been taken, stolen from her in a selfish act of manipulation. She had professed to him, the embarrassment she'd felt after she had given herself to Morgan. It was difficult for Grayson to listen to her speak of her laying with another man, even from her past, and despite believing him to have been her husband. She claimed Morgan was gentle with her and did not harm her, but he'd also never made her feel the way she did when Grayson touched her. From what she described, Grayson knew Morgan had never introduced her to the full pleasures of the marital bed, and selfishly, Grayson was glad for it.

Grayson intended to remedy that as soon as Ann felt ready. It was near to killing him, holding and kissing her every night, but unable to reach that pinnacle of fulfillment he so longed to deliver them both. He would wait until she was ready, though, for he wanted to ensure she only ever felt cherished and loved under his touch.

This night, he sensed something different in Ann. She wanted to join him as one, he was positive of it. She was taking turns being the bold seductress and then pulling back with uncertainty. He thought perhaps, she was unsure of herself. He could feel the need radiating within her, as strong as it was within him. He knew she desired him; she turned molten in his arms with every touch. She just needed his confident direction to teach her how to take her pleasure. And he had no qualms with being the one to lead her there.

Grayson felt her shiver delectably as he kissed her ear and ran his tongue down the soft lobe. She closed her eyes, absorbing the rapturous waves tingling through her body. But she wasn't ready to succumb yet.

She cleared her throat nervously, "Perhaps some chickens too."

"Ann."

"Hm?" She answered shyly.

"Stop talking. Let me love you."

He brought his hand up under her heavy breast and thumbed at the bud of her nipple there. He felt it bead under his artful fingers, eliciting a moan from her kiss-swollen lips.

"Show me..." He heard her whisper, breathlessly.

He covered her hand with his and slid her fingers down to rest them over the bulging of his trousers. Deftly he unfastened the ties at his waist and slipped her hand inside. Tentatively, she began to stroke him there and he prayed his throbbing cock, growing in her hand, didn't frighten her away.

He brought his attentions back to rousing her. He knew she liked the feel of his rough, bristled jaw against the delicate flesh at her neck, so he started there, burying his face against her bared shoulder.

He stripped her of her blouse, ever thankful she chose to wear the far easier to remove pull overs men wore. She didn't bother with corsets or undergarments of any kind out here in the isolated, uncivilized world they lived. Another reason Grayson had to give thanks for his mountain home.

Life couldn't be any sweeter than this, he thought. He was so thankful to have found this woman who had given him so much life to look forward to. She was the fire to his ice, the sunshine in his winter. Her fighting spirit along with her laughter had brought his dull existence to life.

He realized he must have become distracted by his thoughts and appeared to be staring dumbly at her breasts. He looked to find Ann gazing up at him coyly beneath her lashes, wearing a bold and wicked smile.

"If you're not going to focus," She purred, "I may just have to resume regaling you of all my plans..."

Vixen. He answered her devilish taunt with a grin and a friendly nip to her full bottom lip and began showing her how focused he could be.

He resumed brushing kisses along her neck, working his way to her now fully exposed breasts. His deft fingers stripping away layers of both his and her clothing as he did.

What paradise he'd found. Indeed, he hoped to spend the rest of his life loving Ann under the very stars covering them where they lay now: in his Vixen's Valley.

Ann smiled serenely up at the sky above, as Grayson's expert touch flew her higher and higher until she thought she might join its glittery depths. In her peripheral vision she could just see the rocky points, stark white against the black of the night, towering above, reaching too for the stars. Funny, how those white peaks surrounding her valley had once housed only bleakness and desolateness.

But now they sheltered her very heart.

<u>Readers!</u>

Thank you for taking the time to read my book. I hope you enjoyed Ann and Grayson's story. Please feel welcome to leave a review as it would greatly assist me in discovering your likes and dislikes about Ann's Valley as well as insight into what you would like to read from me next. Your support and feedback are invaluable to me as a writer!

You may be happy to know; I am working on a sequel to Ann's Valley; a four-book series following the lives of each of Ann and Grayson's children. And Book 1 is <u>available now</u>!

Read on for a preview of <u>Seduced by the Saint</u>; the story of Kit Stone and Benjamin Price, and the first in the *Stone Ranch Series*!

Cayt Lawson

Seduced by the
Saint

Excerpt

Ann's Valley, Unorganized Territory
Stone Ranch
July 12, 1851

"I don't see why I have to go." Kit grumbled. "I'm nineteen
years old; a woman grown. Why should I be forced to attend
another year at that wretched school?"

Kit's sister Lavinia, or Livvy, as family and friends called
her, continued flittering about the kitchen like a dainty,
energetic, butterfly; serving coffee to their brothers, Luke and
Logan, and their brother's friend, Benjamin Price.

Or *Saint Price*. Or some such nonsense. Kit sneered as she
was forced to step over the arrogant Brit's shiny boots, crossed
at the ankles before her.

"For all you are supposed to be a '*Saint*' your manners
certainly do not reflect such."

In the recent, but rare, visits her brothers deemed worthy
to bestow their family with since their time at University,
they'd been accompanied by the smooth-tongued, aristocrat

before her. And, apparently, the annoying Englishman had decided to attach himself to them for life!

Impudently, Price slanted his green, almond shaped eyes at her. His eyes weren't the vivid green of fresh spring leaves like her brother, Luke's. They were more the color of the sagebrush that grew to the far north of them by the Platte River along the trail to Independence. The trail that would deliver her back to the Female Academy of Columbia.

Was she never to have adventures of her own? Her brothers used to include her and Livvy on theirs, before they'd left for University several years ago. Prior to that, and all growing up, her brothers had dutifully catered to their sisters' every whim.

Kit scoffed, well, for the most part they had. Other times they were complete rascals.

Their time at University had changed them. Suddenly having their sisters tag along was inappropriate. Kit understood how society worked, but that knowledge didn't prevent her from finding the situation most unfair.

Kit glared back to The Saint for good measure, his dusty blue-green eyes returning the stare with fervor. He'd find out soon enough, that no one could beat Kit Stone in a match of stubbornness. She crossed her arms over her white cambric blouse - one of her brother's old shirts, her usual attire - and got ready to stare him out. Then to her shock and dismay, his peach hued lips quirked up to one side in a smirk and he winked at her. Winked at her! The man was vastly irritating. And far too handsome. He was irritatingly handsome.

It was a new development, Price getting under Kit's skin. It started when he returned from California with her brothers and it was then she noticed him looking at her differently. Before that he never looked at her at all. Didn't speak overly much to her either. She always assumed him a shy sort. Then again, Kit wasn't particularly engaging, herself, as a young teen. Truth be told, she still wasn't. And Kit had never received marked attention from a man.

Unless one counted Thomas. Thomas was one of the new ranch hands her parents hired on last summer. Her parents had had to hire help, as her brothers were always gone, making them fairly useless around the ranch they were to inherit. Thomas was one of a handful who stuck around.

Kit rather wished he hadn't. She often felt his eyes on her from a distance, and he liked to materialize next to her from seemingly nowhere whenever she thought herself alone at the barn. In those moments, Kit grew gooseflesh and found his presence quite unsettling.

Price was unsettling for an entirely different reason. When he looked at her, his gaze was full of tenderness, as well as something else Kit couldn't quite identify. Sometimes he looked at her in a way that left little fires over her body, wherever his eyes traveled. It invoked strange feelings within her, she'd never before felt. She found it thrilling! And that was the unsettling part.

Her sister's voice sounded with confidence from the other side of the kitchen. "You're wrong, Kit. Benjamin is simply Benjamin Price. His father is the Earl of St. Vincent. His elder brother may have a courtesy title, however Benjamin, is just a second son and is afforded no title."

Kit heard her brothers chuckle. Luke, the eldest by a mere few months, added to Livvy's insult, "That's correct. Price, here, is certainly no Saint!"

"Well, then why do all of you call him, 'The Saint'?" Kit tried to disguise her frustration, lest her family realize she was discomfited over being made to look foolish. Not that she could blame anyone but herself. She supposed she deserved to look foolish since she was the one who had resorted to childish name calling.

Logan's sincere voice answered, "Because of the family name he descends from in part, but also, because he made the highest marks at University."

"Yes, and all the instructors fawned over him," Luke interrupted with a grin, then added, "Thankfully, for us! Logan and I would have been sent home early on more than one occasion if not for our association with 'The Saint'."

Kit noticed Price averting his eyes from the conversation, as if uncomfortable discussing his academic talents. Strange, she would have thought him one to preen over such admissions from his friends.

Luke proceeded to laugh at his own jest, and even their far more serious brother, Logan, twitched his lips in a hint of a smile.

Kit noticed Price's lips quirk as if he were forcing himself to smile and join the banter. She supposed the others wouldn't recognize the action as she did. Kit found herself feigning laughter as the butt of a joke often enough to know it well. She watched as Price played into their teasing, attempting a boyish pout at the insult. The look came off decidedly more rakish in Kit's opinion, however, and she felt her belly tighten.

Perhaps she would be ill. She never felt quite steady around the man. Benjamin Price was so damnably perfect- from his tailored gentleman's attire that never seemed to dirty- to his oil shined boots. His sandy blond hair was short, but not nearly as close to the scalp as her brother, Luke's, blond hair, and yet it never seemed to be out of place or creased from a hat. Of course, he didn't wear a beaver hat like her brothers and she herself did.

His face was perfect as well, with brows, a darker shade than that of his wheat colored hair, arched faintly over light hazel eyes accented by dark, long lashes. It should be a crime for a man to have such lovely eyes, thought Kit.

As if to offset the prettiness of his eyes, his chiseled features-from his blade straight nose to his cut cheekbones and flesh toned lips-practically made women weak at the knees. Well, not Kit; she didn't have time for such weaknesses.

Even as she told herself that, her eyes drew to his lips. The bottom one was slightly fuller than the top. Just like everything else about the man, he seemed a mixture of soft and hard. Dotting around his soft lips and lining his jaw was the dark, new growth of rough hair. It was probably the only feature about him that wasn't impeccably groomed.

His one imperfect feature was one that only made him that much *more perfect*. Kit found everything about the man quite aggravating!

Price's half pouted, smiling lips spoke then and his eyes lit with more teasing, "I do have a courtesy title actually. There are some occasions where I may be addressed as the *Honourable* Benjamin Price."

His gaze grew intently on Kit and a warm spiral tingled through her body.

"My, my, how humble we are," Kit angled her head condescendingly, ignoring the tingles, "And, here I was under the impression, you thought yourself a Prince."

Logan shook his head as if unamused by the others' jesting and brought the conversation back to panning for gold; the topic they had been discussing prior to Kit's interruption.

Price's tongue wetted the bottom of his upper lip as if he planned to continue their banter, but instead returned his attention to her brothers seated opposite him around the table.

Kit made her way to the stove to procure a cup of coffee for herself. Their mother and Livvy were the only ones in the house who drank tea.

From the counter, she heard Logan's steady voice.

"We already mined in California and each made a small fortune. Why should we head to Cherry Creek to work like dogs in mud and slop again?"

Luke scratched the back of his head in thought, a grin growing across his face.

And the Stone household knew that when Luke Stone flashed his pearly whites and dimples appeared in either cheek, trouble was about to spew forth.

Therefore, his response came as no surprise, "Why, for the adventure!"

Logan shook his head again. For all Luke was the eldest, Logan was often the more comported.

Price smiled encouragingly to his boisterous friend.

Kit would perhaps have been smiling too, if her own life wasn't being decided for her and completely out of her control. *She* was not allowed adventures.

Surlier than when she had first come down the stairs seeking her mother, she turned to trek off in search of her once more. Kit was tired of her brothers having all the fun. It was high time Kit was able to decide for herself.

Before she could get to the front door, she felt her sister's slender fingers at her elbow. Everything about her sister was lovely and lady-like, while Kit had toughened sausage fingers from preferring men's chores to her "Lessons of Refinement" as their mother called them.

From all she had been told, about her mother's poor attitude towards such lessons prior to having children, Kit gleaned that Ann Stone was a complete hypocrite!

"I don't think you should speak to mother right now. Perhaps wait until after her tea."

"You are just afraid I will ruin *your* plans to attend the academy again. You don't care for the saddle and you get carriage sick. What could possibly be so attractive about the school that you would be willing to endure traveling all the way back east for it? The very place where -might I remind you- the good *ladies and gentlemen* thereof, spurned our brother Logan; treating him so maliciously Luke nearly dragged him home to flee them."

"Yes, well, that was terrible. But not all the people there are of that mindset, or so cruel. Certainly, none of my friends despised Indians."

Kit had forgotten how many friends Livvy had there. They were probably the reason Livvy wanted so badly to return. Not to mention, all Livvy's dance partners, Kit rolled her eyes.

That lifestyle just wasn't for someone like Kit. She was too course. She didn't care about dining cutlery except for which utensils could most swiftly shovel the food to her mouth. She didn't care for dancing either. Although, admittedly, that was due more to the fact that she was terrible at it. She was athletic and direct. Movements that served her well in the Stone Stables, where she helped buck out and train the fresh two and three-year-old horses from their mother's proud breeding line. But on the dance floor? Well, on the dance floor she *still* looked like she was breaking out a young colt.

Livvy, however, had taken to the city life like a bird to the air. Kit sighed. She supposed she didn't want to prevent her sister from living as she desired. There should be a way they could both get what they wanted.

"And do call me Lavinia. Livvy is so juvenile."

Kit rolled her eyes. She suspected her sister's recent aversion to her childhood name had to do with the professor Liv- *Lavinia* had grown quite chummy with. Not that Livvy would discuss such harbored affections with Kit.

She and her sister never used to keep secrets from one another. Livvy used to be Kit's partner in mischief and greatest champion. Kit missed those days. She couldn't help but think the lofty school had changed her sister. Now she had her fancy friends and dandy professor. She was too good for the likes of Kit anymore.

It didn't escape Kit that there was a shred of jealousy in her heart. Her sister was all that was refined grace and elegance, a true lady. Whereas Kit was course and awkward amongst sophisticated society. Kit is the one who felt the juvenile; especially compared to her sister. But she'd fit pull her own teeth out before she'd begin ordering people to call her by her full name, Catherine, and walk around superior-like wearing stiff dresses.

Let *Lavinia* have her life of sophistication.

And let her brothers go off on their adventures without her.

She didn't need anyone! She had her horses. Horses she understood, and they understood her.

Kit was too late to retort on her sister's snootiness. More than likely Livvy knowing Kit would respond with a snippet of her own had intentionally gravitated back to their brothers to listen to their exciting plans and ignore Kit. Kit shook her head, irritated with all of her family members-including their friends!

Deciding, not to heed Livvy's warning, Kit exited onto the wrap around balcony where she knew she'd find her mother sipping her morning tea.

Tea was one of her mother's fondest indulgences and a tradition she adamantly upheld from her life in England before traveling to America in pursuit of Kit and Livvy's father.

As she turned the corner on the deck, she saw her parents against the rail overlooking the stables and horses. Her father stood to her mother's back, with her enveloped in his arms. Kit hesitated. Perhaps, she was interrupting a passionate interlude. Her parents, she thought with equal amounts mortification and disgust, were not shy with their affections to one another. Kit personally felt they could be a tad more private with those affections. They were ever being discovered in less than proper states. She was about to turn around and disappear, when she heard her name in their conversation.

Well, if they were discussing her, perhaps it wouldn't hurt to hang back silently and hear what they had to say...

"I do despair over our children." Kit heard her mother's soft voice.

"Luke and Livy: charismatic and carefree - a terrifyingly reckless combination. Then there's Kit and Logan."

Kit's ears perked up even more.

"Equally serious and stubborn. Can't tell either of them anything."

Not true, thought Kit. *Logan wasn't nearly as stubborn as she.*

"All set to run their own lives even though I could manage them all for the better." Her mother's voice continued in exasperated fashion.

Manage them better, indeed. It was all Kit could do to keep from grunting her strong opposition to the idea.

Her father guffawed, then. His gruff laughter echoing across the morning air. She couldn't see her mother's face, but Kit rather thought it probably reflected annoyance for having been laughed at.

Her father rubbed her mother's shoulders, soothingly, but said, "Lest you forget. You charged clear across an ocean and another continent just to see things done *your* way when you were their age. I'd say our children are smooth as churned butter compared to you."

Not pleased to be reminded of her youthful foolishness, her mother responded, "Well that is why they should heed my wisdom. And *you*, you old goat, had better start waxing some flattering compliments to make up for your insulting tongue."

Her father began to nuzzle the back of her mother's neck. Livvy was right, her mother's morning tea was not a good time to discuss matters. Kit hurried and fled back in the direction she'd come without being heard. She started returning to the kitchen, then thought better of it. She had no wish to be in the company of her siblings, all free except her, to do as they pleased with their lives.

Not to mention *The Saint* was still in there, with his arrogant smirks and grins he reserved only for her, because he knew how exasperating she found him. Kit didn't have time for troublesome males in her life. Unless, of course, the male in question was a horse. Speaking of which, she had a new colt to see to at the barn, wherein resided the company Kit preferred.

Thank You

Thank you for reading. If you enjoyed my books then be sure to sign up for my newsletter at www.caytlawson.com, where I offer free giveaways and exclusive excerpts from my upcoming books!

Again, I'd like to encourage you to leave an honest review and I sincerely thank you for choosing to read my book!

<u>**Acknowledgments**</u>

I would like to thank all my friends and family for their encouragement during this crazy endeavor. My aunt for her time and emotional support. My mother and grandmother for an adventurous childhood and for providing strong female role models to look up to. I would also like to thank my sisters for not scoffing when I told them of my plans to write a novel, but who instead joined in my excitement and enthusiasm. A huge thank you to my Dad, father-in-law, and stepmother in-law for all their continued love and support throughout the years. This definitely would not have been possible without them! And finally, thank you to my husband and children, for their unwavering faith in me to achieve this goal.

About the Author

Cayt Lawson is an avid reader of Historical Romance, favoring stories set in Regency England and the American Frontier. She was raised on a quarter horse ranch in the state of Michigan and traveled the rodeo circuit with her parents as a young girl. The modern cowboy lifestyle she grew up in greatly inspired her love of the American West, and the romanticized time in history sparked her desire to explore other remarkable periods of the past.

Cayt currently spends most of her time trying to keep up with her three energetic, young, children and -much to the detriment of her husband's sanity- adding animals to her growing hobby farm. When Cayt isn't reading or caring for her beloved children and critters, her time is spent researching and thinking up new stories.

To read more about Cayt Lawson visit her website at www.caytlawson.com.

www.ingramcontent.com/pod-product-compliance
Lightning Source LLC
Chambersburg PA
CBHW051544250626
47157CB00001B/174